NO SAFE PLACE

ANNE MOROZ

POPULAR LIBRARY

An Imprint of Warner Books, Inc.

A Warner Communications Company

POPULAR LIBRARY EDITION

Popular Library® and Questar® are registered trademarks of
Warner Books, Inc.

Cover art by James Warhola

Popular Library books are published by
Warner Books, Inc.
666 Fifth Avenue
New York, N.Y. 10103

 A Warner Communications Company

Printed in the United States of America

First Printing: September, 1986

10 9 8 7 6 5 4 3 2 1

This book is dedicated to the memory
of the crew of the space shuttle *Challenger*,
Mission 51-L, January 28, 1986

Francis R. (Dick) Scobee
Michael J. Smith
Ronald E. McNair
Ellison S. Onizuka
Judith E. Resnik
Gregory B. Jarvis
Sharon Christa McAuliffe

We will miss you

"GOD HAVE MERCY!"
KATE WHISPERED.

The man who called himself Kagen was Rory.

"Is that any way to say hello to a friend?" Kagen asked, gently mocking. Yes, he was Rory, with his coal-black curly hair cut short, those bright, bright blue eyes that had laughed with her and looked at her with affection...he *was* Rory, down to the scar that drew one side of his mouth up in a permanent half-smile.

Trusted friend, confidant...even lover....
She could taste the betrayal like bile in her throat.

"No, no, Rory is dead—*you were not in all those places!*"

There was a pause while he studied her. "No," he finally agreed. "I was not. Rory and his brothers are merely LSH units."

"But he couldn't be—he *moved*, he-he *thought*, he—"

"He loved?" Kagen's face was inscrutable.

This was impossible! Lifelike Simulated Humans could not do what Rory had done—could not be what Rory had been!

"Frankensteins," she breathed. "You have *thinking* Frankensteins!"

ACKNOWLEDGMENTS

First, I want to thank a group of people who are very important to me, and who had a lot to do directly with this book being written—and, more important, finished!

The Whileaway Writers Co-op:
Ann Crispin, who knew when the time was right
Kathy O'Malley, for her faith, her patience, her nagging, and her judicious use of red ink
Debby Marshall, whose fault it was (only she knows why!)
Teresa Bigbee, for her interest and encouragement

Dr. Katie Woodbury, of NIH, who "loves to b.s. about the brain"
"Doctor" Roddy Gabel (Gabelus Roddyi), for his Latin assistance.

Second, but never last, I want to thank people who have encouraged me over the years, because without them I would never have started writing.

Walter and Alice Moroz, my parents, for being there
P.J. Moran, who had a dream a long time ago and never gave it up
Alberta Moran, who always knew I could
Judy Carr, who made sure I would always do it correctly
Harlan Ellison, for being himself and keeping me honest (and for occasionally curing what ailed me)

And a special thanks to the gangs at the Systems Techniques and Integration Division and the Endangered Species Propagation and Laboratory Investigations Section for not complaining (too much!) when certain people occasionally didn't come to work.

1

A slow hissing broke the silence in her head, and she recognized the movement of air across her face and body. She was on the beach, the hot sun baking her naked body, shining brightly against her closed eyelids. Waves sounded in the background. . . .

"Sky jockey, this is Control Central. Engage grapples—now!"

The sudden loud voice jarred her from her reverie, and a thin line of light traveled across her vision as her eyelids parted slowly. She stared up into painful whiteness.

"Okay, sky jockey, reel 'er in now, nice and slow. And stop the procedure after Step Three—we can't break the seals until further instructions come in. Repeat, stop after Step Three. Do *not* break the seals."

Kate Harlin blinked once, very slowly, and thought carefully about her next breath. This was obviously not the beach.

"L.P.S. *Black Opal* lifeboat, this is Control Central for deep space station *Orphic Angel*. Do you read?"

Kate's first sound was garbled, not even loud enough to be picked up by the transmitter. She reached for the water tube on her right and took a long pull. So very thirsty . . . She used the sides of the hibernation unit, which was already

1

open, to pull herself up to a sitting position, and removed the sensor patch from its place beneath her collar bone. Her skin was irritated, and she rubbed it absentmindedly.

"Repeat, *Black Opal* lifeboat, this is Control Central for the *Orphic Angel*. Do you read?" After a pause, "What does the scanner say? She awake yet?"

"Yes, she's awake," Kate rasped. "If you guys are all hooked up, why don't you pipe some water in here? The stuff I've got tastes like it's twenty years old!"

She wondered how long she'd been locked in this little box. As sick as she felt, it must have been months. Too long to depend on a lifeboat. She was lucky, really.

"Sorry, *Black Opal* lifeboat, it'll have to do for now." The response was curt.

"The name is Harlin, Control Central—Kate Harlin," she snapped, making a face over the water, which really was pretty stale.

"Officer Harlin?" A new voice came over the speaker. "This is Dr. Norton, the *Orphic Angel*'s chief of medicine. Can you answer a few questions?"

She rose from the couch. "Sure. Mind if I get dressed?"

"One favor before you do, if you don't mind. Are there fresh sensor packs in there?"

"Probably." Kate rummaged around in a cabinet. "Yeah. Now what?"

"Put a sensor patch on, please."

She obeyed, feeling the contact slide into its tiny sub-cutaneous receptacle. What she really wanted was an icy cold glass of water. "And now?"

"Just sit comfortably."

Kate sat in the pilot's chair and reclined it slightly. She might as well find out as much as she could about her situation while she was forced to wait. She powered up the board and switched on the console. *Orphic Angel*—she had been here before, though not often. One of the smaller deep space stations owned by Guil-Pro, it was in orbit at an angle to the plane of the solar system, and about 500,000 kilometers out beyond Pluto. That put it at the outer terminus, the farthest border of the human race's attempts to create permanent settlements. Fifty years ago the outer terminus had changed every few years because the urge to explore and stretch the limits was still strong. That was no longer true. Deep space stations were still the jumping-off points for interstellar travel, but this one was not on the most used commercial spacelanes.

The COACH subsystem presented its familiar menu to her, and she made her selections, scanning the information they produced. Her lifeboat was hooked up to the main computer on the station. With a sinking feeling she noted that her only primary connection was a power hookup. She was not on station life support—why not?

"Thank you, Officer Harlin. That's all," Dr. Norton's voice came again.

She blinked, startled. "What d'you mean, that's all? What's going on here? Why the long-distance medical exam?" Suddenly she felt clammy. "What did you find?"

"Not a thing," he said blandly. "You have a clean bill of health."

"Yeah? So what about that nice cold water I've been waiting for?"

"Sorry, you'll have to wait a little longer."

She ran her hand through her hair distractedly, then remembered that as long as she wore the sensor, she was being recorded by somebody's medical scanner on the space station. Best to remain calm in this situation—she had no cause to worry, they had just told her there was nothing wrong with her. Don't give them anything to make them change their minds. She pulled off the sensor.

"Officer Harlin, why did you do that?"

Kate smiled grimly. "Privacy."

"Six months in a lifeboat wasn't privacy enough?"

"Doc, don't play the local shrink." Kate rubbed the bridge of her nose tiredly. Six months! Hell of a long time to be asleep in a tin can—a lot longer than she'd thought possible.

"Sorry, but it's standard procedure for unusual reentries to be interviewed."

Kate sighed. "Look, I'll answer all the questions you want after I get some fresh food. Do you realize the synthesizer in this thing is shot?"

"We can't break any of the seals on your craft until we

get some orders from upstairs." It was Control Central again. "Besides, you're only connected to us by magnetic grapples and power cables. We don't have any way to get supplies to you short of a personal delivery."

"Yeah, so what's wrong with that? The doc said I'm all right." She moved around, beginning to dress. Her jumpsuit was even more wrinkled than when she'd taken it off so many months ago. Smelled about as bad, too.

Control Central cleared his throat. "Don't you know you were broadcasting a disaster beacon?"

"Of course I was. I wanted to make sure somebody would pick me up!"

"Broadcasting a Type A Quarantine isn't exactly the way to get rescued. Most ships'll pretend they didn't even hear you!"

Kate licked suddenly dry lips. "I didn't put out a Type A Quarantine." Her voice sounded small and scared in her own ears.

But the comptuer obviously had. SINS—the Symbolic Inferencing Networked System—that damned "rational" machine, had played one last trick at the end of a time when everything had gone insane and turned against her—the ship, the computer, especially the crew, some of them friends she had known and worked with for years. . . .

Not that she had planned to just glide up to the nearest deep space station and go aboard, perhaps bringing with her the horrendous thing they had found out there that had made them all . . . change . . . so much, all of them except her. . . . But she'd also had no intention of arriving unconscious and at the mercy of whomever found her first. She had programmed the lifeboat's computer to wake her upon receiving signals that indicated she was nearing the outer terminus and signs of civilization again. From that point she would've taken control herself and . . . Well, one of Guil-Pro's space stations was *not* the first place she had planned on docking. . . .

The computer had changed all that, it seemed. SINS must've overridden her careful programming and ignored all signals from the outside until she'd been safely located and pulled in by Guil-Pro. By the time she had awakened from hibernation, it was too late to do anything.

"Officer Harlin, are you all right?" It was Dr. Norton.

"Why shouldn't I be?" She bent over to seal the flaps on her deck shoes, very glad that she had pulled off that giveaway sensor. "But I could sure use a cold beer right now."

"We'll see what we can do about that." The doctor sounded a bit more cheerful. "We're expecting a Guil-Pro corporate representative to arrive within the hour. Maybe we can get some decisions." He paused. "I hate to ask you this, but while we're waiting around with nothing better to do, would you mind reapplying a sensor patch? We'd like to maintain a continuous reading on you."

"Oh, you would? Well, I've decided I need my privacy just a little longer."

"Officer Harlin, please be reasonable. . . ."

"Fuck you, Doctor." She closed the circuit before he could argue.

"Officer Harlin? Harlin, are you there?"

Kate snapped her eyes open. She'd been dozing in the pilot's chair—most deep spacers didn't care to sleep in the hibernation units unless they were actually in deep-sleep.

"I'd like to know where else I'm supposed to be. What's up?"

"Guil-Pro's corporate representative just disembarked down in the main receiving area. His name is—Martin Baker." Control Central sounded highly unimpressed. "He acts like a very important person."

"Good, put him on. I certainly want to talk to him!"

"Harlin, I'd go easy on it if I were you."

Something in Control Central's voice made her listen to him more closely.

"Are you alone?" she asked.

"I'm broadcasting on a tight beam, if that's what you mean."

"Fine, but is anyone with you there?"

A sigh. "No, just me. Goddamn, but you're a hardnose!"

"There's a reason for it." She paused. "Where are you in relation to me right now? Can I see you?"

"You should be able to, because I can see your top lights. Look up, about—oh, say one o'clock. That big amber area?"

"Yeah. So that's you?"

"Well, more or less—I'm right in the center of it. It's like a big picture window."

Kate cocked her head to one side, her ear tuned. "I know you, don't I?"

"Y'might. Watson is the name—"

"Billy Watson! I *knew* I recognized your voice! What d'you mean, I 'might' know you?" She and the young black man had shipped out together several times on the short hops that deep spacers sometimes took between their longer voyages outside the solar system. They all needed the change every now and then, and it was nice to get paid well for a job that didn't require you to deep-sleep away two or three years of your life.

Billy Watson had taught her to play a decent game of poker, though she'd lost her shirt several times during the learning process. Despite the fact that he was ten years her junior and had a reputation for being wild, they'd always gotten along well. The people they worked with had even assumed they were sleeping together. Kate had never bothered to confirm or deny the rumor, even though they were not; in a world where everyone was identified down to voiceprint, retinal patter, and sexual preference, she figured some things were nobody's business.

She laughed. "You could've let me know who you were a little earlier, you know!" She pitched her voice down half an octave. "'This is the voice of Control Central, brought to you by these local stations.' C'mon, Billy, you never used to be a snob!"

"Aw, Kate, it's the damn job. And look who was in here with me, too. Sometimes you've got to be a professional, y'know—and a professional Control Central sounds like a snob!"

"Yeah, don't I know that. So when did you get promoted to the hotseat?"

"Well, I lost a leg a year ago, and..."

"Oh, Billy, that's terrible!" For a moment she forgot her own considerable troubles. "Was it...?"

He talked right over her. "I've got a pretty good replacement for it, but you know Guil-Pro's rules about deep space travel."

She knew, and she thought about how this station wasn't even on the main spacelanes. "Do you miss it?"

"Sometimes, sittin' here talkin' to everyone on their way out or on their way back... But it's not too bad. Two other guys in the accident died—I can't complain."

No, she thought, *nobody ever complains when they get screwed.* "Well, do you hear some good stuff out here, at least?"

"Pretty much." She could almost hear his shrug.

"Good, then maybe you can tell me—what the hell is going on here?"

"Hey, *you* know that better than anyone else. I wasn't out there, sweetheart."

"That's not what I mean. I want to know what *you* know, what you've heard about what went on."

There was silence.

"You still there, Billy?"

"Yeah, I'm here." Another silence. "Well, we know the *Opal* was abandoned out there. And we knew a lifeboat was coming back, though we didn't know who'd be aboard her."

"Is that all?"

"Well... you're not supposed to know this, I guess, but SINS was spyin' on you guys—transmitting data back during your whole mission. We even picked up some of it here." He sounded embarrassed. "There were rumors at first, y'know, about an equipment failure that made the whole crew desert. I tried to follow what was happenin' because I knew you were out there."

"Did you really?" She was surprised.

"Sure. But don't say that to anyone, y'know? I wasn't supposed to be listening, and you aren't supposed to know about any of this."

"Yeah, I see." She tugged at a short, reddish brown curl. "Then what? Something must've changed."

Indeed, he told her, the last transmission from SINS had changed the story considerably. The *Black Opal* had been abandoned on the last planet she had visited. Transmissions were garbled—many of the computer's inferencing circuits had been damaged when someone had deliberately disabled the ship—but it seemed that all hands had been left aboard except for one who'd escaped. It was unclear whether the deserted crew had been dead or alive, but speculation was rampant. At that point the transmissions had stopped.

"Y'know it's not normal to have continuous monitoring on a mission, Kate. You're right, I get to hear a lot of stuff sittin' in the hotseat, even though we aren't a busy station, and I *know* Guil-Pro doesn't monitor most of the missions that go out. You guys were special."

For long moments Kate stared at the console and chewed on the end of her finger. "Yeah, I bet we were. So special that they aren't even trying to stop any of these stories, right? Is Guil-Pro going along with all this stuff?"

"You got any enemies, Kate?" Watson's voice sounded funny.

"Hey, everybody loves me. At least, last time I checked..." She took a deep breath. "Is it really that bad?"

"It's shit, baby."

There was another long pause.

"Billy, you know that what you've heard isn't the whole story. Would you believe me if I told you my part?"

"Well, I'd expect you to try." He was being cautious. "I mean, you were there."

"You mean you wouldn't believe me. Okay." She leaned forward, even though he couldn't see her. "I have the *Opal*'s black box recording. Billy, you *know* nobody can mess with what SINS puts in that!"

"All right, Kate, what do you want me to do?" He sounded exasperated. "What do you think I *can* do?"

She thought quickly. "You're Control Central. You're in charge of all station's communications when you're on duty, right?"

"Go on." He wasn't giving anything away.

"You said we were on a tight beam right now. Can you receive transmissions that way?"

"Well, yeah..."

She rushed on, not giving him a chance to doubt what she was saying. "Good, I'll transmit to you, and you'll have a copy! You can hold on to it until I'm gone and things've died down a little. You know *I* won't be able to leave here with anything."

He was silent, and she could imagine what he was thinking. "Look, Billy, I know it's asking a lot. There's no telling what'll happen if we get caught, and—"

"I could lose my job, is what could happen!" he interrupted. "No one's supposed to handle that stuff except the Board of Inquiry. You're talkin' about breaking the law, Kate—that's how serious this is!"

"Goddamn right it's serious! For chrissakes, Billy, I abandoned a shipload of *people* out there! Do *you* think Guil-Pro is going to come up with something to get me off the hook? I've *got* to protect myself, and this is my only chance." She laughed bitterly. "Look at it this way, Billy. You could always copy the information now, just to humor me, and then not do anything with it. How would I know?"

"Dammit, Kate, cut that out!" He sounded a little embarrassed. "Look, uh—what you've got there is really just a copy, right?"

"Well, strictly speaking I guess that's true. But why—?"

"If it's just a copy, Guil-Pro can fight it. They could say you altered it as you made the copy . . . right?"

"But I didn't make the copy, SINS did! The system dumped everything into the lifeboat when I was priming it before I left. It was an automatic function—I didn't even find *out* about it until later!" She rubbed her eyes. "Billy, it's all I can do. Don't you see that? I'm not going to let Guil-Pro walk on me—I've *got* to do something!"

She could hear him sigh over the connection. "All right, Kate. But I figure you owe me one for this."

"Billy, I owe you a dozen!" She couldn't help but grin. "Is now a good time? Do I need to do anything special?"

"How many cards do you have?"

"Just two." She stared at the small rectangular pieces of plastic that fit so easily into the palm of her hand.

"Only two?" Even Billy was surprised. "That's not very much—unless it's compressed data. This could be tricky if we've got to deal with compression *and* decoding . . ." His voice trailed off into mumbling. "Okay, let me get something ready here, then you do exactly what I tell you."

Kate obeyed her instructions carefully, and watched the green telltale light on her console that indicated the transmission was proceeding successfully. She had no idea how long it would take, but she knew the light would blink off when it was done.

"I'm counting on you, Billy," she whispered. "This is the only way anyone's going to see *my* side of the story."

Her eyes had begun to burn from the strain of staring at the telltale when it changed suddenly to a bright amber. The transmission had been interrupted from Billy's end. She was about to ask him what was wrong when he came back on the air.

"Officer Harlin, Mr. Martin Baker of the Guilford Production Consortium corporate headquarters is here."

Guil-Pro had arrived. . . . *Oh God,* she thought frantically, *please don't let him see what we were doing!* The amber telltale drew her eyes as she tried to compose herself.

"Good morning, Officer Harlin." The voice she heard was properly British.

She cleared her throat. "Yes, Mr. Baker. I assume you've come with orders to release me?"

"A bit anxious, are we?" If she could believe her ears, he actually chuckled, and it was not a nice sound. "Not to worry—the first thing we're going to do is get you off the shuttle and into an isolation chamber on this station. Once we've sterilized you and the craft, then we can worry about what happens next."

"Well, I'm real glad we've got my life so conveniently organized for the next day or so, but I'm more concerned about *now*. For starters, there's no fresh food on this craft. There isn't one good reason you can't get me something to eat—Dr. Norton told me I was healthy." She folded her arms tightly across her chest. "And I'd appreciate it if you took my situation seriously. I don't like being patronized."

Baker's voice was stiff. "I assure you I'm perfectly aware of how serious this is, Officer Harlin. I'm sorry you've had to wait so long, but you'll simply have to be patient. There are procedures we must set up to handle this situation."

"You're acting like this has never been done before! There are isolation chambers on every deep space station Guil-Pro works out of!"

"Officer Harlin, please stop behaving as though you've been exposed to nothing more serious than a common cold virus. Must I explain the significance of what's already happened to you?"

She took several deep breaths, trying to calm herself. "I'd like to know how the hell you know so much about it!"

"I'm surprised at you, Harlin—don't you think we keep tabs on missions of importance?" She could almost see the smile on his face. "Let me begin with this. You are an experiment, Officer Harlin. We are obliged to see to your comfort and health as far as we can, since you were under contract to the Consortium when this unfortunate incident occurred, but that is *all* we are obliged to do. You, on the other hand, are obliged by the terms of that very same contract to cooperate fully with any decisions we make during the course of this experiment.

"As I explained to you, we are aware of some of the events that took place on your mission. We know your crewmates became ill and then went insane, and we know that you have not—or at least not yet.

"And that's why you're here rather than on some other station. You may have carried something back with you—and the *Orphic Angel* is well off the traveled spacelanes."

She found she was unable to speak.

"In fact," Baker continued, "if *I* were operations manager here, you'd have been blasted to bits as soon as we picked up your Type A Quarantine warning. The only reason you're alive is that this station had orders from Earth to hold you. You owe your life to the goodwill and scientific interest of the Consortium, Officer Harlin—you *will* cooperate!"

She swallowed, feeling as though she hadn't done so in several hours. "How much longer do I have to stay on this shuttle?" she asked finally. "That's all I want to know—how much longer?"

"I can't answer that. We have considerable work to do

yet just to ensure that we can get you from the lifeboat to the isolation chamber without endangering anyone else. I *do not know* what we are dealing with, Officer Harlin, and my primary concern must be the inhabitants of this station."

"I understand that, Mr. Baker," she began in a husky voice, "but..."

"I don't believe you do. I have been put in charge by the Consortium's Central Board of Directors on Earth—and I will not risk accidentally loosing something on the populated solar system that could be worse than any disease we have yet to experience! We are taking no chances, Officer Harlin, and that is the end of this conversation. Control Central will notify you when we are ready to begin the procedures."

"Mr. Baker? Mr. Baker, wait..." Fear and rage made her voice crack. "Baker? Goddamn you, listen to me!"

But she was left with that peculiar silence on the radio that meant no one was on the other end. As she stared at her console, the amber telltale that had shown there for many minutes turned to green, then blinked out.

"Control Central? Are you there?"

No answer. Even Billy had deserted her.

CHAPTER

2

Kate Harlin walked naked through the open hatch from the lifeboat, through an umbilicus, and into the *Orphic Angel*. Her path was bounded by a ribbed plastic and fiber tube that forced her to stoop as she walked, and stretched endlessly before her down the corridor of the station. Behind her she heard the hatch close and seal; ahead, she could see nothing but whiteness.

From the tube she stepped into what looked like a shower stall. The computer voice instructed her to close her eyes tightly, stand with her arms away from her sides, breathe through her mouth, and to maintain that status until further notice. It then proceeded to count down from fifteen. At zero, she was drenched in a beating shower. The bitterness of the liquid made her gag.

"Thank you," the voice said when the spray had stopped. "You may now open your eyes and breathe normally. Please note the light above the door. When it shows green, you may exit."

Spluttering and spitting, she felt herself buffeted with warm air and watched as drops of moisture evaporated from the walls. A light above the exit glowed bright green, and the door unsealed with a small whoosh.

The isolation chamber was a small section of the infirmary sealed off by double thicknesses of glass and formed plastex. It contained a bed, a chair, a video communicator, a self-contained toilet, numerous pieces of medical equipment, and a water spigot.

Kate nearly drowned herself, drinking so fast that she came close to choking, but the water was cold and fresh, and she couldn't remember ever having been so thirsty before in her life.

Her most immediate need taken care of, she suddenly became conscious of her nakedness. There were two large windows in the chamber that ran from deck to ceiling, leaving her in plain view, yet she had seen no clothes lying ready for her. She examined every drawer and cabinet in the isolation area and could find nothing. Even the sheet on the damn bed was attached at one end!

"This is bullshit!" she muttered, jabbing angrily at the keys on the video communicator.

"Dr. Norton here." His face appeared on the small screen.

"Where the hell are my clothes?"

"Clothes?" He looked blank, then his face cleared. "Oh, Officer Harlin. They didn't leave any for you? I'll see what I can do."

"Doc, in most languages that means 'forget it.' Don't tell me I can't have any clothes!"

"Well, I'm not really in charge...."

This was not the last time she would hear responsibility

for her situation passed on to a higher authority. It seemed there was a problem with getting anything to her now if it hadn't already been provided.

"Only until we know it's safe to break your isolation, you understand, of course," he finished.

"What about that shower I just went through? Didn't that make me any safer?"

Norton explained that the shower was only the first step in a long and complicated process. The bitter liquid had swept away whatever was on the surface of her skin and the top layer of skin as well, though nothing had been killed or sterilized. The machinery would distribute samples of the runoff into human cell cultures—a fairly standard procedure for contamination studies. Scanners would then study the cultures over the next twenty-four hours, noting any changes. If there were changes, if she indeed carried something with her, then they would worry about the next step.

"What kinds of cultures?" she asked.

"Oh, the usual. Epidermal, bone and bone marrow, various organs, especially the heart and lungs, nerve tissue—and of course brain cells."

Kate wiped away a sudden sheen of sweat from her upper lip. Brain cells? The *Black Opal*'s medic had been convinced that the brain was affected by the disease, and then it had gotten her, too, and she'd no longer been capable of any coherent thought. . . .

"Something wrong?" Norton's question interrupted her thoughts.

She shook her head. "No, I'm just . . . real tired." She straightened her shoulders. "Besides, I haven't eaten in six months."

"There's a small food synthesizer in there, and some supplement tablets." He hesitated. "I'm sorry about the clothes. But you shouldn't be there for very much longer."

She stared at him, realizing that she was seeing him for the first time—he was no longer just a voice over the radio. Extremely thin, with a fringe of light brown hair that probably circled a bald spot at the back of his head, Dr. Norton looked more like a skinny Friar Tuck than a space station's chief of medicine. His face had a woebegone expression, as if he truly were sorry for her situation.

"No, I guess not." She made herself smile as she broke the connection.

Whom was he trying to kid? She knew she would be in that chamber for the rest of her life—however short that turned out to be—just like she knew what would happen to that brain-cell culture. It would change like the crew of the *Black Opal* had changed. Twisted grotesqueries would replace those normal, innocent cells, and her fate would be sealed. Guil-Pro would have their goddamn virus matrix or whatever the hell SINS had called it, and she would be locked in isolation until she went crazy, or until they could find out why the madness had gotten everyone but her. . . .

Distractedly she went to the food synthesizer. Two cans of cold beer and a meal satisfied her hunger and made her feel a little better. With a third can in hand she lay down on the narrow bed, one foot tucked under her other leg, and stared unseeing out through the double thickness of glass.

Above her head, she knew, concealed in the ceiling panels, medical scanners hummed quietly, noting her condition and passing it on to those who were interested in such things.

Kate finished the fifth repetition of her daily exercise regimen and paused for some orange juice. Her hand shook as she drank, and she noted this with concern.

She felt as though she'd been in this chamber forever; yet, even without the luxury of a clock, she was aware that her twenty-four-hour reprieve was ticking away more rapidly than she liked. The memory of that amber telltale continued to haunt her—had Billy been able to copy all her information? She hadn't been able to talk to him again before they'd whisked her off the lifeboat, and no one had come to talk to her here.

What would happen when the time was up? She knew full well that her fate depended totally on what they would find in the lab-test chamber. And she knew they would find something in the brain-cell culture—she knew it in her heart. They were *looking* for it, she *knew* the bastards were looking for it, because they knew *something* was there, had known before the *Black Opal* mission had ever left Earth orbit! And she could prove it, too, if only Billy had gotten all that information. . . .

Worse, she couldn't sleep. Every small whisper of noise made her jump, sure that one of her former crewmates was rounding the corner, madness glaring from too-wide eyes. She even had waking nightmares—when she wasn't paying attention, Alicia Chavez, the *Black Opal*'s medic, would come into the infirmary and turn off the air supply to her isolation chamber. Or it would be Rory, and he would . . . But it was impossible, of course. Alicia's body was trillions of miles away, sprawled in the corridor where Kate had left her. And Rory . . . she couldn't even think about that. But she felt as though she must be constantly vigilant, and so she exercised.

"Kate?"

She jumped as though electrocuted. "Billy! Don't *do* that!" Clutching at her chest, feeling her heart slam against her ribs, she sank onto the bed. "Holy hell!" she muttered.

He looked nearly as startled as she felt. "Hey, I'm sorry. I thought you saw me coming."

How to tell him she'd seen only a madman with eyes the color of killing? Billy was a friend, after all—how to explain it to anyone? *My God,* she thought, *am I going crazy too? Is it finally getting me?*

"No problem," she finally managed to say. "I'm just— a little jumpy, I guess. It's *real* good to see you!"

He smiled crookedly. "I'm not on duty all the time, you know. I thought you could use the company."

"Yeah, sure. I'd offer you a drink, but . . ." She raised her hand in the direction of the isolation wall.

The gesture was not lost on him. "Pretty boring?" he asked.

She shrugged. "Bad enough. You got the time?"

"Seventeen fifty hours."

She nodded and pulled at a lock of hair.

He looked away briefly, and she thought she saw him blush. "Kate, wouldn't they even give you anything to wear?"

"Can't break quarantine, baby. Or are *you* volunteering to open the door?" She smacked her fist on the counter. "No, no, I didn't mean that, I'm sorry. Not your fault."

"I can leave if you'd feel better."

"No! I mean, please—I haven't talked to anyone since I've been in here! Not even what's-his-name—Norton. Besides, I—" She couldn't help it, she had to bring it up. "Billy, did it finish—"

"Finish?" He looked at her with such sudden and deliberate blankness on his face that she knew immediately she had made a mistake.

She faltered, staring at him, trying to read his face. He shook his head very slightly and raised his eyes to the ceiling before looking back at her.

"Are you comfortable?" he asked. "Looks pretty bare in there."

"It could be worse," she said slowly, still trying to recover from her blunder. Did he mean someone was listening in on their conversation? "I'm only supposed to be in here until they can finish running tests to make sure I'm clean."

His face had relaxed, though he still looked worried. "Suppose you're not? Then what?"

She was taken aback by this bald statement of her own fears. "I—I don't know. I'm trying not to think that far ahead."

"Don't blame you." He took a few steps toward the plastex barrier, peering at it curiously. "You know, the airlock you came in here through has been permanently sealed. And they blew your lifeboat." He spoke so quietly it was almost a whisper. "Towed it out two klicks and blew it right away."

Is that what you came here to tell me? she thought, squeezing her eyes shut as if she could see the fireball that destroyed *Black Opal* Lifeboat 1. *So they've found something! Why else would they blow my ship? I'm not immune, not safe anymore . . . and maybe Billy's not either. . . .*

Billy looked at her in dismay and rubbed the back of his neck distractedly. "Look, I don't think they've found anything. I'm sure they'd beam a priority message back to Earth, and they haven't! I'd know about it!" He smiled a little unsurely. "It was only a lifeboat, Kate. It was probably cheaper to blow it than try to sterilize it. You know Guil Pro—I'm sure it was just the money. Shit, maybe I shouldn't've told you about it."

"Now that's not fair." She folded her arms across her

chest. "I have a right to know what happened. You just surprised me."

"Yeah, I guess that's true. I just didn't expect you to get ... well, all weird." Again his eyes moved to the ceiling, as though he were trying to remind her they might be overheard.

"Sorry if I worried you." She made herself speak offhandedly. "I guess I'm kind of stressed."

"Well, you just better watch it, is all," he said uncomfortably, "or people'll be saying you're crazy, too."

She stared at him. "You mean they're already saying it."

He shook his head sharply and gave her a hard look. "I'm not *tellin'* you anything, Kate. But don't be acting off center—and watch who you sound off to. Know what I mean?"

"Billy, whose side are you on?" she asked very softly.

"Are there sides?"

She looked away from him, unwilling to answer that question even in her own mind.

"Kate, I have to go now. In case I ... don't see you again, will you remember what I said?"

She smiled a little. "Don't worry about me."

"Yeah." He raised his hand in a slight wave and walked away.

She did doze once, sitting up, her head slumped to one side, smiling slightly. Only to start suddenly awake, a name dying on her lips. "Rory—?" But no one was there.

Kate watched as Dr. Norton entered the main infirmary. At least he was alone.

"How're you feeling?" his voice filtered through the speaker.

"Same as always. What's up?" She could feel the blood pounding in her ears.

"You'll be happy to know that none of the cell cultures showed any change whatsoever," he said quietly, and smiled. "Apparently you didn't bring anything back with you from out there. You're okay."

She sat down suddenly, knowing her legs were about to go. Such a small thing, those two words *you're okay*, but they were the most wonderful words she had ever heard, and the last she had expected.

"No change? Not in *any* of them?" She had to ask, even though it was what he'd already told her.

"That's right, not a one."

"I can get out of here?"

Norton shrugged. "As far as I'm concerned."

"Then—"

They were interrupted as a slightly built man rushed in from the corridor. "You were not supposed to come down here without me!" It had to be Martin Baker—she recognized his voice immediately, though this was the first time she had seen him.

Norton turned. "That was my decision to make as chief of medicine."

"And I specifically told you not to say anything to her unless I was present. That was an *order*, Dr. Norton. Perhaps you need to remember who you work for!" Baker's pale blue eyes blazed incongruously in an evenly tanned face that spoke of many hours in a tanning booth.

Kate had walked up to the glass that separated her from the rest of the station, and Norton now turned in her direction. "Officer Harlin, this is—"

"Mr. Martin Baker, of course. Thanks, Doc, but I couldn't forget a voice like that."

Baker turned his head slowly toward her and just as slowly stared at her from head to foot and back again, as if he had just noticed her. Then he smiled, though it didn't touch his pale eyes. "Why, thank you, Officer Harlin. But the pleasure is mine . . . quite."

Her face darkened at this none too subtle reminder of her nudity. "Listen, Baker, I don't have to take any shit from some backwater sector director. Do you have something to say to me?"

His smile turned cold. "Indeed, Officer Harlin, I have quite a bit to say to you. But to start things off properly, perhaps I should tell you just who I am. My name is Martin Baker, as you so accurately surmised, and I am Geoffrey Kagen's personal assistant."

She raised her eyebrows slightly. "So?"

"Geoffrey Kagen is the executive director of research for the entire Consortium," he finished smugly. "You were working for him on this last mission."

Her lips curled up slightly. "All right, I made a mistake. You're not a backwater sector director, you're an executive director's ass-kisser."

"You should consider that I'm charged with accompanying you back to Earth. I expect it to be a trying journey, certainly," he looked her up and down again, "though possibly with some compensations."

She ignored this. "When do we leave?"

"Dr. Norton will detail some additional medical tests we'll need before we can break the isolation seals. Norton, I expect to be notified *before* she's been released, not after," he said pointedly. "Officer Harlin, remember you are still an employee of the Consortium, and that you will remain a part of this experiment until we decide that you've satisfied your contractual obligation." He left abruptly.

She stared after him. "What a pompous son of a bitch!"

"I suspect he enjoys it." Norton cleared his throat uncomfortably.

Kate turned her back to the infirmary and walked over to the bench containing the medical equipment. "Let's get started," she said. "The sooner I finish, the sooner I'll get out of here. What do I need to do?"

Later, she pulled her arm from the diagnostic cradle and rubbed it briskly. "So what was this all about?"

Norton explained that she had spent the last hour giving samples of all her bodily fluids—blood, lymphic fluid, mucus from various places, urine—samples that researchers would analyze to see if they could discover why she was apparently immune to the substance that had infected the rest of the *Black Opal*'s crew. They needed the samples now, before she left the sterile environment, to ensure that no outside contamination took place.

"Oh come on! They don't even know what they're looking for!"

Norton shrugged. "You wanted to know."

"My mistake. What's next?"

Norton operated some controls on his workbench, and

with a hissing sound a door she hadn't even noticed slid open. She stepped through it gingerly, and gooseflesh rose on her skin, though she knew her freedom was only relative.

"Hang tight and I'll get you some clothes." The doctor rummaged in a drawer and handed her a set of surgical scrubs. "Not very glamorous, but it's all I've got."

"Thanks. Glamour was never my strong suit." She dressed quickly. "Shoes?"

"Surgical boots—at least until you can get to General Stores." He handed her a pair.

She straightened after putting them on. "Aren't you going to call Baker? I hate to admit it, but if he's from Guil-Pro's central offices on Earth, he can probably kick ass pretty good. I don't want to get you in trouble."

"You mean that? I thought you might want to . . . well, have a little time to yourself."

"Thanks, Doc, but where could I go? This is a small station—he could find me without too much trouble. Even the Port Authority office couldn't help me much way out here."

Norton shot her a look, but thumbed the video-com. "Infirmary for Mr. Baker."

Kate stepped around in front of the screen and folded her arms, waiting. When Baker's face appeared, she smiled. "I'm out, Baker. If you want to see me, I'll be at Stores— well, actually, I might be in the mess. The officers' mess, of course. Why don't you check both places, just to be sure?"

As Baker stuttered into the speaker, she winked at Norton. "Suppose we meet in the mess in half an hour? *After* I've got some real clothes!"

Baker finally managed to speak. "If you leave that infirmary before I get there, I'll have you arrested! Norton, I warned you!" The screen went blank.

The doctor looked a little chagrined. "Better wait. I don't think he was kidding."

She sighed, shrugged, and made herself comfortable. "No sense of humor."

Norton shook his head.

* * *

Kate had hoped to see Billy Watson once more before Baker whisked her off the *Angel*, but Kagen's personal assistant made sure she had no chance to see anyone. After one night spent in real quarters, with real guards posted outside the door, she was hustled with one small pack of newly purchased belongings onto Guil-Pro's luxury liner the *Lady Pluto* for the trip back to Earth.

The good news was that the trip would take nearly four days, long enough for her to get the few facts at her disposal organized into a coherent story. The bad news was that she and Martin Baker were the only passengers on board.

CHAPTER

3

When Kate opened her eyes this time it was dark. That was okay, she thought with a sigh. She was on night cycle, secure in bed in her own private quarters on the *Lady Pluto*, headed back to earth. Yeah, that was okay. She rolled over, snuggling into her comfortable pillow, and tried to go back to sleep.

But it *wasn't* okay, she realized, and opened her eyes again. It smelled wrong in here, stale and closed in. Her bladder began making insistent demands. No wonder she couldn't sleep.

Annoyed at her nervous expectations, Kate sat up quickly to make her bathroom sojourn and get it over with. Her forehead slammed brutally against the closed cover of her safety-secured bed.

"Goddammit!" she yelled, falling back onto the pillow. She rubbed the tender spot, feeling a hard knot rising just below her hairline. Carefully she raised a hand over her face, straight up, now expecting the resistance she met some thirty centimeters above her. She was stuck in her own bed.

Well, wasn't that just dandy? Now she'd have to go and

make a nuisance of herself to the captain trying to get out of here. She'd been aboard the passenger liner *Lady Pluto* for two days, and nothing had gone right yet. She hadn't bothered to meet any of the crewmembers other than Captain Dickenson, and that only at Baker's insistence. The man had been taciturn and ungracious, and she wondered how he had ever become the captain of a luxury liner, where he would be called upon to socialize with the passengers and be charming.

Her bladder was really complaining now, as she groped for the headboard that formed the top end of her cocoon. It was damn dark in here!

Red and green telltales winked on to her left, the familiar console of a luxury liner Passenger Protection System. It was almost always built in to the bed so as not to upset squeamish travelers who didn't care to be reminded of the "dangers" of journeying outside their planet's atmosphere. The normally efficient system would seal a passenger into a safe and self-contained environment whenever the computer determined there was danger to the ship. In cases of serious trouble, or if a ship was damaged far from help, it could function as a hibernation unit, since people in deep-sleep used fewer life-support resources than people who were awake and panicky. The PPS was usually called a cocoon, but Kate had her own name for the things, which could be quirky and malfunction at the most inconvenient times. Like now.

"All right, all right, enough of this," she grumbled, punching controls and sending orders to the unit to release her. Even though she wasn't a member of the *Lady Pluto*'s crew, she was a working deep spacer with access to codes that, during a real emergency, would allow her to identify herself and her special status to the computer. The cocoon would then open, or so the theory went, freeing her to help out in the crisis. This, of course, was not a real emergency, but it would be soon enough if she couldn't use the bathroom.

"Please remain calm. You are enclosed in a Passenger Protection System. You are in no immediate danger. Please remain calm."

"That was *not* the right answer!" she told the stubborn machinery, and keyed in the commands that would make it display its diagnostic screens so she could locate the program error that was causing the system not to respond to her I.D. She was more than uncomfortable now, and she was beginning to get angry.

"You are becoming agitated," the machine said. "Please remain calm. You are in no personal danger. Further information will be supplied as it becomes available. Please remain calm."

The system did not display the diagnostics she had requested, so Kate keyed in her personal identification number again and the override codes that were supposed to break through the machine's passenger protection programming and allow her access to command mode.

—INVALID OVERRIDE CODE—COMMAND IGNORED—

"Oh, for chrissakes—" She jabbed at the keyboard again, by now feeling it was a futile gesture.

"Please remain calm..."

When the protection system began its litany for the third time, she clapped her hands over her ears. The goddamn machine was going to drive her crazy! It was like being on the *Black Opal* again, with SINS misreading her requests and ignoring her command codes....

Wait a minute, she *was* dealing with SINS, or a piece of it. All the SINS computers were exactly alike, parts of a giant whole, and they were installed on *all* Guil-Pro ships. Of course SINS controlled the protection systems along with everything else. The PPS worked even better in conjunction with SINS, because the more advanced computer could be so precise about what might endanger the passenger....

Or it could be so very clever about creating situations just like this one....

"Keep calm, keep calm," she muttered, wiping sweat from her eyes. "Don't think about that, don't even *think* it!"

There had to be a way out of this. This was just a *classic* malfunction! She was no green first-time passenger, scared silly and too spacesick to leave her cabin. She could tell when a ship was in trouble—it was an instinct you developed if you wanted to stay in this business. That instinct told her there was nothing wrong with this ship.

The tiny screen to her side was dark now. She was getting no information flow at all—she was completely cut off from the world outside her cocoon. The realization didn't make her feel any better.

Oh, yes, this had to be a malfunction, all right, because if it wasn't (and she already *knew* it couldn't be a real emergency), then there was only one other explanation—she had been trapped in here deliberately. But that was insane! She was on a luxury liner, she was on her way home, SINS was *not* capable of being malicious, he—*it*, for chrissakes—*it* was only a computer. . . .

Kate forced herself to listen to the insistent voice of the protection system, for fear she might miss something important. It was asking her if she wanted a sedative. Nothing to make her sleep, just to help her relax.

"Sedative? Hell *no* I don't want a sedative! Pay attention to this, you miserable son of a bitch!" She rolled over on her side to face the small screen. "I know there are voice-activated circuits in here. My name is Katharine Harlin. My personal I.D. number is 99734-23-KH. I'm under contract to the Guilford Production Consortium, work order number PX-2287-99734-KH, my rank is second pilot. . . . Let me out of here, you stupid mutha!"

The screen simply flickered and went dark again, while the mechanized voice repeated its question about a sedative.

This wasn't going to work, Kate realized; she had to remain calm. Talking to the system was getting her nowhere—why should it *listen* to her if it was going to ignore her command codes?

The little telltales seemed to blur out of focus, then came back in again. She rubbed her eyes, which only made it worse, then she started to forget what she was going to do next. The persistent ache low in her abdomen faded into the background. She felt sleepy again, and almost yielded to the overwhelmingly sweet, noxious odor that surrounded her. . . .

"No!" she yelled, "I said I didn't *want* a sedative, goddammit!" She began to pound on the lid with her fists, but the blows weakened quickly. "You have to . . . let me out. . . ." Her fists loosened and her sphincter relaxed at the same time. Her hands lay casually on the pillow by her face, and in her drugged sleep she was unaware of the acrid odor from her wet bedclothes.

A very faraway sensation began to annoy her. Where the hell was that sound coming from? If they didn't stop that tinny, scraping noise she'd never get any sleep!

Bright lights blazed through the transparent cocoon lid, and an ugly, distorted face was peering down. . . . She made small mumblings and tried to cover her eyes. She could distinguish a grating, too-loud voice.

"Harlin? Harlin, sit up! Come on now, you must sit up!"

"Wha'?" She felt helping hands, and struggled to sit with their aid. "Wha's goin' on?" Her head flopped helplessly, like a newborn's. A hand supported her neck. It was warm.

The voice kept making demands. "That's it, sit up. Open your eyes, now."

"Sleepy . . ." she murmured.

"Dammit, no, you can't sleep!"

Kate gasped as she was slapped several times, and she forced her eyes to open so it would stop. Staring hard at her rescuer, she could see short, curly, dark hair, a face that softened into comfortable, familiar lines—even down to the little scar that drew his mouth up into a slight smile on one side. She breathed in hard, several times, feeling a silly gladness wash over her, and tried to hug him. She couldn't quite manage. "Rory? Rory, that you?"

He smiled. "Now, Katie, who do you think it is? Here, breathe in."

She felt a mask cover her nose and mouth, and she obeyed him. After all, wasn't it just like Rory to show up in the nick of time and pull her ass out of the fire? God, how she'd missed him. Trusted friend, confidant—even lover, sometimes, in the cold depths of space far away from home. God, how she *still* missed him!

Rory had been the *Black Opal*'s engineer, and he had died billions of miles away and a long time ago. He had died and she still had not stopped mourning him. She knew this man couldn't be Rory, but she was enjoying the illusion too much to let go.

She was sitting in a chair now, on her own, and becoming too aware to maintain this fantasy. She turned despondent, bitter. "Thissiz not funny," she slurred. "Who are you, really?"

"Don't worry about it."

"You *can't* be Rory!" She tried to stand, and he caught her as she nearly fell. "Don' help me, I don' wannyur help. . . ."

"Take my advice, Katie, and keep your butt in that chair."

She followed the suggestion of his helping hands, and felt him adjusting the chair, reclining it. He had Rory's face and Rory's voice, but Rory was dead. Who could this be?

"You're okay. Try to sleep for a while. Got me, Katie? Sleep now."

Rory had been the only one who could get away with calling her Katie.

When she woke, she had a raging headache and a stiff neck. She was still in her quarters on the *Lady Pluto*, slumped in a reclining chair, her mouth as dry as moondust, her oversized T-shirt damp with sweat and urine, her legs sticky and nasty-feeling. She rubbed her forehead and winced when she touched the tender goose egg. She had a very hazy recollection of how she'd gotten here, and a jumbled memory of a terrible nightmare.

Why was she in her chair, for one, and not her bed? Had she been drinking? No, not that kind of headache. She looked at the clock and realized it was 0700 hours—almost time to get up! Had she spent the entire night in this chair? Kate stood shakily, worried a little at the nausea welling in her stomach, and stumbled over to her bed. It was half-closed (*What a pessimist*, she thought distractedly, *why not* half-opened?), gaping at her as though it had jammed in that position . . . and then she began to remember.

She leaned over her bed and took a deep breath, and a whiff of something sickly sweet from inside almost overwhelmed her. Turning her head away, she breathed open-mouthed for a moment, then deliberately turned to sniff at the cocoon again. This time it was very faint.

Now she remembered being trapped inside this damn thing somehow, and knew the system had tried to poison her! She'd been rescued. By . . . whom? She veered away from that recollection. *Therein lies madness*, she thought with a shiver, and rubbed her arms.

There would be some other explanation of her rescue,

if she thought about it long enough. Perhaps she had finally been able to free herself. Yeah, well, why did she keep remembering Rory's face? True, she missed him terribly, but why should she *see* him, as though he had really been there?

Idly she touched the controls on the side panel of her bed and watched as the cover slid back smoothly, disappearing into the decor. By now the faint odor she had first noticed was completely gone, and she could detect only the acidic urine smell. Yeah, right, she remembered that much, not being able to get up and having an accident in her bed.

For a moment she debated telling a crewmember about her trouble, but it occurred to her that all her evidence had disappeared. Besides, what could she say when they asked her how she had gotten free?

She moved toward the shower to wash away the urine, the sweat, the sick feeling, the crazy memories.

She did *not* have the *Black Opal*'s disease, she was *not* going crazy. She couldn't be; she hadn't been sick yet, and all of them had gotten sick and then recovered before they'd lost their minds. All of them. She turned the water on as hard as it would go and tried to stop thinking.

After the shower, breakfast, and lots of black coffee, Kate decided her main problem was a bad case of cabin fever. It seemed to her that all she'd done since waking up aboard the lifeboat was sit and wait for things to happen to her. Even though Baker had allowed her to hide out here in her cabin these last two days and had not disturbed her privacy, his ominous presence was always there. She was used to being in control of her own life, but now he was.

Still, she had needed this time alone to get her thoughts together. She had to be ready to face a Board of Inquiry, a psychiatric review, or whatever else Guil-Pro might throw at her when she got back home. She'd already filled up a half-dozen minicards with the databoard provided in each cabin, but enough was enough.

Besides, she told herself, *why put it off any longer? You should go out and wander around—meet some of the crew on this bird. There's only staff on board; they must be wondering why you're hiding. It doesn't look good. Can't let a*

*silly dream dictate your behavior. Time to start acting like a
professional and stop being a chicken!*

She slipped the minicards into a pocket. She couldn't
shake the feeling that *someone* (not, most definitely *not*,
Rory) had been in her quarters, and there was no sense in
leaving her personal thoughts lying around. Nothing wrong
with being cautious.

She walked down the spacious, brightly lit corridors,
admiring the opulent luxury reserved for those who had money,
comparing it to the dingy corridors she was used to. How
quiet such a vessel was with no one on board! A ship like
this could carry a hundred passengers and a crew of ten, and
the silence of the empty halls and cabins was eerie.

The observation area always drew her when she was
aboard a ship that had one. It was not something she admitted
to many people. After all, she was a professional; why would
she want to look at stars when she was out there in them all
the time? It was her secret delight, this small pleasure, and
very restful, to watch the stars in normal space, especially
now when she was close to her own system. Maybe she could
even catch a glimpse of Sol after more than three years away
from home. She looked forward to healthy, bright sunlight,
not like the dim haze of her last stop aboard the *Black Opal*. . . .
She would not dwell on that too much, she had the future to
worry about now.

"Looking for the sun . . . Katie?"

Kate's arms stiffened. She leaned into the railing that
separated her from the plastex viewport, refusing to turn
around. She was *not* hearing that warm, comforting voice,
so if she didn't turn around she wouldn't see its owner.

"Mad at me, or don't you answer when someone speaks
to you?" asked the soft voice behind her.

She turned abruptly and faced a man she knew could
not be standing there, but was. Now it was impossible to
argue with the evidence of her eyes and ears.

"What's the matter, Katie, aren't you glad to see me?"
He tilted his head inquisitively.

(On Earth there was a bird called a Loon. Its call was
a high, maniacal laugh. Hence the phrase, "Crazy as a . . .")

"Don't *talk* to me, goddamn you!" She slid sideways along the railing. "You're dead. Very dead. You *know* that!"

"*I* know it? I'm standing right here." He smiled. "What does that tell you?"

(The sound of the Loon grew louder in the background.)

My God, he was right, she *was* crazy! She had to be, standing here seeing a man she knew was dead, and letting him laugh at her for seeing him!

(On Earth, in ancient times, the people who made hats, the hatters, used chemicals to produce their wares, mercury that gradually, insidiously, made them sadly and certifiably mad. Hence the term, "Mad as a...")

Hold yourself together, she pleaded silently. *There's a way out of this.*

"Why did you save me last night?" she asked him. "I saw you in my quarters—I know it was you!"

He smiled again. So warm. So sincere. "I was saving you for better things, Katie."

"Don't call me that!"

She kept sliding along the railing until she reached the end, and then she slid along the wall, feeling the rough surface of it through her clothing. That was real. Rory moved along with her, casually. Smiling. She could feel sweat beading on her face.

(The Mad Hatter slopped his tea, and laughed at Alice with the voice of a Loon....)

"Why are you here? What do you want me to do?" she asked.

"Just admit who I really am, and come here to me." He held out his hand. "Let me help you."

"Uh-uh. Don't need it. I'm not crazy. I don't know who you are, but I am *not* crazy!" (*Don't laugh, Harlin, or you'll lose it. The Loon will win, and you hate tea.*)

She repeated this over and over, this litany of sanity, and glanced about so he wouldn't think she had noticed anything in particular. She was reaching her goal, slowly but surely. Less than a meter...

"Don't you feel it? Can't you tell what's happening to you?" Again Rory held out his hand.

"Stop that! Just stop it! Don't you talk to me like that!"

She'd reached her target without Rory realizing what she was after, and now the wall intercom was right behind her. Kate leaned back, slumped tiredly—and felt the switch move soundlessly. The connection was open, if only someone was on the other end to hear. . . .

"I'm not comin' to you," she said. "You want me, you'll have to catch me."

"Oh, I'm much faster than you think, Katie. Much faster."

He moved, and she never saw it, but there he was, grasping her wrist before she could react. The pain of his grip nearly brought her to her knees.

"You make it very hard on yourself," he said easily. "I come to you as a friend." He showed her something shiny in his palm. "Just to cure that terrible sick headache. . . ."

"God . . . *damn* you, Rory!" She tried to kick him, but he caught her ankle and flung her away from him. She caromed into a wall and lay stunned, helplessly watching him come at her. He grabbed her arm and moved to press the shiny thing against her skin. She struggled in a slow-witted, hopeless way, then suddenly she heard running feet pounding down the hallway deck. Rory heard it too, and snapped his head around, losing his attention long enough for her to summon every bit of desperate strength she could.

She slapped his hand and watched the coin-sized object fly away and bury itself under a grouping of furniture. The running footsteps grew louder; there was no time for Rory to retrieve it. His expression turned hideous, and she could believe in that instant that he was capable of far worse than murder. He grabbed her by her collar and thrust his face close to hers, whispering, *"Just you wait, Katie!"* then threw her against the wall, hard. She had to fight for consciousness as he backed away from her, turned, and ducked around a corner.

"What the hell's going on here?"

When her double vision cleared, Kate saw a bearded young man standing before her. It wasn't Rory, but since Rory hadn't been Rory, how did she know whether to trust this one?

"I—I'm—" She gasped, unable to speak.

"Okay, don't try to talk. Looks like you've had the wind knocked out of you. Just lie still."

"But he'll—" She coughed. It was no use, she couldn't explain in time to have him follow Rory. By now he'd be long gone . . . unless *this* was Rory, come back from the other direction in another disguise. . . . *Stop listening to that bird!* she ordered herself.

"You all right now?" he asked as she stopped gasping.

"I—I think so. Whew!" She sat up and leaned back against the wall. "God, what a headache!"

"I guess! Looks like you took quite a header." He smiled engagingly. "I'm Paul Westman, ship's engineer. What happened?"

"I'm not sure." Best to put him off until she could find out how much he already knew. After all, the only crew-member she knew by sight was the captain—and could she even trust him? "What made you show up?"

"We heard something funny on the bridge intercom. Sounded like a fight—your voice and someone else's."

"What made you think it was me?" she asked quickly.

"You're the only woman aboard this trip."

"But you *did* hear two voices?"

"Sure! I mean, not real clear, but . . ." He looked at her a little strangely. "Why d'you ask?"

"Never mind." She shook her head. "It's over now, and who knows where he is."

"Well, no, actually it's not over." Westman crouched down to look at her directly. "How d'you feel?"

"A little winded, and I'm sure I'll be sore tomorrow. Why?"

"The captain wants to see you right away."

"Oh yeah? Well I don't want to see him. This is a personal problem, Westman. Tell him to talk to Baker. He probably knows more about it than I do anyway."

Westman shook his head. "Sorry, I got orders. The captain can't afford not to investigate strange things happening on his ship. And he counts this a pretty strange thing. Besides," he grinned, "the captain doesn't like Baker. Not at all."

"At least he's got good taste." Kate eyed the nearest furniture grouping, then slapped at her pockets as though looking for something. "Shit," she complained, and started patting her hands along the carpeted flooring. "Lost my rank pin." She crawled over to the furniture that had swallowed Rory's little weapon. (Not *Rory*, the *Rory-thing*.) "It's my good-luck piece," she explained, reaching underneath, touching something cold and hard. She moved it carefully in case it decided to bite. "Got it." She palmed the small thing, slid it into a pocket, and grunted as she got slowly to her feet. "Glad to hear the captain and I have something to share a conversation about. Okay, Westman, lead the way."

Kate Harlin sat in the captain's quarters, cradling a cup of coffee in her hands.

"Before we get started," she began, "I'd really like to thank you for your hospitality. Until this incident today, everything's been more than I could ask for, especially coming off a pretty dirty three-year mission."

"Don't sweat it." He shrugged. "I've got my orders, too."

She looked away from him. "Well, it's nice to know who your friends are."

"What makes you think you have any here?"

She set the cup down with a thump, ignoring the splash of hot liquid across the back of her hand. "Look, I came to you because your engineer is a nice guy, and he told me you're concerned about 'strange things' happening on your ship. If you're going to act like a prick about it, I'll just get myself out of your way!" She stood abruptly.

"Now you listen to me, lady!" Dickenson was a short, stocky man, and she towered over him by half a foot, but he put his face centimeters from her own. "I got pulled off a very lucrative passenger contract to come out here and haul your ass home like you were some big-shot explorer with a new find—!"

"And all you got was a lowly second pilot, and a woman at that. How disappointing for you!"

"No, Harlin, it's even worse. I got stuck with a spacer who turned chickenshit and ran, leaving a whole crew behind, that's what I got! So you tell *me* how I should behave. You're bad news!"

She stared at him, her lips stretched into a thin line.

"You think so?" she asked softly. "Spacer, you haven't *seen* bad news! You want to know what kind of a crew I left out there? I'll tell you—bugfuck *crazy*, every last one of 'em, except for the lucky ones. They were already dead!" Her voice trembled, and she felt herself perilously close to tears. "So don't you talk to me about bad news!"

Dickenson stared at her, his jaw tight. "So—" he finally let out a long, slow breath, "you got a story." They both sat down.

Kate bit down hard on her lip, determined not to cry, either in anger or in grief, in front of this man. "Yeah, but it's for the Board of Inquiry. Period."

"Well, that's your business, I guess. Paul, get my bottle. Three glasses."

The engineer obeyed, pouring three generous glasses of scotch.

"Here," Dickenson held a a glass in front of her, "you look like you could use this."

"I don't need your—"

"Drink!"

Kate drained the glass in three swallows. Westman poured three fingers' worth more, and Dickenson said, "Sip. I don't want you drunk, we need to talk."

"Why? You've already made up your mind!"

"No I haven't, goddammit!" Dickenson shoved his hands in his pockets and started to pace. "Look, I'm sorry I blew up at you. I ought to know better than to jump feet first into a story Guil-Pro has anything to do with. God knows I've been working for them long enough!"

"They've made a formal statement?"

"Well, no, I don't mean that, either. But they're not coming to your defense. It makes you look pretty bad, Harlin, when your own employer won't stick up for you. I thought I was coming out here for a real loser!"

"Thanks for the vote of confidence." She rubbed the bridge of her nose tiredly.

"Now wait a minute! I've had a hell of a lot to put up with, you know. What's-his-name—that little bastard who thinks he's running the whole show—Baker! If he's not careful, I'll wring his skinny neck before we make Earth orbit!"

Kate had to smile. "Sounds like his normal self."

"Yeah, well, he's going to put *me* in the loony bin if I have to listen to him much more!" Dickenson scowled. "I'd be careful of him, Harlin. He's talking you up all the time, wondering if you're going to get sick, wondering if maybe you'll go crazy—and he never finishes a damn sentence, so nobody knows what he's talking about!" He scratched his head. "He acts like he's real concerned, but I don't know."

"What does he say?" She was no longer smiling.

"Things he should never say to anyone else, regardless of what's going on." He looked at her. "Did you ever have a breakdown?"

"Hell no! How could I get into space after something like that?"

"You could lie about it and falsify your medicals. Baker implied you were perfectly capable of such a thing."

"Oh, come on, you have to be an expert to get away with something like that!" She laughed bitterly. "I couldn't even get SINS to do what it was supposed to!"

"He seemed to think it was worth investigating."

She was silent.

"You know it doesn't look good for you," Dickenson said. "I hope you have a real good story for the Board of Inquiry."

"Or the shrinks?" Kate took a long drink from her glass.

"Why don't you start by telling me what happened up in the observation deck?"

"Because I—I'm not sure." Strangely, she felt close to tears again. He had *been* Rory, until that last look of utter hatred. (The Loon chuckled somewhere behind her. . . .)

"Paul and I heard some of it from the bridge. Was someone in my crew bothering you?"

"I couldn't say." She swallowed fiercely. "Look, this isn't going to work. Thanks for the scotch." She rose to her feet.

"Uh-uh. Sit down. Look, this is my ship, and I'm going to find out what's going on. If we have to, we can run a lineup with the crew. There's only ten of us. . . ."

"No! No thanks." She couldn't stand the thought of having to identify her attacker, when she knew she wouldn't see Rory's face anywhere she looked. "That wouldn't work. But, look, if you want to help me with something—" She dug in her pocket and pulled out the coin-sized object Rory had threatened her with. "I think this is a pressure hypodermic. He—whoever it was—tried to use this on me. Paul showing up was the only thing that saved me. Maybe you can find out what's in it." She handed it to Dickenson, who examined it curiously.

"Ugly-looking little thing. Yeah, we can put the medic right on it. Paul?"

The young engineer took the hypodermic gingerly in his hand and left the room.

"Harlin, what's going on with you?" Dickenson asked softly. "Who is so mad at you that they'd send someone after you with one of those things?"

She shrugged. "I don't know."

"I'd like to help you, Harlin. I can't do that if you won't talk to me."

She looked at him for a long moment. The words *help you* lingered in the air so invitingly it made her heart ache. Could it really hurt to tell someone? She could consider it practice, a dress rehearsal for the Board. She wiped a finger in the moisture on her glass, working up her nerve to actually begin.

"Suppose you start by calling me Kate, all right?" she asked.

"Sounds good to me, Kate. Call me Jim. Now," he settled back, "what's this shit all about?"

"It started out pretty normally," she finally said. "The *Black Opal* was a standard prospecting mission, with a crew of six. I was the pilot, and we had two exo-geologists along for the ride."

"You knew those people?"

"All of 'em. We'd crewed together a lot."

Dickenson grunted assent.

"It took us a year to get out to the target area, so we had just about a year to explore three planetary systems there."

"What were you looking for?"

"There were good predictors for ore deposits in that area—and I mean rich ones!"

Dickenson's eyebrows went up. "You guys must've been hot stuff. Guil-Pro doesn't usually operate just on predictors."

"Well, it wasn't *just* predictors. Vince Rochenko, our captain, had done a lot of research, and he hit on an area where there was already some work going on. Not a played-out area, of course, just busy. You know, rival companies and such. Guil-Pro really liked that idea. And, of course, that was part of the problem. Here we were with all this reputation and all these predictors, and the mission was a bust. Eleven planets we had to look at, and nothing."

"You guys operate on commission?"

She nodded. "You sign for a certain percentage of the find, depending on your reputation, how many years you've been in the business—and if you've got an agent, well . . ."

"So you were going to be out money."

She looked at him. "It was worse than that. Vince was in some kind of trouble. He picked this mission because he knew it would hit, and he was able to convince whoever he owed that it would hit. They were willing to wait, I guess.

"But he was frantic when we didn't find anything." She took a mouthful of scotch, savored it briefly. "We had the worst luck! Equipment failures, system foul-ups, communication breakdowns—you wouldn't think so much could go wrong on one mission! When it was over, we only had a month and a half left to spend in the target area, and a year to get home. So Vince went into SINS's registry for another area we'd have to pass on our way back. He found one."

"Is that legal?"

She shrugged. "No. An unauthorized stop can get you in a lot of trouble, *if* you don't run out of fuel or supplies, and you're lucky enough to make it home . . . but we decided it was worth the risk."

"You *all* decided?" the captain asked, suspicious.

"Hey, if you don't find anything, nobody gets paid. That's a very persuasive argument."

"So you went."

Westman slipped quietly back into the room and sat down. Dickenson acknowledged him with a nod.

"We went. And when we finally arrived, indications were good that it would be worth the trouble. Yeah, it looked *real* good. We were on the bridge, and Vince was dancing around like an excited little kid. . . ."

CHAPTER

4

"SINS was giving us strong indicators of heavy ore deposits, fairly pure stuff that wouldn't require too much refining," Kate continued. "That's why Vince was so excited. But once we'd landed, Greg—that was Gregor Kidd, our chief researcher—found something even better." She paused. "Artificial structures."

"Ruins?" Dickenson asked.

"No, Captain, *buildings*, not just a pile of ancient rocks like the *Moonstone* expedition found on Cygni Two."

"Rocks! Now wait a minute!" Dickenson disagreed. "Those artifacts were the first evidence we had of life-forms higher than microbials!"

"I'm not knocking the Cygni artifacts, Captain. But those were cave paintings compared to what we found! These structures enclosed a sealed environment, and the interior atmosphere was *different* from the planet's. The buildings were not native to that world."

"You're sure they weren't human built?"

"Not with that atmosphere!" She shook her head. "But none of the materials were recognizable, either. I only saw it from the viewscreen, myself, but the structure looked alien! It was—" she waved her hands vaguely, "it was different. The proportions were wrong." She shook her head in frustration. "I can't get the right words. You'd have to see it. But the atmosphere was proof enough! It was close to ours, but not breathable."

"That's incredible!" Dickenson rubbed his hands together as though he'd been there.

"Yeah," she smiled faintly in memory, "we were wild, like kids, especially when SINS declared it a virgin find. That's worth a big bonus right there."

"So how come nobody else found it before?" Westman asked. "You said it was a busy area. How could all these other companies miss out on something like that?"

"Who knows? Maybe they were smart enough to stay away. We sure weren't." She shrugged. "I don't mean we were careless, though. We sent the robot probe in first, because SINS told us the structures were over five hundred years old. Boswell said they were sealed and sound, safe enough to explore."

"Who was Boswell?"

"The robot probe." Kate grinned self-consciously. "He walked right in through an airlock. Not your normal opening, either, but something that kind of twisted and was just there. The place was real eerie—it didn't even look deserted, more like they'd just left for the weekend. We all had this feeling the owners might come back from vacation any minute and want to know what we were doing there.

"The floor was covered with this stuff that looked like tile fragments. Boswell was having trouble negotiating them in some places, because they were kind of piled up. They looked like bits of slate, but they were a little spongy. SINS said the stuff was inorganic, though he—I mean, it couldn't analyze the substance precisely. It looked almost like some kind of packing material. We wondered if the tenants had left in a hurry, and that's why it was lying all around."

She looked a little distant, and smiled crookedly, remembering. "But the air was clean. No microbes, no viruses, no life-forms of any kind. Alicia, our medic, guessed there was an incredibly efficient purification system at work." She winced. "Rory said he was going to figure the thing out and get a patent for it."

"Rory?"

She swallowed. "Our engineer. A friend of mine."

Dickenson nodded.

"Anyway," she continued after a pause, "that's what gave

Vince wild ideas. The native atmosphere was lethal, but the atmosphere inside the structure was totally different, and similar enough to our own that we could be pretty sure it had once supported organic life. A few trace elements would make it safe for us. Vince wanted to do that right away so we could work unsuited. He figured it would help us get out fast, and we didn't have much time."

"Doesn't sound like a reasonable man's decision," Dickenson remarked.

"That's what I was worried about. We were already breaking the law—Vince wouldn't even let me file a flight plan for that part of the trip—and now he was talking about relying on a completely alien environment. Who *cared* if we could breathe the damn air? The place wasn't made for human beings!" She made herself slow down. "Alicia agreed with me. She said just because the air was pure when we examined it the first time was no guarantee it would stay that way. After all, this system wasn't designed for us. Just our being there might be enough to disturb its balance!"

"Sounds like you didn't vote on this issue."

"No, but we did compromise. After we tampered with the atmosphere, we agreed that the first team should go inside fully protected. One member would strip right away, the other would remain suited until we were sure everything was okay.

"Rory was going to be on the first team, because we wanted a good study of the structure's mechanical systems. He volunteered to be the first test—if I went with him."

"Oh?" Dickenson asked.

She nodded. "We worked well together, and he knew I could keep a cool head if anything did go wrong. It's funny," she hesitated, "Vince took Rory's advice pretty frequently, and he knew we were a good team, but he wouldn't go for it this time. He insisted on sending one of the researchers in there. That's what the regs said—specialists were to accompany all initial contact teams. This, from a man who was breaking the rules by being on this planet in the first place." She smiled quickly. "He wanted to know what were we paying them for if not to take duty like this. I wasn't complaining; I didn't want to go. I thought the whole business was crazy, and I wasn't making any secret of it."

"You're not in it for the excitement of discovery anymore?"

"I like excitement just fine. This was insanity!" She shook her head vehemently. "So we went by the book, and our other exo-geologist, Kishu Mishima, went with Rory. They had cameras and a ton of monitoring equipment, extra oxygen for the suits—you name it. Aboard ship we had set up watches, and someone was always on the monitors. Rory unsuited right away."

"And?"

"Nothing. He wandered around, examined some of the tile-looking things on the floor, and showed them to Mishima—they were everywhere. . . ." She gave a sudden shiver. "And we ran tests. For over three days nothing happened. So Mishima unsuited.

"A little while later, I was at the monitors talking to Rory. He was outside exploring. Now you have to understand that by this time we were all pretty relaxed. They had been working inside the buildings for over seventy-two hours, and Rory had been unsuited the whole time. The temperature in there was comfortable, it was an ideal environment to work in. They'd explored several rooms—I think they had five or six they'd made operational. We were feeling pretty smug. I mean," she smiled, "it almost made me sorry I hadn't decided to go out with them.

"Anyway, Rory had discovered symbols on some of the outer walls, and Mishima wanted him to copy them. We didn't have a linguistics expert on the mission, but we figured SINS might have some ideas. So I finished talking to Rory and switched back to the main inside camera." Kate stopped, feeling her pulse begin to race. "I—I had just—" Her voice caught.

Dickenson made a motion and Westman poured her some more scotch. "Can you go on?" he asked quietly.

"Can't stop now." She smiled faintly and took a long drink from her glass. "I had just told Mishima how Rory was doing when the monitors went crazy. There was this wild surge of energy—I mean, it was almost off the scales, and it was a damn *life-form* reading! Organic life, like it had just showed up, like spontaneous generation. It happened so fast that before I could warn Mishima, the—" she swallowed and rubbed her face, "the whole goddamned floor *moved* right in front of me! It just—it was like a black sheet rippled and moved and started crawling up his legs. There were hundreds of these little flat things, shaped like diamonds—the things we had thought were pieces of packing material, that SINS had told us were inorganic—and they just—they just *crawled* on him, up his legs and under his clothes—he started screaming and tearing his clothes off—oh *God*, it was awful!

"I was screaming, too, when Alicia came running in. She managed to stay calm, somehow, with Mishima clawing at himself and shrieking for help." She took another gulp from her glass. "Then we realized Rory was trying to get us on the other channel. I—I told him what was going on, and he wanted to try to help. He thought if he could just get Mishima to suit up, then we could get him aboard the ship." Her voice had hoarsened. "I didn't want him to go in there. Mishima was huge now. This was a *little* man, and he looked like he weighed three hundred pounds with these—these things all over him. I could hardly stand to watch."

"What did Rory do?"

"Alicia thought it was a good idea for him to go inside. She figured he would be safe as long as he stayed suited. And if we could get Mishima back aboard ship, maybe we could get the things off him in a controlled environment. So he went inside.

"Mishima was obsessed with getting those things off. He recognized Rory when he saw him, even through his faceplate, and understood he was there to help. But when Rory tried to talk him into putting his suit on, that was the end of it. Mishima started bellowing again, and ran away." She gave a short, bitter laugh. "Alicia told me then that he was phobic. One of the reasons he worked in space was because he hated little crawly things, especially bugs. The one pest you don't have in space, the thing he went out to get away from, and here he was . . ." She shuddered.

"Mishima started racing from room to room, and he was naked, though you couldn't tell." Her voice grew very quiet. "He looked like a moving ball of swarming bees, and the more he ran around, the more these things came up off the floor like waves to cover him. God, there were so many of them, all moving and fluttering—" She broke off.

"SINS had *told* us they were inorganic, and everybody had seen the readouts, it wasn't just me! Packing material, for chrissakes—I swear, that's what we all thought it was! For *three days* there were no life-forms—" Her voice broke. "There wasn't anything there, and then these things—"

"Let's stop for a minute," Dickenson suggested. "Do you want any more to drink?"

"How about some coffee?" she managed to ask, pushing away her glass. "I won't be able to go on if I have any more of this. Besides, I really have to use your bathroom."

Dickenson showed her where the facilities were. When she had closed the door, he and Westman looked at each other but could think of nothing to say.

"Want to rest a few minutes more?" he asked when she returned.

"I think I'm okay now. I want to talk—but it doesn't work if I start thinking too much." Kate drank her coffee black, and the scalding heat seemed to ease the tightness in her throat a little.

"If you had a sick sense of humor, I guess it was almost funny, watching Rory stumping around in his spacesuit, carrying another one, trying to catch this screaming maniac who was covered with—these things. We started calling them kites, later, once we had a better idea of what they looked like when they weren't dormant. Anyway," she stared at her hands, "Mishima was trying to scrape the kites off. He'd gotten to the area where they were keeping their tools, and he was using everything he could get his hands on. It was a little room with only one door, so Rory had him cornered. It wasn't over yet, but at least Mishima couldn't run away anymore."

"Did Rory get him?"

She went on as though she hadn't heard the question. "By now the rest of the crew was with me and Alicia at the viewscreen. We were all trying to give Rory advice on how to handle him. Sooner or later he'd have to exhaust himself, we figured, and then we'd have him.

"Then Mishima saw Rory again—I don't even know if

he knew it was Rory anymore—and he grabbed this gun we used to shoot pitons into cliff walls. It's not really a piton, it's more like a harpoon, since it carries rope with it so we can climb. . . ." Kate felt her mouth quiver. "Mishima picked this gun up . . . and shot Rory . . ." her voice cracked on his name, "and we couldn't do anything but just sit there at that damn viewscreen and *watch*! Rory was pinned to the wall, waving his arms real slow, like a big bug. . . . I don't think it took him a minute to die—thank God." She took a deep breath and exhaled slowly. "Then Mishima put the gun down and started scraping kites off again. Rory just hung there, all limp like a doll, with the extra suit still in his hand, and Mishima didn't even know he was there, didn't realize what he'd done—" Kate's voice broke in a sob.

Dickenson and Westman stared at each other over her bowed head.

"I'm sorry, I can't—"

"Don't worry about it, we're with you."

She nodded and tried to smile, but bit her lip instead and wiped her nose. "Vince and Alicia went out after him. We didn't have any real weapons, of course, but Alicia had medical stunguns—we knew they'd never get close enough to him to use a regular hypo. We'd never had to use them and didn't even know if they'd work, but it was all we had.

"Vince didn't want Alicia to go at all—he can be damn old-fashioned sometimes—but she said a doctor ought to be there, and he couldn't argue with that. They managed to stun Mishima from a distance, and then they had to get him in his suit. It—it was pretty grotesque. But the kites showed no interest in them at all. We figured later it had to be heat or something organic that attracted them and made them hang on. Oh, they'd investigate a little, maybe crawl up somebody's arm, but they didn't stay.

"We'd made an agreement, before Vince and Alicia went out, that only the two of them would handle Mishima. Greg and I would seal them off in the part of the ship that included the infirmary and the lower airlock they had used. We would stay in the control area, around the bridge and SINS's master console. That way there'd be several layers of sealed bulkhead doors between us, in case— Well, just in case. So there we were, me and Greg, sealed into the ship's control area, watching them on the screens.

"They got Mishima unsuited and into the cryogenic unit in the infirmary. They were still suited, of course, and maintaining quarantine status. They made damn sure none of those things fell off him, either. While they were trying to figure out a way to remove the kites, the things sort of flattened out and started dropping away by themselves. We didn't know if they were dying or going back into a dormant state, but he was shedding them like fish scales. We guessed it was the cold. When they were all off, Alicia used the waldos to move them into a sample case underneath the unit, and sealed them up. Just for the hell of it, she ran another scan on them—and SINS insisted they were inorganic again. Then she began to thaw Mishima.

"We scanned the infirmary, and it looked clean. Mishima's readings were okay too, so we agreed they could unsuit. She had sedated him while he was still stunned, so he didn't give them any trouble when they moved him to the isolation unit after he was thawed. W-we were afraid if he woke up and the first thing he saw was people in suits, he might— go off again.

"Alicia was being the perfect doctor, real detached about the whole thing, which was good because the rest of us were pretty jittery. She was fascinated by the kites, and also by Mishima's self-inflicted wounds. He had some pretty bad cuts from trying to scrape the kites off, but they were already healing, and it had only been a few hours." Kate paused for another cup of coffee. "A few hours..." She sighed. "So little time to make such a big difference. Mishima had only been unsuited about two hours when all this happened. After three days of nothing... we were just lucky Rory was outside when it happened, I guess."

Dickenson nodded encouragingly.

"Then we had to figure out what to do with the kites," she continued. "They were still in the cryo unit, because nobody wanted to risk letting them warm up to body temperature. Vince wanted to fry them right there, but Alicia thought we ought to try to bring at least one back. She was convinced they were harmless if you kept them frozen. Greg and I argued that we had more than enough film footage of the ruins and the kites to prove our claim—let somebody else come back out and figure out what was going on! This wasn't in our contract.

"We couldn't agree right then, so we put it off." She paused. "We talked about going out after Rory, but it looked like the kites were trying to swarm inside his suit—we couldn't really tell from that distance—and the whole thing was so hard to deal with.

"Alicia brought Mishima back slowly. He came up crazy as a loon the first time," (she could still hear Mishima's voice, like a bird, laughing in the distance behind her) "even after he realized the kites were gone, so they kept him sedated. Then he developed flu symptoms, and that really scared us, so they suited up again. SINS said he should stay in isolation for seven days after these symptoms went away—if they went away." Kate leaned back in her seat and felt her tight muscles protest.

"SINS hadn't been much help up to this point," she said quietly. "We kept giving him data, and he kept building it into his model of the situation, but he wasn't giving out many answers yet. All he could say about Mishima's symptoms was that he had a viral, influenza-type infection. For all we knew, that's exactly what it was—the flu! Even that business about the quarantine was just a quote from the regs."

"Well, you were in a new situation," Dickenson said, his voice a little husky from having been quiet for so long. "Even SINS can't operate in a vacuum."

"Yeah, well—" She hesitated, unwilling to tell them how unhelpful SINS had really been.

"Did Mishima recover?" Dickenson prompted, seeing that she would rather not pursue the point.

"Yes. He wasn't sick more than twenty-four hours. The scanners said he was clean, so we discussed letting him out. SINS had specified a seven-day period, but—well, they'd been unsuited when he'd gotten sick, so Alicia figured they'd probably been exposed anyway. Keeping the disease in the confines of the infirmary seemed like the important thing to worry about, not following the regulations. We agreed they could let him into the infirmary with them.

"It was a real nerveracking situation at this point. Alicia was afraid that she and Vince would develop the same symptoms, so it was just a matter of wait and see. It didn't take long. Next day Vince had it, and a few hours after that Alicia. Now they'd been taking samples like crazy from Mishima while he was still sick, and SINS had it all. But the only thing SINS would recommend was"—she almost choked on the word—"aspirin, or some other antiinflammatory drug. Just like a goddamned doctor, take two aspirin and call me in the morning!" She made herself stop for a breath. "Mishima had his hands full with two delirious patients, even though Vince didn't seem to be as sick, and could help him a little with Alicia.

"Greg and I worked like teamsters, pumping SINS for information, sending information to Earth just in case... none of us made it back. Poor Mishima! To have gone through that horrible experience himself, and then have to put up with two sick people who were almost as crazy with fever as he'd been—" Kate paused. "Do you guys believe any of this?" she asked suddenly.

"Like I said a while back, we're with you," Dickenson said quietly. "Go on."

"Mishima wanted us to leave. We couldn't do that, not with Vince and Alicia so sick. Maybe we couldn't be right there to help him, but at least we could work with SINS and maybe get some answers while he was taking care of them. Besides, they'd probably be okay within twenty-four hours. Mishima argued with us; he was vehement. 'Get out!' he kept saying, but we ignored him. Later, I wondered if he'd had some kind of premonition.

"Vince was completely recovered and Alicia was feeling better when Mishima just—lost it, all of a sudden. He started gibbering, and then began running around the infirmary smashing things. They couldn't stop him. They couldn't even get him cornered, so they had to lock him in the infirmary and leave."

"That broke your quarantine."

"We had no choice. He was becoming more and more violent. I think he would've killed them. He must've started slipping some time before that, and we just didn't realize—

because he'd dismantled the stunguns. Alicia and Vince got into a lab a couple of doors down and locked themselves in. Greg and I monitored Mishima from the bridge so we could let them know as things changed. It was terrible. Alicia didn't know what was going on with Mishima, didn't know if it had anything to do with the kites, the flu, or if she and Vince might get it next. Vince ordered us not to let them out of the quarantine area, no matter what happened. We had to agree. It looked like Mishima was gone for good this time. You could see it in h-his eyes, even over the monitors." She swallowed.

"We had to monitor them and Mishima, and he was just getting worse. He was tearing the infirmary to pieces, and his strength was frightening. His voice—" She broke off with a shudder. "And while we were talking, Alicia started to watch Vince. We could *see* it in the viewscreen! He didn't realize it at first, but she couldn't keep her eyes off him. It made a horrible kind of sense—after all, he'd gotten sick a few hours before she had, so she could only assume he'd go crazy before she did. Then he got mad at her and they started to argue. The look on her face, wondering if he was just arguing or raving . . . When he took a swing at her, she ran away from him, out into the corridor.

"It wasn't very long before they both started acting as—as crazy as Mishima. By now he'd broken his way out of the infirmary. And then they came after us." Her voice grew shaky.

"It's impossible to lock most of those bulkheads against someone who really wants to get through. They're designed to seal off parts of the ship if the hull has been breached, not to keep somebody on the other side out. We tried to get SINS to keep them from opening any of the seals, but—"

She stopped again. It had been part of the whole problem, the way SINS had seemed to work *against* her and Greg instead of with them. They'd had control of SINS's master console, yet they couldn't get certain command codes to function, and sometimes they couldn't even get into command mode. They'd been afraid to shut off the intercom, afraid they'd miss something important, and they'd had to listen to

Mishima's laughter echoing through the corridors, that crazy laugh. . . .

"Still with us?" Dickenson asked.

She started, pulled back to the present. "Yeah. I—I wasn't going to tell you this because it's so unlikely, but I have to. SINS was working against us. It had to be deliberate. I *saw* Vince open one of the bulkheads just by pushing a button, right after I'd sealed it through the master console! He opened it and walked right through, and that was one less seal between us and—and whatever it was." Her voice shook. "Alicia looked right at me on one of the monitors and said she was going to kill me. She *meant* it, Captain, she *meant* every goddamned word she was saying!

"I was really scared by now. We couldn't stop them! And Mishima—he got back into the infirmary and—and—" She had to stop and take several deep breaths.

"Go easy," Dickenson advised. "Slow down, we've plenty of time."

"Mishima let the kites out. He let them out and stood there till they woke up and—and crawled on him, just like they had in the ruins! He—he screamed at us over the intercom, he put his face right up against the monitor, except you couldn't see his face anymore, just the kites, and he *screamed* at us, asked us if we were watching, and those things crawled in his mouth and up his nose and—" Her hand moved convulsively, and she dropped her coffee cup. It bounced on the deck, spraying coffee everywhere. They ignored it. "He said he was coming to get us. He walked out of the infirmary just like that, covered with those things, and he was coming after us, to give us the gift of eternal warmth and protection.

"We had three crazy people after us now and couldn't decide who was the most dangerous. We *thought* Alicia and Mishima were still around the infirmary, but w-we'd lost track of Vince. There was only one corridor that led from the infirmary to the rest of the ship. Greg said he would go down there to try and manually jam one of the bulkheads, and maybe it would slow them down. We only had one stungun between us, but I made him take it."

Her voice was very quiet. "I still don't know what happened to him. The viewscreen was tuned to the door he was supposed to work on, but he never got there. I ran out after him, searched the whole area around that bulkhead—" Her breath came more quickly. "I called to him over and over on the open intercom, *begged* him to answer me if he could, b-but he never did. I—I went back to the bridge then, when I couldn't find him." She wiped her eyes savagely. "The only things I had left to protect myself with were the viewscreens and the intercom. I got to watch Mishima walk right through that same door that Greg was going to try to jam. At least I knew where he was again, when I could stand to look at him. The hardest part then was keeping myself together. I'd tell SINS to seal the doors two steps in front of him, and he'd open 'em like I'd done nothing. Laughing, all the time laughing . . .

"I was afraid to leave the bridge again. I knew where Mishima was, but now I'd lost Alicia, and Vince. . . . Well, I still had desperate hopes that Greg would turn up, until Vince showed up on the screen in a place where I wasn't expecting him at all. He was headed back to the infirmary, and he was ranting on about the kites.

"I panicked. I couldn't stand to see *two* of them running around covered with those things—the fact that Vince *wanted* them now, just like Mishima had, was too much. I had to get out of there. But I had to disable the ship first. God, can you imagine a ship full of crazy people covered with kites on its way back to Earth?" She giggled, then made herself stop.

"I took a wrench from the bridge toolkit—it wasn't much, but it was heavy and had a long grip—and I went down into the core module and disabled all the circuits I could get into. I found Alicia along the way, and I surprised her, which was probably the only reason she didn't get me first. I didn't even try to talk to her—you have to understand me, she wasn't Alicia anymore. She'd been my friend for years, but now she was—I don't know what she was. I hit her from behind with the wrench. I—I only hit her twice—I don't even know if I killed her. I've never hit anyone like that before, it was—" She stopped. "I couldn't see straight, I was so scared. The ship had two emergency lifeboats, and I just hit

one of 'em at a dead run and blasted away from the ship."
She looked down.

"And I am still scared to death. I was right there with
Alicia, I *touched* her! She'd never touched a kite, but she
was just as crazy as Mishima. How do I know I didn't get
it from her? That's what I keep asking myself—suppose I
caught it? Just suppose..." She shivered.

"I programmed the lifeboat computer to wake me before
I got to the outer terminus, and I set a disaster beacon so
somebody'd pick me up. SINS changed that programming!
My disaster beacon had become a Type A Quarantine warn-
ing, and I never came to until I was already grappled to the
Orphic Angel." She looked up at them. "That's it."

They sat in silence for long minutes. Kate didn't want
to say anything, afraid to break the spell, afraid she would
start laughing and not be able to stop.

"Whew!" Dickenson settled back in his seat, suddenly
aware that his armpits were wet and his rear numb from sitting
in one position for so long. "I don't know what to say."

"Do you believe me?"

"Well, you were certainly convincing. And I don't think
you're faking it, unless you're better at lying than I'm willing
to give you credit for. I do have one question, though."

"How am I going to prove it?" She looked at him, and
he nodded. "I have a way, though I don't know if I should
talk about it."

"Whatever you feel comfortable with."

"Well, it involves people besides me, but—let me put
it to you this way. I learned an awful lot about SINS and the
way Guil-Pro works after I had left the *Black Opal*. Did you
know that SINS does a complete dump of all the log material,
including the black box, when the lifeboat system is primed
for an emergency? Neither did I. Apparently Guil-Pro wants
to make sure they have all the evidence available in case
there's some disaster, so they can figure out who to blame.

"Well, that system works both ways. I had a long time
to look all this stuff over before I put myself into deep-sleep."
She looked straight at Dickenson. "And you know what I
found? Guil-Pro knew about those alien structures before the
Black Opal ever got out there. The log mentioned a life-form,

too, though it didn't talk about any kind of danger to humans.
Still, Guil-Pro knew what was out there before we got there,
and just didn't tell us. That bothers me a lot, and I think it
might bother the Port Authority, too. All discoveries of alien
life-forms are to be reported upon first encounter—we all
know that. No fair waiting around to see how much money
you can make off it first."

"Didn't you say SINS registered it as a virgin find?"
Westman asked.

"Yes, but that wasn't the only mistake SINS made, assuming it was an honest mistake. I can't prove it, but I'm
beginning to believe SINS deliberately gave us the coordi-
nates to this system when Vince was so desperate to find
another place to go. I—I'll have a hard time ever trusting the
damn system again, on any ship."

"You should be all right here on the *Lady*."

Kate shook her head slowly. "Something else happened
to me, last night. I wasn't going to tell you, but—I was
trapped in my cocoon last night. I think the system tried to
kill me. It seemed like a malfunction at first, but it ignored
all my commands for release, just like SINS ignored me on
the *Opal*. Then it gave me a sedative I didn't want."

"How'd you get out?" Westman asked. "I don't remember seeing anything about a malfunction on my morning report."

She hesitated. No, she would not bring up Rory (the
Rory-*thing*, she reminded herself). No matter how much she
felt she could trust these people, she would not bring that
up.

"I'm not sure. I just remember waking up several hours
later in my chair, and not knowing how I got there."

"Well, I'll check it out."

"I don't think you'll find anything." She rubbed her
forehead. "God, I'm tired! How long was I talking?"

"A little over an hour."

"It feels like most of the day!" She sat forward again.

"Do you have any plans?" Dickenson asked.

"I guess that depends on my escort. I don't see myself
losing Baker very easily. He claims he's supposed to get me
back to Earth safely—not that he's done a very good job so

far—and even though he hasn't bothered me, I have a feeling he's been sticking pretty close."

"What would you like to do?"

"Be an optimist, assume my copies of the *Opal*'s black box will get safely off the *Orphic Angel*, pick 'em up when I can, and go to the Port Authority." She smiled a little. "But that's just what I'd *like* to do. What I'll be able to do is another matter altogether, I'm sure."

"Do you want to try and get hold of the Authority now, to let them know you're coming?"

"And tell them what? Without those copies, I can't prove anything. They won't even listen to me. No, I'll have to do better than that."

A quiet signal interrupted them. Dickenson turned to his video-com. "Yes?"

"Woods here. I've finished the analysis of the substance in that pressure hypo."

"All right, go on."

"It was a pretty powerful hallucinogen, Captain, related to Trilocaine—the stuff we use for deep-sleep in the hibernation chambers. I don't think it would cause any permanent damage, though I'm not positive about that, but it would sure give you a hell of a ride. The victim would probably react very psychotically."

"How about the dosage?"

"Oh, this stuff would've been good for at least a couple of days."

"And you don't think it would've killed?"

"Not a chance."

"Hm. Okay, thank you, Woods, that'll be all. Keep this to yourself, will you?"

"No problem, sir."

"Well!" Dickenson sat back in his chair. "Somebody sure wanted to tip your brain sideways!"

Kate grinned. "Yeah. And you know what that tells me? Somebody wants me to look crazy when I get back to Earth. That means they know goddamn well I'm *not* sick now!" She took in a deep breath and let it out slowly. "I wonder if this whole business about keeping me in quarantine on the *Angel* was just for show, to keep me off balance? I'll bet Baker hired somebody to jump me this morning!"

"What *I* wonder," Dickenson said slowly, "is whether or not Baker's boss knows what he's doing."

Kate thought of the Rory-thing on the observation deck (Had he really looked so much like Rory, now that she thought about it? Couldn't it have just been stress, not knowing if she was sane or crazy, thinking she could tell no one her story?), of how he told her he had saved her "for better things."

"Well, right now I don't care. *I* know I'm all right, and that's all that matters. Guil-Pro be damned, I've got my side of the story to tell, and that Board of Inquiry is going to have a lot of investigating to do."

"We'll certainly do our best to keep you safe and sound until you get there." Dickenson smiled. "We're a little more than two days out, yet. Suppose we lock you in your quarters and post a guard? We can even keep your video-com channel open so we can see if anything goes wrong—if you don't mind the lack of privacy."

"Hell, that beats what I've been through so far!" She laughed. "I think I can put up with it."

"Good." Dickenson rose to his feet. "Westman, if you'll escort Officer Harlin to her quarters, we can do the rest from the bridge. I'll talk to the crew about posting watches."

"They—" She hesitated. "They're all reliable, aren't they?" *God,* she thought, *am I being paranoid?*

"I've worked with all of them for some time. That's the best I can promise."

As long as one of them doesn't look like Rory— Stop that! "That's good enough for me. Captain," she stood and held out her hand, "I want to thank you, and you, too, Paul. I feel—just a tremendous relief, now. I'm ready for that Board."

"We'll do our part." Dickenson smiled and took her hand.

A short time later, Kate and Westman paused outside the door to her quarters.

"The red button on the back of your com unit, down near the bottom, will keep your channel open permanently, and we'll patch it into the bridge. Also," he finished, "I think you should stay out of your cocoon. I'll check my reports again, but there's no sense taking chances."

"If you find anything, you'll let me know?"

"No problem." He peered around her quarters as she opened the door. "Need anything?"

"I think I have plenty to keep me busy for two days. If Baker—"

"We'll tell him you're resting. Doctor's orders. Woods'll go along with it—he's a good guy."

"Thanks again, Paul." Kate closed the door behind her.

Westman gazed at the door for a few moments, then walked off down the corridor. From around a corner stepped a trim man with short, curly, dark hair and a little scar on his face that drew his mouth up into a slight smile on one side. Rory's blue eyes were cold as he stared at Westman's retreating back.

"Ah, Katie..." he whispered.

CHAPTER

5

Martin Baker typed furiously on the lapboard in his quarters, paused to think, then typed furiously again. At this point he wasn't sure if he was writing his resignation or his eulogy.

Damn, but he'd been so *sure* of himself! *Yes, a fault Mr. Kagen has warned you of many times,* a wicked little voice reminded him. *"I don't pay you to think, Baker, but to obey orders."* That's what Mr. Kagen thinks of you!

He had expected a frightened woman, someone easy to deal with, who would do what the Consortium wanted without too much persuasion. It was what Kagen had *told* him to expect...but Kagen had been wrong. Kate Harlin was a dangerous woman. She was too confident for someone in her position, too willing to fight back, and that was a real problem. His boss, who was always right, had been wrong this one time; he, Martin Baker, had been left on his own to make decisions . . . and he had decided to eliminate Kate Harlin.

With the "emergency pack" developed by Guil-Pro's engineers, and an electronic key that would allow him to alter the signals of any Consortium-built system, even Martin Baker, who was not a whiz at anything computerish, could control a Passenger Protection System unit without invoking SINS and sending out warnings. This was not the first time Baker had had to escort one of Geoffrey Kagen's "guests" and use his device, but he had always had strict orders to use it for control only—and this time he had tried to kill.

Kagen had plans, Baker knew, that had their beginnings long before the voyage of the *Black Opal*, but he couldn't understand why insignificant Kate Harlin would be important in such far-reaching schemes. Baker *could* understand that Kagen wanted an easy mark, someone compliant to do his bidding. But anyone would serve in a plan as thorough as Kagen's (not that Martin Baker was privy to many details), and Kate Harlin was no victim by any stretch. If she could not be cowed, then she was too dangerous. He had decided to eliminate her and then prove that she was unnecessary by the very fact that Kagen's plan would continue unaffected.

But he had failed. Oh, she'd been trapped in her cocoon, all right, and the appropriate sedative overdose had been fed in through her air supply—that much he had heard through the crew's grapevine—but somehow she'd managed to escape the trap. He had seen her himself at breakfast the next morning, looking like a hungover college student but very much alive . . . and he knew then he'd made a serious mistake. Harlin could not have survived without help, which meant someone else had figured out what he was trying to do. Yet, because she had not been completely freed—she was still here on the *Lady Pluto*—he understood that her rescuer must also work for the Consortium. If that was true, Kagen would already know of his aborted attempt at independent thought, and he wondered if he shouldn't be fearing for his career, or maybe his own life.

The video com at his elbow burred softly.

"What is it?" he snapped.

"Captain Dickenson, Mr. Baker. Sorry if I interrupted," came the dry voice. "Message for you from Equator Station—Guil-Pro communiqué."

"Transfer it here, please." Baker was uncharacteristically mild, feeling the perspiration drip down his sides under his shirt. A Consortium communiqué. Could it mean—?

But no, the bland face on his screen was only that of a clerk, telling him what to expect when he arrived at Equator Station.

"Newsmedia?" Baker interrupted the woman. "Where? Absolutely *not*! Yes, yes, I understand. Thank you."

He stared at the now blank screen. This was completely unacceptable. To be hounded by the newsmedia in the Consortium's own docking area? Kate Harlin could *not* be allowed to say anything except what Kagen wanted publicized. If he were to permit *that* to happen . . . Baker thumbed his video com.

"Captain Dickenson? When are we scheduled to arrive at the station?"

"In about four hours. Do you need something?"

"You're sure about that time?"

"We should hit the station's orbit at eighteen hundred hours. If you set your clock to Earth Greenwich Time when we announced the change, it should read just before fourteen hundred hours. Will that do?"

"As long as we stay on schedule, yes. And I *do* need something, Captain. There may be newsmedia on hand when this ship docks, and Mr. Kagen wants to avoid out-of-context publicity. I will need a bullet transport in which Officer Harlin and I can travel to the station in advance of your arrival."

"We have bullets, of course." Dickenson sounded evasive. "Will you need a pilot?"

"No, Officer Harlin is perfectly capable."

"When would you like to leave?"

"How far will we be from the station fifteen minutes before our arrival?"

"Less than a kilometer. All we're doing at that point is final lineup and docking procedures."

"Excellent. That will be plenty of time."

"And what am I to tell the media when they ask for Harlin?"

Baker chuckled. "Tell them she wasn't feeling well, and we moved her early so she could have better care." *That ought to give them something to broadcast*, he added to himself.

"I prefer not to lie to them."

"You have about four hours to get used to the idea, Captain." Baker broke the connection and sat back in his chair. He might still be in trouble with Kagen, but at least this time he had reacted quickly and, in his opinion, rather well to an unexpected situation. He hadn't completely lost his touch.

"Who is it?" Kate rose from her chair at the sound of the door buzzer.

"Westman. The *Lady* will dock shortly—we need to talk."

She recognized his voice, but scanned the corridor outside with her video com anyway, berating herself for being overly paranoid. Nothing had happened since she'd last talked to the captain; no one had even attempted to talk to her other than Westman or a new guard coming on duty. Why she still felt she had to search the halls before letting in someone whose voice she recognized...

"What's new?" she asked, waving him to a chair.

"Good news and bad. We're about four hours away from Equator Station," he said, and told her about the communiqué Baker had received.

"The media? That's great! After I talk to them, there's no *way* Kagen can—"

"Well, that's the bad news, actually." He looked at his hands. "You won't see the media. Baker wants to take you out of here on a bullet so you can avoid them. Guil-Pro's not ready for the publicity yet, he says."

"I guess they're not!" She smacked her fist into her palm. "He can't do this, goddamn him—I've got the right to defend myself against the rumors *they* don't have the guts to stop! Look," she touched his arm, "there's a way around it. When does he want to leave?"

"Fifteen minutes before we're scheduled to dock."

"Good. Ten minutes before that, I'll sneak off here in my *own* bullet, before he knows what's going on. I know ways into Equator Station he's never heard of!"

"Where would you go after that?"

"There's a Port Authority office on the station. Or I could go to the Guildhall and get sanctuary first. Don't worry, there're plenty of places I could go."

"Are you so sure? I mean..." Westman's voice trailed off. "It's a funny thing, the stories going around. Nobody knows anything, which doesn't stop 'em from guessing, of course, but—"

"What are you trying to say?" she interrupted.

"I wouldn't go to the Guildhall expecting to get sanctuary."

"But they *have* to grant me that—it's the law!"

He shook his head slowly and wouldn't look her in the eye. "You deserted a crew out there, Kate. People who were still alive and maybe could've been helped. That doesn't go over too good with the Guild—especially since you were an officer, you know?"

"But I *told* you what was happening!"

"Can't you see?" He waved his hand distractedly. "Nobody else knows that!"

She stared at him. "They'd turn me away?"

"Maybe not." He shrugged. "But if you ran from here you'd need help fast. I mean, where would you go if they *did* turn you away?" He looked at her. "I wouldn't risk it."

"But I've got to get out from under Guil-Pro!"

"I think you should wait for the Board of Inquiry," he said stubbornly. "You'll get to tell your side of the story, and the Board is a disinterested third party. It'll be a matter of public record."

"Suppose I don't get that far? *I* think whoever's been trying to hurt me worked for Kagen. Either Baker hired somebody, or..." She thought of the Rory-thing, and felt cold. "I want people to know I'm here. I want to break this thing wide open so people will know I'm still alive and still sane, and that what happened out there was not my fault. *That's* the kind of protection I need, Paul. That's why I want to talk to the media."

"I don't think it would work," he repeated.

She looked at him for a long moment. "Nobody would help me," she said softly. "Is that it?"

He reddened. "Dickenson wants to, but... Look, protecting you while you're in his care is one thing. He's got the right to do that, this is his ship. And besides, he's not supposed to know the whole story. But openly defying orders?" He shook his head again. "That's something else."

"Yeah." She stared into her lap.

"Look, uh," he floundered, "if I turned my head right now, you could probably hit me pretty hard before I knew what was coming. You know where the bullets are, don't you?"

She raised her head and smiled, a little embarrassed. "Thanks, Paul. But I couldn't do that to you, or to Dickenson, either. Nasty things happen to people who cross Guil-Pro, and there's no reason you should take on my troubles. The fact that you listened to my story and believed me went a long way to making me feel right again." She straightened. "Baker can do what he goddamn well pleases, I'll be ready for him!"

Westman sighed and rose to his feet. "You know we wish you the best of luck, Kate. Me and the captain'll be there when you and Baker launch off—someone has to man the interior controls, anyway."

"Hey," she smiled again, and shook his hand, "you've done a lot for me, the two of you. I won't forget it."

"Captain, I assure you the honor was not necessary," Baker said stiffly. "Launching a bullet transport cannot be on your list of priorities so close to docking at the station."

"I've a perfectly able pilot standing in, Mr. Baker, you needn't worry about a collision." Dickenson's response was just as stiff.

"Besides, we wanted to make sure you got started off in the right direction." Westman smiled blandly.

"We will have no problems in that area, Mr. Westman.

My pilot is just as able as yours." He gestured. "After you, Officer Harlin."

She preceded him through the tube leading to the transport bay. Once they'd entered the bullet, the hatch sealed automatically behind them.

Kate sat before the controls and slipped on the headphones. "Bullet A ready for breakaway sequence," she said quietly.

"Magnetic grapples dislodged—now!" came Westman's voice in her ears. "Proceed under your own power, Bullet A. Good luck."

Kate glanced sidelong at Baker as she took the bullet out in a long arc away from the *Lady Pluto*. "You're the captain, Baker. Where am I headed?"

"Around the other side of the station. And don't make the mistake of thinking you can fool me, either. I know exactly where I'm going."

"Done this before, have you?" She eyed the control panel.

"This is not the first time."

"What *is* your job anyway, Baker?"

"No concern of yours. I am established as Kagen's personal assistant—that is sufficient."

As they pulled away from the *Lady Pluto*, which faded quickly off to their starboard side, Kate shot the bullet straight out away from the station, then began a slow, very wide turn back in.

The station was an impressive sight from this perspective. Named so because it was in orbit directly over the Earth's middle, Equator Station was a tremendous city in the sky. It was the major waystation and starting point for all interplanetary flights, as well as for deep space ships leaving for the outer terminus, which was the last stop for all interstellar travel.

The station's central portion consisted of the first orbiting space station ever built, but the complex had grown up massively around the original core. Equator Station now housed four hotels, a very large section of the Earthside Port Authority, the Guildhall of the United Interstellar Space Workers, communications and tri-vid networks for Earth and space broadcasting, research labs, two hospitals, and quarters for all commercial deep space workers.

As Kate continued on her long, slow arc around the station, Baker appeared unperturbed, and she was beginning to wonder if he really did know what he was doing. She had a very specific destination in mind, and she *knew* she was more familiar with the outside configuration of the station than he was—if she could get them to an airlock of her choosing. . . .

"There's our lock." Baker pointed to a splash of bright green on the side of the station.

Kate scanned the entire length of the station. "You sure? I think we need to go at least another full quarter of the way around."

"Officer Harlin, you would be much better off simply doing your job and not trying to trick me. I know precisely where I'm going, and we *will* arrive there on schedule."

"You're mighty confident for a little man." She turned her head to look at him. All she would have to do right now was hit him upside the head. . . .

As though he could read her mind, Baker opened the palm of his hand to show her a pressure-hypo identical to the one the Rory-thing had attacked her with on the *Lady Pluto*. "Please do as you're told. I don't care to pilot this in myself, but I can do so."

She looked wordlessly back at the controls, and as they approached the airlock in the side of the station she saw why he had been so sure of his destination. The bright green resolved itself into a clever logo at a certain distance, very different from any of the station's other markings. She began to wonder if it weren't Kagen's own private entrance.

Their docking maneuvers were not handled by Equator Station Control Central, but rather by a voice on some unfamiliar communications channel that Baker had given her. They were greeted by two Guil-Pro security guards and escorted immediately to her quarters.

"I must make arrangements for our transport on to Earth. Please see that Officer Harlin stays in her quarters and has no visitors," Baker said to the guards as they stood outside her door. Then he turned to her. "I expect to return in an hour or so. Don't bother trying to contact anyone or use your computer terminal. Everything is being monitored and can be cut off immediately. Do I make myself clear?"

"Hey," she smiled and saluted him, "loud and clear, Captain. I will anxiously await your return." She placed her palm on the I.D. plate and disappeared inside.

As the door slid shut behind her, Kate gazed around the familiar rooms and smiled sourly. Home again. Big deal.

Home meant quiet privacy, a few friends over to play some cards, the chance to read without interruption—not an hour's brief stay with an armed guard outside the door. Damn! Why hadn't she jumped Baker when she'd had the chance, back when they'd been alone on the bullet? She'd been so stupid to let that little pressure-hypo intimidate her—for all she knew, the damn thing'd been empty anyway!

But that hypo had reminded her of Rory and of her own still-precarious sense of sanity (the Loon was never very far away, it seemed), and she hadn't been able to do anything against that threat. So here she was, trapped in her own home, forced once again to wait for someone else's decision before she could proceed with a life that wasn't even hers anymore.

She bent to pull off her shoes. Might as well relax until the little bastard got back—who knew when she'd get the chance again?

There was the smallest of noises from a corner, and she jerked straight up, rigid and listening. There it was again! She was not imagining it—there was a noise in her bedroom. Still holding one shoe in her hand, she hesitated.

It was a trap, and she knew Rory was waiting for her in the next room. Baker had led her into a trap in her own goddamn house, and she had walked into it as blind as though nothing had ever gone wrong in her life. She was a fool, and now she was going to pay for it.

Maybe she could call the guard—but that wouldn't work, he was there to keep her *in*, not to help her. Maybe if she burst through the door at high speed she could get away before the guard figured out what was going on. She couldn't face Rory again, she just *couldn't*, that was asking too much....

Resolutely she put the shoe down and straightened her

shoulders, then turned and walked toward her bedroom, though she was shaking and cold on the inside.

"Hello, Kate."

That voice . . . her relief was so profound she nearly passed out. "Lars, what are you doing here?" she asked weakly, sinking down to sit on her bed.

"That's a hell of a greeting for an old friend!" He crouched next to her. "I heard you were in town, heard there might be some trouble. From the looks of you, I heard right. What's doin'?"

"Oh, *God*, it's good to see you!" She hugged him suddenly and fiercely, and tears squeezed from beneath her closed eyelids.

"Hey, now, it's all right," he said, feeling somewhat inadequate. "Ease up, there."

"I'll be okay in a minute." She wiped her eyes. "Whew! Sorry, babe, but you will never know how glad I am it was you!"

He smiled slightly. "Normally I'd be gratified to hear that, but I think you mean something different."

Kate finally caught her breath. "Well, you must know *something* about what's going on, or you wouldn't have been hiding in the bedroom."

"Let's just say I knew there were gonna be a couple of goons from the Consortium standing outside your door *after* you were inside, so I figured I'd better get here before that happened."

She looked at him and sighed. Jon Lars was her ex-husband. They had divorced several years ago (or was it longer than that by now?) because they'd finally run out of reasons to stay together. Not that they'd been unhappy, they just never saw each other much. She worked strictly in deep space, while he had slacked off years ago. Their between-job breaks coincided rarely—which might not've been so bad if they hadn't both believed in fidelity—and so they had gradually realized over the years that there was no point in keeping it formal anymore. They had been friends since the split, but she hadn't seen him in more than three years.

"How *do* you know so much about what's going on?" she finally asked.

Lars gazed at her thoughtfully. "I happened to come in through the *Orphic Angel* a couple weeks ago. Ran into an old buddy of yours—the name Watson ring a bell? He said you'd remember him." His face was bland.

"What'd he say?" she asked, hardly daring to hope.

"Not a whole lot. Said you need to take it easier, not work so hard." At the expression on her face, he smiled a little. "And he gave me something you'd left with him—he said you'd know what to do with them."

"You don't have them with you?"

He shook his head. "Not with Guil-Pro goons running all over the place. Don't worry, they're safe."

"Don't hang on to them, it's too dangerous! Take them to the Port Authority."

"Must be pretty serious to have you running to the government." He paused. "Want to tell me about it?"

"I'll try, but we have to watch for Baker. He'll be back soon, and you *can't* be seen here."

"Don't worry, I rigged the intercom." He smiled. "How do you think I could hear you coming?"

She returned his smile. "I should've known."

As she moved around the room, changing her clothes, combing her hair, she began to tell him the story of the *Black Opal*'s last mission. It was easier to tell while she was occupied with something else; although, growing further and further from the actual happening of it as she was, she could recite it now without much emotion. The horrible, wrenching feelings she'd experienced when telling Captain Dickenson were gone, leaving only the dry facts.

Lars listened with quiet interest, head tilted to one side, making appropriate noises.

"There's something you haven't explained yet," he said when she paused for breath. "I know I surprised you by being here, but you were a lot more rattled than I expected. You were so relieved it was me—who did you think it was?"

She looked hard at him, and for just a minute the sound of the Loon was right in her ear. "I want you to know I've decided that I'm not crazy."

His eyebrows went up slightly, but he merely said, "No arguments from me."

"I've talked to you about Rory." At his nod, she continued. "He . . . he was the first to die. When Mishima went crazy . . . Well, since then, since I've been back inside the outer terminus, I—I've seen him twice. It wasn't hallucinations. He saved my life on the *Lady*," she paused and Lars nodded again, "and then he almost killed me the next morning."

"Now, are you sure—"

"Let me finish!" she insisted. "Yes, I'm sure it was— at least, it was someone with his build made up to look like him. The first time, I could've imagined it. I'd been gassed in my cocoon when it malfunctioned, and he's the one who got me out, so I could've dreamed that. But not the next morning. He attacked me then, when I was on the ship's observation deck. I managed to open the intercom to the bridge when we were . . . when we were fighting, and someone else *heard* two voices, mine and another. He was gone by the time Westman got there—"

"Paul Westman?"

She nodded.

"I know him. Go on."

"Well, that's really all there is." She shrugged. "I can't explain it, but I know I wasn't seeing things. Someone's trying to make me crazy, or at least make me think I'm crazy, and it almost worked. If Paul hadn't heard that other voice over the intercom . . . Well, someone knows that Rory and I were close friends and had worked together a lot, and they've tried to use that against me."

"So," he said with sudden understanding, "you thought it would be Rory waiting for you in here."

She raised her hands. "I was trapped. There's a guard outside the door who's probably been told to ignore anything he hears from in here as long as I don't try to get away—it was the perfect setup. And Baker would've planned it that way, too."

Lars rubbed the back of his neck and frowned. "It's an odd way to go about things. You have to wonder what they're up to."

"I suspect I'll find out in a very short while." She smiled faintly.

A small telltale next to the intercom flickered briefly, and faint voices could be heard in the corridor outside.

"Turn off the intercom," he mouthed, and she obeyed.

In the last seconds before the buzzer sounded, she caught him in a quick, impulsive hug, and they kissed. She knew full well this might be the last time she saw him for a long while, if ever again, and suddenly she missed him a lot as he disappeared into one of the back rooms.

She went to release the door, then stepped back.

"May I assume you are ready to travel?" Baker asked, sweeping into the room, seemingly unaware that anything had been going on before his arrival.

"I'm ready."

"Excellent." He looked her up and down. "Shall we?" He motioned her to precede him from the room, and the guards fell into step beside her.

As the door slid shut, Lars stepped from his hiding place and sat in the chair Kate had just left. What a fantastic story she had just told! The discovery of a real artifact, a whole, self-contained environment, not simply the ruins of Cygni II. An alien life-form—*real* life, not just microbes . . .

Assuming her story was true, there could be no dispute over the Epsilon Indi find. Life that could appear as a non-living substance to the most sophisticated monitoring equipment available. Life that was deadly to our life.

Life that Kate Harlin was convinced Guil-Pro had known about *before* the *Opal*'s mission had ever left the outer terminus.

That's what he found so hard to comprehend, that Guil-Pro could have known about a life-form this sophisticated, in a system as close as Epsilon Indi, without anyone else knowing. A consortium of five smaller companies, Guil-Pro was just too big to keep that kind of a secret—or so he'd thought, anyway. *If* Kate knew what she was talking about. *If* she wasn't just too damned messed up because of what had happened out there . . .

He shook his head, then rose to his feet and walked over to the wall intercom. For a moment he stared at it, then he removed the small data card from the intercom and slipped it into his pocket. It never hurt to have too much information when you had to deal with the government, and a recording of Kate telling her story, when it was obvious she had no idea she was being recorded, could end up being a lot of help. Too bad she hadn't been able to finish.

He waited half an hour, then left, locking the door behind him.

CHAPTER

6

Kate stood quietly between her two escorts in the lobby of the second tallest building in London—headquarters of the Guilford Production Consortium. Baker conferred briefly with someone on a video com, then turned and motioned to the security men, who took her arms again. Gently, not at all obviously, they escorted her to a big bank of lifts.

The ride to the 225th floor, even in a high-speed elevator, seemed interminable. Once they had arrived, they had to go through a palm-print identification, two total body scans, and a retinal pattern check before they were allowed into the executive suite area.

"So good to see you, Mr. Baker!" The receptionist smiled brightly. "Mr. Kagen has been waiting anxiously for your guest. These two gentlemen," she indicated the guards, "can wait in the next room." She pressed a button, and a paneled section of the wall slid open. "Go right ahead, Mr. Baker."

Well, Kate thought, *at least I'm to have some company.* For the first time, she was actually glad of Baker's presence— because she was beginning to realize, watching the man, that he was just as terrified as she.

The door slid shut behind them, and she glanced around an office almost bare in its simplicity and extreme functionality. What kind of man did it suit?

"Ah, I've been waiting for you—Katie."

She turned without wanting to and faced the owner of that voice, seated at a desk across the room from her. She could only stare, her jaw slack with disbelief, as she began to understand just how thoroughly she'd been had. Her vision darkened as her mind tried to shut down in self-defense; she stumbled uncertainly, and Baker was forced to support her.

"Pull yourself together, Harlin!" he said in her ear, jerking roughly at her sleeve.

"God have mercy!" she whispered.

It was Rory.

"Is that any way to say hello to a friend?" Kagen asked, gently mocking. Yes, he was Rory, with his coal-black curly hair cut short, those bright, bright blue eyes that had laughed with her and looked at her with affection . . . he *was* Rory, down to the scar that drew one side of his mouth up into a permanent half-smile.

Trusted friend, confidant . . . even lover . . . She could taste the betrayal like bile in the back of her throat.

"How—?" She could barely make her voice come out.

"How what?" His voice was gentle, his smile malicious. "How did I beat you home?"

"But you *couldn't*—!"

"Couldn't I?" He shook his head, seemingly in regret. "I tried to help you on the *Lady Pluto*, Katie, but you wouldn't trust me."

"No! No, I don't believe you!" She felt Baker's hand tighten on her arm. "Rory is dead—*you were not in all those places!*"

There was a pause while he studied her. "No," he finally agreed, "I was not. Rory and his brothers are merely LSH units."

"But he couldn't be—he *moved*, he—he *thought*, he—"

"He loved?" Kagen's face was inscrutable.

This was impossible! LSH units could not do what Rory had done—could not be what Rory had been!

Lifelike Simulated Humans—LSH units—had been in existence for a number of years. The mindless creations were used mostly for medical research, because they could be made to mimic closely the human anatomy. Even the brain function was mimicked to a certain extent, with enough of the autonomic functions to keep the units alive without external assistance. Some of them could even move around, stiff-legged and clumsy, with electronic guidance, which gave birth to the popular name for them—frankenstein.

"Frankensteins," she whispered. "You have *thinking* frankensteins!" But Rory wasn't like that. Rory . . . She would not think about it right now.

"Yes." He nodded. "What do you think of my children?"

His question was so matter-of-fact that she almost didn't realize what he was asking. "Your . . . children?" She stared at this man who had dared to create in his own image, and she began to laugh, until tears streamed down her face and her breath came in deep, aching sobs. While Kagen watched with clinical interest, she collapsed into a chair and hugged herself, rocking back and forth. Even she didn't know if she was laughing or crying.

If she didn't stop soon, she realized in some small, sane corner of her mind, she wouldn't be able to. And the last thing she wanted, in that small, sane part of her, was to lose control here in corporate headquarters, in front of her highest superior. She began to gasp, then cough, in an effort to stop herself. Gradually it worked, and she was able to straighten up and wipe her eyes.

"My God, Kagen, you are a vain son of a bitch!" she said weakly, still trying to catch her breath.

"I'm glad you found that so humorous." For all his urbanity, Kagen was beginning to sound impatient. "Martin, fix her a drink. Scotch, I believe?"

She stared at him. How could he know that?

"These are not the normal LSH units—we have incorporated some cloning techniques with the usual biomechanics. In addition to minor things such as appearance, our process carries with it the adult thought patterns of the donor who provides the basic genetic material," he said softly, watching her face. "Rory—all the Rories—think like I think, act as I would act. They *are* me, after a fashion."

She took the glass of scotch in her cold hands and gulped at it, a small dribble running from one corner of her mouth. It had no taste.

That *thing* had been her lover, and this man before her knew it as surely as if he had been there himself. Maybe he *had* been there. Maybe these *things* (yes, she must think of Rory as a *thing*, now if ever), so close to their "father," could transmit information, even sensation, as they experienced it. Maybe . . .

"You bastard!" she said in a low voice. "You're a peeping Tom—you're nothing but a fucking *voyeur*!"

His face hardened, and from the corner of her eye Kate saw Baker's color go white.

"How observant, Officer Harlin; I commend you," Kagen said stiffly, and slid away from behind his desk.

He was in an automated chair. Supported below the waist, he appeared to be sitting in an executive chair when the desk was in front of him. It was a clever ruse, and a necessary one, she realized, for a man in his position. He did have legs, but they were dangling and useless, too small for his body. His right hand appeared perfectly normal. His left, while not shrunken as his legs were, seemed atrophied.

"You see," he continued, "there was a reason I designed the Rory units. They do much for me that I cannot do myself. Martin," again that faint note of impatience was in his voice, "fix me a drink."

Kate was mesmerized.

"Now," Kagen swirled his ice cubes carefully, "we can discuss business in a civilized manner. And I shall begin with you, Martin." The chair turned with a jerk, making it appear an angry motion. "You are a fool. You *persist* in thinking for yourself, and you are miserable at it. I find I cannot trust you anymore, Martin."

"B-but I—"

Kate had never seen Baker when he was not in complete control of a situation; the thought chilled her as she remembered how much in his power she had felt. If Kagen could turn this man into a stammering fool with so little effort, then how much power must *he* in turn have?

Kagen turned to her. "I feel obliged to apologize for him, Officer Harlin. He was responsible for that regrettable incident with your cocoon aboard the *Lady Pluto*. He had express orders to bring you home safely, but he thought he had a better grasp of the situation than I did, and he acted upon that mistaken belief."

Kate stared at Baker. It had been *his* idea. . . . "I ought to break your nose, you little bastard."

She was glad to be distracted from the tension she felt between herself and Kagen—in fact, her anger felt so good that she began to feed on it. She let it fill her, excite her, and with fists clenched she began to advance on the little man.

Baker drew himself up, though he didn't say anything. She noticed a tic in his left eye that she knew hadn't been there before, and she turned away, half-disgusted with herself, her fists relaxing.

Kagen's expression was imperturbable. "We can finish this discussion later, Martin. You may leave now."

"Mr. Kagen—"

"You may leave, Martin."

Kate watched him go; he passed right in front of her as though she didn't exist.

Kagen gazed after him for a moment, then turned his attention to her. "I apologize for bothering you with petty details. But now we can get to the true point of this meeting, Katie."

"Don't call me that."

"I beg your pardon?" He tilted his head, his smile charming, and familiar.

"I said don't call me that." Her hands started to shake. "I don't care who you are, I don't care why you created Rory, I don't care *how* you created him—he *was* my friend, I choose to remember him that way, and he is the only person who can call me by that name."

There was a moment of silence, then Kagen nodded. "I understand. We all have our illusions." He moved back behind his desk.

She took another deep drink from her glass and felt it burn all the way down. She could even taste it this time— Chivas Regal, she thought—and was impressed in spite of herself. It was very hard to get. Some of the quivering in her gut stopped, and she relaxed a little, even to the point of feeling bold.

"All right, I'm ready to get down to business." She took

another sip of her drink and positioned herself comfortably in her chair. "You owe me some answers."

"And you've caused me a great deal of trouble," he responded.

"Me?" She smacked her open hand on the chair arm. "Ever since I hit the outer terminus, people have acted as though everything that's happened is my fault. I was not responsible, goddammit—stop trying to lay this on me!"

"But who better to blame? It is, you must admit, one way to deal with an ethical woman who knows too much. Even though I am the actual owner of your present contract—"

"I have no present contract with the Consortium!" she interrupted him. "My contract ended when I stepped out of that isolation chamber on the *Orphic Angel!*"

He shook his head, smiling. "I see you neglected the fine print—it is for me to say when your duties have been fulfilled. At any rate, we both know I cannot trust you, either."

She swallowed her outrage for the moment, and reminded him, "I've worked for Guil-Pro for twenty of the last thirty years, and you've trusted me for all that time. Why stop now?"

He folded his hands in front of him. "Before we destroyed your lifeboat, my experts made a thorough examination of its computer system. They had to get the black box recording, you realize, along with other information." He smiled at her. "You covered your tracks very well, for the most part."

Her palms grew damp.

"But they did discover that copies had been made of select portions of the *Black Opal*'s logs, and some data from areas in SINS that were restricted. However, we are also aware you brought nothing with you when you left the shuttle for the *Orphic Angel*. Perhaps," he regarded her with a sly expression, "we should examine Control Central's logs of transmissions received for the period of time you were there."

Please, God, don't let him bring Billy into this! She

wiped her hands on her pants. "You're bluffing. You don't know any of this!"

He shrugged. "What we don't know we will certainly find out."

"Even if I *did* have this information," she asked after a pause, "what could I actually do with it?"

"That information tells a great deal more about the Consortium than we would wish to have made public. For example, the Research Division has been working in the field of intelligent cybernetics for almost twenty years." Kagen spoke with obvious pride. "*We* developed the thought-transfer process and the cloning and the advanced bio- and micromechanics that made possible such a being as Rory—he is the prototype."

"And he's a thinking frankenstein," she whispered.

"The 2070 Genetic Controls Conference in Geneva was very explicit on several topics, even though it was ahead of its time," Kagen agreed with her. "'Cloning shall not be used to create whole human beings; cyborgs shall not be invested with the power of independent reason; artificial intelligence research must remain separate from the field of cybernetics.'" He quoted the precepts put forth by the Geneva Conference as though he had more than a passing familiarity with them. "Amazing, when you consider that in 2070 their cyborgs were rudimentary at best. LSH units didn't even *exist* then. As far as they knew, there was nothing for them to worry about."

"What does this have to do with the *Black Opal*?" she asked tiredly. "Nobody on that ship knew Rory was an LSH unit. We were," she had to swallow hard, "we were all fooled."

"You're in the middle of something far more important than the events of the *Black Opal*'s mission," he said. "That was only a small incident in something that's been going on for a long time. You were no different from any mission we've sent out over the last fifteen years."

"Oh yes, we were!" She leaned forward. "We were different because we *had* Rory—you planted him in our crew! Why? Because you knew something was going to happen? Because you already *knew* something was out there?"

"Don't be ridiculous," he said mildly.

"Why would you plant such an expensive prototype on

a routine mission," she insisted, "to see if he could pass? Come on! Guil-Pro is too *cheap* to waste that kind of money without good reason. You knew damn well what was going on out there, and you wanted to monitor the situation."

He raised his eyebrows, nodding slightly. "A very impressive leap of understanding, Officer Harlin."

Kate ignored his sarcasm. "Somebody else got there before we did—who was it? What happened to them?"

He gazed at her for a long moment before speaking. "The original discovery was made several years earlier by a forerunner ship, a three-man prospector. Do you remember the *Hercules*?"

"The *Hercules*!" She nearly choked on her drink. "But I thought—"

He continued as though she hadn't spoken. "They discovered what appeared to be an alien structure, supporting a perfectly sealed environment. That discovery alone would've meant a large bonus for all of them, and they knew it—just as you aboard the *Black Opal* knew it. Don't get the idea that they were innocents who happened on this by accident, either. This crew developed the original predictors for Epsilon Indi—they knew exactly what they were doing. We pay well for such discoveries when they benefit our research. The crew of the *Hercules* thought they had a better than average chance to find something we'd be interested in." Kagen paused.

"Their log records indicate that they elected to bring several of the—kites, I believe you called them?—aboard their ship for further study. It seems they weren't as cautious as they might've been, and someone was infected. After that, one of the crew piloted the ship away from the planet and destroyed it. Travers, I believe. He thought he'd been exposed as well, and wasn't sure he could trust himself if he got sick. They all died."

"If they died, how do you know this?" Kate asked softly.

"When things started to go bad, they jettisoned a marker buoy with their logs."

She sat in silence, thinking of all the stories that had circulated several years ago when the *Hercules* forerunner mission hadn't returned.

If you were just two weeks overdue, everyone figured

you had probably misjudged your light-plus jump—not a difficult mistake to make on a long mission. A month or so late, and you'd probably stayed to check out an extra prospect. That was frowned upon by higher authorities, but nobody ever did anything about it. After all, some of the best finds had been "extra's."

If you were much more than two months late getting home without reporting in, even from a forerunner mission, all sorts of stories started cropping up. Kind of like what had happened to her with the *Black Opal*, now that she thought about it, although the *Hercules* stories had been a lot worse.

There had been a strong accusation that the crew of the *Hercules* had jumped their claim and run off to sell the profits without so much as notifying Guil-Pro or whatever interested clients might have been involved. Interstellar piracy was a favorite myth used to explain many mysterious disappearances. She could still remember the ridiculous cartoons of pirates in bandannas and eyepatches, crawling around in zero g, knives clenched in their teeth, that had circulated about six months after the *Hercules* had last been heard from. Rumors of mad chases in the asteroid belt and through the slummier parts of the Martian colonies were very popular, as were stories of bounty hunters hired by either Guil-Pro or some outraged and less-than-reputable client. The endings of such tales always had the *Hercules* crew hunted down one by one and either killed or prosecuted and ruined forever, depending on whose story you heard.

"I don't understand why you went to so much trouble to discredit them," she finally said. "Wouldn't it have been easier just to say they died on duty instead of making up all that crap? Especially Travers. That was a heroic thing he did."

"Perhaps, in retrospect," he admitted. "But dying in the line of duty raises too many questions. Especially since they had found something we wanted to keep secret. The *Hercules* crew were very cocky, and they talked too much."

"And besides," she interrupted dryly, "you fixed it so they had committed a criminal act, so you didn't have to worry about their pensions or any other survivor benefits. No profit from crime, right? You didn't have to pay their families a dime."

He ignored her comment. "As I said, the crew talked too much. Consortium management decided it was necessary to countermine anything they might have said."

"So you ruined them."

Kagen shrugged. "We hadn't planned on finding life. Once such a discovery was reported, management decided to keep the results within the Consortium. And, of course, we hadn't planned on their dying out there, either. What they found was easy to keep secret—their deaths were not. We had to explain their deaths."

"How unfortunate for you," she said softly.

He raised his eyebrows. "Had the government discovered that the *Hercules* crew had actually died out there, they would've demanded an investigation. An audit mission would've uncovered our secret, the one thing we deliberately failed to report—that we had discovered alien life. You know as well as I the trouble that would have caused."

"Couldn't it still cause trouble, once this goes public?"

"No. According to the story circulated, the *Hercules* never got as far as Epsilon Indi on this mission. No one outside the Consortium is aware of exactly where they were when they 'broke contract' and ran. One of our better-kept secrets." He smiled slightly. "And it will stay that way."

"What did they find out there? What could possibly be so important to you?" She could only remember Rory pinned to the wall, and Mishima, kites swarming over him. . . .

"A breakthrough in biological engineering. The science officer on the *Hercules* was not a trained biologist, but he thought the kite creatures were bio-engineered rather than naturally occurring. Look at their abilities—to appear non-living, and then become alive—amazing!

"But we didn't know enough. The *Hercules* logs were detailed, but her crew weren't there long enough to really study the creatures. For instance, we knew they changed from nonliving to living, but we didn't know why. Or how long it took."

"But you knew they would change. Why didn't you *tell* us we were dealing with a living thing, for God's sake?"

"Telling you would've destroyed the mythology we'd set up for the *Hercules*. Every part of that story was very delicately balanced—one slip would've tumbled the whole thing. We had no choice but to send out a second mission, and it was imperative that your discovery appear to be an accident."

"So you set us up to protect a lie. You're a bastard, Kagen!"

"Your crew were perfect. Not too smart, but not stupid, either. You worked well together, had done so many times for us in the past, and you had what we felt were the necessary professional skills—as well as the necessary flaws."

"Flaws?" Kate's forehead wrinkled. "I don't understand—" Then she stopped. "Vince's gambling?"

Kagen inclined his head.

"You knew he needed money—you knew he'd go for the long shot."

"There are some temptations no gambler will turn down."

"You arranged his *debt*?"

"Some things cannot be left to chance."

"But he was trying to quit," she said softly. "You're disgusting!"

"No, I simply believe in making use of the materials at hand."

"Alicia's favorite subject in medical school had something to do with the nervous system, didn't it?" Kate spoke almost to herself. "Greg was an exo-geologist, the obvious choice, I suppose, and you must've thought the same about Mishima." She laughed suddenly. "Yeah, we were the perfect crew, all right—we had a phobic on board! How did that happen? Somebody fucked up, Mr. Kagen."

Kagen stiffened. "Mishima's phobia was not the type to prevent him from space travel. Besides, he was not to have been the host for the creatures."

"The what?" She sat forward. "What did you say?"

"Mishima was not to have been the host for the creatures. We were aware of his phobia, and—"

"You mean you *planned* to let them—let them attack someone without even *telling* us?"

She almost couldn't go on, she was so overwhelmed by

the vision of Mishima as she had seen him in that monitor on the *Black Opal*, when the small, black, diamond-shaped *things* had risen from the floor in wave after living wave to engulf him. "You *wanted* that to happen? My God! You could have told us—we could've been ready, we would've been more careful, at least—"

"You didn't let me finish," he interrupted gently. "We wanted samples of the creatures, and they had to be activated by living warmth. We could not ask someone to volunteer for such a duty."

"You think it was better as a surprise?"

"It had to appear as an accidental discovery," he reminded her.

"Why couldn't Rory have been the host?" she asked. "He probably wouldn't even have cared!"

"I wanted him in control."

"A hell of a lot of good *he* did! You didn't count on Mishima going bugfuck crazy and killing him, did you?"

"You obviously were not listening to me earlier. Mishima was not to have been the host. As you so truthfully point out, even Rory could not control him in his panicked state." Kagen gazed at her. "You haven't yet asked what *your* role in the mission was to've been."

"My role? What's that got to do with—" Kate swallowed several times. "You were going to use me?"

"Your psych-profiles made you the obvious choice. You were never afraid of insects or other small creatures. True, the sensation would not have been pleasant, but Rory had orders to place you immediately in the cryo chamber. When the creatures dropped off, he would've released you. Quite simple, really."

"You bastard!" She stood abruptly. "You can't *do* that to people!"

"Are you presuming to tell me my business?"

"Your *business*! People died out there because you were so worried about your fucking business—and you *killed* them!"

"Don't exaggerate." He shrugged. "You signed a standard contract—you know what the risks are in exploration."

"That's a lie! *You* knew what was going on and *you*

deliberately didn't tell us. You can't put this one off on any-body else—not Rory, not Baker—nobody but *you*, you son of a bitch!" She was shaking. "Five people, Kagen, five people *died*, and you can't blame anyone else—oh, no, this one's *yours*!" Sweat mingled with her tears, and she took a step toward him. At that moment she could've killed without regret.

"Don't do anything foolish, Officer Harlin."

She hesitated, and in that moment of hesitation she knew she had lost.

Kagen gestured with his good hand, and she turned, only to see Rory standing not five paces behind her. His face was oddly expressionless, and he did not react to her at all, except for his eyes, which watched her. There was no scar, no half-smile that she was beginning to hate, and strangely it made him even more unnerving to look upon.

"An earlier version, before we had perfected the thought-pattern transfer. Not very bright, but very good at his job, and very loyal. An excellent bodyguard." Kagen smiled. "I advise you to be on your best behavior."

It was hard not to listen to him. She stared at him, shivering, her sudden rage just as suddenly drained away. What could she do to a man with *this* at his call?

"Then don't push me," she said quietly. "I won't be much good to you dead, and you've gone to an awful lot of trouble to get me here alive. Don't push me."

"Don't think so highly of yourself; you will serve in either capacity. But you're quite correct, I would prefer you alive." Kagen's mobile hand toyed with a pencil—he looked almost normal. "Please sit down."

She obeyed. The Rory-thing behind her had not moved, and she carefully avoided looking at him—*it*.

"So far, we have sent two missions out to the Epsilon Indi system." Kagen spoke as though to himself. "The first obtained information, but no sample of the life-form. The second was to obtain a sample, but failed due to events I could not control. The third mission will not fail—I must guarantee that." He raised his head to look at her. "I want you to lead that mission."

Her first reaction was unthinking. "But I'm not even commissioned!"

"A small matter." He waved his good hand. "Think of the mission, Harlin, think as a leader! You have the potential—don't mire it in details someone else can take care of for you!"

"Details like the loss of five lives?" she murmured.

He went on as though she hadn't spoken. "You're a survivor, Harlin, and that's what I'm looking for. Think of it, your first command!" He leaned forward, suddenly intense. "Your own crew, your own vessel. Yourself in complete control of every aspect—not like last time."

She stared at him. The offer had caught her completely off guard . . . enough to make her actually consider it for a moment. "Complete control? Can you guarantee it?"

"Of course. Why shouldn't I? Talking with you this morning has given me some insight into you, Katharine. I see now how I *should* have structured the crew for the *Black Opal*. Her mission would have been successful, and chances are no one would've been hurt." He warmed to his subject. "You were correct when you asked why Rory could not have been the host. I was afraid not to have him in control of the situation, but I see my error. He should have been the host and *you* the captain. The infectious agent, which we did not know of from the *Hercules* mission, would not have affected Rory, I think."

"But you're not sure, even of that," she said. "How can you guarantee I'll be in any better control of the situation?"

"Easily. Your host will be a *legal* LSH unit," he could never bring himself to use the term *frankenstein*, "simply a warm body. There will be nothing for the disease to affect. You and your crew will know what you are out there to do. No secrets—no surprises."

Kate listened as his persuasions went on. He sounded sincere, and his arguments were certainly reasonable. . . . Not that she wanted to go back out to the scene of her worst nightmares, but she had a feeling she was getting off light after his earlier veiled threats and the tense trip home from the *Orphic Angel*.

Maybe she wasn't in such a bad situation after all. Maybe

she had built this whole thing up in her mind because of the strain she had been under. Sure, he was asking her to go back out to the place where this had all started, but . . . maybe there were worse things in life. She had survived, after all. And, as he'd said, she would know what she was heading into this time. . . .

Kate glanced off to her left and saw the Rory-thing standing quietly. Funny how easy it was to think of this creation as a *thing*, yet still she couldn't quite bring herself to think of the frankenstein on the *Black Opal*, or even the one on the *Lady Pluto*, as anything other than her *friend*. After all, the *Black Opal's* Rory had never betrayed her (although perhaps that statement shouldn't be examined too closely), and the *Lady Pluto* Rory *had* saved her life, even though he—it—had tried to kill her afterward . . . but he had only saved her life so she could end up here, so what was that worth?

Kagen was still talking in that softly persuasive tone, and she realized she had missed part of what he was saying. And when he had called her "Katie" again, she hadn't even reacted.

She made herself *listen* to him, to what he said and how he said it, and she began to hear Rory in his tone of voice. Not just Rory, but Rory as she was sure he had talked only to her, in the late nights when they'd been far away from home and lonely, or after they had made love and felt closer than any other two people in the universe. She looked back again at the Rory-thing standing slightly behind her. And she noticed that he never blinked.

This is what Rory really was—an expressionless, mindless creature that existed only to give his creator legs that worked, and some twisted semblance of manhood in a world where strength was power and weakness fatal. *This* was Rory. Blank eyes staring at her, no recognition in them, no familiarity, no warmth . . . a creature whose very existence was against all laws. *This* was a truer picture of the man who was talking to her now, trying to make her believe him. . . .

"Wait a minute. Stop right there. You're trying to confuse me with your pretty words. Do you think I can just forget everything and come back to work for you like nothing ever happened?" She could feel herself begin to shake inside. "Is that what you really think of me? Offer me a good enough deal, a chance to save my ass, and I'll be yours forever?" She raised her fist at him. "Fuck you, Kagen!"

He looked surprised, but only for a moment, and then he chuckled. "As I said earlier, you are an ethical woman. But, before you decide irrevocably, may I make my other offer?"

"I'm not interested."

"Don't be hasty, my dear; you really have no choice but to hear me." His smile was not pleasant. "My primary interest for this mission is transportation of the creatures safely back here. Of course, we have talked about using a legal LSH unit, but that was only a condition of your leading the mission. If you are not captain, well . . . LSH units are expensive creations, even if they can't think for themselves, and I'd really prefer not to use one for so dangerous a purpose. If you do not lead the mission, then you will be the host."

Kate dropped her drink. Mishima, looming before her, black diamond-shapes swarming over him, opened his mouth wide as a cavern, as if to swallow her whole. He laughed hysterically with the voice of the Loon, and the sound of it was deafening. . . .

"You're very quiet."

She could hear Kagen's voice, but she could see only Mishima, who smiled and beckoned to her. Behind him was Rory, stuck to the wall, arms waving weakly. (The voice of the Loon was behind her now, very faint, but threatening to grow loud again.)

"Please, take your time. It's still morning yet."

His prosaic statement caught her attention, drew her away from her waking nightmare. "You can't make me go back out there!"

"Can't I?"

"You'd never get away with it!"

"And why not? Who have you told you were coming here—a few friends, perhaps? Without proof, whom could they convince?"

"There are people who know where I am—and they *do* have proof!"

"Careful, my dear, I know of everyone with whom you've had contact since you arrived at the terminus."

She stared at him, stricken. How could she have been so stupid?

He began to trace a careful design on the top of his desk, his hand trembling slightly. "You remember meeting Rory on the *Lady Pluto*, I'm sure."

"What about it?"

"You escaped him—but you must have seen the hypodermic he was carrying?"

"Oh, he showed me, all right. He enjoyed showing me—you must've given him your twisted sense of humor."

"Do you know what was in it?"

"He took great pleasure in telling me," she lied. To tell the truth, to admit she had found the pressure-hypo and had it analyzed with the express understanding and permission of the *Lady Pluto*'s captain, would tell Kagen just how involved Jim Dickenson had been—which was too involved.

"So you must be aware of what the drug would've done to your mind."

"I know it was an hallucinogen."

Kagen nodded. "Had Rory succeeded in his task on the *Lady Pluto*, you would've been carried off that ship a raving madwoman, strapped to a stretcher, completely restrained. Not a permanent condition, but sufficient to convince anyone who might've seen you that you had not survived your trip home in good health. At that point, I would've had two choices. Either we would have run tests to determine, if we could, exactly what did happen out there, or we would have frozen you and simply shipped you back out with the next mission as the host. It would've been a simple matter to find a crew who would not pay any attention to the body in the freezer."

"Why are you telling me this?"

"Because I want you to know what might've happened."

"Why are you dealing with me at all? Why not just hide me away somewhere? Who would miss me? Even you said as much."

"Much as we do not like the situation, the *Orphic Angel* is not a secure station. None of them are. It really can't be enforced. What that means, as you seem already to have heard, is that the story of what happened to the *Black Opal* is *not* secret, nor is your existence as a survivor. As to the condition of that survivor, well—we had hoped to show the newsmedia a very sick woman. Instead, we had to spirit you away and simply tell them you were ill. Not half so convincing, I'm afraid. But whatever happens to you now must be explainable, particularly to a Board of Inquiry. The drug could still do that—but I want that sample, and I want you to lead this mission."

She stared at her hands and desperately wished herself to be somewhere else. The Loon still chuckled in the back of her mind, tempting.

"Believe me, Officer Harlin, the choice is yours."

"All right, I'll go." Her voice was soft.

"Excellent! I knew you'd see reason."

The taste of scotch was still on her tongue, and she nearly gagged on it. She'd never be able to drink Chivas again. (The Loon whispered in her ear, but she couldn't understand him.) *Get away from me!* she thought angrily, and then, *My God, I'm talking to him! Can't do that . . .*

"Much of your ship is already outfitted."

Kagen was talking again, and she realized she'd missed the first part.

"I think you'll like the *Pegasus*. As I told you, we've been preparing for a return mission ever since the first reports of trouble started filtering in." He sipped his drink.

"When do we leave?" She decided she might as well show some interest. Even though she hadn't exactly volunteered, it *was* her first command.

"In twelve hours."

She stared at him with dark-rimmed eyes. "Twelve *hours*? Come on, Kagen! I was out there for three years, for God's sake! You can't make me turn around in less than a day!"

"The decision has been made. Beside," he smiled faintly, "I'd rather you had as little time as possible to throw a spanner into the works. You've proven too good at doing that."

She sighed and rubbed her eyes. "Don't give up on me yet."

He ignored her. "The *Pegasus* will carry a crew of six,

including yourself. Four will be standard contract hires—all eager volunteers, I assure you—and the fifth will be a genetics researcher for the Consortium. His job will be to study the biological situation for us—and to keep an eye on you."

"After all this, you still don't trust me?" She almost giggled at her feeble sarcasm.

"My dear, I'm not a fool."

"I don't suppose you'll tell me which one he's going to be?"

"I'm sorry, did I say 'he'?" Kagen smiled. "I'd hate to ruin the surprise for you, though I'm sure you'll find out soon enough who it is."

"Bastard!" she muttered.

"Only you and our researcher will know the full background of the situation. It will be up to you, of course, as captain, to tell the rest of your crew as much of the truth as you see fit. Obviously, I won't be there to stop you."

She nodded. "You remember that, too."

"Ah," he held up his hand, "but let me finish. I was going to offer some advice. True, what you say will be entirely up to you. But let me remind you of the way your crew will perceive you as you go into this mission. They won't know what really happened on the *Black Opal*, but they've all heard the stories."

"I'll bet you made sure of that!"

He raised one shoulder. "I simply thought I would remind you that an officer—even though you were not the captain—who deserted her crew, however horrible the situation, is not one to inspire confidence in her leadership. Then, too, your experience out there was so terrible it probably left you a little...oh, shall we call it obsessive about certain things. Perhaps *paranoid* is a better word. In any case, these people have entrusted their lives to you over the next year and a half or so. Don't make them regret it."

"I'm not a fool, either, Kagen." She stared straight at him. "I'll do what needs to be done."

"Excellent attitude!" He smiled. "But did I mention that the researcher might not be the only crewmember in my employ? *Might* not. But perhaps you'll behave yourself if you don't think you can trust anyone...eh, Katie?"

She had thought she might try to kill him if he called her that again, but she found she hadn't the energy or the desire with the blank stare of the Rory-thing at her back. So she swallowed her words, deciding it might be best to let him think it no longer bothered her, and forced herself to smile. "Don't push your luck."

"Do you have any more questions?"

Kate shook her head.

"Very well, to the last item, then. There will be a press conference at the shuttleport here before we leave for Equator Station. The newsmedia know you've been here today—though we would've preferred they didn't—and we've been forced to promise them a statement from you this afternoon."

She looked up quickly. "No."

"I beg your pardon?"

"I said no. I won't do that for you."

He shook his head at her. "The time for this behavior has passed, Captain Harlin. By agreeing to lead this next mission, you have officially extended your contract and continued your employment with the Consortium. As your employer, I am ordering you to make a statement to the newsmedia regarding this mission. Or, if you prefer, I can have Rory hold you now while a medic administers the drug we discussed earlier. I'm sure the media people would understand if we told them you were still not feeling well and might be having a small relapse." He cocked his head. "You will go back out there, one way or the other, Captain Harlin. Make no mistake—I want you to lead this team. I have a perverse desire for you to be fully aware that you are working for me, and that you are doing this job because *I* want you to do it. But I can do without you if I must."

"God *damn* you!" Her voice cracked. "If I talk to them?"

"You'll lead the team as I promised."

"Complete control?"

"Within reason."

"Okay, but I want to see the frankenstein loaded. I want to see it hooked up to life-support by a qualified tech—and I want access to that room!"

"Very well." He nodded.

"All right, I'll give your press conference. What do you want me to say?"

"I don't care, as long as you convince everyone you're leading this mission of your own free will. Just make yourself appear to be a perfectly satisfied and loyal employee of the Consortium, and I will be happy."

"They'll think I'm crazy, going back out there!"

"As long as you convince them you're doing so willingly. After all, that is what's important."

She frowned, staring at her hands. He kept speaking of loyalty. . . . "What's going to happen to Baker?" she asked.

"Are you so concerned for him?"

"Call it curious."

"In all likelihood, nothing. He will be by my side, as always, doing my bidding," he paused briefly, "and worrying about when I will punish him. I needn't do anything—he will do it to himself."

"You're a cold bastard."

"Oh, Martin will have every chance to redeem himself." He smiled slightly. "Much as you will on this next mission."

Kate felt a muscle in her cheek twitch. "Don't rub it in. You've got me."

His smile broadened. "I know."

CHAPTER

7

Two shuttle limousines settled at the curb in front of the London Shuttleport Passenger Terminal. Kagen exited first, in his automated chair. Kate followed, escorted by four security men in plain clothes. Several other Consortium executives came from the second car.

"Don't forget, Katie." Kagen's voice was so low that only she could hear him as he signaled one of his security men, who gave her a brief glimpse of what he held in his hand—a small pressure-hypo.

"I know the rules," she said between clenched teeth.

"Good. Let's see a smile, then. You're a new captain, remember?"

Slowly they made their way down the long concourse of the terminal. Kate could see a large knot of people ahead in the distance.

As they reached the edge of the crowd, members of the newsmedia parted respectfully to let them through. Kate thought regretfully of her missed opportunity earlier in the day—was it only that morning?—to be interviewed without the very real threat of censorship sitting next to her in an automated wheelchair.

A small podium had been readied for them, and some public relations flunky took the microphone. Kate stood immediately to the woman's right, with Kagen by her side, and the others were arranged in a half-circle behind them. She was effectively hemmed in.

"Good afternoon, ladies and gentlemen. We don't have but a few minutes to talk with you, because there's a lot of work left to be done before the *Pegasus* can break away from Equator Station. But we can give you a little background."

Kate listened as the woman droned on about that "well-known *Black Opal* disaster" (was it *that* well known?) of a little over a year ago, briefly touching on the various rumors that had been circulating; undoing some, but not all, of the bad Guil-Pro had said about her for the way she had handled the situation. They left just enough in doubt so that she would seem appropriate for such a return mission, yet not entirely blameless for what had happened. Funny how *they* managed to come away sounding vaguely paternal and supportive about giving such a valued employee a second chance.

And the crowd ate it up. Members of the electronic printmedia were typing fast and furious notes on steno-boards for direct relay, their faces rapt with attention at the new story unfolding just for them, while the network tri-vid remotes had homed in on her with unerring expectancy, broadcasting her face to the watching billions of Earth and the lunar and Martian colonies.

A young man sat alone in his darkened office at the Earthside Port Authority, staring at a tri-vid screen. All day long the newscasts had promised this event—a media conference with the survivor of the infamous *Black Opal* mission. The buildup had been typical media hype, but Patrick Meitner had every reason for wanting to watch.

He had been given the responsibility for forming and leading the Board of Inquiry that was to look into the *Black Opal* mission and its strange outcome. So far he had received minimal cooperation from the Guilford Production Consortium—as little as they could give him and not break the law, as a matter of fact—and this would be his first chance to get a look at Second Pilot Katharine Harlin. After all this crap he was hearing from the Consortium's P.R. representative, it would be real interesting to hear what she had to say for herself.

"As I said, ladies and gentlemen, there's a lot of work left to be done before the *Pegasus* is ready for breakaway, but Captain Harlin has agreed to say a few words before we'll have to close."

Kate's ordeal began in earnest when she had to clip a small microphone to her lapel and speak to the hungry crowd. She'd never considered herself good at improvisation; within the bounds of what she and Kagen had talked about on their way to the passenger terminal, that was exactly what she had to do now.

Perversely, her restrained manner as she told her rehearsed story was far more convincing than she could ever have hoped to make the truth. She realized this, and cursed herself for not even trying to push Kagen's limitations.

"The director of the Research Division has told me we have time for a few questions," the publicity representative spoke again. "You, sir, back in the corner?"

"How come you're going back out *now*? We know your last mission was almost three years long, and a pain in the ass besides. What's the rush? Why not take a break first?"

"Guilty conscience, hey?" another voice shouted, but was silenced quickly.

The publicity rep interposed herself smoothly into the situation with a standard answer about bonuses and "making it up later" that earned her a few catcalls.

"Hey!" shouted a new voice from the back. "I'm a Guild representative. Guil-Pro can't *make* you go back out without your paid furlough unless that's the way *you* want it! If they're putting the pressure on, say something now!"

Kate hesitated noticeably. She'd been in the spotlight too long and was beginning to feel light-headed and queasy. She was drenched in sweat. No one had anticipated this angle—not Kagen, not the P.R. rep—nobody—and she wasn't ready for it. Especially not after Paul Westman's convincing warning that she shouldn't expect any help from the Guild because of what she had done. And here was help. . . . The temptation to give in was overwhelming.

"Don't forget," the voice continued, "there has to be a Board of Inquiry within a certain period of time, too! You'll have to be present for that!"

The publicity rep knew how to answer *that* one, and she stepped in neatly before Kate could open her mouth. While the woman was talking, Kate felt a gentle touch at the small of her back and glanced over her shoulder. Kagen wasn't looking at her, but his threat was clear. The security guard beside her held the pressure-hypo casually; if his grip tightened . . .

"Please!" She raised her hands and forced herself to smile, knowing she was the only one who could silence this line of inquiry. "I know this sounds a little crazy, but I'm doing this all on my own. Believe me, after what I went through out there, nobody could make me go back if I didn't want to!" This provoked brief laughter. "Thanks for the concern, really. But the best way for me to work through a bad experience is to get right back on it. I have to, so I don't lose my nerve. You can't afford that in this business." Kate forced herself to smile again, and it made her face hurt. For a moment her queasiness almost overwhelmed her.

"No more questions, thank you!" Kagen moved to break up the conference himself. "Captain Harlin is very tired, and she still has a lot of work to do. Thank you very much!"

There was some applause as they turned away and proceeded to the Consortium's official shuttle. Tri-vid cameras recorded the event for the world to see; few would forget the expression on Kate's face as she turned for one last look at the crowd before disappearing through the hatch.

In his office, Meitner stared at the tri-vid screen and memorized that stunning closeup. Dark-circled eyes in a pale face stared back at him. He wasn't sure which parts of her speech were truth and which were not, but he knew she was in trouble.

"Do I have to be followed every goddamn minute?" Kate exploded as they stood in Guil-Pro offices on Equator Station.

"You've behaved so far," Kagen conceded. "What would you like?"

"I need to pack, and tend to some personal things," she said more quietly. "I'd like to go alone."

Kagen regarded her measuringly. "Very well, you may be alone for three hours. I will even grant you the privacy of your quarters, which, I remind you, I need not do. But you *will* be under surveillance. Records will be kept of everyone whom you see or speak to. Those people will also be watched, to make sure they do nothing foolish after you have gone. So be cautious, my dear." He smiled. "Don't get any of your friends in trouble."

She gazed at him in silence, arms folded tightly across her chest.

"You may go now."

She turned to leave.

"Remember, Katie—three hours. Your escort will let you know when your time is up."

She continued across the office without pausing, without bothering to turn her head, and Kagen let her go.

An older man turned away from the viewport and regarded Kagen thoughtfully. "Do you trust her?"

"Of course not." Kagen busied himself at the bar, and servo-mechanisms moved smoothly to assist his inept hand.

"And you let her go?"

"She can't go anywhere that I won't find her, and she knows it." Kagen powered his chair to the other man's side and handed him a drink. "Besides, she's afraid of me. Didn't you see it?"

"You're very sure of your pawn, Geoffrey." The man chuckled.

"I know how her mind works, Mr. Guilford." Kagen was imperturbable.

"I must say," Guilford sighed, "I envy you that confidence."

He watched Kagen take two small tablets with his drink. "Heart bothering you again, Geoffrey?"

"Occasionally. I'm afraid I'm about due for another transplant. Blasted expensive things!" Kagen shook his head. "You would think they'd have developed longer-lasting units by now. With the exorbitant fees they charge, I'd expect to be served a lifetime, not a mere three years or so!"

"Surely you can afford it—"

"That's not the issue. It's the principle I object to!"

Guilford's eyebrows rose slightly. "You could always look into it yourself. A bit of legitimate research for a change?"

Kagen ignored the gibe. "I've thought of that, actually. Perhaps our next project . . ."

"Mmm, yes." Guilford glanced at his watch. "Geoffrey, I'm still worried about that Harlin girl. Doesn't she have friends?"

"I'm sure she does." Kagen sipped his drink. "An old crewmate of hers is one of our Control Central staff on the *Orphic Angel*, as a matter of fact. Watson, his name is."

"And she came back through that station! Geoffrey, are you sure—"

"Mr. Guilford, please don't concern yourself with the minor details. Billy Watson lost one of his legs in an accident several years ago because he tried to save someone else's life. The man died anyway. Watson is a very detached individual—his psych-profiles confirm that. He won't stick his neck out again. Especially not for Kate Harlin."

The older man was still concerned. "But doesn't she have a husband?"

"Former husband, yes. He wasn't man enough to keep her, and she insulted him by leaving him. Why should he put himself out for her now? They never see each other."

"Well, I trust your judgment of the situation." Guilford made one last attempt. "But are you sure you at least don't want her quarters monitored?"

"It's not worth the effort. Besides," Kagen allowed himself a frosty smile, "I can tell you exactly what you'd hear."

"Oh? What's that?"

"Two hours of glorious sex."

Guilford was plainly puzzled. "How can you be so sure?"

"She's from the working class, Mr. Guilford. Would you expect her to be reading a book?" He thought for a moment, then smiled as though at a private memory. "Besides, I know Katie *very* well."

"Kate? Kate—dammit, woman, don't run away from me!" It was Lars, hailing her from a side corridor.

"Jon!" She stopped, undecided. Her head still ached from frazzled nerves and Kagen's scotch, and he looked angry. She wasn't sure she was ready to handle that right now. "I—I'm glad to see you."

He grabbed her in a big hug. "You'd better be," he whispered in her ear, nuzzling her. "This is supposed to be the first time we've seen each other in over three years, remember? Be real glad, baby, in case somebody's watching."

She obeyed, made herself laugh and chatter about nothing as they stood and looked at each other, noting how neither had changed, asking how long *had* it been, after all . . . knowing all the while that he was furious with her.

"Let's go someplace quiet, lover. Want a drink?"

"No!" Damn, but the man was frustrating! "My head aches, I need to rest—and I'd like to be alone!"

He gave her a look. "We have to talk."

She sighed. He was so determined! There was no avoiding him. Besides, Kagen *had* promised her the privacy of her quarters. . . .

"All right, let's go. But I don't want to fight."

"You know what I'm going to say, then."

"Jon, please don't—"

"Why the hell are you going back out? We haven't seen each other in close to four years, I've got some leave stockpiled—you haven't even been home twenty-four fucking hours, and you're going straight back out for at least another two years!"

She backed away from him. "And why the hell do you think we split up? Don't run all these arguments by me again, Jon, I'm too tired and I have too much to do."

"This is *not* the same old argument, goddammit—look at you! You're as pale as a basement bureaucrat, and the circles under your eyes are deep as craters! What the hell are you trying to do to yourself?" He broke off to follow her into a lift.

"And what the fuck difference does it make to you?" She turned on him as the lift began to move. "Just who the hell are you, yelling at me like this out in the goddamn hall, when I don't need to—" She had to stop, afraid she would start crying. This was not how she'd wanted this to go, not how she wanted to remember him. . . .

But he seemed to realize he had gone too far, and he stopped. "Kate," he said softly, "you haven't answered my question. You can at least do that. Why are you going back out? What happened?"

She took a deep breath to steady her voice. "You saw the broadcast, didn't you?"

"Damn straight—and I was so surprised you could've knocked me over! That was the *last* thing I ever expected to hear you say!"

They had reached her quarters, and with a persistence Kate had rarely seen in him before, Lars followed her right inside.

"Can we talk?" he asked. "Or is something wrong?"

"You tell me something first," she said unsteadily. "Are you really mad, or was this just a show for the cameras?"

He looked annoyed, but had the grace to blush. "A little of both, I guess. I really *didn't* expect you to go back out there. And I didn't figure on your coming across so much like you support what they're doing. You surprise me, Kate. You caught me off guard, you were so damn convincing."

"Now you know how I've been living my life since I got back from out there," she said flatly. "Let me tell you how it really is. Kagen said I had three hours to be alone from the time I left him just a few minutes ago. He also told me I would be under surveillance everywhere but here—and I don't even know whether to trust him that far or not."

"Kagen? *The* Geoffrey Kagen?" Lars pursed his lips, then motioned her to be quiet. While she watched, he removed the cover from her intercom and played with some of the internal controls. Although he was an officer now, he had signed into the space services many years ago as an engineer, and he'd always kept up with the technology. After a few moments' work, he shook his head and smiled as he replaced the cover. "Guild law *says* that company quarters have to be completely independent units, which is supposed to keep the bastards from getting any ideas about surveillance networks to keep tabs on their employees, but it doesn't hurt to be careful. Looks like we're clean."

"Kagen's no fool. He knows it's not worth the risk of getting caught—no spacer would ever work for Guil-Pro again!"

"So you actually saw Geoffrey Kagen?" Lars asked. "Do you know how unusual that is? The man is seen so little in person that every few years or so rumors crop up that he's died, or that he never existed in the first place! Are you sure it was him?"

"Believe me, it was him." She opened her kit bag and dumped out her dirty clothes, then turned to her closet.

"Oh, shit!" she murmured.

"What's wrong?"

Her duty ship for her last five missions had been the *Black Opal*, and that's how all her old uniforms were marked. Besides, she'd just gotten the equivalent of a field promotion, and her new uniforms would have to reflect her new rank.

Ship's captain was like no other rank, and only captains wore a deep royal blue, the color of status in the space services.

Her old uniforms were a light tan.

"I forgot I'd have to call Stores," she explained. "Need new uniforms."

"Shouldn't they have been provided?" he asked.

She shrugged and activated her video com.

"General Stores, Cooper here."

"This is Captain Harlin of the *Pegasus*, personal I.D.

number 99734-23-KH. You have an order for new uniforms for me?"

"Hang on a minute, ma'am." The voice was polite but disinterested. "Sorry, ma'am, I got no orders for any issue to a Captain Harlin. Hmm—I do have a Second Pilot Harlin, listed for the *Black Opal*. Work-order number PX-2287-99734-KH—that you?"

"You'd better update your records, mister," she said evenly. "Do you have the *Pegasus* listed at all? GPC-1242, class J?"

"Uh—yes, ma'am. Crew of six. Uniforms issued for . . . hmph, only five issues. No, wait, there's a note. . . ." Another pause. "That's right, ma'am. Only five issues. The sixth is a PIA."

"What the fuck is a PIA?" she demanded, a little louder than she'd intended.

"Uh—that's 'previous issue applies.'" The voice was now faintly apologetic.

Kate's face stiffened. "Who ordered that?"

"Somebody in the front office. That's all I know."

"How long would it take you to issue me new uniforms if you started right now?"

"Let's see . . . you'd have to get authorization, then they'd have to be made up, delivered . . . at least twenty-four hours, ma'am."

"Twenty-four hours," she repeated. "Sorry, not good enough. Thanks, Cooper." She broke the connection without waiting for his reply.

"Welcome to the bureaucracy." Lars kept his tone of voice light.

"Bureaucracy, my ass—that was deliberate! Kagen's trying to make me look like an unprepared fool!"

He thought it best to say nothing as she raged silently for a few moments. Then her anger was gone as suddenly as it had come, and she sighed deeply.

"I guess I'll have to wear the old ones," she said matter-of-factly. "At least they're clean. But I wish the color difference wasn't so obvious."

Quickly and methodically she folded the uniforms and

undergarments and packed them along with a few personal effects. Let them think what they wanted.

Lars had watched her closely for the last few minutes, and he thought that now might be a better time to try his questions again. "You all right?"

"I'm fine."

"Sounds like your interview with Kagen was pretty traumatic."

"Look, I told you I don't want to talk about it," she said quickly. "Things didn't turn out like I expected, and I don't think it's a good idea for you to be involved."

"I'm already involved, whether you want me to be or not."

She stood with her back to him for long moments, then her shoulders sagged. "Jon, I'm worried about Billy. Kagen is suspicious that I was able to get information off the lifeboat before they blew it up—he even hinted he knew how I did it, which would put Billy right in the middle.

"Do you know what he said to me? Anybody I see or even *talk* to today will be kept on record, to make sure they don't do anything 'foolish' after I've gone. You *know* damn well they've already seen us together this time at least. So you're right, you *are* involved."

"Doesn't that give me the right to know what's going on?"

She turned to face him suddenly, her eyes bright. "I am so fucking scared I can't see straight!" She squeezed her eyes shut and stood there, biting her lower lip.

Lars pulled her to him. She didn't protest, but she was rigid against him, unyielding—determined not to break down. "Oh, Kate," he murmured.

She raised her head a few minutes later and looked at him. Her eyes were dry. "I'm sorry. You shouldn't have to deal with this."

"When are you going to get it through your thick head that I *want* to deal with it?" He looked at her searchingly. "Tell me what happened with Kagen."

She told him about the interview, about how the *Hercules* had discovered their "virgin" find years ago, and what had happened to her crew. She described the deal she had worked

out to get her first command instead of a free ride back to
the stars in a freezer. She told him about everything but Kagen
and Rory—she couldn't bring herself to talk about that yet.
Besides, Lars knew who Rory was, though he'd never met
him, and to have someone else know what Kagen had done
to her, even Lars . . .

"Got you locked in airtight?"

"For now."

"What're you going to do?"

"Do? What the hell d'you think?" She shook her head.
"I'm sorry, Jon. But it's not like I've got a choice."

"Well . . . you could try to get out of here."

She laughed. "Run? How far do you think I'd get? Shit!"
She jammed her hands into her pockets. "I don't really care
now, anyway. It's just another job, and once I get out there
again, I'll have some control over the situation. What bothers
me is that I'll never have the chance to get Kagen for all of
this. If I could just *get* him, I'd feel like some of it was
worthwhile."

"How would you get him, if you could?"

She clenched her fists and held them up before her. "With
these."

He looked somewhat taken aback. "That's not like you."

"Why shouldn't I want to make him pay for what he did
to those people? And to *me?* What's the matter—don't you
like me like this?"

"No, I don't think I do."

"Would you rather I curl up and die because Guil-Pro's
got my ass backed into a corner?"

"No, but—dammit, Kate, do you have to go charging
in there fists first? There must be a happy medium—"

"Must there?" She turned away from him and beat her
clenched fists on the wall. "How do you think I got *into* this
mess in the first place? I am sick and fucking tired of happy
mediums!"

"Wait a minute, Kate, I didn't mean—"

"Oh, Jon, I know what you meant, and that's part of the
problem. There *is* no happy medium with the Consortium!
You either shut up and take it, or you stick 'em every chance

you get, until they get tired of it or pissed off and they get rid of you. And I'm tired of taking the shit."

"How long have you been working in the service?"

"Almost thirty years, and a lot of it with Guil-Pro. See what I mean?" She smiled tiredly. "I've been around more than long enough to know what goes on with them—I know it isn't any different with any other company, either. I didn't mean to say I was perfect, Jon. I know I've let stuff slide before. But this time it was too much—too goddamn much." She thought of Rory. "So I decided I was going to fight back, and that's why I'm in trouble now. I guess," she smiled at him, "you think I'm crazy."

The look in his eyes hurt her, and she turned away from him. "Well, I can't blame you if you don't like what I'm saying, but," she shrugged, "I never asked you to like it, either."

"You're right, I don't like it. Dammit, I don't want you to give up on your principles, but I don't want you to get hurt, either. Can't you . . ."

"Jon, I have to fight them this time. It's as simple as that. And wherever I end up, I'm going to drag Kagen with me. Don't you see, I've got to get *something* out of this! If all this hell was for nothing—"

"No." He walked over and touched her shoulder. "It won't be for nothing, because you won't let it. And I'll be right behind you. You're right, I don't have to like it. But I'll be here when you need me." His grip tightened briefly. "What can I do now?"

Her smile trembled around the corners. "I hope . . . I hope someday I'll be able to tell you how much this means to me."

"Just make sure there *is* a someday. That'll be enough for me." He brushed a tear from the corner of her eye. "Seriously, is there anything I can do for you now?"

She shook her head. "Just deal with the stuff Billy gave you. Get it to the Port Authority—they'll be in charge of the Board of Inquiry. I don't have a contact, I don't know if the information is coded or not—just get it to them without getting yourself killed. And *wait* before you do anything. I know Kagen'll have you watched, probably for some time after I leave." She shook her head, murmuring, "I hate to have you anywhere near this."

"Speaking of old arguments, let's not get into *that* again. I'll do my bit—you just keep *your* ass out of trouble!" He smiled at her. "How much time do you have left?"

She glanced at her watch. "Almost two hours."

"You probably need some time by yourself. I'll come back to see you off . . . if you like."

"That sounds real good—but don't get caught."

"Ah, now, I'm better than that!" He chuckled, then grew sober. "Good luck, Kate. Be careful."

"Don't you doubt it."

She was a tall woman, but still he had to bend to kiss her. She hugged him tightly, then pulled away and smiled. "You be careful, too."

He touched her face lightly, then slipped out the door.

"Your crew is in the next office, signing their contracts. I thought now might be a good time for you to meet them."

It was a little over two hours later, and she again stood before Kagen in the Consortium's Equator Station offices.

"That's up to you, Mr. Kagen."

"Please." He smiled and gestured. "I'll wait for you here—I understand how important first impressions can be."

I'll bet you do, she thought, glancing down at her uniform as she walked to the door, which slid open ahead of her. She passed down a short corridor with a sharp turn to the left. Then she stood, momentarily unnoticed, in the doorway of a conference room.

There were five of them, sitting or standing about in casual uniforms. Documents were spread on the table before them. The tradition had become law for the various spaceworkers' guilds—contracts must be written out and signed on hardcopy in order to be valid. Official copies, of course, were stored in microform, but men and women whose lives were distorted by Planck's constant and the law of time dilation wanted something solid and unalterable to document what they were and who they worked for. Contracts were printed on paper and signed in ink, and there were no questions asked.

The closest to her was an older man, red-haired and slightly graying, an engineer by his navy blue pants. Certainly looked experienced, and she was glad for that. Next was a short, middle-aged man, wiry, with sandy hair going gray. Looked impatient, but she hoped, noting the tan jumpsuit, that he would make a good pilot. She wanted all the experience she could get for this mission. The next wore a brown T-shirt and pants, indicating the nonbiological sciences, and he reminded her of Lars—tall and blond and not too hard to look at, with a muscled chest under the tight brown T. Engaging grin. Pretty obvious about eyeing the only other female in the crew, a tall young woman who wore the silver colors of a computer specialist.

Young indeed! Kate doubted if she was even twenty-five. Light-colored hair cut short, blue eyes—ill-at-ease, too. And staring with covert admiration at the fifth member of the crew, a young man in green with a medic's insignia. He was of medium build with blue-black hair (she winced; it was the color of Rory's hair) and gray eyes, good-looking—and knew it, too. Kate was briefly amused at the thought of a triangle developing before they even broke orbit, until she remembered that one of her scientists was probably Guil-Pro's genetics researcher, and her keeper. Three scientists in the damn crew—and she had no idea which ones to trust.

Just then the young woman looked up. "Captain Harlin?"

"Am I the last to sign?" she asked, stepping into the room. She felt suddenly awkward, aware that her uniform was wrong in all the obvious ways—color, rank, insignia. . . .

"It's your honor." The red-haired engineer grinned and held out a pen for her to take. If he'd noticed something wrong, she couldn't tell, and it made her feel better.

Kate scanned the standard Guilford Production Consortium document, wondering why Kagen had even bothered with the formality, unless it was to preserve appearances. Her eyebrows lifted slightly as she noted the extra sweeteners. Not only was she to receive two and one-half points of the gross proceeds of this mission, but she was also to get three points of the next large transport run instead of the usual single point. She signed quickly, wondering if she'd live to collect the bonus.

Miraculously, a secretary appeared to take the documents as she finished signing. "These will be placed on the Consortium's standard database for all contract documents. Hardcopies will be stored with our Records Management Section, and additional hardcopies will be forwarded to you at the appropriate mail stops. Are there any questions?"

"Yeah, how much time left before breakaway?" asked the sandy-haired pilot.

The secretary consulted his watch. "Eight hours, forty-two minutes."

"Great! Time for one last bender!" He laughed, though no one else did.

Kate smiled. "As long as you're sober for breakaway, Mister..." She paused. "Let's introduce ourselves now. I don't like to call people 'hey you' if I can possibly avoid it. My name is Kate Harlin—and I don't stand on rank. Okay?" She saw several assenting nods. "Good. We can start with you." She looked at the man who had just spoken and wondered how far off her initial judgments had been.

"George Grayson, ma'am. Pilot and navigator. A little in the Science Section if you need it, though we look pretty overloaded with science-terrifics for this trip." Again, his remark didn't receive the laughter he seemed to expect.

Kate sighed inwardly and added *crude* to her earlier assessment of *impatient*. "Welcome aboard, Grayson." She moved to the next man in line.

"Alfredo Juli, ma'am. I'm your exo-geologist and pasta specialist in the galley." The blond young man grinned at her.

God, she thought, *this is just a lark for him. Was I ever like that?* "Experience?" she asked. "Aside from the pasta, that is."

He smiled appreciatively, then grew serious. "Mostly inside the outer terminus, ma'am, though I had the chance to study some of the Cygni artifacts under Coulson. I know what we're going out there for."

She nodded, beginning to relax into her role a little. "Glad to have you, Al—or do you prefer Alfredo?"

"Al is fine, ma'am."

"I'm glad to have your experience, too, Al. I have a lot

of respect for Julia Coulson's work." She shifted her gaze to the next person in the group.

"Teresa MacKessen, ma'am," said the tall young woman. "I'll have the computer station, but I also know communications, and some engineering in pinch."

Kate was thoughtful. "You look pretty young to've been in all those areas of expertise." *And awfully young to be a spy,* she continued to herself. *But it wouldn't be the first time. . . .*

"I've been in the service for five years!" MacKessen was defensive.

"Ease up, Teresa," Kate said lightly, "that wasn't a put-down. If you know your stuff, I don't care how old you are. Okay?"

MacKessen nodded, but still looked uncomfortable. *I hit a nerve somewhere,* Kate thought, *and I don't think it's just her age. . . .*

"How many times have you been in deep space?" she continued.

"Once. I mostly did inner-system exploration for the old Red Planet Research Associates."

Kate vaguely remembered that the small company had been gobbled up somewhere along the line by one of the firms that was now a part of Guil-Pro. Should that mean something? she wondered. "Did they ever freeze you?" she asked.

"No."

"Good enough." Kate moved on. "Next?"

"Peter Schweitz, ma'am. I'm your engineer."

"You've been around for a while. What's your line?"

He smiled. "I used to ride shotgun on the three-man forerunner ships Guil-Pro sends out to the real unlikely prospects."

From the corner of her eye, Kate saw MacKessen change color and look away. "I like that kind of experience, Pete," she said. "I'm looking for people who are used to seeing the unusual. And," she smiled a little, "I was on one of those myself, once. Changed my mind about *that* line of work for good!" She glanced again at her computer specialist, who was now staring fixedly ahead, then nodded at the last man.

"Kenneth Luttrell, ma'am. I'm an MD, and I'll be in

charge of our extra passenger." The young man smiled, and it was a gorgeous smile.

And I was right, Kate thought, *he knows it, too.* "You've been in deep space before, Ken?"

"Kenneth, please."

She nodded. "Of course, Kenneth."

"Yes, ma'am, I've been in deep space a number of times."

"Good. By the way, where will we be keeping our extra passenger?" she asked, making a mental note to find out later how many of her crew knew that the passenger they referred to was a frankenstein, and, for that matter, how many of them cared.

"On Deck 2, just off our main life-support center. Convenient for monitoring."

Deck 2, right next door to the centralized life-support center where their own hibernation units were located. *Convenient indeed,* she thought, and then wondered why the idea bothered her so much.

"All right, I guess that'll do for now. We have slightly less than eight hours before station breakaway. That would make it twenty-two thirty hours Earth Greenwich Time. I'd like to meet everyone aboard the *Pegasus* at twenty-one hundred hours. That should give us plenty of time to go through final checkout on a new ship." She nodded briefly and left the room, trying not to worry about whether they were staring at her.

There were many other questions she wanted to ask her new crew, but they could wait until the *Pegasus* was far from Equator Station and whoever might be listening.

CHAPTER

8

At 2050 hours Earth Greenwich Time, Captain Kate Harlin approached the access umbilicus that led to the airlock of her first command, the Light-Plus Ship *Pegasus*. Better to be early than late for such an important first appointment. A Guil-Pro security guard was on duty, and she flipped him her I.D. card.

"Whoa, ma'am, sorry!" He caught at her arm. "I got my orders."

"Oh, you do? And what might they be?"

"You've got to be searched, ma'am."

"What?"

"Mr. Kagen's orders, ma'am."

"What does he think I'm going to do, carry a bomb onto my own goddamn ship?" she asked, her voice rising slightly. "I'm the *captain*, for chrissakes, doesn't that mean anything around here?"

"Sorry, ma'am. Orders is orders."

She muttered something vaguely obscene, but submitted to the search.

"Okay, you're clean." The guard stepped back and reattached the portable scanner to his belt.

"Just what the hell were you looking for?"

"Didn't find anything—what're you worried about?" He shrugged.

She made a disgusted noise and walked past him.

"The bridge is that way," he called after her, pointing even though she wasn't looking.

"Don't do me any favors!" She walked on up to the access umbilicus and disappeared without looking back.

Annoyed, Kate strode through the corridors without

bothering to see if any of her crew were aboard yet. Searched before boarding her own ship! Kagen couldn't have picked a more demeaning way to send her off.

Well, best to try to shake it. The sooner she got away from him, the sooner she could feel in control of the situation. She entered her tiny quarters and jerked open the door to her locker. There before her were five standard royal-blue uniforms, just as she would have arranged them, all emblazoned with the *Pegasus* markings and her new rank of captain. She reached out to touch them, hardly believing they were there.

On closer inspection, she saw collar pins with the *Black Opal*'s emblem on them, rimmed in black. Her throat tightened for a brief moment, and she swallowed hard. *Damn Kagen, anyway!* she thought, and almost ripped them out. Then she stopped to think. She had a right to mourn her friends, and this was an appropriate and acceptable gesture. She would hardly be the only spacer ever to wear some remembrance of a mission past.

Kate stripped quickly. The new uniforms were a perfect fit, and once again she found herself wondering whether she'd been the victim of a bureaucratic screwup, or if Kagen had arranged it just to embarrass her—or if she was being too paranoid about the whole thing.

Teresa MacKessen paused at the entrance to the bridge and looked around her. Straight ahead was the main viewport, a large, many-paned window that now looked out into the starlit blackness of space. The bridge itself was on two levels.

Immediately in front of her was the command area, split in two by a narrow aisle. To the left and slightly below the level of the aisle was the captain's seat, and to the right was the pilot's; both were surrounded by control panels for the ship's major functions. The master computer console was to the left of the captain's seat, forward and slightly lower than the command deck, so that the seat itself was in a well, encircled by three monitors and the array of SINS's controls. Everything was in muted shades of blue, gray, and green, with occasional bright splashes of red.

She walked out to the end of the command deck, ducking under ceiling fixtures, to the top of the two steps leading down to the mid-deck. Here were seats and myriad control panels for the engineer and the two mission specialists, their exo-geologist and the physician/biologist. She knew that the engineer had additional controls in his area down in engineering on Deck 3. She also knew that the ship could actually carry eight, and that there were two seats beneath the command deck that wouldn't be needed on this trip. All had a direct view from the main port; all were within view of the captain from her seat above. A convenient arrangement, but very cramped.

Teresa walked back from the forward end of the command deck, nearly bumping her head again, and stepped down into the well that contained her seat and SINS's master console. The seat itself was comfortable, with a high back, and moved at the touch of a button. Up and down, back and forth, tilt, swivel—she stopped, suddenly embarrassed that someone might think she was playing with her chair. Her age almost always branded her as "the kid" on a mission anyway, so she certainly didn't need to be caught acting like one. After all, she was a professional.

The master console . . . now that was a different matter. Playing with that was her job. This one, in keeping with the rest of the ship, was newer and a little cleaner than she was used to, but still very familiar. Idly she tapped in a few commands, bypassing the COACH subsystem that only got in her way, and watched the results display across the monitor—must be one of the newer superhigh-resolution screens. She began to think about this mission she had signed on for.

What would it be like working for Kate Harlin? she wondered. She'd never worked for a woman before, and would've looked forward to the opportunity in any case, but . . . well, there were just so many stories going around about the *Black Opal* mission and its sole survivor. Some were good, many were bad, most were confusing—and then there was the story Guil-Pro had put forth at the newsmedia conference, different again from any of the earlier stories. Had Kate deserted her crew out there? Had they been dead or alive when she left? Would it have made a difference either way? True to form, Guil-Pro hadn't cleared up the confusion.

Then again, did any of it matter? Captain Harlin looked

like a sane and reasonable person, and certainly acted like one, so what was the big deal?

Then why did she show up in her old uniform, with her old ship's name and her old rank? What was she trying to prove? a nasty little voice nagged at the back of Teresa's mind. *You'd better hope she knows what she's doing, because you're stuck with her for two years out there!*

"Oh, go eat it!" she muttered.

"I beg your pardon?"

Teresa looked up from her seat and blushed furiously. The captain was standing above her, on the deck level. "Sorry. I—I was talking to myself."

The older woman smiled a little. "No problem." She moved away.

Teresa stared after her and blinked. Had she been seeing things earlier? Harlin was now dressed in royal blue. The name *Pegasus* was emblazoned on both shoulders and across the breast, and her rank pin was plainly that of captain, not second pilot.

Then she saw the small remembrance pin. That certainly had not been there before, though there was nothing unusual about it—in fact, she'd have wondered if the captain *hadn't* elected to show some respect for dead comrades. It didn't match at all with the image the woman had presented earlier, appearing in an old uniform, seemingly with no respect for her position, her ship, or her new crew.

Curiouser and curiouser, Teresa thought, turning back to her console.

Kate's next stop was Deck 2 and the cubicle where the frankenstein—*brain-dead LSH unit,* she reminded herself—was to be kept. The bright red door didn't slide open as she approached, and she very nearly walked into it.

"What the hell?" she muttered, stepping back. SINS should've recognized her image as she approached (after all, she *was* the captain) and, at the most, demanded a palm print as further verification. The system was *not* supposed to let her walk into the door!

She slapped the palm plate, and nothing happened. She pressed her palm tightly on the plate, allowing SINS plenty of time to verify her print, and still nothing happened. Annoyed, she inserted her I.D. card in the slot.

"Please state your name." SINS had a very neutral voice, which made him—it—sound bored most of the time. Another little quirk that annoyed her.

"Can't you read the goddamn card?" she asked.

"That name is not recognized."

Damn implacable machine! "Katharine Harlin, captain, Light-Plus Ship *Pegasus*, personal I.D. 99734—"

SINS interrupted, "That name is not cleared for entry to this area."

"What do you *mean* not cleared? Listen, you cockeyed piece of electronic junk, I'm the captain of this ship! Didn't your goddamn programmers ever tell you what command rank meant?"

"Processing."

When she realized that SINS was going to spit out a definition of *command rank*, she yanked her card and strode off down the corridor. Kagen was going to hear about this. If she couldn't get to him, *somebody* was going to get an earful.

When she entered the bridge moments later, she noticed that several more of the crew had appeared. Al Juli, Schweitz, and Luttrell were standing in a huddle near the pilot's console.

"MacKessen!" she snapped, startling the younger woman. "Tie me in with Guil-Pro's Control Central on the station. I need to speak to Geoffrey Kagen."

"Yes, ma'am." MacKessen obeyed quickly.

Kate was a little surprised at how easy Kagen was to reach.

"Captain Harlin! I didn't expect to be hearing from you so soon. Do you need something?" He smiled innocuously from the tiny screen.

"You're damn right I do! Why don't I have access to the cubicle where the fr—the cyborg is to be kept? That was part of our agreement."

A frown crossed his face briefly. "It certainly was. Are you positive?"

"Very. SINS wouldn't verify my image, my palm print, my voice, or my I.D. card."

"Is your engineer aboard yet?"

"He's here."

"Perhaps he could help you out. If he has no success, please let me know, and we'll send up a specialist."

"Thank you," she said abruptly. "You'll be hearing from me, I'm sure." At her signal, MacKessen cut the connection.

"Schweitz, will you come with me, please?"

"Let me just get my toolkit here . . ." he muttered, going hastily through his bag. "All right, ma'am, where to?"

"Follow me."

"Now," Pete Schweitz said when they'd arrived, "you want to show me what happened?"

"Sure." Kate walked up to the door, and it slid open obediently. From the corner of her eye she saw Schweitz exchange glances with Kenneth Luttrell, who had apparently tagged along to watch.

"Well now," Pete said easily, "let's check out the whole thing, just in case there's a glitch somewhere. Back off and walk up to it again."

Kate did so, and the door slid open before her.

"Now I'll try it. I'm probably not cleared for image verification." Schweitz walked up to the door, and nothing happened. "Well, that works. What'd you do next?"

"Hit the palm plate."

"Could be it just needs cleaning." He shrugged. "Try it."

She did, already knowing what would happen before the door slid open in front of her.

"And then?"

"My I.D. card." She almost asked him why bother, but figured she might as well follow it to the bitter end. She knew her card would be accepted as well—once she'd passed that initial image verification, SINS wasn't going to balk at any of her other identifications.

Once again the doors opened for her, and she felt her color begin to rise slowly. "Sorry to trouble you over nothing, Pete, especially since you haven't even been to your quarters yet—"

"No problem, Captain. It's just like any other hardware

problem—soon as you call in the specialist, it goes away. Like going to the doctor when you're sick, y'know?"

"Thanks, Pete." She smiled at him as he turned to walk away. He was going to make her life on this mission a lot easier.

Kenneth Luttrell was still watching her.

"Don't you have anything better to do, Doctor?" she asked.

"Yes, ma'am, as soon as they load my patient—" He paused, turning to look behind him.

Around a curve in the hallway came two technicians with a portable hibernation unit between them, mounted on an a-grav carrier. Kate stepped forward and opened the door for them. Lights came on inside the bright white cubicle, and they moved inside. After positioning the unit, one of the technicians touched a control on the carrier. Their burden settled slowly to the deck.

"How much does that thing weigh?" Kate asked.

"'Bout seven hundred seventy kilos."

After anchoring the hibernation unit to the deck, the lead tech turned to her. "Who's in charge of this thing?"

She jerked her thumb at Luttrell. "He's the medic."

"You know how to read these gauges?"

He nodded.

"Why don't you show me, just in case?" Kate suggested.

"Sure thing." The technician explained the entire system to her. "You want to make sure he's still good and frozen," he finished, "this is the monitor to pay attention to. He's not animate, so you don't need to worry about brainwaves. But as long as this stays in the green, you're okay. And you can get all this stuff on the bridge, too, through SINS, if you don't want to bother with coming down here."

"Thanks, tech. Appreciate it."

"Anytime, Captain." The two men nodded and walked away.

Kate peered curiously at the hibernation unit. Half the top was transparent plastex, though most of it was iced over. She thought she could see Rory's face, but it was hazy.

"Are you satisfied, Captain?" Kenneth asked softly.

She regarded him thoughtfully. "I think so. Yes, I think

I am." She made a small gesture. "He's all yours, Doctor. I'll be on the bridge if you need me." She consulted her watch. "Final checkout is in forty-five minutes."

"Aye, aye, Captain." Luttrell turned to his business.

Kate stared at him a moment longer, then left.

In less than an hour, the last crewmember had boarded, and the *Pegasus* was on its way to the outer terminus. After almost four days of travel in normal space, they would reach just beyond Pluto orbit in the area of Station *Windjammer*. Once there, they would set in a final course for Epsilon Indi, fire up the light-plus engines, and go into deep-sleep for seven long months.

Kate made a final check with First Pilot George Grayson and locked in the automatic pilot. "Teresa, get hold of engineering, will you? I want a crew meeting in the mess in forty-five minutes. And make sure you dredge up the doctor—I haven't seen him in a while."

Dr. Luttrell made a few final notes on his clipboard, then set about detaching his portable scanner leads from the hibernation unit on Deck 2. Their nameless patient was doing just fine, for what it was worth. With a brain-dead LSH unit, you had to worry about fewer than half the normal life signs. For instance, the entire bank of brainwave monitors was dead flat, except for those indicating autonomic function. Heart was fine, other internal organs okay, respiration an exciting two breaths per minute—he certainly had his work cut out for him on this trip.

But what was he going to do about Katharine Harlin, he wondered as he put his equipment away. He was familiar with her psych-profiles, and his first meeting with her had borne out what those records said—she was a tough woman who wasn't going to be as easy to manipulate as Kagen had insisted. Of course, Kagen had probably intimidated her, as he did everyone else, which was bound to give him a warped outlook on the way most people behaved. Luttrell was beginning to think he should just lay it on the line with her.

Do me a favor, Captain, and keep your cool. Don't sound off at the mouth too much, and don't do anything stupid to sabotage what we're out here for. We'll all get along a lot better if this mission works, and that bastard Kagen won't have us for dinner when we get back home.

Then again, if he *wanted* to work on her undercover, she had left him a few promising openings. That silly bit about not being able to get in here to see the LSH unit (though she'd sounded sincere), and her obsessive curiosity about the hibernation unit and its contents—at least he had something to work with.

"Luttrell, you down there?"

The voice over the intercom interrupted his thoughts, and he thumbed the switch. "Right here."

"This is MacKessen. Captain wants a meeting in the mess in forty-five minutes."

He frowned. "Already? What about?"

"How the hell should I know? Just be there." Teresa sounded bored. "Bridge out."

The doctor leaned against the wall, arms folded. Maybe things were starting earlier than he'd expected. Now he might *have* to do something.

Kate walked slowly down the corridor to the mess, wondering just what the hell she was going to say. Maybe just what Kagen had suggested—as much of the truth as she saw fit. But how much was that? She smiled a little. If she was careful, she might even smoke out her spy. Just maybe...

"Captain?" Luttrell came up behind her, touching her arm.

"What is it?" She continued to walk.

Teresa, a few paces ahead of them, listened with vague interest. Sometimes eavesdropping was the best way to find out what was really going on. Sometimes it was the only way.

"Captain, I need to speak with you," the doctor insisted.

"You have my ear for two minutes, Doctor."

He glanced at MacKessen's retreating back and decided she was sufficiently out of range. "I don't know what you're planning to say in this little briefing, but I thought I might remind you to be careful."

Kate glanced at him. "What're you talking about?"

"Let me be frank. I've had access to the psych-profiles for everyone in the crew—yes, even yours. It's part of my job on this mission, aside from watching over the patient. And," he hesitated, "you have a reputation, however undeserved, to live down. This crew needs to trust you, Captain; they probably *want* to trust you. But you've already left one crew behind to save yourself—that trust won't be easy to build up."

Her jaw tightened. "Let's not talk about that, shall we, Doctor?"

Ahead of them in the corridor, Teresa's eyes widened, and she began to pay more attention to the conversation.

Luttrell shrugged. "Just some advice, Captain. Give these people a chance to trust you—"

"I don't like your attitude, *Doctor.*" Kate's voice grew a little louder. "You sound too much like Geoffrey Kagen, and I don't like that either. You wouldn't be working for him, would you?"

"We're all working for him on this mission."

"That's not what I mean." She looked at him, slowing her pace a little. "Kagen told me that someone on this mission was working directly for him, to—how did he put it?—make sure I behave. I think you're that person."

"Don't be silly."

"Can you prove to me you're *not* working directly for him?"

"Now, Captain, I think you're overreacting—"

"I won't tolerate a spy, Doctor. Come out into the open or give me some proof that you're not."

"Okay, let's say I am." He sighed. Perhaps the direct approach would have been better from the start. He had not, he supposed, been very subtle. "Consider this, then. Mr. Kagen has some pretty high stakes riding on the success of this mission. Don't you think he'd be real unhappy if you talked too much about . . . well, about certain things you know?"

"I appreciate your honesty, Doctor." Her lips smiled, but her eyes were hard. "Now, don't you think you're starting on me a little early? I mean, we're just barely under way."

Luttrell felt sweat on his upper lip. "Don't take this too

lightly. Our employer means business, and he wants this mission to succeed. Badly. I would be very careful if I were you."

She shoved her hands deep into her pockets and quickened her step. "Is that a threat?"

Ahead of them, Teresa felt her ears begin to burn. She should not be listening to this conversation. It was like what passed between shrink and patient, or priest and penitent, and it wasn't any of her business. But it sounded serious. She continued to listen, strained to hear, in spite of herself.

"You don't have to take it that way," Luttrell was saying. "I'm doing my job, and I'm giving you some friendly advice on the side. You've worked for Kagen before, you know he can be a real bastard when he's pushed."

"Sounds to me like you're trying to save your own ass, Luttrell, and to hell with this mission." Kate hunched her shoulders and frowned. "So let me give *you* some advice. Get off my back. I'll say what I damn please, and don't ever threaten me again—I don't care how friendly it is."

He shrugged. "Whatever you say . . . Captain."

Ahead of them in the corridor, Teresa turned into the mess room. Her face was expressionless, but she had a knot in the pit of her stomach.

Al Juli poured coffee as each member of the crew took a place at the table. If anything was the same across all space missions, whether short hops to the moon or thirty-year trips to the edge of the galaxy, it was the coffee, in unending supply. And no amount of nonsense about caffeine and health could talk them out of it.

Kate warmed her hands over her steaming mug and tried to remember how long it had been since she had last thought to eat. Her head ached dully.

"I don't want to keep you long," she began slowly, "because I know we all have work to do. But I wasn't given time for a full preflight briefing, and we have to get some things out of the way. This is mostly for me," she smiled disarmingly, "since I wasn't home long enough to find out what's really going on. And I also have some things to tell you from Mr. Kagen." Her gaze flickered briefly in Luttrell's direction, but he was staring at the table.

"I need more information about these creatures we're out here to get," she continued. "I realize this request may sound a little strange to you, considering that I've been there before, but you really do know more about these things than I do. You've had access to log notes I haven't had time to look at yet—and believe me, when I was out there I was too busy trying to keep people alive to worry too much about the particulars of what we were fighting." She looked around the table. "I'm not even sure where I should start. Who's my resident expert?"

Pete Schweitz shook his head slightly and stretched back in his chair. This discussion would be out of his depth, he could tell already.

"Do we really have one?" Teresa asked before anyone else could say anything. "All due respects to Al and his work with the Cygni find, but—I mean, this is our first discovery of a life-form you can even see with the naked eye. I know what I picked out from the initial scans that SINS made. . . ."

"Oh, I don't think it's as difficult as our computer specialist makes it out to be." Kenneth Luttrell smiled professionally. "My background is in biology, Captain. I would guess I qualify as your expert." He glanced questioningly around the table. Teresa scowled, but no one else moved.

"You have the floor," Kate invited.

He began to lecture them about the little creatures the crew of the *Black Opal* had discovered (Kate noticed he made no mention of the *Hercules* mission) and quickly warmed to his subject. He had obviously studied everything available from the previous mission—possibly even some records the rest of the crew had not been given access to. It seemed to her, although she'd been right there when things had happened, looking over Alicia's shoulder or listening to Greg and Mishima talk about the ruins, that Luttrell certainly knew more than she did about what was out there.

There was a pause when he had finished, as though everyone was absorbing the tremendous amount of information he had given them.

"I have a question, Kenneth," Teresa finally spoke up.

The doctor looked attentive.

"Where did you come up with the idea that the creatures were bio-engineered instead of naturally occurring?"

"Well, now . . ."

Was it Kate's imagination, or did Luttrell hesitate a little overlong before he spoke?

"It wasn't in any part of the *Black Opal*'s logs that *I* read," Teresa continued.

"Perhaps to the untrained eye . . ."

"No, it wasn't even in the biological data," she added, as though she were thinking aloud, as though he hadn't spoken.

"I tend to agree, Ken," Al spoke up.

Teresa narrowed her eyes. "Don't tell me you're *guessing*, Doctor?"

Kate watched the exchange with interest. The good doctor had picked the wrong crewmember to patronize, it seemed. Or maybe some of the patina of those good looks and gorgeous eyes had begun to wear off. Teresa was no dummy, certainly. And with Al Juli's support . . .

"If you'll let me explain," Kenneth said calmly, "of course this is just a theory. But it's perfectly justified by several of the log entries, if you bothered to pay attention to the initial scans as compared to what SINS recorded when the creatures came alive the first time and engulfed—"

"I think that's enough for now," Kate broke in, pushing her mug over to the coffeepot. Pete refilled it for her. "Unless there are any more questions along those lines, shall we move on to the next topic?"

"Which is?" Luttrell asked quietly.

"I want to talk about risk taking. Does everyone know why we're headed out to Epsilon Indi?"

It was interesting, Kate noted, that the question seemed to stump all of them for a moment. Even the doctor looked more surprised than anything else.

"Well, actually, I thought it was pretty clear," George Grayson finally said.

"I just want to make sure. What exactly did Guil-Pro tell you?"

The group exchanged glances, except for Luttrell, who was looking at her in a distinctly unfriendly manner.

"Do any of you remember what they said?" she prompted

"Not a whole lot . guess. George finally admitted "Besides, who pays that much attention to it, anyway? Okay, so we're getting a specimen for the Department of Health and Contamination, in case this disease, or whatever, is contagious. And, I guess, knowing Guil-Pro," he grinned faintly, "we'll see if there's any money in it for them, too. I mean, as long as we're out there, right?" He winked.

"Almost right," Kate agreed, tempted to wink back. She found herself beginning to warm to the gruff little man. "Actually, they already know there's money in it for them, or we wouldn't be going out there, no matter *what* the government wanted. I'm sure a contract somewhere has already been signed, executed, and delivered."

"Yeah, so?" Grayson looked at her expectantly.

"I don't know if you're aware that the Research Division, with whom we signed our contracts, is heavily into genetics research right now. But they're particularly interested in cloning and intelligent cybernetics."

"They made that thing down on Deck 2, right?" Pete asked. "That frankenstein?"

Kate nodded. "You also know that it's illegal to own any kind of frankenstein *except* one that's brain-dead?"

"*Is* there any other kind?" Teresa asked.

"Captain," Kenneth interrupted softly, "is this important to the mission?"

She stared at him. "I've decided that it is. To answer your question, Teresa, the doctor was right—there *is* a strong theory that the kites are bio-engineered. Guil-Pro is interested in samples of them in order to further their—and probably others'—research into areas that may not be legal."

"For instance?" Kenneth interrupted, almost as if daring her.

"Combining artificial intelligence with cybernetics, maybe making a thinking frankenstein. A good-quality one, so good you might not even recognize it for a frankenstein." Her gaze around the table was challenging.

"But why?" Teresa wanted to know.

"To assist in exploration, to work or travel where it may be dangerous for humans to go, yet where the 'human' touch might be needed—" Kate shrugged. "How many ways in the colonized worlds are there to make money? This is just another one of those ways."

"But we don't *know* this, right? They just *might* be breaking the law." Teresa shrugged. "I can't see letting it eat my lunch. This probably isn't even the first time they've done this kind of thing. What *I* don't understand is why they couldn't just tell us, instead of going through all this crap to keep it covered up."

"Why should they trust you?" Kate came back immediately. "You might really work for someone else—a rival. There's more money and reputation in this game if you're the best, and you get to be the best by being first. Guil-Pro wants very badly to be first."

"Seems like a lot of trouble to me," George Grayson remarked. "Suppose they get caught—suppose *we* get caught, I guess I should be asking. Then what?"

"*We* are not doing anything strictly illegal on this mission," Kate explained. "If they get caught? Well, intelligent cybernetics is a forbidden research area. The penalties are pretty tough, I think."

"Seems to me you're doing a lot of speculating, Captain," Luttrell said. "That could be dangerous itself."

"Could it?" She gazed directly at him. "I was told *your* specialty is genetics. Were you ever involved in an intelligent-cybernetics program?"

"You needn't make this sound like a cross-examination, Captain."

"I could order you to answer me, Luttrell," she said very quietly.

"It's an area I've always been interested in," he admitted, "but as far as I know, the opportunity for research does not exist anywhere—inside Guil-Pro or out."

She merely nodded. There was an extended and somewhat uncomfortable silence after that.

George finally spoke. "I, ah . . . I appreciate your letting us in on all of this, Captain. It's a real change to work for somebody who tells you things instead of keeping 'em under wraps all the time. But—well, it makes me kinda wonder why you're the captain. You obviously don't buy into why we're out here. Seems to me there's a *lotta* things you don't buy into, if you know what I mean. And, ah . . ." He hesitated. "What I mean is, the rest of us just got a job to do. I understand the way you feel about this stuff, being one of the first ones out here and all, but I'd, uh . . . I'd sure hate to see it fucked up for the rest of us, if you take my meaning."

"Yeah, I take it," Kate said bleakly. "But I guess you missed my point. Of course I'd like it if you all agreed with me that this *might* be a terrible thing we're contributing to, but I know that's a lot to ask. I'm just satisfied that now you have *all* the information about why we're out here, not just part of it, so you can make any decisions you feel you have to make. I think it's my job to keep you completely informed, because in some situations not being informed can get you killed—" There was a sudden catch in her voice, and she had to stop. Of all the times to remember Rory, pinioned to the wall of the alien structure, arms waving weakly. Even if he *had* been only a frankenstein, goddammit . . .

"Captain?" Dr. Luttrell's voice was quiet, but to her ears the warning was unmistakable.

"Sorry," she said flatly, and looked up again. "You asked what *I'm* doing out here, leading this mission. I have an agreement with Guil-Pro because of some . . . past incidents." She stopped again, but this time her voice didn't betray her. "I don't want to be here, believe me. I'll have nightmares about what I saw those creatures do for a long time to come. But part of my deal with Guil-Pro was leading this mission. Satisfied?"

"Hey, that's fine with me." Grayson's brow cleared. "Your deal with them is none of my business and I don't want it to be. This is just another lousy job I'm gonna get paid for, and you're the captain. As long as you do your job and let us do ours, I don't care why you're doing it."

Everyone nodded slowly.

"Well," Kate smiled faintly, "if you can accept me on those terms, I guess we're even. I've given you the facts; you can do anything with them you want."

There was a silent exchange of glances.

"Anything else?" Kate looked around the table one last time. "If not, that's all I had. Resume your stations, please." She was the first one to leave the room.

Luttrell caught up with her moments later outside.

"Captain, we need to talk."

"So talk. Or can't you do that and walk at the same time?"

He stiffened. "Don't push it, Captain. I tried to be nice—"

"If that was nice, I don't ever want to see you nasty."

"You really don't want to cooperate, do you?"

"You're catching on."

"Look, Captain, you may not've believed me earlier, but my ass is on the line the same as yours. If this mission doesn't go, Kagen'll hold me just as responsible for it as he will you."

"No, Luttrell, you've got it all wrong. You'll be *more* responsible, because you're supposed to make sure I behave!"

"Either way. But if we could make a deal—"

"What kind of deal?" She turned on him. "My good behavior in exchange for what?"

"Staying alive, for all I know!" Luttrell was exasperated. "You think you can handle what Guil-Pro would throw at you if you fuck this mission up?" He laughed. "It's not just you and me you have to worry about now. We'll *all* catch hell if you piss Kagen off—all six of us. You want that on your head, too?"

"What do you mean 'too'?"

Luttrell smiled slyly. "Come on, Captain, do you really believe Kagen doesn't know who's already tried to help you? You think they'll get away with that?"

She shivered, remembering Kagen's oblique reference to Billy Watson. "Who are you talking about?"

"I can't name any names. I'm just warning you not to add five more people to the list because of your stubbornness."

"Tell me who!" She grabbed him by the collar and raised her fist in his face.

"Easy, Captain, we have an audience."

Kate let him go. The rest of the crew were leaving the

mess now. It was too late to undo the scene they had already caused—best not to make it any worse.

"Get out of my sight!" she hissed. "And if you bring this up again, I'll beat your ass through the hull—*Kenneth!*"

They stared at each other a moment longer, then Luttrell turned and walked away. Kate spun on her heel and headed for the bridge.

The rest of the crew walked slowly down the corridor, staying well behind the confrontation. Teresa, hands pushed deep in her pockets, could feel the tension easing as the captain and the doctor went their separate ways.

"Well. Did you see that?" George finally muttered.

"Yup. She almost belted him, by damn." Al shrugged. "We all agreed it's none of our business, I know—but I do wonder what's going on between them."

Pete looked concerned. "I don't know, maybe we *should* make it our business. If the captain has a problem, it affects all of us."

Teresa shrugged. "What makes you think it's her with the problem?"

"Ah, you women, stickin' together—" George tried to make light of it, but Teresa wasn't having any.

"I suppose you think you're an expert?"

"Hey, hey, easy now, just tryin' to take the edge off." Grayson backed down quickly. "Seriously, why wouldn't it be her? She's the one been through all the hassle—it'd make sense."

"Yeah, sure." Teresa started to wander away. "I don't want to talk about it now."

George started after her, but Pete caught his arm. "Leave the kid alone, will you?"

As she walked slowly back to the bridge, Teresa brooded on the argument she'd overheard between the captain and Dr. Luttrell. It colored her view of the entire mission now, especially after the things the captain had brought up at the briefing. Attuned as she'd been to the situation, she hadn't missed the frequent and unfriendly glances that had passed between the two of them. It was like they shared a secret that the rest of the crew knew nothing about. She didn't know which idea scared her more—the thought of an overtired and unstable captain, or the thought of something going on behind her back—behind all their backs—that she didn't understand.

Well, one thing was for sure. Her first impression of Dr. *Kenneth* Luttrell had been dead wrong. Gorgeous, yes. But what a son of a bitch! A shame his personality didn't match his face. She *hated* being condescended to, and he was a pro at that! But she had noticed something else for the first time since the crew had gotten together over a month ago for preflights. Al Juli seemed like a real nice guy. . . .

Dr. Luttrell slumped over a microscanner in the sickbay and rubbed his forehead. Make-work wasn't going to tell him anything he didn't already know. It didn't even help to pass the time anymore.

Goddammit, where had he seen Teresa MacKessen before? Her face was very familiar, he had realized, and it bothered him that he couldn't remember. Worse yet, he had a feeling it was important that he remember. It might have an effect on this mission, which, as the captain had so rightly pointed out, was really *his* responsibility. Well, best not to worry about it now. If it was really important, it would come back to him. It always did.

Kate sat tiredly on her bed. End of the first shift of the first day—things had not started auspiciously for the new captain. She removed her shoes and massaged her tired feet. Her head hurt.

Luttrell was going to be a pain in the ass. No question about that. As for the rest of them, well . . .

She felt a little better after a hot shower. Wrapped in a warm robe, she prowled about her quarters. This was the first chance she'd had to really find out what was where. Ship's quarters were always small, though the captain's were more generous than most. The ceiling was low, which didn't bother her, and all the furniture was built into the bulkheads, except for a desk and her narrow bed. Narrow, but comfortable, she noted, bouncing experimentally, and plenty long enough for her.

Her computer terminal was situated on the small desk

at the foot of her bed, with enough room left over for work if she needed it. Idly she turned the unit on.

Kate sat abruptly on the end of her bed, staring at the amber screen. There was a single message in the middle of it.

—I AM WATCHING YOU—

Four harmless little words. As she stared, unable to move even to turn the power off, the message faded. She began to doubt that she had seen anything.

Quickly she turned it off.

You're tired, she told herself. *Rough first day, that's all.*

She began to unpack her kit bag, removing the small things she hadn't had time to put away earlier in the day. As she opened a drawer in her bedside table, something rolled to the front with a quiet thump.

It was a bottle of Chivas Regal.

With a note attached.

"Katie," she read silently, *"thought this might make your journey a little more pleasurable. Rory."*

"You bastard!" she muttered. Of course the note was Kagen's. Of course it was.

She stared at the bottle for long moments, then set it on the nightstand and completed her unpacking. Any good she had gotten from her shower was completely gone now. She could feel tight muscles down her neck and across her shoulders. Rory had known what to do for that. Hadn't he.

Angrily she tossed her kit bag onto the floor of the closet and slammed the door. She was wide awake.

Well, what the hell? Kate pulled a glass down from a cabinet and ordered ice cubes from her small food synthesizer. One glass wouldn't hurt. She had to get to sleep, didn't she?

The scotch tasted good. True, she hadn't thought she'd be able to drink Chivas again after her traumatic interview with Kagen, but this did taste good.

By the time she'd finished the glass, she was beginning to feel sleepy. Good, just what the doctor ordered.

The next night, she had two glasses before bed. It wasn't until the third night that she noticed the bottle was still full. Then she stopped counting how many glasses she had before bed.

CHAPTER
9

Travel in normal space was routine, especially in the well-charted commercial lanes, so Kate had a lot of time to think on their way to the outer terminus. She noticed that their registered course was via the *Orphic Angel*'s orbital plane, though they would be a quarter of her orbit away from her—a small matter of almost nine billion kilometers. A little too far away for idle chatter with Billy.

Bored, she stretched back in her seat and looked around. She sat somewhat higher up than the rest of her bridge crew, and it was easy enough to see by their postures that they were occupied with tasks equally as important as hers—and about as interesting.

She noted with grim amusement how the crew avoided any mention—in her presence, anyway—of their first briefing. What an introduction that had been! Not that she knew exactly what she'd hoped to accomplish by bringing in some of Guil-Pro's sordid past exploits, and hypothetical ones at that. Now they probably figured her as a radical and a rabblerouser, with a rat-on-the-company-to-save-the-world and a screw-your-paycheck attitude—not exactly the way to gain the respect of this pragmatic bunch (though she held out a little hope for Teresa).

Let's face it, they were all used to putting their asses on the line for a corporation that paid well but didn't always play fair. Everybody would take a little shit on the job, and if nobody cared about the bigger issues, well, life was tough.

At least she'd smoked Luttrell out, although that scene in the corridor after the briefing might have blown any credibility she could've hoped to have. She'd have to watch herself with the good doctor in the future. He had a way of pushing the right buttons that made her nervous.

"Captain?" Teresa's voice broke into her thoughts. "Private message."

"Switch it over, please." Kate put her headset to one ear. What she heard was a recording, over a day old with as far from Earth as they were—an official Guil-Pro bulletin. As she listened, the color drained from her face.

"Captain? Captain, you all right?" Teresa was bent over her, shaking her shoulder.

"Huh?" She snapped to. "Yeah, yeah, I'm fine." She put her headset down. *Is this what Luttrell meant? Anybody who helped me?*

"You sure? Christ, you look so white—" Teresa stepped back. "Bad news?"

"Guil-Pro bulletin, couple of days old already. There was a freak accident at Equator Station." Kate swallowed. "One of the ships docked there sprung a leak in a maintenance lock. A crewman was killed while trying to get his captain out of there. Neither one of them made it."

Teresa made a face. "Bad way to go. But why send an official bulletin as a personal message?"

"I knew them. Somebody wanted to make sure I found out what happened."

"Who were they?"

"The captain was Jim Dickenson of the *Lady Pluto*. Paul Westman was his engineer."

"Wasn't the *Lady* the ship that brought you home from the terminus?" Grayson asked suddenly.

Kate nodded.

"Jesus, I'm sorry," Teresa said softly.

Kate's eyes were dead as she stared out the viewport. "So am I."

Moments later, Kate turned her attention back to them. "George, when're we due at the outer terminus?"

"ETA in six hours and thirty-two minutes."

"Thank you." Kate activated the COACH subsystem and went to work.

She was terribly afraid for Lars. All of a sudden, Luttrell's seemingly idle threat had turned to reality. If Kagen had been able to find out enough about her involvement with Dickenson and Westman to think they should be eliminated, what was to stop him from discovering that Lars was involved? She was already worried enough about Billy Watson. He was beyond her help, though the very nature of his work, so much in the public eye, would, she hoped, serve to save him.

But Jon Lars didn't have the protection of the public eye, and she had to warn him, had to tell him that the *Lady Pluto* accident was no accident. He *had* to back off, leave it alone—stay out of her problems! If anything happened to him because of her, she couldn't live with it.

She spent several minutes composing a reasonable message that would convey what she wanted and yet be innocuous enough if the wrong person got hold of it. When she'd finished, she had no idea whether she'd succeeded. But she fed the message into one of the *Pegasus*'s three transmitter buoys, then wrote a small program that would cause it to launch automatically after the *Pegasus* had gone into light-plus for the long journey. The buoy would fall free of the ship's interference field and into normal space, and transmit its information on a private link she knew Lars would have access to on Equator Station. With the *Pegasus* well started on its journey, Guil-Pro should no longer be monitoring their communications. Her tight-beam transmission just might get through.

This one's for Jim Dickenson and Paul Westman, she thought, and locked the program card into the auxiliary transmit station on her board. If all went well, Lars would get her message and would be safe, and it wouldn't matter if she were light-years away. Maybe it wouldn't even matter if she died now. *If* she could trust SINS not to sabotage her efforts.

It was the best she could do, at any rate, but there were so many if's. . . .

* * *

Kate stood outside the entrance to the central life-support core, feeling a little ridiculous. She had no good reason to be here. They would reach the outer terminus in less than two hours, and she'd be down here then, with the rest of the crew, preparing for their long journey in deep-sleep. Why not wait until then?

She was scared. The shadow of the Consortium seemed to be everywhere, much farther reaching than she had suspected. She didn't feel safe even this far from home, near the orbit of Pluto, and perhaps that was why she had come here.

Resolutely she slapped the palm plate and watched the door slide open before her. The central core wasn't security-locked—why should it be? The lights came up automatically in the clean white chamber (*probably the cleanest place on the ship*, she thought), and she walked in. Eight hibernation units were lined up in two neat rows, their clear plastex tops open wide, comfortable cushions waiting. . . .

She walked slowly down the chamber, scanning the units carefully. Each was labeled with the vital statistics of the crewmember it would support in deep-sleep—name, height, weight, resting pulse—all the information SINS needed to calculate the right mixture of cryogas for a given journey. There were only six of them on this trip, which left two empty.

Impulsively Kate moved her bio-chart from the unit between Kenneth Luttrell's and George Grayson's to one of the unmarked ones. Quickly she reset the controls and entered the new data, instructing SINS to mix, from scratch, a compound appropriate for one Harlin, Katharine, height 183.2 centimeters, weight 71.4 kilos, resting pulse 63. . . .

SINS gave her a signal when the change was complete, and she double-checked her work carefully. Her figures, generated by hand-held calculator, agreed with those SINS had made, and she felt better. Now all she had to do was blank the unit that had originally been designated as hers, and no one would ever know she had been there. But she would know.

It was funny, now that she thought about it, but it would never have occurred to her to worry about her hibernation unit if she hadn't had the trouble with her cocoon on the *Lady Pluto*. Of course, Baker had been right there to do his dirty work on the *Lady*, but did he have to be? Wouldn't it be just as easy for someone to program SINS to do the same thing Baker had done by himself? Her distrust of SINS ran deep after her experience on the *Black Opal*. At least now she knew that the life-support mix designed to keep her alive for the next seven months *would* keep her alive.

Once she was out in the corridor, Kate felt herself drawn to the smaller chamber next door, where the frankenstein slept his frozen sleep. For long moments she stood outside that bright red door—this was not her first visit down here since they'd left Equator Station—then slapped the palm plate and entered. The door gave her no trouble this time, either.

Lights came up in the small chamber, and she peered through the frosted plastex lid. She thought she could see Rory's face, but she wasn't sure. Experimentally she breathed on the cover, and for a moment a small clear space appeared. Yes, it was Rory, asleep—she could see just that much before the frost clouded the opening again. For a moment her throat closed as she remembered happier times; then, reminding herself what she was really there for, Kate examined the gauges closely. Everything was as it should be. Not Rory but a mindless LSH unit slept in this chamber, and she would do well to remember it.

She left the chamber and walked quickly away down the corridor.

Teresa stirred cream and sugar into her coffee and took a seat at the mess table. She and Al had come in together, and George Grayson followed shortly.

"I hope things get more exciting than this," she grumbled.

George snorted. "You'll get outta that soon enough! Excitement on this kind of mission only means one thing—trouble. And trouble's the last thing you want in deep space, believe me!" He stubbed out his cigarette. "Nothing'll happen anyway until we come out of light-plus on the other end. Enjoy the boredom while you've got it."

"Mmm." She stared into her cup. "Easy for you to say. You've been out here before."

Grayson rolled his eyes at Al, who grinned. "You'll outgrow it, Mac."

"Mac?"

"Yeah, Mac." Grayson lit another cigarette and inhaled deeply. "You don't like it, I won't use it."

"No. No, I kind of like it." She smiled.

They sat in agreeable silence for a few minutes. This was the longest period of time she'd spent with Grayson that he hadn't annoyed her. She hoped he wouldn't do anything to ruin the mood.

"Say, Mac, how old are you?" Grayson asked.

She spoke without thinking. "Twenty-four."

"*How* long did you say you'd been in the service?"

She reddened. "You heard what I told the captain. Five years."

"So you were nineteen when you joined, huh?" Grayson blew smoke rings. "When *I* went in, you had to be twenty-two."

"That hasn't changed," she said evenly. "I lied. I'm tall, and," she grinned briefly, "I can look real mean."

Grayson chuckled. "I believe it! But why'd you bother?"

"What do you mean?"

"The whole thing. It's a lot of trouble to go through for a job that ain't no piece of cake. 'Specially for a woman, if you don't mind my sayin'. Most nineteen-year-olds have other things on their minds."

"Especially nineteen-year-old women, right, George?" she remarked dryly. "I was tired of being on Earth. There's no place left to go down there, and . . . I had a lot to get away from."

"Family problems?"

"Part of it." Suddenly she grew defensive. "What's it to you?"

"I'm nosy. Besides, I kinda like you."

"Some excuse. But," she smiled faintly, "thanks."

There was another silence. No one seemed to want to go back to work—there wasn't much work to go back to.

"What d'you think of the captain?" Grayson asked suddenly.

"Who, me?" Teresa's eyes widened.

"Yeah."

"I like her."

"How about the way she runs things?"

"We haven't had much of a chance to tell yet, have we?" Teresa fiddled with her coffee cup. "She knows what she's doing, and she's taking care of us. That's enough for me right now."

"Mmm. What about *Kenneth*?"

Teresa made a face. "He's a pompous asshole."

"Captain must think the same way."

"Since when d'you gotta get along with everybody?" Al spoke up. "I don't really like him, either, if you want to know."

"But still, don't you think she was a little hard on him?"

"When?" Teresa asked innocently.

"Oh, come off it!" George laughed shortly. "She got all over his case in the hallway after that briefing."

Teresa shrugged one shoulder. "Looked to me like he got what he deserved. He was being a shit."

"That's still running pretty tight. She looked like she was gonna throw him into the nearest bulkhead!"

"But she didn't," Al pointed out. "Besides, Mac is right, he *was* being a shit. So the captain lost her temper—it ain't against the law."

"Yeah, I know." Grayson lit another cigarette.

"And you'd've never thought twice about it if she was a man," Teresa said. "You guys always get away with that kind of stuff."

In spite of himself, George grinned. "Got a point there. But I tell you, the way she looked then, *I* wouldn't want to be on the receiving end of one of her fists, either!" He shook his head. "I wonder what she was trying to get at in that briefing."

"*I* thought it was obvious. And it's just what I was talking about!" Teresa insisted. "Guil-Pro lied, and she went out of her way to make sure we knew what was really going on. I admire her for that."

"You're right. And *Kenneth* can be a pain in the ass." Grayson blew a lungful of smoke rings and watched them dissipate. "I just hope this mission doesn't go bad. All I want to do is get the job done, stay outta trouble, and get home in one piece to collect my big fat paycheck."

"So I gathered," Teresa said dryly.

"Ooh!" Al winced. "She's got your number! But seriously, I don't think we've got anything to worry about. The captain's been with Guil-Pro for a long time, and she must be pretty reliable to get to that rank. They don't mess around with that kind of stuff. Especially not if there's money involved."

"Hey, look, I got nothin' against her—I'm sure she's good! But don't you think what happened to her on the *Black Opal* put her through some hard changes? Come on, guys, anybody would be a little closer to the edge after that kinda shit!"

"You're right, Grayson, and I got damn close to that edge, too." Kate walked into the mess. "But I'm not there yet, so I'll thank you not to rush me along." She poured herself a cup of coffee and sat at the table.

Grayson slowly turned red. "Sorry, Captain, I didn't mean that the way it sounded."

"No, you're not out of line. You've got the right to worry about my sanity—I'll be running your life for the next couple of years. And I mean running, too. But as far as what happened to me on the *Opal*—shall we leave it?"

Grayson raised his hands. "Hey, okay by me."

Teresa watched the exchange curiously. The captain gave no indication of how much of the conversation she'd overheard, beyond her reaction to Grayson's last remark. Nor did she seem at all upset that her personal competency was being discussed behind her back. The woman was very calm now, very controlled, and Teresa found herself inordinately pleased by that.

They turned the conversation to things that had happened on Earth while the captain had been gone for over three years. Teresa finished her coffee and listened. After a while, Al moved around the table to sit next to her, and they talked quietly together. When he gave her a quizzical sidelong glance, she nodded and smiled a little.

Kate keyed in a series of codes and waited for acknowledgment. It came quickly. "All right, everyone, Outer Terminus Control Central has our position, and we're far enough past the safety zone. Engineering?"

"Schweitz here."

"Ready to fire up the big ones, Pete? We've gotten a go from Control Central."

"All readings are green, Captain," Pete's voice came back through the speaker.

"Good. George, is our final course laid in?"

"Laid in and locked."

"All right, let's take it out!" Kate kicked in the light-plus engines, and the *Pegasus* faded from normal space. They were officially under way.

"Do we still have a check on our destination, George?"

"Aye!" the pilot barked. "All vectors are green. We'll be right on target when we come out."

"Okay. Teresa, set life-support systems for Phase One shutdown." She looked around her. "We're about ready to close up shop, ladies and gentlemen. Power off and meet me in the life-support core in fifteen minutes. You get that, engineering?"

"Engineering, aye! Fifteen minutes."

"External scanners on auto-record. Life support ready for shutdown. Support core condition green, all units prepped," Teresa reported. "Oh, shit!"

"What's wrong?"

"Nothing, I just lost a telltale." Teresa glanced at her watch. "I've got a little time, so maybe I'd better change it now. It's one of the first ones I'll need when we come back up."

"Okay," Kate agreed, "but don't take too long. SINS gets cranky if anything throws off the shutdown cycle." She closed down her board and swung herself up out of her seat, nearly hitting her head on an overhang. Damn, this bridge was small!

Teresa started digging around for spare lightbulbs, swearing under her breath at the goddamned cheap Guil-Pro equipment that never worked when you needed it. She was going to have to pry the whole cover off her damn board!

Everyone else headed for central life support.

Some minutes later, Teresa paused at the entry to the life-support core chamber. The rest of the crew were already there in various stages of undress. The eight hibernation units were open and waiting, and it occurred to her how much like coffins they looked.

Kate glanced up and saw her. "Here!" She tossed her a sterilized packet containing her medical sensor. "Get that telltale fixed?"

"Yeah. Took me a while to get the cover back on my board after I'd changed it, though. Damn thing didn't fit right!" She began to strip down.

"Some advice for you, Teresa, since you've never gone under before," Kate said as she climbed into her unit. "It's a little scary at first—you'll find it hard to breathe. The cryogas is heavier than air, so don't worry about it. Just take deep, even breaths, and you'll be out in seconds. SINS knows what it's doing. You know about the sensor patch?"

Teresa nodded, unconsciously fingering the vesicle of the tiny subcutaneous receptacle just under her collar bone before she placed her sensor.

Kate sat up, waiting for the rest of the crew to climb into their units and lie down. "Good night, everyone. See you in about seven months." She thumbed a switch that would be her last willful contact with SINS until her awakening seven months later, then lay back. Lights in the chamber dimmed into darkness. The cover of her hibernation unit slid over her silently, sealing her in. It became very cold, very drowsy. . . .

Kate stared up into the darkness, eyes wide open. As the cold and heavy gas seeped in around her, she tensed, fighting the lethargy—knew she was fighting, and couldn't help it. Suppose, just suppose, Kagen had tricked her again. . . . Sleep overtook her.

Lights all over the *Pegasus* flickered and went out. The ship cooled gradually because no heat was provided; power was concentrated on the light-plus drive and the life-support core. Soon all was still, quiet, frozen.

CHAPTER

10

Kate opened her eyes to blinding whiteness. For just a minute she hadn't the faintest idea where she was, then her head began to clear. There were few times in life when you felt this bad and weren't dying, and coming out of deep-sleep was one of them. She sat up slowly, stripping the medical sensor patch from her chest. As usual, the vesicle of the subcutaneous receiver was a little irritated after such long contact. Her feet touched the cold deck, and she groaned. Why did thawing out *always* have to feel like the godawfullest hangover? Grabbing a towel, Kate scuffed off to the showers to try to wake up. She'd instructed SINS to wake her first; the others weren't even stirring yet.

As she fixed a pot of coffee in the mess some minutes later, she found herself thinking of the *Black Opal*. She hadn't checked *Pegasus*'s position yet, or done any of the other things that should be a captain's first concern upon waking from deep-sleep (at least, she supposed they should be), but she *knew* they were in orbit around the second planet of the Epsilon Indi system, and she knew the *Black Opal* was somewhere down there, below them, waiting. Rory would be there. And the Loon, if she wasn't careful . . .

You have a job to do, she reminded herself. *Don't get wrapped up in the past, or you'll never get out of here alive.*

Grimly Kate finished her first cup of coffee and glanced at her watch. She still had about fifteen minutes before the others would wake up, so she headed for the bridge. Like it or not, now was the time for all those little chores that were the captain's responsibility. Besides, she wanted to find out what had happened to the program card she had left locked in her console seven months ago. It should have run its course and erased itself, leaving no evidence of the transmitter buoy that would be long gone by now.

Kate activated the main bridge consoles. SINS had already displayed the most important information on the bridge master monitor, including a view of Epsilon Indi and the navigation charts with their position marked. They were home free.

But what she saw at her own console made her heart skip a beat. The program card—she knew that was what it was without looking too closely—was on the deck by her seat, crushed.

"Kagen one, Harlin nothing," she muttered, collecting the fragments. They had been smashed almost beyond recognition.

Well, she should have known better. Kagen had warned her; Guil-Pro would keep watch, even out here. But who the hell had done it? Luttrell was the obvious choice, but he had no knowledge of how to run a ship or what you could do from the captain's console—she didn't think he was capable of figuring out enough of what she had been doing even to realize he should try to stop her. And he hadn't had the opportunity anyway.

On the other hand, there was Teresa. . . . *She* had stayed behind to replace that indicator when the rest of them had gone down to central life support. And she knew computers— she could certainly have recognized what Kate was trying to do. No doubt there had been opportunity.

But motive? Teresa had been genuinely concerned when Kate had received that bulletin with the bad news. Kate shook her head. There was more to the younger woman than you could see on the surface, but not this. (She squelched the insistent voice in her head that kept asking, *Why not this?*)

"Well, shit," she muttered, examining the broken pieces. The card looked as though someone had crushed it with the heel of a boot or a hard-soled shoe. She found herself trying to remember what footwear the various members of the crew had been wearing, until she realized how futile such an effort was.

Her problem was that she wanted it to be Luttrell, and the doctor didn't fit the bill. So it had to be someone else.

Well, no time to worry about it now. She had one more task to do before heading back to the mess and the rest of her crew.

Once more, Kate stood outside the red door on Deck 2. It was ridiculous, she kept telling herself; she could just as easily have checked this out on the bridge (in truth, she knew she didn't need to check it out at all), but she wanted to see for herself that the frankenstein was still frozen in deep-sleep.

Nothing had changed. The cover of the portable hibernation unit was still frosted over; the monitors still read as they should for a brain-dead LSH unit in hibernation—the room looked completely untouched, and she was comforted.

Now she could tend to business, and she went swiftly back to the mess. The rest of the crew would be stirring, and it was her duty to make sure everyone was all right.

Grayson, taciturn as ever, was the first to appear. "Mornin', Captain."

She nodded and pushed a cup of coffee over to him. Caffeine first, then conversation. The others filed in slowly, none the worse for wear.

"Everyone come out all right?" she asked.

"Ohh ... I think so. Am I supposed to feel like shit?" Teresa gulped her coffee black and scalding hot. "This is worse than my last hangover!"

"That's about right," Kate said with a chuckle.

"Not exactly well rested, I have to agree." Luttrell sipped his coffee gingerly. "What's up, Captain?"

"George did a good job," she informed them. "We came out right on the money, in a long orbit around Epsilon Indi. Our target is the second planet, about half a day away from our present position." She put her hand in her pocket, felt the broken fragments there. But this was not the time to mention that, if there ever would be a time.

Grayson inhaled deeply on his first cigarette. "So what's next?"

Kate took a chair and poured herself another cup of

coffee. "Setting down will be pretty tricky, George. We'll try to put down as close as we can to," she hesitated briefly, "the *Black Opal*. She was in a good base position for exploration work."

Grayson nodded. "I remember the scans. It shouldn't be too bad."

"Once we're down," Kate continued, "we'll need to take a look at the alien structure, see what the interior conditions are like after a year, and determine our next move."

"I think we should go into the *Opal* first," the doctor spoke up.

"No." She said it without hesitation, almost without thinking.

"But why not? There were creatures in there, we might be able to learn—"

"I said no." Kate had a sudden image of the *Black Opal* with Mishima still alive, still covered with kites, wandering the corridors and laughing with the hysterical cry of the Loon.

"But don't you think—"

The look on her face stopped Luttrell in mid-sentence. There was an uncomfortable pause she couldn't interpret, and she began to worry that she'd been too hard too quickly— the last thing she wanted them to think was that she was *afraid* to board the *Opal*. She couldn't afford to have them think she was afraid of anything.

"Teresa, you, Al, and I will be on the first team out," she said tiredly. She hadn't really planned on being on the initial team, but it would show them she wasn't shy about going into that place. "We'll travel in groups of three—three on, three off. A fourth will go outside only in a drastic emergency, and one person is to be aboard ship at all times. George, you've got the main board; Kenneth, keep an eye on the medicals for him. Pete, I want you on standby, but while you're at it you could check out the equipment for moving the frankenstein." She hesitated briefly.

"I'm going to issue laser pistols to the outside teams," she went on slowly. "I don't know if they'll be effective— we didn't have any to use last time. Let's not count on them, just in case. I'd rather everyone be extremely careful." She looked around at them. "Is that clear? I don't want to have to report any deaths because somebody got careless."

Everyone nodded.

"Are we looking for anything in particular?" Grayson wanted to know.

"Not really. Our first priority is to set up the monitoring equipment. So long as the airlock on the structure operates smoothly, we shouldn't have any problem."

"Any chance we could use the equipment that was left in there from the *Opal*?" Teresa asked hesitantly. "I mean, if it still works, that'd save us some trouble, and we could use the stuff we brought with us for backup."

Kate looked at her for a moment before replying. "That's a good idea. If it works it'll save us from carrying all that crap, which would take several trips, even in the jalopy." She referred to the small multiterrain vehicle they carried in the cargo bay. "We'll check out the old equipment first. Anything else?"

"I hate to bring up bad memories," Al began, "but has anyone thought about what to do with Rory's body? I mean, if we go into all the rooms that are opened to look for the old equipment, well . . . we're bound to find him, don't you think? Shouldn't we give him a decent burial, or something?"

Kate hoped she was able to keep a neutral expression on her face. *She* had thought about finding Rory's body—had thought about it from the time she'd first come aboard the *Pegasus*, back at Equator Station. But she had just been so opposed to exploring the *Opal*—could she afford to avoid this issue as well, now that it had been opened?

"I think I have the solution for that," Luttrell said quietly. "I was privy to some discussions among Consortium management on this subject, and I'm sure you'll agree with their recommendation, Captain. They thought it best to simply seal the room off and leave it as a memorial to the men and women of the *Black Opal* who died here. It was what Rory's family wanted."

Rory's *family*, indeed! Kate was outraged at the lie, yet tremendously relieved that Luttrell had taken her off the hook this time. It was a moment before she began to realize what he had said. Of course Guil-Pro wouldn't want the rest of the crew to know about Rory, and this was the perfect way to avoid it.

At one time she'd had the vague notion of deliberately letting the rest of the crew find Rory's body, of letting them see that there was almost no decomposition. Perhaps they would even see some of the biomechanical construct underneath the skin layer or around the working organs. It would be the surest way of demonstrating what she had talked about in that first briefing.

Oh, yes, this could be her perfect opportunity to prove to them that there *was* such a thing as a thinking frankenstein, that Guil-Pro's technology really *had* come this far, that she hadn't just been talking stuff. *See this? This is important! I wasn't just talking about research and possibilities and things that don't affect your lives! See how Guil-Pro lied to me? They could do it to you, too! How do you know they haven't already?*

And she could end up with her entire crew suspicious of one another, if she wasn't careful. After all, if Rory had been a thinking frankenstein, couldn't one of *them* be just as easily?

So, for all that revelation might help her cause, she was glad of Luttrell's solution. She really did not want to be reminded, either.

"Yes, Doctor," she finally said, "I think that's an excellent idea. There was no equipment in that room we'd need, no reason to disturb the remains at all." She looked around the table. "Is that all?"

No one moved.

"All right, everyone finish dressing and get to your stations, please. We'll break orbit in half an hour." Kate drained her mug and left the room.

Luttrell shook his head. "It's best this way," he murmured.

"What's best?" Teresa wanted to know.

"Closing off that area without moving the body."

"You'd better believe it! *I'm* sure not interested in hunting up a year-old corpse!"

"They were very good friends," Luttrell continued, almost to himself. "I think his death disturbed her greatly. I would hate to bring back unpleasant memories when it's not necessary."

"I don't think any of us want to do that if we don't have to," Teresa said quietly. "Aren't you making a big deal out of nothing?"

"Yeah, Kenneth, what're you trying to say?" Grayson asked.

Luttrell laid his hands flat on the table as he rose to his feet. "Simply this. Let's not put too much pressure on the lady in charge, okay? She's got enough to carry around on this mission without any extras."

The rest of them stared after him in puzzled silence as he left the room.

The landing on Epsilon Indi's second planet had gone about as smoothly as any procedure does in space, and Kate was in a pretty good mood on her way down to the main airlock vestibule. She'd been in this line of work for a long time, but she could still experience the excitement of an initial contact team. Sure, this wasn't virgin territory anymore—not by a long shot—but *she* had never been outside on this planet before, and that was enough.

"Captain Harlin?"

She turned and saw Teresa following her down the corridor. "What is it?"

"I don't know if it's important or not, but we're missing one of the transmitter buoys."

Kate's eyebrows shot up. Maybe her plan *had* worked, if the buoy had been launched. "Yeah?"

"Well, after I found out about it I checked the scanner history, and SINS registered a small explosion. Apparently the pod released from the ship after we hit light-plus, and blew up almost immediately."

Kate hid her disappointment.

"Do you think it could've been a malfunction?" Teresa was asking.

"The explosion certainly was," Kate agreed carefully. "It's strange the maintenance crews wouldn't have picked up on a problem like that before we left."

Teresa shrugged. "Those guys can be real screw-ups,

sometimes. We're lucky it didn't explode while it was still in the ship. But I guess it's too late to do anything about it now."

"By about seven months." Kate sighed. "Well, thanks for the report. And—would you mind keeping it to yourself for a while? No sense worrying anyone with it."

"Sure."

Kate thrust her hands into her pockets and felt the fragments of datacard there. Would Teresa even have brought the subject up if she was responsible for it? *Easy enough to find out*, a little voice spoke in her head. *Watch her face when you show her this*. Slowly Kate withdrew her hand and extended it toward the other woman, palm upward, the broken bits of plastex and magnetic media displayed.

Teresa stared at it curiously. "May I?" she asked, reaching out to examine it.

Kate nodded without speaking, watching her closely. Teresa took a piece of plastex in her hand and turned it over and over.

"It almost looks like someone stepped on it. But—" She looked up at Kate, puzzlement in her eyes. "Where did you find this?"

"On the bridge, right after SINS woke me up." Kate never took her eyes from the younger woman's face. She saw nothing suspicious.

"That's funny, I don't remember leaving a program card—"

"How did you know it was a program card?" Kate jumped on her immediately.

"I didn't," Teresa responded evenly. "I was guessing. Why? Do you think I did this?"

Kate was beginning to regret having brought the subject up. "You had the opportunity. You were the last one to leave the bridge before we went into deep-sleep. You know computers—you could have figured out what I was trying to do better than anyone else in this crew." Teresa looked hurt, a reaction she hadn't expected.

"Why do you think I would do this?" the younger woman finally asked.

Kate shrugged. That was the one question she'd been

unable to answer herself. She could assign plenty of motive to Luttrell, but as far as anyone else was concerned...

"Look," Teresa insisted, "do you have a reason for thinking I'd do something like that?"

"No," Kate was forced to admit. "It was just a shot in the dark, really." She sighed. "I felt obliged to say something, just to reassure myself. Obviously, I was wrong. I'm sorry."

"Hey..." Teresa shrugged uncomfortably. "I can see something is going on. It's with you and Luttrell, right? Isn't that what this shit is really all about?"

"Yeah, that's part of it." Kate decided to admit some of her doubts. "I'd love to pin this on him," she indicated the broken datacard, "truth be known. But I can't. He had no opportunity, for one."

"You really don't like him, do you?"

"No. I don't trust him, either."

"Why not?"

"He was pushed on me by the Consortium." She almost laughed. "You didn't think *I'd* pick an asshole like that, did you? Not that I had any choice in this crew, but I was warned about him, and I couldn't do anything about it."

"Is he watching you?"

Kate raised her eyebrows. "What makes you think I need watching?"

Teresa refused to back down. "You overheard part of that conversation we were having with George—he's not the only one to figure out you're running pretty close to the line. I mean, look at the way you just jumped me.

"And besides," she continued, "you already told us you've been in some trouble with Guil-Pro, and you just said they pushed Luttrell on you. So maybe they don't trust you. And ... well, he's a doctor, and we've all heard the stories."

"Think I'm a little crazy, do you?"

"I don't, no."

"Oh? Why not?" Kate asked quickly.

"I just don't." Teresa thought about it for a minute. "Crazy people don't worry about the things you worry about. You're too careful of the people who work for you, for one."

"I appreciate that." Kate nodded. "Well, I'll confess. You were right," she indicated the fragments in her palm, "this was a program card. I programmed it before we left the outer terminus. It was supposed to fire off one of the message buoys after we went into light-plus, then beam a message back to Equator Station. I'm real sorry it didn't work."

Teresa's eyes widened. "The buoy that exploded?"

"I'm afraid so."

"You think it was rigged ahead of time?"

"No, that doesn't make any sense." Kate shook her head. "The buoys are frequently needed for legitimate business, when you're too far away for radio contact but you need to get a message back pretty quick. A lot of claims are staked using those buoys."

"So you think someone in the crew did it."

"I don't have much choice but to think that." Kate chewed thoughtfully on a forefinger. "I just don't know who."

"You—you don't think I did it?" Teresa asked hesitantly.

Kate smiled. "No, I don't think you did it. Like I said, it was a shot in the dark, and not a very bright one at that."

They continued together toward the main airlock vestibule, where they would suit up for their first trip to the surface. Kate was thoughtful. Well, it didn't *seem* as though Teresa was responsible for destroying the transmitter. Unless she was playing a very deep double game . . . Kate didn't even want to think about that. One down, four to go . . . maybe.

"By the way, Teresa, I said once that I don't stand on formality, and I meant it. You can call me Kate."

The younger woman smiled.

The outer airlock door opened, and they stepped out into a dim, hazy sunlight. It was late morning where they had landed.

"According to SINS, the artifacts are over that way." Kate pointed in a roughly northwest direction. "Shall we head on down?"

She operated the controls, pushing oversized buttons with her gloved fingers, and the ramp slid out and came to rest on the surface with a light puff of dust. They walked down the slight incline.

"It's awfully quiet," Teresa remarked. "Not even any wind, that I can tell."

"Oh, there's an occasional storm, but we didn't experience much weather last time, either," Kate agreed. "Just this damn eternal haze."

"How far do we have to go?" Al asked.

"Not more than a hundred meters, according to SINS," Teresa replied.

"Maybe we should've used the jalopy."

"Ah, c'mon, you lazy lump! A hundred meters is nothing in this gravity!" Teresa teased. "If we had to carry that monitoring equipment, it might be a different story. But just to save you a walk?"

"It was only a suggestion."

"I think you'll live." Kate chuckled. "George, can you read us?"

"Coming in loud and clear," Grayson reported from back aboard the ship. "You could be standing right next to me, Captain!"

"Good. Let me know if you start to lose us, or anything else peculiar. How's your visibility?"

"You're real clear right now. According to SINS, we can pick up visuals on the main scanner to at least two klicks."

"The artifact must be behind that formation, then, since we can't see it from here. Thanks, George." Kate turned to the other members of her landing party.

"Let's take it a little easy on this trip, okay? I don't particularly want to push any limits this time around, but especially not our air."

They both nodded. Guil-Pro rules were that no one stayed out in a suit for longer than three hours—and to follow up, they made suits with three and a half hours of air, including the reserve. It was cheaper that way.

"Okay, George, we'll move on now," she reported.

The three of them trudged together over the dusty surface of the planet. They could see few distinguishing characteristics in the landscape—mostly low, rolling hillocks, with what looked like some taller cliffs in the background, including the one they assumed was blocking their view of the alien structure. Everything was a uniform, grayish brown color, very dull. Soon the line of cliffs grew closer, and as they rounded a curve they lost sight of the ship. The quiet, except for their shuffling footsteps, was eerie.

"Kind of like breaking the old lifeline," Al remarked, peering behind him. "I sorta hoped we'd be able to see the ship from the building."

"None of that, now," Grayson's voice crackled heartily in their earphones. "I'm right here, and you're still coming in loud and clear. SINS just finished a topographic—you're going around a good-sized cliff. Keep bearing to the left, and he says you should see the artifact soon."

"Do you remember what it looked like, Cap—uh, Kate?" Teresa asked.

"I've never been able to describe it."

Suddenly the cliff turned sharply away from them, opening into a large flat plain.

They saw it.

Even from this distance, it was huge. Parts of it looked almost like a natural formation, layered and heavy at the bottom, of the same dull, gray-brown colors as the landscape, with walls sloping gradually inward like the defensive bulwark of an old Earth castle. Jutting up from this base was what appeared to be a portion made of large square shapes, obviously artificial, but looking as though it had been thrown together hastily instead of carefully built. Odd, uncomfortable angles hurt the eyes after only a few minutes of gazing. Above this, impossibly delicate, towering spires pushed so high into the hazy sky that their tops could not be seen.

Grayson cleared his throat over the radio. "You guys all right? It's awfully quiet out there."

"Oh boy," Teresa muttered, "where're my headache pills?"

"What do you mean, pills? Is something wrong?" Grayson demanded.

"I know what you mean," Al agreed. "It's—it's fascinating, but my eyes sure do hurt."

"Are you guys all right? Goddammit, *talk* to me!" Grayson sounded truly worried now.

Kate was still staring at the structure, unable to pull her gaze away. True, she had seen it from the cameras on the

Opal, but that was nothing compared to this. Finally she blinked and turned away.

"Sorry, George. Everyone's okay, except for a good case of the we-just-saw-our-first-flying-saucer heebie-jeebies. The structure is very...uncomfortable-looking. Pictures wouldn't do it justice, and, I see now, neither did the *Opal*'s cameras. You have to see it for yourself."

"Well, all I ask is, next time, will you guys come to a little earlier with the radio? All I could hear was heavy breathing."

"Don't worry, it won't happen again." Kate glanced at the structure sidewise, then turned fully around, putting her back to it. "Well, Al, you're the geologist. D'you think you can handle it?"

"Maybe up closer, where I don't have to stare at the whole thing."

"That's a point," Kate agreed. "George, make sure that gets into the records, will you? There's a lot of discomfort in looking at the whole structure from a distance, which may go away as we get closer and can no longer see the entire thing."

"Captain," a new voice spoke in their ears, "this is Dr. Luttrell. Is it possible that your discomfort could be from something psychological rather than the physical appearance of the place?"

"Not a chance!" Teresa broke in. "This is an odd building, Luttrell. It wasn't built by humans, so it wasn't made for human eyes to see or human minds to understand."

"It was just a suggestion." The doctor sounded miffed.

Teresa ignored him. "If you don't mind, Kate, when we get back to the ship I'd like to do some studies on the shape of the damned thing. Maybe SINS can figure out why it's so painful to look at."

"Good idea. Now, let's move on. George, we're going in a little closer, then we'll circle the building clockwise. We've approached the thing from an unfamiliar angle, and I don't recognize anything from the *Opal* films." Kate began to walk, and the others followed her. "Does anyone see anything resembling an airlock?"

It seemed to Kate that they had walked quite some distance before Al pointed to what might be an opening in the side of the structure. She had seen the airlock through the cameras on the *Opal* mission; why couldn't she recognize it now? Perhaps there had been more than one—but surely they had gone more than halfway around by now?

"Well, that could be it," she agreed. "Let's find out."

They approached the area slowly.

"How do you suppose it opens?" Teresa asked.

"Boswell—that was our robot probe—just walked right through. Maybe we can do the same."

Kate took a few steps forward, then cautiously held out her hand. Was it her imagination, or did she feel a warmth through her suit? "George, did you notice any temperature change just now?"

"Uh, no, but I wasn't really watching."

"Watch this time." Again she passed her hand close to the proposed entryway.

"Copy. A slight temperature gradient on the left hand. What was that?"

"I passed my hand close to the entrance—if that's what it is. Keep a special eye out for that, will you? I don't want to get fried if something decides I don't belong here."

"Want to back out and wait for Oscar?" Grayson referred to the *Pegasus*'s robot probe.

Kate sighed. "No, I guess not. We had absolutely no trouble of any kind last time, and I can't see where anything would've changed in just a year or so. Our initial surface scans indicated everything was status quo. It's not like the owners of this place came back while we were gone."

Resolutely she extended her hand again, this time holding it in position instead of brushing it by. She could feel the warmth through her suit again, and then, with an odd twisting motion, an opening appeared. It was better than double her height, but very narrow. The airlocks on the *Pegasus* were wider than this opening.

"Al, scan this, will you? I want the temperature, size, and any other parameter you can think of. George, I want you to get the same information." Somewhat gingerly, she stepped through. It remained open behind her, rather to her relief. "Well, seems safe enough so far. It's even lit. I guess you can come on."

"The height is about three point three meters, width about two-thirds of a meter," Al reported. "If there was a temperature gradient, I didn't catch it. I don't know how that opening worked, either—I'm not getting any indications of a power source at all. Must be magic." Al chuckled a little nervously as he followed Kate through the opening. Teresa came behind him.

They stood in a small foyer that matched the shape of the opening itself. Very high and narrow, it made for pretty cramped quarters, especially with three of them in there.

"Now what?" Teresa asked.

Kate shrugged inside her suit. "Let's find out. An airlock isn't much good without two openings, is it?" Cautiously, Kate reached out to the wall opposite where they had come in. With the same odd twisting motion, the opening behind them spiraled shut.

"Goddamn!" Al turned as quickly as he could in the close space.

"George! George, do you still read us?" Kate signaled frantically on her radio.

CHAPTER

11

"No problem, folks, you're still coming in loud and clear," Grayson's calm voice informed them. "*Kenneth* tells me there's a lot of elevated breathing and pulse rates in there—what happened?"

Kate laughed shakily. "Nothing unusual, if I'd stopped to think about it. When I extended my hand to the wall opposite the one where we came in, the opening behind us closed up real quick. But, of course, if this is an airlock, that's exactly what *should* happen. I guess we're all a little nervous right now. You didn't get any kind of energy reading when that happened?"

"Not any more than when the first opening appeared." Grayson sounded puzzled. "I wonder what kind of power source they use if we can't pick it up?"

"Maybe we'll let Pete play with it. That should be right up his alley—eh, Pete?"

"You let me out there, ma'am, I'll figure it out for you."

"Good man." Kate smiled, though Pete's eagerness reminded her of Rory's boast that he would figure out all the puzzles this structure held, and make money on those puzzles in the bargain. "Al, how about an atmospheric?" she asked, as much to change the subject as to get the information.

"Look at the dust on the floor!" Teresa interrupted.

Indeed, the dust was blowing about as though air were moving.

"Al?" Kate repeated.

"Right. Yep, it's changing, all right. The outside atmosphere was pretty heavy methane, with carbon dioxide second on the list. We're now changing gradually to . . ."

"Go on," she prompted.

He cleared his throat. "Earth-normal atmosphere."

"That's impossible!" Grayson's voice came over the radio.

"No, no, it's not," Kate said quietly. "We changed the atmosphere inside here a year ago. It was close to Earth-normal when we arrived; all we had to do was add trace elements to make it breathable. Vince wanted to do that so we could work without our suits, so we could work faster. It was all in the records—you should have seen that."

"Well, yeah, that's true," Grayson admitted. "But I didn't figure it would *still* be Earth-normal after over a year. I mean, we're talking alien machinery here, designed to manufacture and maintain *their* atmosphere, right? So how come it maintained ours instead?"

"Perhaps they're close enough to composition," Kate said slowly. "Or perhaps it's designed to maintain whatever atmosphere is in here. When we got here on the *Opal*, the internal atmosphere was still different from the planet's outside, and this structure is over five hundred years old. For all we know, the atmosphere had been maintained inside for that long! It'll be something else for Pete to look into when he gets his chance out here."

They were interrupted when the inside opening formed. Peering curiously through, they could see that the inside of the structure was also lit, though somewhat dimly for their preference.

"This fits," Kate said, stepping into the structure. "We had to add extra lighting when Rory and Mishima went in. We were missing too much on the cameras."

Kate stopped so suddenly that Teresa, right behind her, ran into her. "What's wrong?" the younger woman demanded. "What's the matter?"

Kate stared at the large room the airlock had opened into. The entire floor was littered with what looked like slate-colored tile fragments. They were small and diamond-shaped—she could feel the sheen of sweat on her face, the dampness in her armpits and on her palms, and knew the medical scanners would show Luttrell every giveaway sign of her discomfort. Before her very eyes those diamond-shaped devils rose in waves from the floor and engulfed a helpless figure who stood among them. She watched Mishima run, and heard the Loon screaming in her ear.

"Kate? Captain!" Teresa shook the woman's shoulder violently. "What is it?"

"Nothing." Kate abruptly came back to the present. "Let's just be careful."

"What's that stuff on the floor?" Al asked.

"Those . . . are kites," Kate said softly.

"But they're not living!" Al exclaimed.

"And what's the temperature in here, Al?"

"About minus forty degrees centigrade."

"Pretty chilly. We could heat it up, of course."

"What are you talking about?" Grayson wanted to know.

"I'm talking about how easy our jobs would be if we could work in here without our suits," she said. "I'm talking about exactly why we can't even *consider* doing that. Those harmless-looking kites are roused by heat, as far as we could tell, and dormant—lifeless, that is—in the cold. That means we work in our suits in here, and we keep it cold, just in case. As cold as it is right now."

"I don't think anyone wants to do otherwise, Captain." Luttrell's voice came to them, level as always. "We certainly have no desire to duplicate earlier mistakes."

The others had crowded around her into the room, and Teresa now walked out ahead of her, scuffling through the layer of dull, lifeless-looking diamond shapes. "I know what all the reports said, but—but they look so *dead*!" She bent to pick one up. "*Look* at this thing! How could you possibly ever think this could come to life?"

"Let me scan it." Al walked over to her. "George, you picking this stuff up?"

"You're green, kid. Let me have it."

"No indications of life," Al said quietly. "Not a flicker. This is incredible!"

"SINS doesn't make much of what you sent back, either," Grayson said. "Except to say he recognizes the pattern. Obviously those are the same guys you found a year ago."

"Oh, I didn't doubt that," Kate said softly. "I didn't doubt that at all."

"Over here!" Al called suddenly. "I've found another door!"

"Where does it lead?" Kate asked.

"Into another area with our good atmosphere."

"Well, Rory and Mishima opened up several rooms when they were working here. You've found the same path they followed."

"There's another opening over here—a sealed one," Teresa said. "Why don't we explore here first? We already know what's down that way, pretty much."

"That's true," Kate agreed. "Of course, our main reason for this first trip was to see if we could recover and use the old monitoring equipment from the *Opal*."

"Oh, I know, but we can do that on the way back, can't we? Let's just go in here and look around for a minute!"

Kate chuckled appreciatively. "I guess it couldn't hurt to break some new ground on this trip. We'll take a detour in there, look around, and then leave it for a later party. How's that?" She did not say that she was happy to put off for as long as she could their necessary travels along the old path. Even though they were going to seal the room containing Rory's body without entering it, she wasn't eager to be reminded of what had happened there.

"Sounds good to me," Al said.

"Just be careful in there, you guys," Grayson warned.

"After all that buildup, suppose we can't get it open?" Teresa asked suddenly. "Suppose there's a safety feature, and the door won't open because the atmosphere on both sides is different?"

"Let's not make problems for ourselves," Kate suggested.

The door spiraled open at her touch, as easily as the others had. Dust on the floor blew about briefly as the air shifted, and they could see lighting come on in the next room.

"Shall we?" Kate stepped through the opening first.

The room they entered was similar to the one they had just left. A tall ceiling arched over them, up into the shadows, and Kate resolved that they would improve the lighting on the next trip out. She didn't like the idea of something being up there with them unable to see it, even though she knew her fear was groundless.

"Well, there's still a mess of kites in here," Al remarked, flipping a few of the diamond shapes with the toe of his boot. "They must not have been very important to these people, to just leave them lying about like this."

"Who can say?" Kate murmured.

"Over here!" Teresa's voice rose with sudden intensity. "Over here, quick!"

"Are you all right?" Kate demanded, though she could see the young woman plainly.

"What's going on?" Grayson wanted to know.

"Sorry, no problem—I'm just excited," Teresa apologized. "Look what I found!" She pointed.

There was a large opening in the floor, about the size and shape of the doorways they had passed through. They could see down about two meters, then all was blackness. What looked like the beginning of a staircase extended down from one side.

"We've discovered what may be a stairway down to

another level," Kate reported back to the ship. "Hard to tell at this point, because there's no lighting down there."

"Damn, I wish you'd brought a camera!" Grayson swore.

"That's our next priority, I promise." Kate unsnapped the portable lamp from her backpack and shined it down into the opening.

"Those are stairs, all right!" Al said excitedly. "See, they spiral down to the left!" He peered over the edge.

"Careful!" Kate grabbed at his arm. "Stay away from the edge—we have no idea how far down that goes! Five-eighths gravity wouldn't be *that* generous to someone your size in a long fall!"

"Yeah, right. The floor looks firm enough, but these damn kites are kind of slippery," he admitted somewhat abashedly.

"Let's try it this way." Teresa got down on her hands and knees. "Grab my ankles, somebody. I want to check out how sturdy these steps are. See, the sides are real smooth, so my suit should be okay."

"I'll grab her boots, Al, and you can hang on to mine for insurance." Kate scuffed her boots in the kites until she cleared enough of an area for her to lie down on the floor without interference. She then dropped flat to her belly behind Teresa, and Al followed suit behind her. Kate wrapped her gloved hands firmly in the ankle straps on Teresa's suit, which were designed for just such a need, and felt Al doing the same for her.

Slowly Teresa inched her way to the edge of the opening and continued until she was extended almost halfway out over the spidery staircase. Then she put both hands, palms down, on the top step and pushed. There was a cracking sound they could hear through their suit helmets, and a large piece of the step fell away into darkness. They all slid forward at the sudden release of support.

"Okay, back me up!" Teresa gasped. She had gotten the most incredible sense of vertigo watching the piece of step fall away, especially when she had felt as if she would follow it. Her heart was racing.

"Everything okay?" Grayson asked. "*Kenneth's* got a bit of an elevated pulse on you, Mac."

"Yeah, I bet he does!"

Soon they were all back on their feet on solid ground.

"Well, that settles that," Kate said. "As soon as we reopen the areas that were opened on the ˙*Opal*'s mission, we're going to bring extra lighting and the winch and find out what's down there."

"Those stairs must be awfully old, to have collapsed like that," Al remarked.

"Either that," Teresa said, "or the original tenants weighed so much less than we do that those stairs supported them without any trouble."

Kate nodded. "Could be, considering the evidence we have of their apparent size and shape. There's a reason those airlocks are tall and narrow."

"I hate to interrupt, but are you guys gonna get around to those other rooms?" Grayson asked. "You've been out there nearly an hour and a half, and *Kenneth's* telling me he's getting signs of lack of nourishment in everybody."

"You tellin' me it's dinnertime?" Teresa asked, laughing a little.

"Need to hear the noise in my stomach?"

"We can do without that," Kate said, smiling. "He's got a point, though, gang. We've still got a bit of work to do. Shall we check out the old equipment?"

The trip back through the passages and rooms previously opened by the *Black Opal*'s crew was relatively uneventful, and Kate found it depressing. When they reached the room that SINS identified as the one that contained Rory's body, they simply did not enter.

"We'll mark it for now," Kate said quietly. "Maybe later, if Pete can figure out how the doorway mechanism works, we can seal it permanently. Or we can use our weapons, if we need to."

The monitoring equipment in the remainder of the rooms proved to be in good working condition, though some of it needed a little cleaning. Pete promised he would take care of that on the next trip out, when it would be his turn to join a landing party.

"I think that does it for this trip," Kate said as she

straightened from inspecting the last piece of equipment. "I hope you got everything that was going on out here, George."

"No problem, Cap'n. We opened up a whole new section of SINS's library just to hold the data from our trips outside."

"Good thinking." She looked around her. "We'll be heading back now."

"Captain?" Luttrell broke in. "Any chance of bringing back a kite for me to look at?"

Somehow Kate managed to keep her voice level. "Out of the question, Luttrell. We didn't even bring a sample case this time. Besides, I'm not at all sure I want one of those things on my ship."

"But, Captain, we're here to study them. How can we not have a sample?"

"I'll think on it. But we can't do anything now—we've nothing to put it in." She turned to Teresa and Al. "Let's move out."

Kate pushed her feet into a pair of clogs and made her way from the showers to the messroom. Sometimes, she decided, the worst part of this job was having to run things; what wouldn't she give right now for somebody else to be in charge! She was so tired.

It never works that way, though, does it? she asked herself as she entered the messroom.

"Where's Dr. Luttrell?" she asked, pausing in the doorway.

"On Deck 2 with the patient. Said he'd be right up." Al was pulling steaming plates of food from the processing bays.

"He'd better hurry." Kate poured herself a cup of coffee and sat at the table. "Pass me some of the blue shit, please."

Grayson laughed. "Sorry, Captain, not until you've eaten your vegies. That blue shit happens to be dessert, according to SINS's menu."

"Could've fooled me," she grumbled, reaching for something else.

Luttrell paused in the doorway. "Good, just in time for dinner."

"No, actually, you're late," Kate informed him curtly. "This was supposed to be a meeting, remember?"

Grayson looked up, as if a little surprised at the curtness of her tone, but said nothing.

"My apologies." The doctor took a seat at the table and began to serve himself.

"I trust the frankenstein is okay?" Kate asked.

Luttrell looked directly at her. "I would have reported a problem with the LSH unit, Captain."

She returned his look but said nothing.

Teresa washed down a mouthful of indeterminate substance with beer and made a face. "Good God, what did I just swallow?"

Grayson cocked a speculative eyebrow at the remains on her plate. "I believe that was the Polynesian hash," he said primly.

"What you *mean* is SINS's leftover special!" Teresa said in disgust. "God, why can't they make this stuff more like real food?"

Pete laughed. "Guil-Pro doesn't want to spend more for it, that's why. We're not paying passengers, remember?"

Kate finished the last of her dinner and decided to forgo dessert after all. None of it was appetizing enough to tempt her right now.

Luttrell glanced up. "You know, Captain, we're going to have to get a sample kite sooner or later."

"That's my decision to make," she said. She was perfectly aware that in order to study the true nature of the creatures, they would have to see them both dormant and living. As far as they knew right now, the kites were aroused by warmth—specific warmth, like body temperature—so they could not see the creatures living outside the *Pegasus* without exposing someone to the dangers of being overwhelmed by them.

Their only alternative was to bring a sample aboard the ship and allow it to come to life where they could have some measure of control over it. But even in that situation, Kate did not want any kites aboard her ship, dead or alive, until she couldn't possibly avoid it, until the time came when they had to collect the specimens to return home.

"I would prefer," she said, "to learn as much about them as we can in their own environment before we have to bring them into ours, *if* we have to bring them into ours at all to study them. My first priority is to clean and connect the monitoring equipment. On the trip after that, I want to look into the area Teresa found today."

Luttrell poured himself more coffee. "Captain, I honestly don't know if we can find out any more than we already know about these creatures by studying them in their own environment. I really believe that in order to discover anything new and helpful, we must bring one aboard ship."

"Your request is noted, Doctor," she said evenly. "But *I* will make the final decision."

"But, Captain—"

"Put some work into the data we've already collected, and stop worrying about getting a specimen we're not ready to handle." She finished her coffee. "Discussion closed."

"You know, I was thinking," Al began after an uncomfortable pause.

"Hard work?" Grayson said, snickering.

Teresa covered her eyes and made choking noises.

"As I was saying," Al started over, "I think we ought to name the place. I'm tired of calling it 'the structure,' or 'the building,' or 'that thing out there.' What say?"

"Yeah, that's a good idea," Pete agreed. "What should we call it?"

"You always ask the easy questions," Al grumbled. "Hell, I don't know!"

"How about *Titanic*?" Luttrell suggested.

"Oh, come on, there's enough bad luck here already!" Teresa protested, as the others made disparaging noises.

Kate sat back and watched as several other choices were derided.

"What do you think, Captain?" Grayson asked.

She merely smiled and shook her head.

"Roanoke," Pete said suddenly. "You know, the Lost Colony?"

"Never heard of it," Grayson started.

"Sure, I know the one!" Al said excitedly. "The old British empire was colonizing what used to be the United States of America. Over five hundred years ago, wasn't it, Pete?"

"That's right." The engineer nodded. "It was an island colony off the coast of... let's see, that would be North Carolina, I think. Lasted less than two years, and disappeared without a trace. They don't know if the colony was wiped out by illness, or starved, or tried to survive by joining the local natives, or what. But they never found any of the people."

"Sounds good to me," Grayson said. "It's even about the same age, right?"

They all nodded.

"So, how does it sound, Captain?" Teresa asked.

"Roanoke it is," Kate agreed. "We'll make an official note of it in the log." She smiled. "Not a bad piece of work, Pete. I didn't know you were interested in history."

"Got to have something to do down in engineering when things are going smooth." Pete looked a little embarrassed at being found out. "Damn machinery is too well behaved these days to keep a man very busy."

"Roanoke." Grayson rolled the name around on his tongue. "I like that. So, now it's got a name, who gets to visit Roanoke next?"

"You, Pete, and me. Teresa, I want you on the main board. I don't see any need for you to go out, Doctor, until we have all the environmental stuff set up." She looked at her watch. "We'll leave in two hours. If there's nothing else, you're on free time till then—unless you've got work to do." She looked pointedly at Luttrell. "Teresa, hang around for a minute, will you?"

The computer specialist lingered after the rest of them had cleaned up their dishes and gone.

"I'm curious." Kate poured herself another cup of coffee. When she looked up, Teresa was still standing nervously. "You want to sit down? I'm not going to chew you out."

Teresa obeyed a little sheepishly.

"I think," Kate said slowly, "we'd better get something straight right now. You already know what's going on between me and Luttrell. I'm *going* to ride his ass; there's no way around it. Don't you go taking it personally, okay?"

Teresa spread her hands. "I'm working on it, I promise. But it still makes me uncomfortable."

"You'll get used to it, I'm afraid." Kate smiled ruefully. "But, enough of that. How are you and Al doing?"

The younger woman blushed. "Are we that obvious? You're the second person to say something."

"Oh?"

"Yeah, George has been yanking my chain a little. We're, uh, we're doing fine. I mean, it's nothing. . . ."

"Okay, okay!" Kate laughed. "Don't go into details, it isn't any of my business! I just like to see my crew getting along."

"Oh, I get along with everybody." Teresa thought about Luttrell. "Well, almost everybody."

"I'm glad you said that. Shows you're picky." Kate's smile faded. "Actually, I *did* want to talk to you about something else."

Teresa raised questioning eyebrows.

"I want to know a little more about what you plan to do with studying Roanoke's—what did you call 'em—geometric parameters?"

The young woman's eyes brightened. "Sure! I want to use SINS to look at the way the structure is put together. The system has some pretty complex graphics capabilities, and I don't see why I can't use some of them to figure out why the angles of that structure are actually painful to look at." Teresa began to sound very earnest. "We have a lot of perceptual assumptions when we look at a three-dimensional object. Luttrell probably had a point when he asked if there was a psychological component to our discomfort—there *are* certain things we expect to see. But he was going about it all wrong. We're not having problems looking at the structure just because it's alien, but because we're used to seeing certain components in a three-dimensional object, and either they weren't there, we weren't seeing them for some reason, or they were changed, different enough to be disturbing."

"So why is SINS going to help you with this?" Kate asked. "Why won't it be fooled by what we were seeing—or what we thought we were seeing?"

"We have camera images from the *Opal*'s mission, but this time SINS only has access to the images Al's portable scanner sent back. A camera can only see what's there, but

the scanner data is enhanced. SINS has a lot of special inferencing circuits that make it different from most computers,
and that's where I expect to get the extra help from.

"You said yourself that the image you saw from the *Opal*
didn't do the structure justice—I think the system used its
inferencing logic to mask out parts of the image it thought
wouldn't make any sense to us mere mortals studying it. But
I can override that mask and use SINS to make sense of what
was really there." She paused. "I think, anyway. I'm really
just guessing. I'll be able to do more when I have some current
visuals to use for comparison. But there's no reason I can't
start with what I've already got."

Kate nodded. "It sounds like you've thought this out
pretty well, so go ahead and study away. But do me a favor,"
she looked at the younger woman, "if you *do* come up with
something, let me know before you tell anyone else."

"Sure." Teresa reached for a cup of coffee. "You think
Kenneth would be interested?"

Kate smiled briefly. "I see George started something."

"Luttrell asked for it."

"I suppose he did." Kate stared at the table. "You're
right, though. Just to be safe."

Teresa nodded and rose to her feet, seemingly more at
ease than she had been. "That all?"

"For now."

"Then I'll go work with SINS for a while. Luttrell won't
need the subsystems I'll be using, and I'll secure all my data
in case anybody gets curious."

"I'd appreciate that." Kate nodded. "Keep me posted?"

"Yeah." Teresa headed for the door.

CHAPTER

12

Time passed slowly on the bridge. Kate rubbed the crease between her eyebrows, trying to shake a headache. She was waking up with one every morning now. She deliberately did not attribute it to the scotch she had been drinking every night to get to sleep.

The crew of the *Pegasus* had made their second trip to the planet's surface, during which Pete had cleaned and reconnected the *Black Opal*'s monitoring equipment. They now had camera and scanner capability in most areas of Roanoke except the sealed room that had become Rory's crypt.

"Damn!" Teresa smacked her console and pushed her seat back abruptly.

Kate looked over at her. "Something wrong?"

"No, I just feel like I've been working for hours without getting anywhere. I've been trying to analyze the geometry of that structure, and the images SINS is giving me are almost as bad as looking at the damn thing itself! I've got a headache."

"Take a break," Kate advised, glancing at her watch. "We're about ready to go outside again, anyway. We have to look at that staircase you discovered."

"Mmm. I could use the exercise."

"Coffee!" George returned to the bridge with three steaming cups.

"Ah, bless you, kind sir!" Teresa sipped gratefully at hers.

Kate glanced up and noticed that Luttrell had followed Grayson onto the bridge. Teresa saw him too, and casually reached over to blank her console screen.

"We're scheduled for another trip out soon, aren't we, Captain?" Luttrell asked.

"That's right."

"Am I to go?"

"You're not." She raised questioning eyebrows. Amazing how arguing with the man helped her headache to go away.

"I believe I'm the only member of the crew not to have visited the artifact yet."

"That's true. But you're not scheduled to go out this time, either."

He folded his hands carefully in front of him. "I thought I would remind you that, aside from our primary mission of returning to Earth with sample kites, our research while we're here involves studying them as well. If you continue to refuse to bring a sample aboard ship, I'll have no choice but to go there. Yet, I have not been given that opportunity. Captain, I cannot get my work done."

Kate's jaw tightened. "If you check the duty roster, Doctor, you'll see your name on it for the trip out after this one. Is that soon enough to satisfy your scientific curiosity?"

"I suspect it will have to be. Thank you, Captain." Luttrell turned to leave.

"Doctor," Kate called after him.

"Yes, Captain?"

"Can you handle the primary scanner monitors?"

"Certainly, Captain."

"Good. That's your station for this trip out."

Luttrell nodded and left quickly.

"Touchy bastard," George remarked. "I guess that means Al's going out again this time?"

"What's the matter, mister, don't you read the duty roster, either?" Kate asked, but her smile was teasing. She was definitely feeling better. "That's right, Al, Teresa, and me."

"Well, no wonder he's complaining!" Grayson laughed. "So far you've been on every outside trip, and both Mac and Al have been out before."

"Privileges of rank. Besides, it's only right that Teresa gets to explore what she discovered." Kate turned back to her work. "You know we'll have the portable camera with us this time. I'd like you to handle it from this end."

He grinned. "Good. I really want to see what's down that damn stairwell Mac found!"

Al and Teresa set the winch up over the stairwell, using a crossbeam framework Pete had constructed for them to support it. The crossbeams extended far beyond the edges of the opening in both directions, in case the flooring should prove to be weak. Pete, who watched them from the main cameras set up in each room, instructed them on just what to do. Teresa then struggled into the winch harness and allowed Kate and Al to fasten the camera to the breastplate of her suit.

"The scanner's attached to the bottom of the camera," Al told her. "All you have to worry about is turning the equipment on and off."

"Great. Are my straps tight?" she asked.

Kate checked the harness a second time. "Everything looks good."

"Can I have a check on the scanner?" Luttrell's voice came through their earphones. "I need to make some fine adjustments."

Teresa set switches as Luttrell repeated calibrations to her. "Okay," he finally said, "you're green from here."

"George, how's the portable camera?" Kate asked.

"If Mac will kindly turn the power on—okay, looks good to me. Nice clear picture."

"Pete, have you got a good visual from the big camera?" Kate asked.

"Green from here. The extra lighting we set up helps a lot. Teresa, don't forget to check the winch before you use it."

"You expecting problems?" she teased.

"With *my* equipment?" The engineer was all pretended outrage. "Hell no! But I wouldn't trust anything Guil-Pro supplies us with, not without checking it myself."

Kate knelt carefully and touched a switch on the winch. About half a meter of cable unreeled before the mechanism ground to a halt.

"I won't get far on that," Teresa remarked. "Good thing you had us check it out, Pete."

"See, what'd I tell you? And I even checked it out earlier, myself!" He sounded chagrined. "Doesn't take much with that crap."

"I hope we don't have to go back and get the spare, after all this!" Teresa bent down, and together she and Kate popped the casing that protected the main hoist mechanism. Teresa poked her gloved finger inside. "I am really gonna be pissed if we have to go all the way back to the ship—hold on there!" She clutched at something and obviously missed it, as they could all hear her muttered curses over the radio.

"What's wrong?" asked Al, who hadn't seen the bright object fall away into the shaft.

"I don't know. Something fell out of the main gear works. I hope it wasn't important. Shit!" Teresa sat back on her haunches. "I sure wish you were on this trip, Pete!"

"Talk about timing," Kate agreed. "Well, let me look. At least I've used these things before." She peered inside. "Nothing's missing—I'd stake my reputation on that. See the shiny marks here? Something was probably rubbing on this place and jammed up the works. Let's try it again, unless you'd rather just go and get the spare, Teresa."

"No, let's go ahead and use this if it works. The damn thing has been inspected to death!" Teresa tested the winch several times, even halting it with the manual brake once. It worked perfectly. "I guess that fixed it, whatever it was."

"I think you should come back and get the spare winch anyway," Luttrell advised.

"What for?" Teresa protested. "There's nothing wrong with this one!"

"Captain?" Luttrell paused expectantly.

"I don't think there'll be a problem. We've both examined it, and everything looks fine." Kate was confident.

"I still don't think—"

"Ah, will you leave it, Luttrell?" Teresa said. "*Some* of us have work to do."

"Very well," he murmured, obviously annoyed.

Kate and Al replaced the winch casing, while Teresa unhooked her portable lamp from her backpack and attached it to her helmet. "Here goes," she muttered, clambering carefully over the lip of the opening so that she hung free. Much to their relief, the framework didn't even slip.

"Lower away!" she called.

The winch started smoothly, and Kate watched the line play out. Everything seemed to be working as it should.

As she descended, Teresa reached up and switched on her lamp. The walls of the "stairwell" glinted back at her, smooth as glass. She wondered what kind of tools had cut with such precision. The stairs themselves were mounted on this shiny surface, suspended, it seemed, by a mere filigree of support. They were beautiful, but incredibly delicate—no wonder she had broken off a piece with her full weight!

"George, are you picking up these stairs? Aren't they beautiful?"

"I can copy, but it's a little dark in there. Can you describe what you're seeing?"

"Sure. The stairs are *very* delicate—they look like they can barely support themselves, much less anything else!"

"Maybe they aren't stairs at all," Kate murmured.

"I'm wondering how the opening was cut—looks like the surface might have been melted," Luttrell remarked. "Scanner doesn't pick up any radiation, though."

"I'm so relieved," Teresa said dryly. "I wonder if we're looking at layers of the planet's surface? I've gone down a long way, and I'm still in a shaft. At least I don't *think* they would've made a floor so thick."

"Can you see anything below you?" This was Kate's voice.

"Yeah—a lot of dark." Teresa peered downward. Her lamp seemed to glint off shiny walls as far as she could see, with no bottom in sight.

Without warning, the shaft flared open beneath her, and the chamber into which she dropped came alight with the colors of the rainbow. She was seized with a terrible vertigo.

"Holy shit!" she gasped. "Stop, stop, that's enough!"

"What happened? Are you all right?" Kate demanded. "What's that light down there?"

Teresa looked straight up, following the line that held her until it disappeared into the black hole that was the opening of the stairwell shaft, and clenched her teeth to keep them from chattering.

"Teresa?" Kate repeated.

"Whew! Yeah, I'm okay now." She looked down again. "It was just such a surprise. C-can you see this on the camera, George?"

"I'm not sure what I'm getting, Mac. I don't think we have enough range on the lens, more's the pity."

"I'll try to describe it." Teresa took a deep breath. "I'm hanging about two meters below the ceiling of this huge chamber. The ceiling is arched—I think I'm at the highest point. The stairs curve sharply away from the opening and follow the line of the ceiling down toward the floor, a long way away from where I am. I guess the best way to describe it is the whole chamber looks like a dome . . . but the *colors* in here—my God, it's *beautiful*! The entire room is iridescent, and much more brightly lit than the other areas we've been in. There's also stuff on the walls farther down, but I can't really see what it is from here."

"We can see a little of what you're describing now that it's lit down there," Kate said, a slight catch in her voice. The bottom was a *long* way down. "We can also see you, hanging straight below us. Quite a dizzying view!"

"You're telling me!" Teresa agreed.

"How far above the floor do you think you are?" Luttrell asked.

"Oh, lord, I don't know. Maybe thirty meters? Thirty-five? Something like that."

"Let's do a scan," he suggested.

"Okay." Teresa fumbled for the main control with her gloved hands. "Ready, Kenneth? Mark—now!"

She kicked her feet slightly, trying to make her body turn. The chamber was equally impressive in all directions, she discovered, now that her vertigo was gone and she could look and enjoy.

"Captain," she heard Luttrell's voice, "I'm getting interference on the scanner. It might be echoes from the ceiling; I can't be sure."

"No problem. Teresa, I assume you heard that," Kate

said. "We're going to lower you until the doctor reports no more interference. Ready?"

"Ready," she responded.

"Lowering away!" Al called.

Teresa felt a slight tug as the winch started again. She watched as the opening of the shaft rose away from her. How far down was she going to have to go, for God's sake?

. . . and she was falling, dropping suddenly out of control.

Teresa let out a startled cry and froze, arms up, eyes squeezed shut. She knew she must have screamed, would scream again if that horrible dropping sensation didn't end . . . then her head cracked against her helmet faceplate with the force of her stopping, and everything went dark.

"*Teresa!*" Kate shouted, hanging on to the hand brake with all her might. She'd heard the snap when something went wrong, had seen the cable drift free and whine through suddenly frictionless gears while the line-length counter went crazy. The automatic safeties had failed in quick succession, and she'd gone for the emergency brake by instinct alone.

"Jesus Christ!" Al muttered, scrambling awkwardly around to Kate's side of the winch to add his strength to hers on the brake handle. The two of them balanced precariously on the framework, suspended over the opening, in danger of plunging over the side themselves.

"Teresa!" Kate called. How far had the woman fallen? They could still see her, but . . .

"What's going on?" Luttrell demanded. "What happened?"

"The winch failed!" Kate strained with the effort of pulling on the brake. She was afraid to let up the slightest bit, afraid to move even to give Al better purchase, because the cable might slip again.

"Is she all right? Did you catch her, for God's sake?" Grayson's agitated voice interrupted whatever Luttrell had been about to say.

"I think so," Al said tightly. "No answer yet—Teresa!"

Teresa opened her eyes slowly, blinked. The floor of the chamber, still far below her, swirled dangerously. She groaned, heard the sighs of relief in her radio. "What the fuck happened?"

"Thank God you're all right!"

Teresa closed her eyes again and swallowed until the lump disappeared from her throat.

"Teresa?" Kate's voice was tentative.

"Yeah, give me a minute. Banged my head." She opened her eyes, looked down again. It wasn't so bad this time. "What happened?"

"I'm not really sure," Kate admitted. "Things just let loose. All of a sudden—bam!—you dropped like a stone!"

"Don't those things have safeties?"

"Kicked in and failed. We stopped you with the hand brake."

"Well, at least *something* worked the way it was supposed to!" Teresa forced a laugh. "Can you get me back up? I must've dropped halfway to the floor!"

"I think we'll be okay. But we can't rely on the hoist mechanism at all—we'll have to use the hand crank," Kate decided. "Besides, it doesn't look like you fell that far."

"You're kidding! Even if it's only a few meters, I must weigh a hundred kilos in this suit. Besides, do you know how long it's going to take to haul me up by hand?"

"Well, at least you'll be light as a feather in five-eighths gravity," Al teased.

"We don't really have any choice, Teresa," Kate said.

"I agree," Luttrell said carefully. "Without safeties, I don't think you should trust any of the electronics. We've already made that mistake once today."

Kate chose to ignore Luttrell's obvious dig.

"Nobody's answered my question yet," Teresa said. "How long is this going to take? We've been out here at least an hour, haven't we?"

"Fifty-eight minutes," Luttrell corrected.

"Right. So what's the gear ratio on the block and tackle?"

"It'll take about an hour and a half," Pete broke in. "Give or take fifteen minutes."

"No problem," Kate said. "Even plus fifteen minutes, that still leaves you forty-five minutes of air, counting the reserve."

"Someone can bring extra suit-packs if you need them," Luttrell pointed out.

"Not for me," Teresa said darkly.

"Then the best thing we can do is stop talking about it and get started here," Al said. "Captain, do you feel like you're braced pretty well on this framework?"

"Sure," she made herself laugh, "as long as I don't look down."

Al moved carefully around so that he was opposite her, then took the hand crank in his gloved hand. "Ready? Teresa, the captain's going to let go of the brake, so you may slip a little. Don't let it bother you."

"Thanks."

Al began to haul the cable up, winding it in with painful slowness.

Teresa felt the first jerk and the brief drop that accompanied it, and was very glad Al had warned her. She then put all her concentration on trying to counteract the natural swaying caused by her uneven upward journey. She didn't even think about looking down. The sight was no longer beautiful.

Just when she thought she was about to go crazy, Teresa saw the support framework immediately above her, and reached up her gloved hands to grasp it. Kate and Al grabbed her by the arms and pulled her up the rest of the way. Soon all three of them sprawled on the hard surface of the alien floor, away from the edge of the stairwell.

"Thanks, guys!" she gasped, and was seized by a sudden fit of shivering.

"Is everyone all right?" Luttrell asked, when the silence had grown long.

"Can't a person rest for a minute?" Teresa had recovered somewhat and was sitting up now, unstrapping the camera and scanner from her suit. "George, I sure as hell hope you caught all that on camera!"

"Every last minute, Mac. It'll be out in feature length as soon as we hit Earth orbit, I promise."

"Great, I'll be a star." She began to struggle out of the harness.

"Here, let me help." Al moved to assist her.

"If I may be serious for a moment," Luttrell broke in, "this matter will have to be made note of in the log. Including all the circumstances leading up to it."

"Luttrell, what're you babbling about?" Teresa asked.

"He's referring to my decision to use the winch after we had problems with it," Kate said quietly. "Thank you for reminding me, Doctor."

"Certainly, Captain. And if I may also remind you, you should be starting back shortly. You're about ready to cut over to your reserve."

Kate stared at the winch as they packed it, wondering what indeed had gone wrong. Dammit, she *had* used this kind of equipment hundreds of times! She could take one apart and put it back together again blindfolded, and she knew there was nothing wrong with this one when she had examined it. Luttrell was just trying to make trouble. Even Pete had checked it earlier. . . .

She stopped right there. Hadn't Kagen warned her that Luttrell might not be the only person in the crew working directly for him? Could Pete have lied about the condition of the winch, hoping she would be the first to use it? But that was such a long shot—unless it didn't matter who used it first. She was the captain, after all, and whatever happened would be ultimately her responsibility. Luttrell would see to it that she didn't forget *that*—he was already seeing to it.

But not Pete.

"I think I'm ready to go back now," Teresa said.

"Say, Al, where's Mac?" Grayson asked, opening a can of beer. "I'd have thought she'd want a couple of pops to calm herself down after that little trip."

"Haven't seen her." Al accepted a can from the food synthesizer. "*I'm* the one needs a couple pops—that was a lot of work, hauling her ass up with that crank!"

"Hey, don't complain to me," Grayson chuckled, "*you're* the one told her she'd be light as a feather." He took a long drink from his beer. "So, what do you think the problem was?"

"Hell, I don't know. We all looked at the damn winch,

and Pete checked it over himself before we ever took it out there—what's to think? Guil-Pro fucked up again, I guess."

"Discussing our jinx, gentlemen?" Luttrell joined them.

"I told you not to start with that shit, Luttrell," Al snapped.

"Merely a joke." The doctor smiled humorlessly. "But our good captain does seem to be plagued by such difficulties, doesn't she?"

"What's that supposed to mean?" Grayson demanded.

"You didn't hear?"

"Dammit, Luttrell, why do you have to bring all this stuff up again?" Al asked. "Grayson wasn't even aboard ship when that happened!"

"All the same, he has the right to know what happened, Al. Just as our captain insists we have a right to know what *she* would have us know."

Luttrell related their captain's problem with the door to the cubicle where the LSH unit was being kept. "Of course, by the time Schweitz got there to fix it, there was no problem. Never had been, I'm sure."

"Why are you so sure? What's she got to gain by lying about something that'd only make her look foolish to the rest of us?" Al asked. "It doesn't make sense to me."

"That's my point," Luttrell said smoothly, pouring himself a cup of fresh-brewed coffee. "It *doesn't* make sense. It's something in her head, like this fear she has of bringing a kite aboard the *Pegasus*. She's being guided by her fear and her memories, not by the reality of the situation."

"Christ, how many times do I have to say it—Guil-Pro wouldn't put somebody like that in charge of a mission!" Al insisted. "They don't take that kind of risk, not with money involved, especially!"

Luttrell shrugged. "Kept under control, it wouldn't be that serious. Guil-Pro knows that, too."

"You mean there *is* something wrong with her?" Grayson asked. "Is that why you're here?"

"I can't say definitely that something is wrong, no. I'm to keep an eye out, nothing more." Luttrell stared into his coffee cup. "Take the accident with the winch this afternoon. That could have been completely avoided, had she taken my advice."

"Now wait a minute. Pete inspected the thing himself," Al began.

"No, no, she can't be blamed for the actual failure, I didn't mean that. But once the equipment failed, she should have insisted on using the spare, as I recommended. She made a poor command decision, gentlemen, that's my point."

"Hey, either there's something wrong with her or there isn't. If you ask me, a captain who makes poor command decisions is a pretty goddamn serious problem!" Grayson said.

"Don't get excited." Luttrell raised both hands. "If you know about a potential problem, you can watch for it, prevent trigger situations from coming up. That's the only advice I meant to give." He rose to his feet, draining his cup. "Just be on the lookout. I will be. Good day." He walked out.

"Goddammit, I *knew* she was going to be trouble!" Grayson swore.

"Oh, you knew, huh? Then why'd you sign on this mission, bright boy?" Al asked.

"But that's what she did *last* time," Grayson went on, "made a poor command decision! Running out on a shipful of people she was responsible for—Christ!"

Al stared at him. "You're awful quick to believe that quack's mouthwash. Look, George, I was out there with her today—she didn't make any snap decisions, or do anything without thinking about it first. Cut her some slack, will you?" He rose to leave.

"What's the matter, aren't you worried about your own ass?" Grayson called after him.

Al turned around at the door. "Not so much that I'd start believing every word out of some Earthside desk-jockey shrink's mouth, when he hasn't proved a damn thing. You heard him after the accident—he's out to make trouble. I don't trust him, and I wouldn't pay any attention to him."

"Well, 'scuse me," Grayson said to no one, and got himself another beer.

Very carefully Teresa laid the winch on the engineering workbench and wiped her greasy hands on a towel. She hadn't been able to shake the idea that maybe her accident hadn't been an accident at all . . . she was haunted by the small piece of metal that had fallen from the main hoist gears. So she had gone over the entire hoist mechanism with excruciating care, and she didn't like what she'd seen.

The emergency brake operated on a simple enough principle. The main pulley was attached to a gear with teeth. When the manual brake was applied, a bar dropped down and caught in the teeth, locking the pulley. The shiny marks Kate had noticed had been between the pulley and the gear . . . they had been jammed. If she hadn't accidentally knocked out that tiny piece of metal, the manual brake would have locked open when Kate had used it. She would have plunged to her death. Slowly, in five-eighths gravity, but to her death, nonetheless.

If the hand brake had been sabotaged, Teresa had reasoned, then something must've been done to the main hoist gear as well. Because nobody would fix the manual brake unless he knew it would be needed, and it would only be needed if the main gear failed.

She had been right.

There was a counter on the hoist to keep track of how much cable was being unreeled. The counter could be fixed to release the main gear after a certain length of line had passed it, though she couldn't understand why anyone would want to do so. But she was able to do it herself, right there in the lab . . . it was frighteningly easy. The toggle had been set at about ten meters; five to get down the shaft, and an additional five to get past the scanner interference Luttrell had complained about. She frowned. Luttrell . . .

What frightened her most about the sabotage, though, was what had been done to the safeties. Teresa stared at the sonar analysis graph that crawled across SINS's display. Figures winked in and out, became plus or minus as the bright line traced out a revealing story. She was seeing the results for the third time, and they refused to change. The safeties—those tiny clamps that should've automatically grabbed at and held the cable when it had come free—were all microscopically flawed. And each flaw had been precisely machined to the same failing point, so they would all go at the same time. *Machined*, for Christ's sake! Somebody'd had the skill, the time, and the right equipment—not to mention the desire—to do such finely detailed work that was sophisticated . . . and very, very deliberate.

The scenario had obviously been worked out with great care. If she hadn't been lowered to the release point in the normal course of events, there would be an excuse to lower her farther, until she passed that point. (*Luttrell's echoes on the scanner,* she thought.) Once the line got to around ten meters, the main hoist gear would release. The safeties would engage, and fail, one after the other. In desperation, whoever manned the winch topside would use the manual emergency brake, and that wouldn't work either. Maybe they would try to stop it with their hands. Their gloves would burn on the singing cable as it unreeled despite all their efforts.

And what would *she* feel like? Terrified, helpless—wondering in the last brief moments if five-eighths gravity would be enough to save her. . . .

Teresa shook herself. What was she saying? It hadn't happened.

But it could have, she told herself sternly. *And it didn't have to be you, it could've been anybody.*

But it *had* been she, and everyone had known ahead of time that she would be the one to travel down on the end of the winch line. She didn't want to think about why someone might want to kill her. Didn't even want to think . . .

Lost in thought, Luttrell strode down a corridor on Deck 2. Good God, the complications he was running into! As if it weren't bad enough trying to baby-sit a goddamn obstreperous female captain who wouldn't listen to reason, now he had to worry about the damn stubborn female computer specialist, too! He'd always said women didn't belong in space, and here was proof.

He'd finally remembered who Teresa MacKessen really was. The name, obviously a false one, hadn't triggered him, but the face . . . he never forgot a face, though sometimes it took a while to come back. He *hadn't* forgotten her face, either, from seven years ago. He'd even figured out how to make the COACH subsystem let him into the personnel information SINS had on all of them, and her previous work record confirmed what he had already guessed.

This was important, a possibility Guil-Pro had obviously overlooked completely. Now he had to deal with it, out here in the middle of nowhere, light-years from home and anyone else's advice.

Where the devil would she be, anyway? Come to think of it, he hadn't seen her or the captain since their last trip outside. He had to find MacKessen quickly, before the two women talked to each other and discovered what he already knew . . . that they had a great deal more in common than either of them realized.

CHAPTER

13

Teresa wandered down a corridor and debated where to look next. The captain hadn't been in the messroom, nor had she been in the tiny gym they all used to keep themselves fit. She didn't mind not having found the woman yet—she still hadn't decided how she was going to make her report.

What if Luttrell really did have something to do with it? she wondered. *How can I tell her I think he's trying to kill me, or somebody, or whatever he's trying to do?*

"Officer MacKessen?"

"What?" The question had been put very quietly, but it scared her out of her wits. "Jesus Christ, Luttrell, what the hell are you trying to do, sneaking up on me like that?"

"Sorry, I didn't mean to startle you." He smiled. "Can I talk to you for a minute?"

She regarded him with immediate suspicion. Anyone who picked such an out-of-the-way place to hold a conversation was usually going to reveal confidences you didn't want to hear.

Ain't life a bitch? she thought briefly. *Here I am alone with one of the most gorgeous male specimens I have seen in life, and he's a real jerk!*

She tried to be polite, and succeeded only in being abrupt. "I really don't have time right now."

"I want to talk to you about the captain."

"Oh yeah?" She folded her arms.

Luttrell nodded. "If you'll let me give you some background first, so you can put it in context."

"I just told you I don't have time! Can't you get to the point?"

"I'm sorry, but I don't think this can wait. And you must hear me out."

Something in his tone of voice brought her up short. "All right, go ahead."

"I've been informally keeping track of everyone's mental health on this trip, with psych-profiles and the like. It's an unusual situation. We've never had the chance to study humans when they were actually getting ready to face an alien life-form—especially a known hostile one. It's a unique opportunity."

"For what? You gonna write a book?"

"Will you be serious?"

She looked at him. "If you'd stop trying to sound like a college professor getting cranked up for the next lecture, maybe I could be serious. What's your point?"

He appeared to be struggling to keep himself under control. "I've been paying special attention to Captain Harlin for two reasons. One, of course, is that she's the captain. She's integral to the success of this mission because of the role she's been given by the Consortium."

"Fascinating," she drawled.

"You can be remarkably uncooperative, Mac," he said tiredly, and Grayson's nickname for her sounded unsavory on his tongue. "The second reason, and possibly the more important of the two as far as we're concerned, is that she's already under a lot of stress because of the nature of her last mission out here."

"No shit. And this one isn't turning out to be a whole lot better, is it?"

"That's why I'm concerned. I . . . don't know how well she's handling it."

"What?"

"Her psych-profiles show a trend I don't like. Her reactions to the standard stress points have deteriorated considerably, especially compared to her test runs before the *Black Opal* mission. I ran another quick one a little while ago, and it's gotten even worse."

"My God," Teresa exploded, "what a stupid time to run the test! I could have *died* when that hoist slipped—what the hell kind of reaction did you expect?"

"These tests are designed to discount exceptions like that. It's a statistical average of—"

"Oh, fuck statistics!" Teresa hunched her shoulders. "I could be dead, and you're talking about statistics like some goddamn clinical shrink!"

"That accident really bothered you, didn't it?"

"Don't you try to analyze me!" Teresa backed away from him, hands raised. "Yeah, it bothered me, all right—it still bothers me. After all, *I'm* the one who would've ended up on the bottom!"

"And that's why you were down in engineering, trying to figure out what happened?"

"Who says I was in engineering?"

"Hey, you don't have to hedge with me. We're friends, right?" He smiled disarmingly. "In fact, I . . . well, maybe this isn't the most appropriate time to bring it up, but I kind of thought we could be more than friends, you know? We're both intelligent, consenting adults—you're not bad-looking. Besides, I like feisty women."

"Are you crazy?" She couldn't help it; those were the first words that came into her head.

He shrugged, seemingly not offended. "I've never really had the chance to talk to you alone before."

"So your concern about the captain's behavior was just an excuse?" She didn't know whether to feel flattered or relieved.

"No, no, not at all. I just thought, as long as the opportunity came up . . ."

She stared at him as though he were a lab specimen,

and wondered in that moment how she could ever have thought him attractive.

"You've been doing clinical research too long," she finally said. "It's given you some funny ideas about the way people work—at least about the way I work. I mean, we both know what you're talking about, right?" she asked. "Well, guess what, *Kenneth*. This may surprise you, but right now I wouldn't fuck you for what you've got between your ears, much less for what you've got between your legs."

"Well," he hadn't lost his smile yet, "at least I made the offer. You can keep it in mind."

"You don't take no for an answer, do you?"

"Have it your way. But let me tell you something, Mac." His smile became sly. "If you don't want anyone to know you've been down in engineering, you'd better keep your hands in your pockets . . . or go wash them."

She blushed and looked guiltily at the oily smears on her fingers and palms. "Think you're a real Sherlock Holmes, don't you? So what's it to you?"

"Maybe a lot—and not just to me, but to all of us." He regarded her thoughtfully. "What did you find out about the winch, Mac? You're trying awful hard to keep it secret. Did you find out it wasn't an accident?"

Her face was expressionless. "Like I said, what's it to you?"

"For chrissakes, don't play stupid with me—this could be important! If you found something that serious, I don't think you should tell the captain. At least not now."

"What am I supposed to do, wait until someone dies?"

"Don't be ridiculous, no one's going to die." He began to pace. "Let me explain something to you. The captain's in trouble with Guil-Pro because of some things she was involved with a while back."

"Yeah, she told us that. You forget?"

"Will you let me finish? Leading this mission was one of her options to . . . well, let's say to pay off some old debts, and to stay out of more serious trouble."

"You call coming out here again an *option*? Some choice!"

"She volunteered."

"Right!" Teresa laughed shortly. "Kind of depends on what her other choices were, doesn't it?"

He shrugged. "I couldn't say."

"Yeah. Well, it seems to me she's paying for it anyway, whatever decision she had to make."

"That's my point! She *is* paying, a little bit every day, and it's wearing her down. I think she's a lot closer to the edge than anyone realizes."

"Bullshit."

"I beg your pardon?"

"Bullshit! You're wasting my time, *Kenneth*. Give me some facts, or lay off it!"

"You listen to me!" He thrust a finger at her. "I'm being straight with you. I think you're closer to the captain than anyone else on the crew right now—you're the first person I've talked to about all this."

"Yeah, you just made it up, right?"

"You're a real hardass, you know?" Luttrell made an obvious effort to control himself. "Look, Mac, this is the place where something horrible happened to her. Something only she really knows about, inside her head. She *deserted* five people she had worked with as part of a close-knit team for years!" He looked at her hard. "Whatever her reasons were at the time, and I'm sure she thought they were good ones, she left those people out here. Do you know what it's like to be the survivor of a disaster, and to spend the rest of your life wondering if there was anything you could've done to prevent it? People go crazy for a lot less reason than that!"

"Then why isn't she on furlough, or some kind of medical leave? Why the hell is she out here at all if she's one step away from psychotic?"

"Don't put words in my mouth. I never said she was anywhere near psychotic. And you know why she's out here as well as I do. There's a job to be done, and she knows she has to do it."

"That doesn't sound like a head case to me."

"Why, because you can't see it?" Luttrell waved his hand. "Of course she keeps a lid on it. She's got a lot of responsibility, and she has to! But how long can that last?

It's a lot to ask of anyone." He paused. "I'm sure, for instance, that you have no idea she's drinking too much."

She made herself stop and think about it. She couldn't remember any particular instances—but the captain did look tired most of the time. Whatever was going on, it was pretty plain she wasn't sleeping well.

"And," Luttrell added, "she's checking on that LSH unit constantly. I believe she goes down there two or three times a day." He shook his head. "Not good."

"How do you know she does that?"

"You're so suspicious." He shook his head again. "I've seen her, of course."

"Okay, okay," Teresa finally admitted, "I'll give you a break. Suppose you're right, just for the sake of argument. What do you want us to do?"

He relaxed visibly. "Not much, really. It's more a matter of not doing certain things, I suppose. Taking the edge off here and there, nothing obvious. Like this incident with the winch. You don't *have* to tell her you think it was sabotage, do you?"

"I can't keep information like that from the captain! She has to make informed decisions!"

"Maybe certain decisions could be better made by other people," he said carefully. "Just to get the weight off her shoulders for a while, that's all I mean."

She stared at him. "Do you know what you're saying?"

"Of course I know what I'm saying. It seems perfectly reasonable to me, given her present state of mind. Isn't it better than losing her for good?"

"What do you mean by losing her for good?"

"If she breaks down, that's it. She couldn't be trusted again."

Teresa folded her arms and frowned. "So what do you want? Who's supposed to make these decisions if she doesn't? You?"

"If necessary," he said deprecatingly. "But it wouldn't have to be—"

"Damn right it wouldn't have to be! You listen to me, Doctor. This isn't just your decision to make! Until the captain proves to the *whole crew* that she can't handle it anymore, she's still the captain of this ship—she gets the problems, and she makes the decisions!"

She was working up a good head of steam now. "You're real clever, Luttrell, you almost caught me. But I know where you're coming from now. Go try your ideas on somebody else—I ain't interested!"

"You're being very foolish."

"I don't think so. I heard you threaten the captain a while back, and I've heard some of the things you've told the other guys. I think you're trying to get her removed from her command!"

He stood very still. "You'd better stay out of what you don't understand."

"Oh, I understand plenty, Dr. Luttrell. *You'd* better get off my case, and stay off hers!" Teresa turned to leave.

"What's the matter?" he asked softly. "You afraid your captain can't handle it anymore? You afraid your idol is going to crack up and leave you stranded out here like she did her last crew?"

She stopped, listened to him walking up behind her.

"It's hard, isn't it, realizing someone you admire can't hack it?" he continued. "You can't ignore the signs, Mac— you'd *better* not ignore them!"

She turned to face him. "There aren't any signs. Anything you've seen is in your head, because *you* want it to be there!"

His face changed suddenly. "What does that mean?"

She laughed. "Why didn't you tell Guil-Pro you had the hots to be a ship's captain?"

"What are you talking about?"

"Come on, Luttrell, you don't have a chance of getting her declared incompetent, and you know it! When I tell the captain what kind of shit you're pulling behind her back, she'll have your ass for *mutiny*!"

Luttrell took a quick step forward, his face suffusing with color. Before she could react, he flung her up against the wall and held her there, his forearm pressed tightly against her throat. *"What did you say?"*

Teresa fought a sudden panic. "You heard me!"

"Say it again!" He pressed tighter, and she started to choke.

"Let me . . . go!" She clutched futilely at his arm.

He let up slightly. "What did you say?"

She sucked in great, deep breaths, almost sobbing, until she grew light-headed. "Get off me!"

"Think you're a tough little bitch, don't you? Tell me what you said, or I'll break something!"

"I said *mutiny*, you pig—let me go!"

His face was ugly as he released her. "I don't want to hear that word again. Talking like that is going to get you in a lot more trouble than you bargained for on this trip . . . *Ms. Josephine Travers*."

She whitened. "What? What did you call me?"

"*Travers*. That's your name, isn't it?"

"I don't know what you're talking about."

"Of course you do—why else would you be out here? You know Guil-Pro's looking for you because your brother's case is still open."

"You lie—!"

"You mean you really don't know?" He cocked his head. "It seems your brother and his friends managed to unload some of what they stole before they died." He smiled. "Guil-Pro never recovered the money, the records, the location of the stake—none of it. But they're pretty sure it's still around, hidden somewhere. They think somebody in James Travers's family might know where."

"Like me? That's crazy—I never even *saw* Jamie after he disappeared!"

"I thought you didn't know what I was talking about," Luttrell said softly.

"All right, smartass, so my real name is Travers. It *still* doesn't matter—"

"If it doesn't matter, why did you change your name?"

"None of your goddamn business!" she shouted. Then she made herself stop, made herself think before she said anything else. "The last time I saw Jamie," she said in a low voice, "was before he left for his last mission."

"But Guil-Pro doesn't know that; neither does the captain. And me," he smirked, "I don't care whether you did or not. I just know the official story, and the official story says he saw somebody in his family. As far as I'm concerned, Guil-Pro missed a beat on their security when they hired you for this trip. You've been pretty smart, *Josephine*. Signing up for deep space jobs that were headed for areas your brother scouted with the *Hercules*. What were you doing, following his trace?"

Teresa stared at him, white-faced, her lips trembling. "What do you know about what I was doing? I've never been in deep space before!"

"No, but you tried. I looked up your work record. James Travers prospected Lambda Gruis, and you tried to sign onto the *Noah Webster* followup mission. The *Hercules*'s second stop was Theta Eridani, and you wanted to ship out on the—"

"All right, all right!" She covered her ears with her hands.

"Did you know he was headed for Epsilon Indi next?" Luttrell asked softly. "Did your brother tell you what his plans were? You know they never made it this far—why did you want to come here?"

She was stubbornly silent.

"Have it your way." He shrugged. "But let me tell you something. Leading this mission only canceled part of Kate Harlin's debt. She still owes Guil-Pro a lot for keeping her ass out of the fire." He leaned closer, and Teresa slid away from him along the wall. "They really want that money bad, Mac, and the captain really wants to get clear with Guil-Pro—all the way clear. See what I'm getting at?"

Teresa was shaking now. "She wouldn't do that. Sh-she wouldn't turn me in without—"

"Don't you bet on it." He moved closer to her again, trapping her in a curve of the hallway. "Guil-Pro's a real monkey on her back, love. She may be a good commander, but she knows when to put herself first."

Teresa swallowed. "What do you want?"

"Just a little cooperation. You don't say anything to her about the winch, and you keep quiet about this little conversation. It's like we never talked at all, right? If the captain lights into my ass for any of this stuff, love, you've bought it!"

"But I don't *know* anything!"

"Don't waste your protest on me—Kate Harlin's the one you'll have to convince. Like I said, I don't care. Go ahead, tell her. See which one of us is right." Luttrell walked slowly away. "You think about it, *Travers*," he said over his shoulder. "Think about it real hard."

Teresa stared after him, clenching her fists to keep her hands from trembling. How had he found out who she was? It had been so long ago, and it was supposed to be all over now. Her brother and his friends were dead, in disgrace... and now Guil-Pro wanted to drag it back out again.

Where they really looking for her? Was Luttrell telling her the truth, or was he just trying to scare her into doing what he wanted? But she *had* been hiding, really, using her mother's name all these years... And she *had* tried to get on those missions. Her work record would show that to anyone who cared to pay attention, just as Luttrell had decided to pay attention.

And the captain... how much trouble was she really in with Guil-Pro? Would she believe Luttrell's story, though she disliked and distrusted him? Kate didn't impress her as the type to jump to conclusions. But if she *were* in trouble, if she needed a way to get back into good graces with Guil-Pro ... Teresa shook her head, unwilling to take the risk to find out.

So what are you going to tell her now? the young woman asked herself. *As soon as she finds out about the winch, she's going to ask questions, try to find out what's going on. It'll get back to Luttrell, and my ass will be in a sling. But I have to tell her something!*

She walked slowly down the Deck 2 corridor, past the doors leading to their tiny quarters. Now there was a thought. She hadn't tried Kate's quarters yet.

Kate sat on the edge of her bed and rubbed her face with her hands. She had just come from visiting Rory—what a quaint term, *visiting*. She laughed at herself. *Visiting* Rory, as though she were going to the gravesite of a departed loved one. But she had merely been checking, once again, on the condition of the frankenstein in its Deck 2 hibernation unit. Dammit, why couldn't she call the thing a brain-dead LSH unit? That's all it was, a piece of goddamn realistic-looking machinery. . . . She wasn't quite sure what drove her to check it constantly, but she was uncomfortable if she let it go longer than a day without peeking in.

As always, she had gone down to the room itself rather than use the monitors on the bridge. And, as always, everything there was the same. All the monitors read as they should—the frankenstein was alive, but frozen and brain-dead—and the plastex cover was lightly frosted, so that she couldn't quite see inside. Just the suggestion of dark, curly hair...

She stared at the full bottle of liquor that stood on her worktable. This was not the first time she had wondered where the bottle came from and why it was always full when she looked at it.

Kate was a beer drinker. She liked beer a lot; on a good day she could drink it with liquor by the shot and hold her own with any of the guys in Residential Area 3. Not that she did it very often. But she could appreciate an occasional beer or three, especially after a hard day's work.

That's why this was different. She wasn't dealing with just beer anymore, she was dealing with liquor. Liquor that seemed available to her without asking, in endless refills without her memory or desire.

She could no longer use the excuse of needing it to get to sleep at night—this was the middle of the day shift. Her hands were shaking.

Maybe Luttrell was right. He hadn't said anything up front, of course—that wasn't his way, the bastard—but she knew what he was getting at with that little speech about formally reporting the accident. Perhaps she *had* made a bad decision. It didn't matter that Teresa had been perfectly willing to use the winch—the decision and the ultimate responsibility for the results of that decision were hers, not Teresa's. She recalled her own words at the start of this mission, about not wanting to file any death reports because someone had been careless. Well, maybe *she* had been careless.

Dammit, why was she letting Luttrell do this to her? It was her ship, her command—she had the respect of the crew (didn't she?) and she had her own self-respect. (Didn't she?)

She also had Mishima, and the Loon. She had the shadow of the *Black Opal* only kilometers away . . . and Rory. Rory, whose last gift to her had been the first of many bottles of scotch.

The bottle of Chivas Regal had been full when she'd sat down. Now, looking up a little bleary-eyed, Kate noticed it was about half-empty. Actually, she felt pretty good for someone who'd been drinking the way she'd been, and she wondered, for a fleeting moment of amusement, if someone had been watering her private supply. Maybe her private supplier? No, no, bad joke, not funny . . .

"Come in!" she called in answer to her door buzzer, rather pleased that her voice sounded perfectly normal.

Teresa hesitated in the open doorway.

"I said come in, didn't I?" Kate waved her arm expansively. "Have a seat."

Teresa had a funny look on her face. "It wasn't that important. I'll, uh . . . I'll come back later."

"I don't like to drink alone," Kate smiled briefly and without humor, "despite what this looks like. At least you can keep me company. Or grab a glass, if you want. But sit down."

Teresa took a glass from the small cupboard Kate had indicated and sat in the room's only chair. "What is it?"

"Just what the bottle says—Chivas Regal. Scotch, if you don't know any better."

"Isn't that expensive?"

"Terribly. Know how many bottles I've been through since we broke away from Equator Station? Three—and a half, counting this one. Know what else? I haven't the foggiest idea where it all came from." Kate realized she was babbling, and made herself stop.

Teresa smiled uncomfortably. "I'm a little confused. How can you not know where it came from?"

"Just what I said. Every time I look at the damn bottle, it's full again. Or there's another one in that drawer right there." She pointed to her bedside table. "Check it out. Probably one in there right now."

Teresa obeyed. There was an unopened bottle lying in the drawer.

"See, what'd I tell ya?" Kate grinned.

"Uh, I really think I ought to come back later." Teresa rose to her feet.

"What's the matter, I make you nervous?" Kate pointed to the chair. "Sit down. You came to tell me something. If it was important enough for you to hunt me down, it's important enough for you to tell me right now. Sit!"

Startled, Teresa obeyed.

"I'm waiting." Kate poured a glass for herself and one for the younger woman. Teresa noticed that the captain's hand was perfectly steady and that she spilled not a drop while pouring.

"See, I'm not as drunk as you thought," Kate said slyly. "Feel better?"

Teresa blushed. "I'm not sure."

"Have a drink. It'll help, and you look like you could use one."

Still shaken from her encounter with Luttrell, Teresa couldn't really argue. Though seeing her captain seemingly in just the kind of state Luttrell had described was a bit of a blow. He was such a bastard—but suppose he was right? Suppose Kate *was* in trouble, and drinking herself into worse trouble? Teresa took a big swallow of the liquor and choked.

"Careful."

"Yeah!" Teresa gasped and wiped her eyes. "Powerful stuff!"

"You're used to the manufactured shit, just like I am. This is the real thing." She poured two more glasses.

"Have you been in here very long?" Teresa asked hesitantly.

"Long enough." Kate quirked her mouth sardonically. "But you could tell that, couldn't you? You disapprove?"

"No! No, it's not that." Teresa played nervously with her glass. "I mean—I guess I just didn't picture it."

"Didn't think I had any vices?" Kate chuckled. "Guess

again, kid." She drank, and wiped her mouth on the back of her hand. "So come on, what's on your mind?"

Teresa emptied her glass and was silent for several minutes, looking like a child who'd been caught stealing. "That, uh, that accident really bothered you, didn't it?" she finally asked.

Kate held her glass to the light and regarded it steadily. Then she put it back on the table instead of drinking it. "Accident?"

Teresa swallowed. "Yeah. In Roanoke."

"Ah." Kate nodded. "Whatever gave you that idea?"

"Oh, come on—!" Teresa stopped. "Okay it's your game. Maybe it didn't bother you. But it scared the shit out of me!"

"Accidents happen in this business. You learn to live with it."

"*If* it was an accident."

"That's not something I choose to think about." Despite her words, Kate regarded the young woman curiously.

"Oh yeah? Then why're you tryin' to drink yourself fuckin' blind?" Teresa emptied another glass and stopped to catch her breath. Her first glass had just caught up with her, making her head spin.

"You're doing pretty well yourself, computer specialist. Slow down a little." Kate tried to smile, but her mouth twisted the other way. "All right, if you really want to know, it scared the shit out of me, too." She stared at her glass, watched her knuckles turn white as she gripped it. Teresa winced, half-expecting it to shatter.

"You know why it scared me," Kate continued softly, "aside from the fact that it could've been *me* on the end of that line? Which is a pretty selfish reason, when you think about it. But maybe I could've prevented it. Maybe I *should* have.

"That's what scares me. I should have known better. Protecting this crew is part of my job, and I should have insisted we use the spare winch until that one could be checked out. I fucked up. Maybe that means I'm a lousy commander. Maybe it means I can't hack it out here anymore, period. Maybe everybody was right." She took a sip from her glass. "I used to be better than that."

"I—I wouldn't pay attention to anything Luttrell says," Teresa said quietly. "I don't think anyone else does."

"Oh no? I think you're wrong." Kate topped off her glass. "But I've let you sidetrack me. That's not what you're here to talk about." She looked at Teresa sidewise. "Is it?"

"Well—" The younger woman hesitated. Kate *seemed* sympathetic, but . . . "Actually, I was really looking for something to drink. I'd heard that Al had some real beer, and—and I thought—"

"You figured scotch would do as well? Why'd you want to tie one on?"

"Bored." Teresa gulped her drink quickly. She wished Kate wouldn't keep asking her these questions—she was finding it harder to come up with reasonable-sounding excuses.

"You've been too busy down in engineering these past few hours to be bored." Kate cocked her head slightly. "Besides, you were pretty surprised when you found me like this, so you weren't expecting to come *here* to drink. Am I right?" She smiled. "Come on, Mac, talk to me. That's what I'm here for."

Teresa saw the sympathy in Kate's eyes and felt herself weakening.

"What were you doing in engineering?" Kate prompted.

"Christ, the whole damn ship knows I was down there!" Teresa rubbed her eyes exasperatedly. "I was looking at the winch, if you must know. The accident—well, it wasn't."

"Wasn't what?"

"Wasn't an accident."

"Explain that."

Teresa described her discoveries in detail. "The whole thing was rigged to cave in, right down the line," she finished. "Something would fail, the backup would kick in, and then that would fail. It was only luck that we found the piece of metal jamming the emergency brake, or that wouldn't have worked either!"

Kate's eyes darkened. "You're absolutely sure about all this?" Suddenly she felt quite sober.

"I ran a sonar analysis on the safeties. SINS gave me the same answers three times straight. Those flaws were microscopic and perfect, Cap—uh, Kate. It *had* to be deliberate." Teresa swallowed. Now for the hard part. "I think," she said slowly, "that someone tried to kill me."

Kate raised her eyebrows quite high. Here was a twist she hadn't thought of. "Why?"

"Because everyone knew ahead of time that I was going to be using the winch. And I told you it wouldn't take very long to fix, once somebody decided to do it."

"You're pretty sure it was aimed at you."

"Well, I—" Teresa broke off. "Since I'm the one who'd have been killed, I just . . ."

"Not so obvious, is it?" Kate smiled crookedly. "Who d'you think did it?"

"Luttrell." Teresa spoke without thinking—she had been concentrating too hard on pouring herself another drink. "I mean—oh, hell, I don't know what I mean anymore!"

"Why Luttrell? He's hardly got the ability for something like that."

Teresa swallowed her words. "I shouldn't have said that. I—I've had too much to drink."

"No such thing!" Kate protested, making herself sound drunker than she felt. "Let me help you with that." She finished pouring the younger woman's drink. "There's certainly more here than I can drink by myself." It was a dirty trick, using alcohol to get information, but now was not the time for Teresa to get coy. "Well," she continued the conversation, "you must've mentioned his name for a reason. Why pick on Luttrell?"

"I don't trust him. I—I overheard him threaten you once."

"When?"

"Right before your first briefing, in the hallway outside."

Kate recalled the conversation. "You heard Luttrell threaten me once, so now you think he's trying to kill you? I'm not sure I understand."

Teresa made herself speak very slowly. She couldn't tell the captain the real reason she thought Luttrell might have for wanting to kill her. To do that she would have to tell Kate who she really was, and she wasn't ready for that yet, if she would ever be ready for it. "No, that's just my reason for not trusting him. Anybody who would sneak around like that behind people's backs—"

"So you think he sabotaged the winch?"

Teresa brought her full glass shakily to her lips, and slopped half the contents down her front. "Shit."

"Do you think he did it?" Kate asked again.

"How the hell should I know?" Teresa was finally driven to answer. "You think he left fingerprints? Christ, he wouldn't know what to do with the electronics anyway!"

Kate was inexorable. "Which means?"

Teresa floundered, realizing the corner she'd been backed into. She should never have started drinking.

"Spit it out."

Teresa covered her face with her hands. "Somebody else had to do it. Probably somebody back on Earth. At least the business with the safeties. Those flaws were precise, and that means sophusti—siphos—shit, the right kind of equipment."

"And that means?"

"Somebody high up knows about this. And wants it to happen, I guess."

Kate nodded. "So this is bigger than both of us, right? Good, it's nice to hear someone else say it for a change. But why Luttrell?"

Teresa stared at the bottle on Kate's bedside table. It was almost empty, she noted with sudden interest.

"Mac?" Kate made her voice gentle. "You're still holding out on me."

Teresa looked up, moving her head very carefully. She decided she was not feeling at all well. "I don't think I can talk about it anymore."

"Has Luttrell tried to get you?"

Teresa shook her head, and the room began to move in slow circles.

"Who put the fear of God into you? Come on, Mac."

"Nobody!" She swallowed the sour taste in her mouth. "Look, Captain, I don't have any proof, so you wouldn't be able to do anything anyway. It . . . it's just my word against his."

"Okay, then this is off the record."

"You mean it? You won't get mad and—and do something?"

"You'll have to tell me first."

Teresa couldn't hold out against Kate's persuasive tones any longer. She was too drunk, and dimly angry at herself for letting Luttrell scare her in the first place.

"He told me you were cracking up. He practically came out and *said* it. Talked about your psych-profiles—"

"That's a lie. He's never profiled me. I don't even know if he's qualified to do it."

"Well, he sure made it sound good. He was talking about your stress reactions, and how much pressure you were under—he pushed all the right buttons, Kate. I think he wants to take your command away!"

"Does he really think he can make a case for that?" Kate asked slowly.

Teresa blinked. "He sounded like he did."

"God, I've probably given him more than enough cause. Has he talked to anyone else about this?"

"He said I was the first person."

"Well, I'll just have to make sure you're the last person as well. Dammit, I *told* him I'd break his sleazy neck—"

"Oh, no, please, Captain, don't do anything. He'll *kill* me if he finds out I told you!"

"He won't find out." Kate looked at her closely. "He really did scare you, didn't he? What's he got on you, I wonder?"

Teresa's lips trembled. "Don't ask. Please don't ask me that."

Kate sighed and wondered if finding out would be worth the effort of getting the younger woman drunker than she already was. "All right," she decided, "I won't ask."

Teresa tried to pour herself another drink and spilled most of it. Angrily she wiped her eyes on her sleeve. "Goddamn this stuff. I'm such an *ass* when I drink!"

"Don't worry about it. I'll consider the subject closed."

"Shit." Teresa drank what little she'd managed to get into the glass, and reached for the bottle again.

"I think you've had enough." Kate moved it out of her reach.

"I guess I'm pretty lit, huh?"

Kate heard the soft slurring of words, and agreed silently. "Will you be all right?"

Teresa smiled owlishly. "Hell no. I'll probably get god-awful sick in about ten minutes." She started to rise, and had to catch her balance on the edge of the table. "Well, maybe less than ten minutes," she added faintly.

"Here, let me walk you to your quarters." Kate took her by the arm.

"Nah, I can take care of myself. I used to get drunker'n this in school."

"That's fine. You're not in school now." Kate started to walk, supporting most of the younger woman's weight.

Minutes later, they were at the door to Teresa's quarters. "Think you'll be all right?" Kate asked. "You want me to stay with you?"

"No. Don't like to be sick in public," Teresa mumbled.

"Here, at least lie down so you don't hurt yourself." Kate pushed the younger woman down on her bed and lifted her feet up so she lay flat. "Keep your head turned to the side, okay?"

"Captain, you . . . you'll watch out for Luttrell, won't you?"

"Don't worry, he'll be easy to take care of," Kate promised. *I wonder what it is you know,* she thought as she left.

Christ, she wondered as she walked back down the passageway moments later, *how come you can never get really drunk when you want to?* Oh, she was high enough, all right, and she'd managed to forget exactly how much she *had* drunk, but it hadn't made the world go away, so it hadn't been enough.

Kate stretched, flexing her shoulders and reaching up to the ceiling as she walked. So now Teresa was having trouble with *Kenneth.* It made her wonder how many others in the crew he was trying to get to—what he was telling them, and why—and what she could realistically do about it anyway. For Teresa's sake at least, maybe nothing for now. Oh, hell, what else could go wrong?

She soon found out, when she returned to her quarters. Her stomach began to knot in protest at the outrageous amounts of liquor she had consumed. She suffered silently for a few minutes, and then was finally and thoroughly sick.

Wearily Kate sat on the edge of her bed and unfastened her shoes. It looked as though she had a true ally in Teresa MacKessen—something she wasn't sure she could say about anyone else in the crew. Maybe, as the days went on, she could persuade the younger woman to part with the rest of her secret, whatever it might be.

As she straightened from taking off her shoes, she caught sight of the bottle of scotch on her bedside table. It was almost full again.

"I'll be damned," she murmured. "I wasn't gone but five minutes—if that!"

She picked up the bottle and sniffed. It was scotch, all right.

"Well, what the hell." She took a quick slug, then got up to take a shower.

CHAPTER

14

Feeling better than she had in days, Kate suited up for another trip to Roanoke. They had already made several forays outside since the failure of the winch, while Pete had gone over Teresa's initial findings and completely torn down the faulty piece of equipment. He was pretty sure he'd fixed it, and Kate was willing at this point to rely on him. She found it interesting that he had insisted on examining the backup winch as well, and even more interesting that he had found the same problems with it.

She still refused to allow a kite to be brought aboard the *Pegasus*, forcing Luttrell to examine them outside. Not that it told him much, he often complained, since without exposure to warmth the things resembled nothing more than pieces of slate.

"Sure you're ready to ride that hoist again?" Kate asked, turning to face Teresa, her helmet under her arm.

"Hey, if Pete says he fixed it, he fixed it. Him, I believe."

"Just doin' my job." Pete smiled.

"Nice to know sombody around here feels like that about it." Teresa laughed.

"Mac, you're not cuttin' up on *Kenneth* again, are you?" Grayson's voice came to them over the intercom.

"Sorry, it goes against my ethics to have a battle of wits with an unarmed man."

Luttrell's voice was distinctly absent from the intercom.

"Now, Teresa," Al said, "be nice to your doctor. Never can tell when you might need him."

"You guys knock it off," Kate said mildly.

With the winch fixed, they were going to explore the underground area that Teresa had discovered. Kate wanted four people on this trip—two below and two above to operate the winch—a violation of her own three-on, three-off rule. Despite an argument from Luttrell, she had decided that the situation called for a little flexibility. So, Grayson and Luttrell stayed aboard ship this time, with Luttrell on the monitors. Grayson had assured them he could handle both the main camera and the small, portable one that Teresa would carry with her.

Much as she wanted to see the underground chamber, Kate had decided to send Teresa and Al down, while she and Pete would work the winch from above. Teresa went first.

As the cable unreeled with Teresa on the other end, Kate found herself with mixed feelings. She regretted having to take a back seat in the exploration, yet in a way she was glad not to be the one hanging at the end of the line. If they had trouble again...

"George, are you picking this up?" She heard Teresa's voice. "Can you see what's on these walls?"

"It's blurred, Mac. You're just too far away."

"It looks like giant murals," Teresa's voice went on. "And—oh my God, it's moving!"

"Stop the winch!" Kate ordered. "What's moving? Is something down there?"

"No, no, the *mural* is moving!" Teresa explained.

"Holograms?" Kate wondered aloud.

"Not sure, I'm still too far away."

"Okay, start her up again," Kate said, somewhat absently.

"Can you see any shapes at all?" Al asked after a brief pause.

"Very vaguely. Just dark blobs. And they don't move all the time. One will do something, then stop, and then the one next to it will move. Damn, I wish I could see better!"

"How far down are you?" Kate asked.

"Better than halfway, it looks like. As I get closer to the floor, I can see that the murals are high up on the walls. Over my head, at least!"

"That would fit in with what we've guessed so far about the creatures who built this place, if they really were tall and thin," Kate said. "This stuff would be at their best viewing angle, not ours."

"Can you slow this thing down any?" Teresa asked suddenly.

Kate made a slashing motion with her hand, and Pete stopped the winch altogether. "Why?"

Teresa cleared her throat. "Well, it just occurred to me that we don't know anything about the surface down here. Like, for instance, whether or not it can support my weight? Suppose there's a subbasement, or an old quake fissure?"

Grayson's voice came to them from the ship: "SIN's analysis indicates you'll be on a solid layer of bedrock, several thousand meters thick—no subbasement, and nary a faultline in sight. You should be okay, Mac."

"Sounds good. My little scanner says I'm about five and a half meters from touchdown."

"Start her up again, Pete. Slowest speed you can get."

"Okay here," Pete acknowledged.

"I'm down!" Teresa called after a brief period of silence. "I'm taking the harness off now; Pete, go ahead and haul it up. Damn, it's beautiful down here! George, can you still read me?"

"Loud and clear, Mac," his voice came from the *Pegasus*. "What's up?"

"I'm headed due, uh—no, make that north-northwest. I should be close enough to one of those murals shortly for you to pick up the images on my camera."

There was a brief time when all they could hear was Teresa's breathing as she moved around. Then . . .

"Oh, my God."

"What is it?" Kate demanded. "Are you all right?"

"Yeah, I'm fine. But—have you started down yet, Al?"

"No. Why?"

"Captain, I think you need to see this."

"What is it?"

"You have to see it. I . . . just think you should be down here."

Kate struggled into the harness. "Sorry about this, Al. I'll give you the next trip, I promise."

"Hey," he shrugged elaborately in his suit and smiled, "I can wait."

"Okay." Kate signaled, swinging out over the opening, and felt herself begin to move slowly downward. Very soon she broke out of the shaft at the apex of the cavernous room. It was indeed as beautiful as Teresa had described, but she could not concentrate on that now. She strained to find the other woman, tried to ignore the moving shapes on the walls that had no meaning at this distance, and not long after that she touched bottom.

"Over here!" Teresa called, waving.

Kate stepped free of the harness and approached the far wall where Teresa waited for her. She was fascinated, staring at the huge murals as she began to make out what they depicted. They indeed moved as she watched them, much as Teresa had described, but it was the subjects that held her gaze, not their execution. She was looking at incredibly tall, slender creatures who, she could only assume, were going about their daily business. They were humanoid, with two arms and two legs, and their clothing was some indeterminate dark color—she still wasn't quite close enough to see from where she stood.

As she drew even closer to one mural, she realized why

the younger woman had wanted her to see the moving like-
nesses.

The aliens were covered with kites.

The kites were everywhere, on the aliens, on the ground
around them—they fluttered from the ground to their bodies
and back again as the images before her moved, paused, and
moved again. She was mesmerized.

"My God!" she whispered. "George, can you see this?"
And then the nightmare was on her—there were no alien
creatures before her, but Mishima, swarming with kites, running and screaming, running and screaming. . . .

"Captain, are you all right?" Teresa touched her shoulder.

Kate focused on the mural again. "I . . . I've seen this
before."

"On the *Opal*?" Grayson asked quietly.

"Yes. Only . . ." She stopped, unable to pull her gaze
away from the vision that moved before her.

"Captain," Luttrell's voice interrupted her thoughts, "this
is fascinating! The kites appear to be a part of their normal
lifestyle. Like body decoration, or—or clothing, perhaps!"

"It's true," Teresa agreed. "Look, the things are everywhere, in all these pictures. In fact, I don't see any of the
aliens *without* kites!"

"Could somebody tell us what you guys are seeing?" Al
asked plaintively. He and Pete were the only ones without
access to the camera's view. Teresa tried to describe the murals
as best she could.

"Captain, this isn't like anything we imagined!" Luttrell
sounded very excited. "We *must* have one of these creatures
to study aboard ship!"

"Really, I wouldn't mind looking at one myself, up close,"
Al added. "The dormant version, that is."

Listening to all their voices, Kate began to feel overwhelmed. Somewhere in the background she could hear Rory
wanting to study the "packing material," before they knew
what the kites really were. Then Alicia, preternaturally calm,
studying the creatures they had gotten off Mishima's body
by freezing him, telling her thoughts to SINS for the record.
But behind Alicia's voice were Mishima's screams, and be-

hind that, so faint as almost to be missed, the laughing voice of the Loon. . . .

"All right," she decided, her voice a little husky, "next trip out we'll bring a sample case. But you're only getting one kite, Luttrell, that's all. Just one."

"It will be more than sufficient, Captain." The man sounded disturbingly pleased.

Kate and Teresa explored awhile longer, then traded places with Al and Pete, to allow them to see the alien artwork firsthand. By the time they returned to the *Pegasus*, Kate was exhausted.

Tired as she was—and tiredness had become a habit with her—Kate forced herself to be in the science lab when Luttrell began to study the kite sample. The doctor had gone to collect it himself, he was so pleased to be getting one.

Luttrell began his examination with the creature in below-freezing temperatures, then gradually began warming the sealed compartment it lay in. He had approximated the original atmosphere discovered in the alien structure as closely as he could.

In spite of herself, Kate found she was fascinated by what Luttrell was doing. He was very skilled in operating the computer-controlled waldos, wielding the tools of his trade almost as well as if he were using his own hands.

"What's the temperature now?" she asked.

"Mm, about minus thirty degrees centigrade. Not much warmer than outside. I'm trying to duplicate the conditions created by the *Black Opal*'s crew. The warming process was very gradual, as I recall." He glanced at her sideways. "If you're really interested, you can follow the temperature changes on this gauge right here."

The temperature had already risen to minus twenty-eight degrees.

"I wonder," he murmured, "when we can expect the thing to become animate."

"Rory had been out of his suit almost seventy-two hours before Mishima was attacked, and the place was already warm by then. You might have a long wait."

Luttrell merely raised his eyebrows.

Nearly an hour passed, and Kate grew bored with watching. The kite hadn't stirred, and Luttrell's examinations were getting more minute and less interesting.

"Call me when the thing wakes up, will you?" she finally asked, turning to face him at the door.

"Certainly, Captain." He didn't look up.

Kate supervised another trip to Roanoke while she waited for Luttrell to report on his experiments. Grayson and Al had gone out with Pete to survey the basement chamber; she and Teresa manned the primary monitors and cameras aboard the *Pegasus*. The team set up additional lighting and the permanent cameras in the underground chamber so that their future explorations wouldn't be limited by what they could see on the portable camera. The additional lighting showed the room to be even more beautiful than they had first thought. The very walls themselves were splashed with colors.

"Have you had much chance to analyze the shape of the structure?" Kate asked, pressing the quiet button so her voice didn't carry over the radio.

Teresa shrugged. "I've done a little, but..."

"What's the matter?"

"I'm not sure. I mean, what I'm finding isn't making a lot of sense." Teresa looked at her. "I think the structure is changing."

"How do you mean? There's hardly any weather here to—"

"It's growing."

"You mean it's *alive*?"

"No, not exactly. I think it's more analogous to the behavior of a crystalline structure—you know, some crystals do grow. I don't think it's organic, but I need to do more work before I can be sure. That's why I haven't said anything yet."

"I wonder..." Kate's voice trailed off.

Teresa looked at her inquiringly.

"Do you remember, on our first trip to Roanoke, how I couldn't find the airlock? I couldn't find anything on the outside surface that looked familiar?"

Teresa nodded.

"Perhaps the structure had changed enough in a year for me not to recognize it."

"I'll run that comparison with my next set of scans," Teresa said.

Kate nodded, releasing the quiet button.

"Captain, I think we'll be heading back now," Grayson reported. "Pete's got about everything you could think of set up down here."

"I was just going to say you guys have been out there for a long time."

"Yeah, but this wasn't really worth bringing extra suit-packs out for," Pete said. "Though maybe we should consider leaving some out here, in case we hit a tight spot like Mac was in."

"I'd go along with that, but it's against Guil-Pro policy unless we station somebody out there for the duration," Kate said.

"Oh, for chrissakes, who would know the difference?" Grayson broke in.

"We'd all *know*," Teresa said dryly. "The question is, who'd report us?"

"Aw, shit!" Grayson muttered. "You don't think—"

"Captain!" Luttrell's voice, coming over the ship's intercom, interrupted the exchange. "Captain, can you come down here now? I've found something!"

Kate took a deep breath. "Mac, can you manage all this by yourself?"

"Sure, no problem." Teresa looked disappointed. "Let me know if it's anything neat," she said wistfully.

"Don't worry!"

Several minutes later, Kate arrived in the science lab, struggling to maintain the appearance of calm disinterest. "What's up?"

"Look, here, through the ocular. Can you see?"

"But—the thing's alive!" Kate jumped back at the sight of the living creature. She couldn't help it as her heart pounded with a fear she hadn't expected and, for the moment, couldn't control.

"Not alive, Captain. At least, not living as an animal is

living, so far as I can tell. I'm trying to use the term *animate* for now."

"That's beside the point, dammit! You—you said you'd tell me when it woke up!"

"Captain," Luttrell turned to her, a solicitous look on his face, "you're perfectly safe. We're insulated by several layers of plastex and vacuum. It can't hurt us." He covered her hand with his, until she drew back. "You must control your fear. What would the crew think?"

She stiffened. "You'd like them to see me like this, wouldn't you?"

"I don't know what you're talking about."

"I'll bet you don't." To Kate's relief, her sudden anger at Luttrell made her unreasoned panic easier to control, and she began to feel that she was in charge of herself again. "How long has the thing been alive? All right, *animate*, if you insist."

"Slightly more than half an hour."

"Half an hour? Doctor, I left you with orders to let me know as soon as it woke up."

"I apologize, Captain. I was distracted."

"Well, don't let it happen again. I can't afford to have my people getting distracted so easily." She turned back to the sealed environment containing the kite. "Wait a minute. This doesn't make any sense." She looked at Luttrell. "Why is this thing alive? We haven't even had it aboard ship for five hours yet!"

"I placed a CLT construct in with it." He pointed. The kite had molded itself perfectly to the surface of the small cultivated living tissue construct, covering it almost entirely. "The skin surface on it is similar to that used for cyborgs."

"No, no, I'm not talking about that. The *time*, Luttrell— it should have taken *days* for this thing to come alive, not hours! What's going on?" She folded her arms and gazed directly at him. "Is there something you haven't told me about this yet?"

He made some entries on the console keyboard and studied the results before answering her. "I can only offer a theory, Captain. When you arrived on the *Opal*, the kites had been undisturbed since the *Hercules* mission—several years. We have no data from the *Hercules* at all on how long they were exposed before anything happened. Another difference is the amount of space we're operating with—the rooms in Roanoke are very large, and Rory's and Mishima's body heat probably dissipated very quickly because it was chilly in there as well. This setup here," he indicated the sealed environment, "is very closed in. Not only is the air warm, but the kite can only get half a meter or so from the construct. And the kites were last triggered just a little over a year ago."

"You think it might take less time to trigger them the more often it happens?" she asked.

"Especially in a closed environment such as this. But the time might decrease anyway with the frequency, despite the amount of surrounding space involved." He leaned forward, his face animated. "You have to understand, Captain, this is a new life-form, and we have nothing to compare it to. All life has variables in its cycles. I'll certainly work on it further, but it will probably take years before we can be sure of the timing—if we ever are."

"Terrific." She stared thoughtfully at the kite. "How does this CLT-construct thing work?"

"It's plugged into a life-support board that supplies it with blood and other fluids, to maintain it," Luttrell said. "As far as the kite can tell, it is on whole, living tissue. Which, of course, was the idea."

"Why?"

"Because, despite the small space in the chamber, ambient warmth alone was not enough to animate it. Dr. Chavez's notes repeatedly referred to *body* heat, rather than ambient heat." He paused, turning back to the sealed environment with its faintly pulsing inhabitant. "She was correct, it seems."

Kate continued to stare at the kite, both fascinated and repulsed. "Well, this is very interesting. Was there anything else you wanted to show me?"

"Indeed. Look more closely. I'll increase the magnification."

Ready for what she would see this time, Kate was able to put her eyes to the ocular. Against the dark slate gray of the kite's skin, if it could be called that, she could see darker specks moving about. There were also some on the CLT construct, though they didn't appear to stay for long.

"Those things look like miniature kites!" she said.

"Yes, don't they?" He seemed a little distracted. "I call them 'mites,' though of course I'll have to name them formally for the paper. If you look closely, you can just barely see them with the naked eye."

"You're going to write a paper on this?" she asked, turning back to face him.

"Of course. Probably several, in fact." He looked at her, surprised. "This is one of the most important discoveries there's been, and must be published properly. You . . . don't object, do you?"

"No," she gazed at him for a moment, "no, I don't object. You do what's right." She turned back to the image. "What do you think they are?" she asked, glancing at him over her shoulder.

"I suspect we'll have to make that up as we go along." He smiled slightly, and she could see that his mind was on bigger things, such as the stir his paper would create when he presented it. So, the thought of scientific renown was exciting to the good doctor, was it?

"All the microbial extraterrestrials found so far have fit into already existing classifications. However, these . . . creatures are so much more complex," he continued, "I may actually have to name a new kingdom to be able to classify the nomenclature."

"Kingdom?"

"The highest named grouping of things as we know them. Animal, mineral, vegetable, and now . . . a fourth." His smile grew. "It'll have to be approved, but whatever I come up with will, traditionally, have first consideration."

"What about the kites? Are they related?"

"I don't know yet. All I can say now is that they're similar—living, but not quite alive; not quite animal, but not quite plant."

"Oh." She contemplated them for a moment longer. "Well, what do the mites do?"

"I'm not sure yet."

"You must have some ideas."

"Well . . ." He paused thoughtfully. "They seem to move back and forth between the kite and the CLT construct as though they were designed to behave that way. Since this is only a skin-surface construct and not a living being, I have no way of knowing if we're seeing the entire cycle or not. But I have a feeling that there may be symbiosis here."

"Do you mean," she hesitated, "some kind of relationship between the kites, the mites, and . . . a host?"

"Yes, I think it's a good possibility, especially with the behavior that Teresa described seeing in the murals. Of course, I'll have to observe more before I can say anything definite. I'd like to study the murals myself."

"Well, you've got plenty of time. We've only been here eight days, so you have twelve left." She thumped him on the shoulder. "Keep up the good work, Doctor—you might save your ass yet!" She grinned at him and walked from the lab.

The look he sent after her was not at all friendly.

Luttrell's research took time. It was six days after his original discovery of the mites before he made his next major breakthrough in understanding the complex relationship between the kites, the newly christened mites, and their major hosts, the slender creatures of the beautiful moving artwork.

His initial observation still seemed correct. There was apparently a symbiotic relationship shared by the three creatures. Luttrell had spent hours studying the murals and had gotten some insight into the patterns of the aliens' daily lives, because it appeared that that's what the story pictures showed. To the crewmembers of the *Pegasus*, it made as much sense as the reminders of home most spacers carried.

From the murals he had gotten the idea of setting up an extremely complicated CLT construct, one that allowed him to simulate a small but complete body section rather than just the surface. When completed, it resembled—with some imagination—a pasty, flaccid forearm, with bone, muscles, nerves, and tendons all in their appropriate places. Blood and fluids were channeled between the forearm construct, a lung-cell construct, and a primitive vertebrate brain construct, so that the entire formation was an independent, closed cycle.

He had taken days, with considerable assistance from Pete, to get everything just right, and he was very proud of it, particularly the brain construct.

When Luttrell had finally transferred the kite to his CLT full-function construct ("the arm," as he was fond of calling it), he was startled at how rapidly things changed. The almost microscopic mites swarmed to the surface of the arm, though never far from their kite minor host, and insinuated themselves into the cultivated skin. He hesitated to call it biting; it was more like burrowing. For a long time he completely missed the fact that they then injected a substance and, more important, absorbed fluids in turn. Once he realized this, most of the remainder of his research time had been spent in analyzing this important exchange.

The entire crew of the *Pegasus* was assembled in the science lab for a briefing on his latest discovery.

"First, let me begin with the kites—*platyrhombus thermophilus*." He cleared his throat.

"Platy-whoziwhatsis?" Grayson interrupted.

"It's Latin for flat, square-shaped, liking heat. Is that satisfactory?" Luttrell asked somewhat stiffly.

"Oh, pardon me." Grayson settled back, covering his mouth to hide a smile.

Luttrell continued, "I have determined that the kites here on this planet are not the same as those pictured in the murals. The pictured creatures may well be living animals—I can't tell. Our local kite, however, while indeed organic, is definitely not animal." He paused to enjoy the surprise that this announcement caused. "If anything, its cellular structure resembles that of a plant, though of course it is not truly vegetable, either—not as we understand it."

"A plant? With that kind of behavior?" Al asked. "Then again, I suppose . . ." His voice trailed off.

"Oh, I don't mean for you to think of them as plants. I merely suspect they were engineered from a vegetablelike matter. If that is the case, it is certainly far beyond anything we have accomplished, even in our work with LSH units."

"For what purpose do you think they were engineered?" Teresa asked.

"We may never know for certain, unless we have the

good fortune to meet the builders of this place, but I do have a theory, based on my study of the murals. The kites appear to act as protective body covering, clothing if you will, with a little something extra, as I will explain when we get to the mites.

"The creatures depicted in the murals are obviously not native to this world, but at some point in their history they developed space travel. Perhaps those planetary kites were unsuited for leaving their home planet, perhaps they simply did not perform appropriate functions to allow their major hosts to travel in space. I believe these alien beings engineered similar constructs to protect them as they traveled, and those constructs are what we call the kites. The kites are incredibly tough and resilient, and in the murals we see the aliens wearing layers and layers of them. It is conceivable that they'd be very effective as a spacesuit, especially if they have the ability to transfer stored oxygen. Of course," he shrugged deprecatingly, "this is strictly conjecture. As I said, we may never know more than that."

Luttrell paused to smile at the assembled group, then reached up to flip a switch. "If you'll look at the monitor now, we can discuss the mites. They also appear to be engineered from a vegetable-based cell structure. Incidentally, I have formally named them *microrhombus Luttrelli*, though I will continue to call them mites for simplicity's sake."

Grayson snickered. "Why'd you name 'em after yourself?"

"As the discoverer, I'm allowed to recommend a name. It must be approved, also, like my name for the kites. These names specify genus and species only—from there, we will have to create higher classifications, all the way up to kingdom."

"Kingdom? Hey, as long as you're naming these things after yourself, you can call that Kenneth's Place," Pete suggested with a perfectly straight face.

"Sounds like a bar I used to hang out in," Al muttered as Teresa smothered a laugh.

"All right, you guys, let's get serious," Kate said sharply. "Kenneth is the only one of us who knows anything about these beasties—let's pay attention. We may need some of this later."

"Thank you, Captain." Luttrell cleared his throat. "As I was about to say, the mites burrow under the skin of the major host and release a chemical that is absorbed by the capillaries—the 'something extra' I mentioned earlier. This fluid contains a toxin, lipid-soluble and of very small molecular weight, which also appears to have been bio-engineered. I have isolated it here," he explained as Kate peered at the image displayed on SINS's monitor. They were now dealing with substances so small that the computer's image-enhancement capabilities were needed for them even to comprehend what they were seeing.

"Now, this is definitely a toxin and not a virus, as I had first feared. The reported influenzalike symptoms that certain of the *Black Opal*'s crewmembers exhibited misled me for quite a while before I realized they were mere side effects of the toxin as it traveled through the circulatory system."

"So what happens?" Teresa asked. "You get bitten by a mite, or burrowed, or whatever it does—and this stuff gets into your blood? Then what?"

"It crosses the blood-brain barrier and enters the brain." There was a silence.

"I don't get it," Pete said. "I mean, why would anybody wear something that was going to poison them?"

"We must assume that the chemical is not a toxin for them. We can only guess at what benefits they derive, though it must be important or they wouldn't have bothered to manufacture it. Now, this primitive vertebrate brain doesn't contain all the complexities of a human brain, so I must make some educated guesses as to what happened aboard the *Opal* past a certain point. In this primitive brain, the toxin seemed to have an affinity for certain groups of cells in the cortex. In humans it might be the neocortex or possibly the limbic system."

"Why those areas?" Kate asked.

"Because in humans, progressive destruction of cells in those areas of the brain causes dementia."

"Insanity," Kate murmured. She was beginning to feel a great relief. In Luttrell's simple explanation she could hear

Guil-Pro's first formal admission that something had actually been *wrong* with the crew of the *Black Opal*, and that she hadn't deserted a healthy, living crew. And she was beginning to get a glimmering of why she had been the only one to survive.

"How long do the mites live away from the kite?" she asked suddenly.

Luttrell looked a little startled. "I don't know, I haven't studied them long enough. They do venture away from the kite on the skin surface—I've actually observed that—but I haven't recorded the duration. And as far as their survival away from everything—for instance, in the air or on a suit surface—I don't know."

"But they can survive on the skin surface without a kite?" she persisted.

"I've observed them staying burrowed for a period of time, yes." He shrugged. "But how important that is . . ."

"Of course it's important!" Kate rose excitedly to her feet. "This *must* be why Greg and I never caught the disease on the *Opal*! Alicia and Vince handled Mishima *without* their suits very soon after they thawed him. Some of the mites must've stayed on him after they got rid of the kites, maybe burrowed under his skin, and that's when they were exposed! We never knew anything about any mites—we never got to that level of research. We simply assumed the disease was caused by the kites, and then transmitted from person to person like a virus. Greg and I were always sealed off from them—we were never exposed to the *mites*!"

"Of course that's possible, Captain, but—"

"That's right, Doctor, it's *possible*—about as possible as anything else you've been talking about for the last fifteen minutes. But if I'm right, it means the mites are the danger, not the kites." She sighed. "Have you been able to analyze the toxin yet?"

"No, I had to see what its effects were first."

"Well, you continue that research, but don't get too carried away with your new kingdom." She saw him frown. "I want a way to counteract that toxin or to control the mites. I don't care which answer you find first, as long as you find one of them. We need protection in case there's an accident. That's your top priority."

"Very well, Captain," he said frostily.

"I have one more question," Teresa said.

Luttrell looked at her attentively.

"When the kites are dormant, like inside Roanoke, are the mites dormant, too?"

"I don't know yet. When the mites are on an animate kite, they stay just beneath its surface. The kites go dormant as a survival technique when there are no hosts. The mites may also, but then again," he shrugged and smiled, "they may not."

CHAPTER

15

Time was growing short for the mission. The crew of the *Pegasus* had slightly more than three days left before they were scheduled to leave, and Kate was beginning to look forward to the end of the mission with an actual feeling of accomplishment. After all, they'd had some remarkable successes, when she looked at it. Luttrell had made tremendous strides in his research in a short period of time and in less than ideal working conditions, as he continually reminded her. He had even discovered, rather to their surprise, that the mites were very easy to kill.

"If they've burrowed under the surface of a kite," he had told the crew, "they are virtually indestructible. Somehow the kite forms a protective seal over the mite, whether it is dormant or not. But if they are on the kite's surface, or anywhere else, even water will destroy them. Now I'd advise using something more viscous than water if there's a choice, just to be safe, perhaps a disinfectant foam or a spray with oil or some other substance that will create a film."

So they were safe even from accidents now, and Kate was satisfied.

Of course, Luttrell still had access to SINS and the information it had from previous missions, some of which she suspected she had never seen herself, but Kate always managed not to think about that part of it. After all, wasn't it more important that they were nearly finished here, and no one had been killed or even hurt? (*Don't think about the winch accident, Katie. Depressed? Take another drink before bed.*)

But they *were* doing well here, and that would pay off when they returned home. This mission might have been the best thing to happen to her, after all that earlier mess. Could it be that Kagen had done her a favor? (*Don't think about Mishima, Katie, or what you had to do to Alicia before you left the* Opal. *We're really doing fine here, and Kagen will like that.*)

They were going back out to Roanoke to get Luttrell a second kite for comparison studies. Kate was no longer afraid of the creatures—it was hard to fear something they were actually beginning to understand—so Teresa went out with Pete and Grayson while she and Al sat at the scanners. Luttrell, as always, was hard at work in the lab.

"Pete, you and Grayson collect Luttrell's sample," Kate ordered as she settled herself into position on the bridge.

"Will do," Grayson's voice came back through the speaker.

"Teresa, you wanted to work outside?" Kate asked.

"Right. I want a chunk of Roanoke itself to examine, and I thought I'd look at a part of the exterior away from where we've been working. It's something Al and I are doing together."

Kate cast a quick sideways glance at Al, who sat next to her at the controls, but he was making an adjustment and didn't notice.

"All right, but check in every fifteen minutes," she said.

She watched Al until he finished and leaned back in his seat, then she reached over and touched the quiet button. "What're you two up to?" she asked.

He looked at her and frowned slightly.

"I'm sorry," she said quickly, "I shouldn't have used the term *up to*. I don't mean to sound like you're doing something wrong."

Al relaxed a little. "It was Teresa's idea, really. You know she's been working on the composition of Roanoke itself."

"Mmm. She thinks it's growing."

"Well, she's onto something. And she decided that Luttrell isn't going to be the only one to make a scientific name for himself on this trip. So," he looked away from her, but Kate could see a smile tug at the corners of his mouth, "she wants to run a side-by-side analysis of a kite and a piece of the building."

"Why?"

"She thinks there's a good chance the two are derived from the same substance." He looked back at her again. "I think she's right."

"What made her think of this?"

"Some of the things Luttrell has let drop. He's not all that interested in the kites, you know, not since he discovered the mites. And she's planning to use some of his notes."

"Oh? I didn't think he'd be that cooperative." Kate raised her eyebrows.

"I daresay he wouldn't be. I don't remember saying, though, that she was going to ask him." Again Al hid a slight smile. "She's not a computer expert for nothing."

Kate's brows rose even higher. "I'll be interested to hear the results of all this."

"With luck we'll know more very soon." Al turned back to his monitors.

"We're at Roanoke now," Grayson's voice came over the radio. "Pete and I are going inside, and Mac is proceeding around to our left."

"Okay, I have her beacon on the grid," Al acknowledged. "How far around are you going, Teresa?"

"Until I see something interesting."

Teresa waved at Grayson and Pete as she left them behind, then turned her attention to where she was heading. It was about time they started exploring some new areas. She had been getting tired of seeing the insides of the same eight or nine rooms.

In the background on her radio she could hear the others' conversations—when she was suited, she always kept the volume down so that the constant chatter wouldn't drive her crazy. It was nice to know the others were there, but...

"Al, may I have my computer link, please?" she asked. "I want to date this section and compare it to where we've been hanging around."

When the green light on her hand-held scanner came on, she aimed it randomly at the structure and waited for the results on her tiny screen. Interesting. This section was a little newer, according to SINS.

"Thanks," she called. "You can kill it."

She walked on for a time, with only background conversations and the sound of her own breathing in her ears.

Roanoke was truly massive. Walls jutted up away from her into the misty atmosphere, and went on forever in front of her, so that she began to lose track of just how far she had gone.

"MacKessen reporting in," she called dutifully as the alarm she had set to remind herself went off quietly in her ear. "Any idea how far I've come?"

"One hundred seventy-five meters," Kate reported. "You're not getting tired?"

"No, I just lost track of how long I'd been walking." She paused again and stared upward. The hulking structure was beginning to oppress her, along with the watery sunlight creeping over the horizon. Although it was just after dawn, planet-time (they never went outside the ship at night), she knew it would never get much brighter than this, even at noon. They had never seen what color the sky was.

She was drawn sharply out of her reverie by the appearance of an airlock in the side of the structure. Wondering for a moment if she had completely circled Roanoke, she called her ship.

"According to the locator grid you're not quite halfway around," Al told her. "Why?"

"I've found an airlock. Thought I'd come clear around the other side."

"I suppose you want to go inside," Kate said after a pause.

"Yeah, I do. We can be pretty sure at this point, I think, that there's nothing dangerous in there."

"All right, but I want you to report back every five minutes."

Teresa reset her alarm, then walked up to the airlock. Somewhat gingerly she extended her hand, and felt the familiar sensation of heat. The entryway irised open before her.

"Okay, I'm inside." At that moment the lock shut behind her, leaving her in total darkness. She gasped.

"Are you all right?"

"I'm fine! But it's pitch dark in here."

"Be extremely careful where you step," Kate ordered. "And if the interior itself is dark, I want you to back out. Nobody explores alone in total darkness—got that?"

"Loud and clear." Teresa held her hand out before her again and took a few steps, steeling herself to meet the opposite wall. Again she felt heat, and the way before her opened.

"Well, it's lit," she reported. "Very dimly, but enough to see by."

"How does it look?" Al asked.

"Pretty much the same, like a small antechamber. The atmosphere isn't breathable, though—that means I'm in new territory!" She scuffed her feet on the floor. "Lots of kites, too. Al, let me have my computer link again. Might as well find out how old this part is."

When the green telltale appeared, Teresa began to walk around the perimeter of the small room, aiming her handheld randomly. "Holy shit, this place is less than four hundred years old! That's over a hundred years off our original reading!"

"Sounds like a good place to collect your sample," Al said.

"It'll have to be a small one," she said with a laugh. "I walked too damn far to carry something very big!"

As she worked Teresa could hear in the background the muted conversations as Kate reported her findings to the other party. It made her even more determined that Luttrell was not going to be the only member of this crew to make a name for himself! She couldn't wait until she and Al could start their tests.

"That does it," she reported some minutes later, as she disassembled her cutting tool and put everything away in her sample bag. "I'm going to wander around for a little while. I still have plenty of air, don't I?"

"Almost an hour," Al told her. "But remember, it took you twenty minutes to get there, so don't push it too close."

Teresa immediately headed for a doorway she assumed would lead her from the small antechamber to the main part of the building. She only hoped it would be lit. Even if she disobeyed Kate's order and tried to explore in darkness, her portable lamp wouldn't illuminate enough to make it worthwhile.

When the entry opened before her, she found herself in a room of dizzying proportions. This was bigger than the basement chamber! And in the center was a great crater, with smooth, sloping sides.

"We'll need the winch here," she reported. "There's a huge depression in the middle of the room. It'd probably be all right to walk down without help, but I wouldn't want to take the chance of falling. It's pretty far to the bottom."

"Play it safe and leave it for the next trip," Kate's voice came back.

Teresa walked toward the lip of the crater, watching for signs of crumbling or weakness in the flooring as she approached. Finally she stood at the edge. She couldn't see the bottom, or all the way across, and now she found that the sides were not as smooth or steep as they had appeared from a distance. There were occasional projections at uneven intervals, like upthrust rocks, and the sides looked rather soft. She put her foot over the edge, testing. It came away without leaving a print, but she had definitely not stepped on a natural rock surface.

Something on the slope below and slightly to her left caught her eye. It was an odd-shaped lump, very different from anything else she could see. Forgetting her earlier concerns about falling, she quickly tied a guy line to the nearest projection and began to descend cautiously toward her unusual target, moving diagonally down the slope, slipping once or twice, but never enough to lose her footing. She drew closer, thought she could make out something in the dim light. . . .

"Mac? Goddammit, Teresa, *answer me!*" Kate's voice crackled in her ears.

Teresa shook herself and looked around, realizing that the woman must have called her several times already. "MacKessen here," she stammered, staring down at the incongruous thing that lay at her feet.

"Are you all right? What the hell happened? Couldn't you *hear* me?"

"I—I'm sorry. I lost track of—of time." Teresa quavered, and knew she was losing track of her voice as well.

There was a body at her feet, all too human, encased in a spacesuit not much different from her own. The faceplate was shattered, mercifully lined with thousands of tiny cracks that hid whatever was beneath it. There was a long tear in the shoulder, probably where it had struck the projection after a fall, and it was obvious that kites had been at work long ago.

"Well, don't do that, for Christ's sake! There's reasons for checking in every five minutes!"

"I—I know, I'm sorry. It won't happen again."

"Are you sure you're all right?"

"Yes . . . yes . . ." Teresa felt tears in her eyes as she stared down at the Guil-Pro logo on the figure's chest and shoulders, shining extra-bright in the light of her lamp. And there, beneath the logo, was the name of the ship, glittering like a star in the surrounding dimness . . . *Hercules*. Her brother's ship, the one Guil-Pro said he'd stolen, and died in . . . it was here instead . . . oh, God, they'd died *here* instead. . . .

Teresa backed away hastily, but skidded on the sloping surface and fell. Holding tightly to the guy line, she used her weight and momentum to scramble as far from the corpse as she could before starting to pull herself back up the slope.

"Teresa, what the hell are you doing?" Kate's voice was charged with real concern.

"Nothing! Nothing—I slipped!" Teresa tried to keep the catch out of her voice as she struggled to her feet, fighting for her balance and her hold on the line. She stumbled back up the now-treacherous slope, falling several more times, once nearly rolling back down.

Oh God, oh God, what was Jamie's ship doing here? What was going on? She pulled herself up faster, awkwardly running, until her life-support system couldn't keep up and her faceplate fogged over from her exertions. Finally she reached the top of the slope, scrambled, yanked her line off, and kept going, not paying attention, for the moment, to whether she was moving toward the connecting door or away from it.

"Teresa, stay put," Kate ordered. "I'm coming after you."

"No, Captain," it was Al's voice, "you stay here. I'll get her."

"No!" Teresa almost screamed at them, then swallowed and forced herself to sound calmer. "No, I'm all right!"

She stopped, breathing heavily, realizing that not only could Kate and the others hear her labored breathing, but if she wasn't careful she could get lost. She took several deep breaths, made herself walk, got back in control. Her faceplate cleared and she could see again. It was a good thing she'd stopped running—she was nearly past the door back to the airlock antechamber.

"Do you think you can follow an order now, computer specialist?" Kate's voice was quiet in her ears.

"I—I'm sorry—I'm okay now." She hadn't quite caught her breath. "Don't let Al come after me, please. It's not necessary. I just got turned around in that big room, and I couldn't see the door anymore. I guess I got a little phobic for a minute, and panicked. Then I fell when I started to run."

"You're all right now?" Kate's voice sounded relieved.

"I'm fine, really. Check the monitors. Just a little out of breath still."

"Come on back to the ship, then. You lost five minutes of air running around and panting like that."

"Yeah. Yeah, I'm coming back now." Without a glance behind her, Teresa passed through the dark airlock and out of Roanoke.

When she arrived back at the *Pegasus*, Pete and Grayson

were there ahead of her. Her scare had made them all decide they'd done enough work. Kate too was waiting.

Even before Teresa took off her helmet, Kate could see how pale the young woman's face was—and how expressionless.

"You sure you're all right? You were pretty damn quiet on the walk back."

Teresa removed her helmet and set it aside. Her hair was soaked, plastered to her head and face. She looked for a moment as though she might pass out.

Kate pulled an emergency oxygen mask down from one of the bulkhead compartments and held it out to her. "No arguments, either. Breathe!" She pushed the mask against the woman's face.

Teresa stopped undressing long enough to take several gulps of air before turning her head aside. "Yeah, I'm okay. Thanks."

Kate saw the improved color in her cheeks and nodded. "Take it easy for a while, will you? Pete, check her suit out, just in case."

Teresa finished undressing, left her suit on the bench, and walked away, the precious sample case looped over one shoulder. Kate took a step to follow her, then hesitated.

"If you don't mind my sayin', Captain, something's wrong with that young lady, and it's nothing to do with her suit."

"I know, Pete. But I can't make her talk to me." Kate sighed. "Can I?"

Kate wandered apprehensively about the ship, a flask cradled carefully in a large pocket of her baggy work pants, half-hoping she would run into Teresa. She'd already checked the science lab, but only Luttrell was there.

Something was wrong. Teresa *never* lost her sense of direction—she was the best pathfinder in the crew! As for being phobic, well ... Kate just shook her head as she climbed down the ladder to Deck 2. Mac was going to have to come up with a better story than that.

The passages on Deck 2 were smaller, the lights dimmer than in the main portion of the ship, but Kate barely noticed. To her surprise (she told herself), she found herself outside the bright red door to the frankenstein's cubicle. She rocked back on her heels, took a good slug from the flask, and debated whether to go inside.

Ah, what the hell? she thought, turning away. *The little fucker is fast asleep—why should I disturb him?*

She continued on down the corridor. The taste of scotch was heavy in the back of her throat. "Horrible stuff," she murmured. "Don't know why I drink it."

That was a good question, now that she thought about it. Why was it that every time something strange happened (which was quite often on this trip, truth be told), she felt obliged to drink? She thought she'd improved a little, with things going well, but here she was again, gulping scotch....

"Hello?" She paused in front of a recess in the corridor. Teresa was seated on an access hatch in the alcove, leaning against the wall, sample case clutched in her lap. She looked up. "Can I talk to you?"

"Sure." Kate propped her foot on the edge of the hatch and leaned her elbow on her knee. "What's on your mind?" The flask had disappeared back into the large pocket; with luck, Teresa hadn't noticed it. But the younger woman apparently had other things on her mind.

"Well, it's ... I ..." Teresa's composure crumbled suddenly, and her voice broke. "Kate, I found a—I found some-body—"

"Found somebody? What do you mean?" Kate caught her by the shoulders. "Where?"

"It was a body—a *human* body, in a spacesuit—" She was crying now. "Oh, Kate, the suit said *Hercules*...."

"Where was this?" Kate repeated.

"In Roanoke. In the crater."

Kate leaned back against the wall as sober as she had ever been as she realized the import of what Teresa was telling her. My God, she had thought this was finished. Things had been going so well, and now she was back in the middle of it again. A body, for God's sake! God*dammit*, why couldn't Teresa have left well enough alone....

She covered her face with her hands until she felt more in control, at least for Teresa's sake. It wasn't her fault she'd found the damn body, after all. What a shock that must have been! No wonder she had run, and run, and run. . . .

Kate remembered something then, something she'd almost forgotten in the routine of the mission, in the possibility of success. She didn't want just to survive this mission, just to do a job. That would never be enough. She wanted revenge.

Kate gazed thoughtfully down at Teresa. And now a new puzzle, on top of everything else—one more thing to worry about. Teresa and the *Hercules*. What did they mean to each other?

The younger woman finally caught her breath. "I'm sorry."

Kate leaned sideways, forced herself to relax a little. "I think it's time to talk."

Teresa wiped her eyes on her sleeve. "No. No, I'd better go." She stood. "I'm supposed to be on duty."

Kate pushed her back hard enough to make her sit abruptly. "I'm tired of one-sided conversations, Mac. There's too much at stake for me not to know everything that's going on. Consider this an order—talk to me."

Teresa was silent.

"What's the *Hercules* got to do with you?" Kate pressed.

"Nothing."

"You're a lousy liar." Kate crouched until she was on eye level with her. "I said this before, and I still mean it. If Luttrell's gotten to you, I want to know about it. Whatever you tell me won't go any farther than right here. But I *have* to know what's going on."

Teresa let her breath out slowly. "I lied to get onto this mission."

"About what?" Kate deliberately kept her voice neutral.

"My name. MacKessen's not my real name. I mean, it is, but it's my mother's name."

"And Harlin is *my* mother's name. The women in my family have been doing that for generations. It's not illegal—I'm sure Guil-Pro doesn't care." She tried to reassure. "I don't."

"That's not the problem," Teresa continued doggedly. "My father's name, which is my legal name," she hesitated, "is Travers."

They were both quiet now; Kate watched Teresa, and Teresa watched the deck.

"So you're Jim Travers's little sister," Kate finally said, and rose slowly to her feet.

"I—" Teresa stopped. "You knew Jamie?"

"We shipped out together a couple of times." Kate smiled a little. "We even slept together. We were buddies."

"Th-then you know he was on the *Hercules* when it disappeared."

"I know." Kate's eyes narrowed. "It wasn't his body you found, was it?"

"No. Thank God!" Teresa drew a shaky breath.

"How had this one died? Could you tell?"

"The faceplate was cracked, and there was a tear in the shoulder. It looked like kites had gotten in there, a long time ago. I couldn't see, and . . . well, I didn't really try."

"I don't blame you." Kate was silent for a moment. "Why didn't you want me to know all this?"

Teresa flushed. "Don't you know the story?"

"Most of it. The *Hercules* was prospecting, and her crew jumped a big claim when they struck it rich. Ran off with their stake, their ship, and a lot of potential Guil-Pro profits. Piracy charges were brought, I think." Kate recited the whole publicly known story. "It's a lousy story, but what's it got to do with you? That was a long time ago. You couldn't have been much more than a kid."

"Yeah!" Teresa laughed, and the sound of it grated on Kate's ear. "What do you think it's like, being a Travers in this business after what they said my brother had done?"

"Pretty tough. But it couldn't have been too bad. You're here, aren't you?" Kate hesitated, wondering how to proceed. "I guess I can't figure why you're so uptight about it."

"Did you know that Guil-Pro hired bounty hunters?" Teresa's voice was painfully on edge. "That's how my brother died, you know. They were chased by bounty hunters, and they had an accident, or there was a confrontation—something, the stories were all different." She had to stop for a moment. "Didn't you know that Guil-Pro is still investigating the case? They didn't get all their money back, goddamn them! They think Jamie hid some of it, and told somebody in the family where." She looked up, her eyes bright. "Captain, they're looking for *me*!"

"Oh, God," Kate said softly. "Did Luttrell tell you that?" Teresa nodded.

"What exactly did he threaten you with?"

The younger woman stared at the deck. "He, uh, he said you were in trouble with Guil-Pro, and that's why you were out here. I know you told us that yourself, but—well, he made it sound a lot worse."

"That's because it is worse. But go on."

"He said you still owed them a lot for keeping you out of some other earlier trouble, and—and that you'd go pretty far to get out from under that. To get square with them."

"Oh?" Kate gave a sudden laugh. "Even so far as turning you in, was that it?"

"Well . . . yeah."

"And you believed him."

The younger woman had the grace to be embarrassed. "He was very convincing."

"I bet he was." Kate paused. "He thinks pretty quick on his feet—which makes him more dangerous than I'd thought."

"What do you mean?"

"I figured he was kind of stupid, just somebody following orders. It looks like I was wrong."

There was an awkward silence.

"Then you, ah—you don't care?" Teresa asked hesitantly.

"What? Oh, you mean because you're Jim Travers's sister, and Guil-Pro's still looking for you?" Kate smiled briefly and shook her head. "Teresa, even if I wanted to I couldn't turn you in. Luttrell lied. Guil-Pro isn't looking for you." She sighed and rubbed the crease between her eyebrows. "In fact, they're not looking for anybody, or anything."

"They're not?" Teresa stared at her.

Kate shook her head. "Guil-Pro lied about the *Hercules* mission."

"Well, I—I admit I was a little confused when I saw the body. I know a lot about Jamie's last trip—the *Hercules* wasn't supposed to have gotten this far, though Epsilon Indi was on the original flight plan." Teresa's voice shook briefly. "Do you know what really happened?"

Kate looked at her for a long moment. "Now that's a story, all right." She paused, groping for the right words. "The *Hercules* discovered this place, and reported it to Guil-Pro because of the evidence of intelligent alien life."

"*They* discovered Roanoke?"

"That's right. Only they didn't know any better, and they weren't careful enough, I guess. What they discovered killed them, just like what happened to the *Black Opal*." Kate gave a rueful little smile. "We never seem to learn. But nobody jumped a claim, and nobody stole a ship. In fact..." She paused. "Jim flew the *Hercules* off the planet and destroyed it because he thought he'd been infected." She saw Teresa grimace, and reached out to touch her shoulder. "He was a hero, Teresa. He did that because he was afraid of what he might do if he went crazy."

Teresa took a shaky breath. "I'm glad you told me that," she said softly. "I wanted to know."

Kate nodded.

"What about the *Opal*?" Teresa asked after a pause. "I thought—"

"We weren't any better off. Before we even left Equator Station, Guil-Pro already knew a whole lot about this place. The *Opal* was a dummy mission, to get the one thing the *Hercules* had failed to get for them. A sample."

"So you *did* know about it!"

Kate shook her head. "Oh, no. Our discovery had to look like an accident, even to us. Guil-Pro had already lied about the *Hercules* to cover up the original find—how could they take all that back later? Embarrassing, to say the least." Her lips twisted. "It was easier just to set us up."

"I don't understand."

Kate sighed, realizing she would have to tell Teresa the whole ugly story. "Look, it's too much to go over here. Let's go back to my quarters where it's comfortable, and private. I'll—I'll explain everything."

Teresa sat stiffly against the seat's hard back, staring at the nearly empty bottle of scotch that stood sentinal between her and her captain. "Those bastards," she whispered. "Jamie was just a scapegoat."

"Jim was *dead*!" Kate said harshly. "Guil-Pro could make up any story they needed, and nobody would argue because Jim and his crew were *dead*!"

Teresa winced. "And they made you a part of it, too."

"Yeah, we were the lucky ones, all right, hand picked for the job. Kagen told me as much."

"And what he did to you with Rory . . ."

Kate said nothing. Somehow, moved by Teresa's story, she had found the courage to talk about Rory, and Kagen, and how she felt she had been set up for this, or something like it, many years ago—she and Rory had been friends and lovers long before the last voyage of the *Black Opal*. She had no doubt that Geoffrey Kagen was a man of vision, farseeing enough to have planned a situation like this without knowing exactly what the future would hold.

And in telling someone the *whole* story, finally, Kate could feel her puzzlement and hurt begin to ease, though she would always be angry. But maybe now she wouldn't have to look around every corner, fearing to see that crooked smiling face, those bright, bright blue eyes, the black curly hair . . . or, if she did see Rory, it would be for what he was—a soulless machine, capable only of the deception of love and friendship.

"What he did to me with Rory," Kate finally said, "has damned him forever."

Teresa wrapped her arms about her knees and hugged them to her chest, as if seeking warmth. "You know," she said softly, "I'm really sorry I didn't believe what George told me."

"What was that?"

"Before we hit the outer terminus, I complained because I was bored. He told me to enjoy it while it lasted—and I thought he was crazy." She paused. "God, what I wouldn't give for a little boredom right now!"

Kate looked at her. "I don't mean to insult you, but what the hell are you even doing on a mission like this?"

"I . . . This is going to sound stupid. I'm not even sure I can convince myself anymore." Teresa sighed. "I wanted to find out as much as I could about what really happened to Jamie. The only thing I could think of was to work where he worked, and to make friends with his friends."

"And those friends told you to come out here?" Kate raised a disbelieving eyebrow.

Teresa looked miserably uncomfortable. "I know it sounds dumb, but let me try to explain. I trained for space work, and bummed around until I got pretty good. Then I hired on to Guil-Pro, and I talked to people."

"Could they help you?"

"Not much. I heard rumors mostly. A lot of people thought Jamie had been screwed over."

"But no proof."

"No, there wasn't any proof. Just a gut feeling—but it was enough!" She was defiant, sensing Kate's skepticism. "Goddammit, you *can't* always prove everything! Sometimes you have to—"

"Hey, hey, take it easy." Kate laid a hand on her shoulder. "Don't you think I understand that? Look at the story I've just told you—what proof do you think I have, other than one or two things that may've gone up in smoke months ago? But it's a hell of a gut feeling that makes you sign on to a mission like this—I'm out here because I *have* to be."

"Well, it wasn't all gut feeling," Teresa confessed. "All the stories said the *Hercules* never made it as far as Epsilon Indi, and I was willing to believe it until all this stuff came up with the *Black Opal*."

"But what good did you think coming out here would do?" Kate asked gently.

"I—I didn't know." Teresa hesitated. "When I first signed on, we were only coming out here to find out what happened to the *Opal*. It was strange to me, losing two ships in such a relatively short time, so I checked up on it. Guil-Pro has a real good safety record—they don't lose many ships. So I thought maybe something funny was going on, and maybe it would help me to come out here and see for myself."

"But the mission changed. Why'd you stick it out?"

"Because then it was an even better reason! The discovery of an alien structure and an alien life-form? What better excuse for things to go wrong?" She looked away. "One more screwy hope to add to my fairy tale."

"Fairy tale? Oh, I don't know. You turned out to be right, didn't you?"

Teresa stood abruptly and jammed her hands into her pockets. She walked across the captain's quarters and kicked her foot against the deck. "Believe me, I wish I hadn't!"

"You are rather in the middle of it now, that's true." Kate watched her.

"Luttrell wasn't lying when he said you were in real trouble with Guil-Pro, was he? I mean, it's what we've just been talking about, isn't it?"

"Oh, yes, that's it, all right. I know what happened out here, and Kagen is worried that I can prove it."

"But not while you're here."

"No, not while I'm here. And I've got to hand it to the bastard." Kate laughed ruefully. "He knows he'd be better off with me dead or frozen somewhere, but he also knows he might not be able to get away with it—thank God he's not sure! So he got me out of the way instead. And I'm not only doing a job he wants done, but I'm doing it on his terms!"

"How do you know he won't try to kill you out here?"

"Oh, I expected he would—actually, I suspect he may have tried already." Kate touched the bottle of scotch, but decided against having the last swallow, at least for the moment. "As long as it looks like an accident, Guil-Pro can get away with anything out here."

"How can you be so goddamn calm about the whole thing?" Teresa burst out suddenly.

Kate looked at her in surprise. "What do you want me to do, hide in my quarters?" She leaned back in her chair as the younger woman started to pace again.

"No, but it seems like you ought to be *doing* something!"

"I do. I get roaring drunk, remember?" Kate stretched her arms up over her head.

"Oh, shit that's not what I—"

"Goddammit, Mac, haven't you ever been so bloody sick and tired of something that it just doesn't matter anymore?" Kate said suddenly. "Haven't you ever just wanted to tell the world to get fucked and leave you alone in your little hole?"

Teresa stopped in surprise, shook her head.

"I didn't think so." Kate sighed. "Well, that's where I am right now. Things were going so well, and now this had to happen. Oh, God . . ." She grabbed at the bottle, stared at it briefly, then pushed it away again. "I am so tired of this whole fucking mess. I wish I could just go to sleep and never wake up. At least it would be someone else's problem."

Teresa stared at her, and thought about what Luttrell had said about the captain and her drinking. "Oh, wow, I . . . God, I'm sorry, Kate, I didn't mean . . ."

"Don't worry about it." Kate waved her hand. "It just means my acting is doing the job."

"The captain's always in control, right?" Teresa looked sober.

"The captain has to *look* that way, yeah."

"You don't think we can do anything?"

"What would you like me to do?"

"Cool Luttrell off. Kate, he scares me!"

"He should; he's dangerous. But I can't very well clap him in irons. They don't let you get away with that anymore."

"Not even if he's talking mutiny?"

"Proof, dear. We're sadly lacking in proof."

"What about the winch? We can prove that was sabotaged! And the body I found—we could tell them the whole story!"

Kate was shaking her head. "Proof again, kid. The *Hercules* crew could easily have come here *after* stealing their ship—and believe me, Guil-Pro would come up with that one quick enough if they had to!"

Teresa's face fell.

"And there's another problem," Kate added gently. "Luttrell might not be the only person on the crew who works for Kagen. We don't even know who else we can trust."

"But I can't just sit around the rest of the mission and ignore the problem—I'll go crazy!"

"You'll be busy enough," Kate said dryly, "because we're still going to do exactly the job we were sent out here to do."

Teresa stared at her in disbelief. "Even after all this? You can still even *think* about giving in to Kagen?"

Kate banged her fist against her desk, surprising even herself. "Goddammit, where was that attitude seven months ago? Where the *hell* were you and the rest of the crew when I told you what Guil-Pro was doing? You're not going to let it eat your lunch, remember? It's just another lousy job you're going to get fucking paid for doing—*remember*? Don't give me that bullshit now, it's too fucking late."

Teresa heard her earlier words echoed in Kate's outburst, and she could have bitten her tongue for what she'd just said. And she could never apologize enough for saying it.

"Oh, shit . . ." Kate ran her hands through her short hair. "I'm sorry, that was uncalled for." She smiled a little. "You see, I don't always manage to keep it in."

"No, I deserved that. I had no right to say what I did, not when you tried to do everything you could for us, and we didn't pay attention. It's just . . ." She looked up. "Well, you were right, in a way. I *do* care more now than I did seven months ago. It's gotten personal." She paced rapidly, with long strides. "Is it too much to ask? To see Kagen and Luttrell get fucked over for once, instead of somebody like you or me—or Jamie?"

"I've been asking myself the same question. And yeah, it's probably too much to ask. But it won't stop me from trying." Kate stared through the bottle. "Because I have to live with what Mishima looked like, running through the *Opal*, covered with kites and laughing . . . and I have to live with Rory . . ." She broke off. "But I have five other people on this crew to think about besides myself, and that's why we're going to do this job the way Kagen wants it done. That way maybe nobody'll get hurt."

"You ought to at least give the rest of them a choice. Maybe they'll want to help!"

Kate's voice was frosty. "I've already decided."

Teresa met her eyes briefly, then looked away. "Okay, so we don't tell anyone. We can still collect a sample and just make sure it never gets home. It would be real easy to take care of any notes Luttrell has made. Even SINS makes mistakes, and Luttrell's not very good with the system. . . ."

"Use your head, Mac. You signed a contract, remember? We *have* to bring a specimen home, or we've broken that contract! Sure, we could set up an accident. But Luttrell's watching me for just that kind of thing. Do you know what would happen if he could prove foul on us? Guil-Pro could sue us for breach of contract—not just you and me, but the whole crew! You know what that means? *We* pay off the price of the contract. You could never work for anyone else again—no one would touch you! Guil-Pro would own your soul!"

"What about the Guild?" Teresa asked, but her voice was a lot quieter.

"Sweetheart, nobody wants to mess with Guil-Pro. The Guild would drop us like hot refinery waste if Guil-Pro looked sideways at them!" Kate smiled grimly. "Besides, there's something you haven't thought of."

"I seem to be doing a lot of that today. What?"

"Suppose we pulled it off? Suppose we managed it so well that even Luttrell couldn't prove we'd screwed the works. No specimen, no data—a very pissed-off Guil-Pro." Kate paused. "How many kites do you think are in Roanoke?"

Teresa shook her head. "I couldn't begin to guess."

"Right. So we come home empty-handed. Kagen'll be pretty sure we pulled something, but he won't be able to prove it. He may try to get us anyway, because he'll need somebody to blame, but that's beside the point. What's to keep him from sending somebody else right back out here to finish the job we didn't do? Maybe somebody who wouldn't care as much about what it all means as we do."

"Oh, shit," Teresa muttered. "Well, let's get rid of all of them."

"Now wait a minute, think what you're saying. Do you want to destroy the whole building—all that artwork?"

"Oh, no, we couldn't do that! I didn't mean that at all! The artwork is too beautiful—and it might be the only remaining legacy of that race."

"Or look at it this way. Suppose they're still around. Don't you think they'd be mad if we blew up their property? We have no idea what this place is, how important it is to these people. They might even come looking for us."

"Now you've given me the creeps, dammit!"

"I just wanted to make sure you considered all the issues." Kate smiled. "Why don't you work on it? Maybe there's a clue in that sample you brought back—a way to destroy the kites without hurting the structure."

"But it's so big—we have no idea how big it is inside! And suppose we missed some? Even one left behind might be enough." Teresa frowned. "This is more trouble than I thought it would be."

Kate nodded. "I've been tangling with that one for a while myself." She paused, staring down at the deck for a moment. "Speaking of trouble, I want to show you something." She reached under her bed and pulled out a small strongbox. "You have a quick memory—learn this combination." She demonstrated as Teresa watched. "There's a small laser pistol in here. If there's trouble, especially if something happens to me, this'll be here if you need it. But only as a last resort, all right? It's not in the weapons inventory, and if you pull it out too soon, you'll lose the advantage of surprise. You with me?"

"I hope I don't need it," Teresa said quietly.

"So do I, but I like being prepared."

"Yeah." Teresa looked away and sighed. "What about the body I found?"

"Don't bring it up. Downplay the whole area—the crater, everything. We have enough work to do in two and a half days to keep us plenty busy without exploring over there. And we'll be better off if nobody else knows about what you found for now. And," Kate smiled, "I guess I won't start calling you Travers."

Later that day, long after Teresa had left, Kate pulled the flask from her pocket and stared at it. There was only a swallow left, just like the bottle on the desk. She debated whether to finish them off before she returned to duty. One for the road? For old times' sake? Yeah, for old times' sake, all right.

She tossed the flask, unopened, down the waste chute. The nearly empty bottle on the desk and a full bottle in her drawer followed. (Yes, she'd checked, and there was yet another one.) Let him leave all the presents he wanted, whoever he was. She'd had enough of that.

CHAPTER

16

Kate was tired. Once again she'd sat up too late, long past the start of her sleep period, working with SINS, trying to figure out her options. Her eyes hurt, her neck was stiff, her head ached. . . .

"Oh, enough!" she muttered, and pushed away from her console. She was in the captain's quarters—still hard to call them her own, even after all this time—and the idea that she could use a drink crossed her mind. But no, she'd already won that battle. She wasn't doing herself or the crew any good by drinking, even just to relax before bed at night. Besides, she now had an ally in Teresa MacKessen/Josephine Travers, and it behooved her to treat that relationship with the respect Teresa, at least, seemed to think it deserved.

All the same, she checked the drawer of her nightstand. It contained one full bottle, which she cradled thoughtfully in her hand. She wasn't really surprised to see it there. She had been finding bottles everywhere lately—ever since she had decided to quit drinking, matter of fact.

What bothered her was that the bottles kept appearing, no matter how many she threw away. It seemed she was being tempted to change her mind. And it was tempting right now, lord knows, to go back to the bad old ways.

"Goddamn you, whoever you are," she muttered, "I'm not that easy to get. Go after someone else!" She tossed the bottle down the waste chute.

—YOU ARE GOING TO DIE—

Kate glanced at her console screen, then looked away,

almost missing the five small words that had overwritten the work she had been doing.

"What?" She did a classic double-take, saw the words, read their meaning, and hit the print key, eager to have a record of SINS's eccentricity. Not the first time this had happened, either, she recalled.

The contents of her screen spewed from the printer—everything but the death threat. She looked back at the screen, and the warning was gone.

"Oh, shit." She rubbed her eyes, leaned her head on her hands. After a second she looked at the printout again, stared at it until her eyes burned. Only her own work, nothing more.

"Goddammit, SINS, what are you pulling?" she yelled. Angrily she threw the printout at the screen, but it only fluttered to the deck. Was the whole ship conspiring against her, just the way the *Black Opal* had?

"Shit, shit, shit," she murmured. Useless to scream at SINS. The computer could do nothing without programs—and programs were written by human beings. She knew that as well as she knew how to pilot a light-plus ship. So someone with a strange sense of humor had gotten into SINS's head. Funny.

(The Loon laughed in her ear, very close. "Funny," it repeated. "Funny, just like on the *Black Opal*, where the machine talked back and wouldn't obey . . . Who's gotten into SINS's head, Katie?" the Loon asked. "You know it's not Teresa. Who's left? Rory?")

Rory? Oh, my God . . . She keyed hasty commands on her console, then tapped her fingers anxiously until the image she wanted appeared on her screen. But no, the frankenstein slept peacefully; the readouts on her screen and the evidence of her own eyes showed her that. Nothing had changed.

("But we had to be sure, didn't we?" the Loon asked softly. "We still have to be sure he's all right." Its laughter echoed in her head.)

"Stop it, stop it!" she screamed, covering her ears with her hands as if that could shut out the mocking hoots. "Leave me alone, you fucking crazy bird! You only talk to me when I'm sick, and I'm not sick anymore, goddammit! I am *not* sick anymore!"

—YOUR TIME IS NEAR—

The words glared out at her from SINS's console, in the center of a blank screen. Even as she jumped, reaching for the print key, the message faded, leaving only its ghost behind.

Kate switched off her console, rose silently, and stripped. She took a hot shower, trying to scald out the chill she felt in her heart. It helped a little.

Resolutely she turned out her light and went to bed. Lying on her bunk in the dark privacy of the captain's quarters—*her* quarters, she reminded herself fiercely—she could feel hot tears welling in her eyes and sliding down her cheeks. Crying was a good release, or so she'd been told.

This wasn't supposed to be happening to her anymore. She wasn't supposed to be hearing the Loon, or watching for Rory (but she still was), or reading crazy messages from SINS—that part of this hell was over! She had stopped drinking, she had found a friend, an ally, someone else who understood why Guil-Pro was doing these things. She had no *time* to go crazy now! They only had two days left on this godforsaken mission—just two more days, if she could last that long....

After a while, she slept.

"Grayson? Grayson, d'you have a minute?" Luttrell paused in the doorway of the ship's small gymnasium.

"Yeah, I guess so." Grayson sat up on the bench where he'd been lifting weights and wiped his face. "What's up, *Kenneth*?"

Luttrell made a small face. "It's about the captain. I wouldn't have interrupted you, but I think it's important, and I don't often see you alone."

"Yeah, I like it that way."

Luttrell cleared his throat. "I'm trying to do you a favor, Grayson, since you're second in command."

"Something wrong?"

"Oh, no, nothing definite yet." Luttrell smiled, showing his white, even teeth. "It's just that I've run some psych-profiles on the crew, and the captain is not reacting too well on some of the stress points. I'm a little concerned."

"This isn't the first time you've said something like this." Grayson remembered the way Al had made light of some of his own earlier concerns. "You sure you know what you're talking about?"

"Knowing that kind of thing is my business, I assure you," Luttrell said somewhat stiffly. "You must be aware, as we all are, that she is under tremendous pressure on this mission."

"Yeah, you've told me that before, too. But she was pretty up front about it with all of us."

"Very true, and that was right of her, of course. But it does not change the situation. To admit to her problem did not do away with it."

Grayson grunted, seeming to lose interest.

"She's a very tough woman," Luttrell went on, "and you know it would take a lot to bring her down."

"Are you saying she's pretty close to down?"

"Perhaps not that close, yet. But she could be soon."

"I thought things were getting a little better, m'self," Grayson said, fixing Luttrell with a steady stare. "Can you be specific? All these 'perhapses' and 'could bes' are making me a little nervous."

Luttrell got up from the seat he'd taken. "There's a problem, George—you know I can't exactly be open about the fact that I'm keeping track of her. I'm only trying to clue you that something may happen, since you *are* second in command."

"Yeah, and I'd like to keep it that way, too." Grayson rose from the bench and walked over to stand before Luttrell. He was fully fifteen centimeters shorter than the doctor, but bulky and well put together. "Look, either you've got specifics or you don't." He folded his arms. "I don't like you enough to just go along for the ride, y'know?"

Luttrell smiled weakly and sat back down. "Specifics. All right, I'll give you a few. This is breaking the confidentiality of a patient-doctor relationship, but—"

"I won't tell your secrets, *Kenneth*."

Luttrell gazed directly at him. "She is having trouble sleeping at night, and she's drinking too much."

"Aw, c'mon—" Grayson hesitated. "We all drink. That's no big deal."

"You don't have to drink to get to sleep at night, *every* night, do you?"

"Mmm." Grayson shrugged. "How do you know she does?"

"She's asked me for help."

"Luttrell, she hates your guts!"

"But she can't get drugs unless I prescribe them. As ship's physician, I have the only authorization."

"Okay, fine. What else?"

"Do you remember the incident I told you about soon after you came aboard? How she claimed to have difficulty getting into the chamber on Deck Two where the LSH unit is kept?"

Grayson nodded.

"She is still obsessed with that. She checks it constantly, sometimes two or three times a day. And she goes to the chamber itself, rather than using SINS."

"Why would she do that?"

"Perhaps to make sure it's still frozen—perhaps simply to make sure she can still get into the chamber." Luttrell shook his head. "I don't know."

Grayson chewed on his lower lip. "How d'you know all this?"

"Grayson, I'm trying to help you," Luttrell said quietly. "Can't you at least trust me to do that?"

"I'm workin' on it, man. Now answer my question."

"Every time someone enters that chamber, the information is recorded in SINS. I'm the physician; technically, that unit is my patient. I get the report daily."

Grayson began to pace, his feet making light impressions on the padded floor. "Is that all?"

"Well, there is one other thing." Luttrell hesitated. "I think she and Teresa are having a relationship."

"Having a—" Grayson hesitated. "You mean they're screwing?" He started to laugh, and the sound echoed in the small gym. "I can't wait to hear this one. How do you know? Did they come and tell you?"

"I wish you would try to take me seriously, George." Luttrell had a pensive look on his face. "I've seen it in certain behaviors. The psych-profiles will always show—"

"Ah, c'mon, *Kenneth*, what's the big deal? Nobody cares. The captain is allowed to fuck around—and she can fuck anybody she wants to!"

"Oh, no, you miss my point entirely. I hope you don't think I disapprove!" Luttrell shook his head vehemently. "Not at all. But they're working very hard to keep it a secret, which puzzles me. Teresa has even gone so far as to establish a relationship with Al. I must wonder why."

"Maybe they're private people."

"I wish I could believe that." Luttrell looked down. "I'm afraid the captain is using the relationship to persuade Teresa to her point of view, and doesn't want the rest of us to know she has an ally."

Grayson scowled. "What's to persuade about?"

"Don't tell me you've forgotten that first staff meeting we had, where she ran on about the terrible things Guil-Pro was doing to us, and what they had already done to her— you must remember that!"

"Well, yeah, now that you mention it, I guess I do." Grayson scratched his head. "But I still don't see—"

Luttrell held up a hand. "My concern is this. Up to now, things have gone fairly smoothly on this mission. But if something should go wrong, if she does crack under the stress as the mission comes to a close, we'll have to act quickly. You'll have to take command, she'll have to be treated. If she's got Teresa convinced, somehow, that we're all against her, then we'll have the two of them to deal with. If Teresa has convinced Al of the same story, we may have three of them! That's half the crew—it'll be a lot harder."

Grayson began to pace again. "So what do you think we should do?"

"Nothing for now. I didn't mean to get you all worked up, George." Luttrell rose to his feet and caught Grayson by the shoulder. "I just wanted you to be aware of what was going on, since you're next in line."

"Will you stop saying that?" Grayson pulled away from the other man's grasp. "You're talking up trouble, dammit! I don't want to have to run this show!"

"With any luck, you won't have to. This is just what *could* happen, George, not what will happen. All you need to do is think about it." Luttrell made his move to leave.

"Yeah, I'll be thinking about it, all right. But just remember, *Kenneth*," Grayson pointed a finger at him, "I still don't like you."

Teresa sat before her console on the bridge late into the night shift. Her incentive to find out what Luttrell was really doing with his research had doubled. The man spent all his waking hours in that damn science lab—he *must* be coming up with more than he was telling the rest of them! She was convinced that somehow, between what he had discovered (especially what he wasn't telling them) and what she and Al were doing, there would be a way to destroy all the kites and their deadly mites and yet leave Roanoke and its beautiful artwork intact.

Luttrell's libraries had been embarrassingly easy to break into. He didn't use SINS very well, and his attempts at securing his data had been pathetic, especially to one with her expertise.

By midnight Teresa had discovered the link between her work and Luttrell's. Roanoke was indeed made from the same base as the kites. The structure was a marvel of biomechanical engineering—it grew more like a plant than a crystalline structure, adding thickness to walls, and eventually, over long years, adding new rooms such as the one she had discovered the day before. Imagine, a building that built itself! What would that do for colonization—at least, if the process could be speeded up. The original builders must have had a way to control the growth, but that was a problem for another day....

Feverishly she worked, searching now for the key to destruction, but the answers she needed refused to surface. Frustrated, she keyed in commands that would allow her to access SINS's inferencing mode for a question-and-answer session. She hadn't worked with this facility as much as some of the others—she prided herself on not needing that level of assistance—but she knew that its ability to reason in human fashion was downright intimidating. It must have been such work with SINS that had allowed Guil-Pro's scientists to create the brain that was the core of LSH units like Rory—Teresa hoped she'd never meet a human-made being with that level of intellect.

Her careful questions soon led her off in completely unexpected directions, and she lost track of the time.

Al greeted her at the door to her quarters. "Little late, aren't you?"

"Sorry, I was busy with something. I kind of forgot where I was."

"I was beginning to worry."

"How late is it? Oh, shit, it's after 0-two-thirty hours! I'm sorry, Al, I had no idea—"

"No problem, kid. I was just a little concerned, that's all." He gazed at her curiously. "What're you working on?"

"I'm not sure yet. I'd rather not talk about it right now, if you don't mind."

"Hey, we've got better things to do this time of night, anyway," he murmured, touching her cheek gently. She went to him gladly.

CHAPTER
17

Kate had set herself a last task in Roanoke before they were to leave tomorrow. In their methodical explorations of rooms off the major area that the *Opal*'s crew had made livable, they had discovered an entire wall covered with symbology. This was not the only evidence of written language they had found—symbols were to be seen everywhere—but this was the most massive collection of them in one place, and they had theorized that it might be something important. With the other excitement of the mission, they had never finished recording the wall of words. Kate was doing that now, with scanner, camera, and computer sketchpad, while Grayson and Pete were off dismantling their lights and monitoring equipment.

She paused in her work, stretching until her spine popped with a satisfying crack. Damn, but that was hard to do in a spacesuit. She took a deep breath, realized she was a little winded. How ridiculous—she'd been sitting down for almost two hours! Out of habit, she checked her air supply. About forty-five minutes left. Not bad, but perhaps time to begin thinking about getting back. After all, the other two had been working harder than she.

"Say, fellahs," she called, "I've got about forty-five minutes left. You go along with that?"

"Give or take a few," Grayson answered first. "What's up?"

"Nothing, just double-checking."

"Everything all right?" Teresa's voice crackled in their ears from aboard the ship. "What're you talking about?"

"Everything's fine," Kate repeated, wondering why her air seemed so stale. She glanced suspiciously at her suit gauge. It didn't smell like she had forty-three minutes of air left. "You guys want to start heading toward our meeting place? Say in about ten minutes?"

"Sure thing," Pete agreed.

"Yup, I'm about done," said Grayson.

"What's that?" Kate asked.

"I said I'm almost finished."

"Oh, all right. No rush." Kate went back to copying silently for several more minutes, not noticing at first that each activity, even taking a few steps, was causing her to breathe more heavily.

"Who's panting like a racehorse?" Teresa asked.

"Speak up!" Kate said. "Dammit, why is everyone whispering?"

"I asked who was panting," Teresa said slowly, careful to enunciate.

"Must be me," Kate said, eyeing her gauge again.

"Is your air okay?"

"Gauge says thirty-six minutes, same as everyone else's." She swallowed. "Good air mix, too."

"You dizzy, light-headed?" There was worry in Teresa's voice.

"A little, and I'm working on a hell of a headache. I just can't seem to get a good lungful." She tried, which only made it worse. *Careful, now, breathe shallow. Don't panic . . .*

"Try banging on your pack, if you can reach it," Pete suggested. "Maybe your valve is stuck."

"Right. Then I'll be positive I don't have enough air!" Kate tried to laugh, but it was too much effort, so instead she reached around behind her and thumped on her pack. Nothing happened. She could still breathe, but she was beginning to feel as though she were at the top of a very high mountain.

Like skiing the Andes . . .

"You're sure about the mix?" Luttrell's voice came to her. "I'm reading you a little high on carbon-dioxide intake."

"Tell me something I don't know." She sighed. God, but her head was pounding away!

"You'd better meet now," Teresa said. "Pete, check the fittings on her suit. She's starting to show signs of C-O-two poisoning."

"We'll do what we can," he agreed. "Could be the regulator, the exhaust valve—a bunch of things."

Kate tried to pick up one of her tools and found herself, to her surprise, on her knees.

"Captain, are you all right?" Teresa's voice sounded tinny over the radio. "What was that noise?"

"Nothing, nothing. I'm . . . a little dizzy, is all." Kate took a deep breath and blinked several times, trying to climb to her feet. *Christ!* she thought. *I've got to get out of here!*

"Stay put, Captain, we'll come to you," Grayson told her.

"But I'm farthest from the airlock," Kate said. "If we need to get back . . ."

"Can you walk?" Teresa asked sharply.

"Of course I can walk! What th' hell d'you think's wrong with me, anyway?"

"Stay there, Captain," Pete called. "I'm almost there."

"I've got to get out of here!" Kate mumbled, not realizing she had spoken aloud this time. "Pete? Pete, I—I can't hear you! Don't stop talking!"

"Captain, don't leave that room!" Luttrell cut in on the conversation. "You're only making it worse moving around!"

C'mon, Kate, she thought to herself, *this is just like mountaintop skiing! No problem . . . just keep thinking that . . .* Her feet scuffled through the slatelike dormant kites.

But the harder it became to breathe, the harder it was for her to stay calm. Although she knew that someone would come to help her, she couldn't relax.

Back aboard the *Pegasus,* Teresa and Luttrell watched helplessly as Kate began to wander farther from her two companions. Then she disappeared from the camera's view.

At that, Teresa pushed back from her post at the monitors. "I'm going outside," she announced to Luttrell, and thumbed a mike switch. "Al, meet me in the main airlock with a spare suit-pack." She started from the bridge without waiting for an acknowledgment.

"Wait a minute," Luttrell called after her.

She turned back to him at the doorway. "What's your problem? Can't you run the main monitors by yourself?"

"Of course! But you can't just violate the three-on rule without—"

"*Listen,* you asshole, her life is in danger. She's already breathing close to six percent CO_2. You're the doctor—don't you realize what that means? Go log an official complaint if you don't like the way I follow the rules!" Without waiting for a response, she ran from the bridge.

Al was already in the main airlock vestibule when she got there, with an extra suit-pack propped on the bench. "Want to take the jalopy?"

"Yeah, it's faster. She was starting to sound really bad, Al."

Buried within the depths of the smothering alien structure, a thing that grew and shrank with her every breath, a thing that seemed to envelop her, Kate leaned against a wall.

She imagined its cool surface touching the skin of her cheek, its crystalline colors splashing across her face like water. The thought calmed her; she could feel her breathing slow. She looked around her. Was that the opening to Rory's crypt she saw across the room? Would he come out to meet her?

"Captain." Luttrell's voice came to her, very soft, soothing. "Captain, I have you on the locator. You're back in the rooms with acceptable air."

She had forgotten that until he'd reminded her. But why was he murmuring to her so softly and sweetly, like a lover? The analogy made her shiver.

"Why don't you take your helmet off? By the time the others get to you, it'll be too late—you'll already have brain damage."

He was right. He was a doctor, he understood these things. She reached up and fumbled for a minute around her helmet snaps.

Luttrell's soft voice eased into her confused thoughts again. "—so just unsnap your helmet and take some air. You won't be exposed long enough to activate the kites. There's nothing to worry..."

Kate shuffled her foot through a pile of the slatelike diamond-shapes while spangles of light danced before her eyes. The movement of her foot against the kites made them move, and they seemed to stir with a life of their own. They were waking up, and she had nearly unsnapped the first closure on her helmet!

"No!" she screamed. "I won't do that!"

Aboard the jalopy, bumping across the planet's rough terrain, Teresa and Al exchanged glances, wincing at the sound of the scream. "I'm going as fast as I can," he said.

"Captain, stand still, for God's sake!" Grayson called. "We'll get you out of here, but you've got to stay in one place so we can find you!"

"No, I won't let you take my helmet off!"

"What's she talking about?" Luttrell asked. "I've got her on camera—there's nobody else there!"

"Kate, nobody's after your helmet," Teresa insisted. "Just stay in one place and let them help you! Pete, are you there yet? What's wrong with her?"

"I don't know, Mac. She just started screaming. I think she's losing it."

"Try to keep her calm," Teresa said. "We'll be there in two minutes."

Kate was backed against the wall when she saw two spacesuited figures approaching her, reaching for her. "Don't come near me!" she yelled, holding a digging tool in front of her. "I'll puncture your suit, so help me God, if you touch me!"

"Come on, Captain," Grayson said. "We're here to help you."

Kate stared at them through the sparkles that danced before her. Blackness wavered at the edges of her vision. Now there were four figures coming at her.

"Don't come any closer!" she threatened.

"Take your helmet off," the Loon whispered in her ear.

"Captain," Teresa said as they walked closer, "we have more air. We don't have to take your helmet off—we have an extra suit-pack."

"You—you won't take my helmet off?" Kate asked hesitantly.

"No, of course not. We brought a suit-pack," Teresa said quietly. "Will you let us come closer?"

"Okay." Kate gasped. "I—I think you'd better hurry!" She fell rather than sat as her legs collapsed beneath her. It grew very dark.

"Come on!" Teresa said excitedly as she began to work on the fittings of Kate's suit-pack.

"Here, let me," Pete offered. "There's a faster way." He demonstrated, and the suit-packs were exchanged much more quickly than Teresa could have managed. "Somebody keep hold of this one, so I can look at it when we get back to the ship."

"Her pulse is evening out a little," Luttrell reported from the ship. "Respiration slowing. How soon can we get her back here?"

"We're working on it," Teresa said shortly. "Kate? Kate, how do you feel?"

Kate concentrated on her breathing, in and out, slowly,

until her head cleared and she felt somewhat in control of herself again.

"Captain, how do you feel?"

"Wonderful!" The woman sighed and tilted her head back. "Do you know what fresh air is like after you've been breathing five-year-old engine exhaust?"

"Christ, you had us all scared!" Grayson said. "I thought you were gone for a minute, running around like a nut-case! Pete and I had a hell of a time figuring out what room you were in because you kept going!"

"Guess I was hallucinating," Kate said, though she remembered very clearly the sound of that insidious little voice in her ear. "Sorry if I gave you guys a hard time."

"Think you're ready to stand up now?" Teresa asked.

"Yeah, I think I can manage that."

Kate struggled to her feet with the help of several pairs of willing hands. "You guys are lifesavers. I appreciate this."

"I just wish I knew what happened to that pack," Pete said worriedly. "I don't like stuff that *I've* inspected going bad like this. I don't want you to think I'm not doin' my job, Captain."

"That hadn't even occurred to me, Pete," Kate said tiredly. "Let's worry about it when we get back to the ship."

"Why don't I drive you back?" Teresa offered. "You're still a little weak."

"Oh, I don't think that's necessary," Kate began to protest.

"We've already got the jalopy here," Teresa insisted. "Besides, Luttrell doesn't think you should exert yourself too much right now. And he *is* the doctor."

"Yes, isn't he?" Kate murmured. "Okay, I'll ride in style. I guess my knees are still a little shaky."

"See you guys back at the ranch!" Teresa waved at everyone minutes later as they started away in the multiterrain vehicle.

They rode in silence for a few minutes. "Captain," Teresa began, "switch over to private mike, will you?"

"Sure." Kate did so. "What's up?"

"Do you want to talk about what happened?"

"I don't remember very much, except that I must've been hallucinating."

"I've heard that line before."

"Mmm." Kate stared fixedly into the distance ahead of them. She was not going to tell anyone, even Teresa, about the voice in her head. They would think she was crazy! And maybe she had been, hearing the voice of the Loon again for the first time in days.

"You don't want to talk about it," Teresa said.

"Don't need to."

"Have it your way." Teresa pulled up next to the *Pegasus* with a jerk and signaled the ship to drop the cargo-bay ramp so she could drive the jalopy up inside.

By the time the rest of the crew arrived, Kate was sitting in the airlock vestibule with an oxygen mask over her face while Luttrell, looking concerned, gave her a cursory examination.

"Well, everything seems okay," he reported.

Kate pulled the mask away from her face. "Good. Pete, do you see anything there?"

The engineer had been examining her suit. "Sure do. The valve on your C-O-two regulator is a little sticky. See?" He demonstrated. "It started venting oxygen to the outside along with your C-O-two when your suit-pack got below a certain pressure, so it's not something you'd notice until you'd been in the suit for a while. And of course as you used more air and the pressure in your pack got even lower, the air mix would get worse. Which it did."

"Can you fix it?"

"Don't see why not."

"Good, I'd hate to waste a perfectly good suit-pack." She rubbed her temples with shaking hands. "Pete?" She hesitated, almost afraid to voice her question. "Could that valve have been damaged deliberately?"

"I—" He stopped. "Deliberately? Well, yeah, if a guy knew what he was doing. But why would anyone want to do that?"

"Doesn't matter. It *could* be done—that's what I needed to know." She was staring at Luttrell, and everyone could see it.

The doctor raised his eyebrows. "Don't you think you should get some rest, Captain?"

"It can wait."

"In fact," he continued, "I have a better idea. Maybe you should come down to the infirmary for a more detailed exam."

"Now? What for? I'm just a little tired."

"Well, so you say, but..." He lowered his eyes.

Kate folded her arms, repressing a strong urge to stand up and punch him. "What do you mean, 'so I say'?"

Luttrell shrugged.

"*Answer* me, Doctor! What are you getting at?"

He looked directly at her. "Captain, if you removed your helmet for even the briefest period of time—"

"*Removed my helmet!* Are you crazy?" She tried to stand, but her knees gave out and she couldn't.

Luttrell continued insistently. "Right before the rest of the crew got there, I saw a marked change in your physical signs on the monitors here. Your pulse and respiration began to subside toward normal—all the indications that you had some good air to breathe, if only for a moment."

Kate could feel the stares of the rest of the crew as they paused in what they were doing. "I did no such thing, *Doctor*," she said slowly, now positive that his was the voice that had whispered to her. "Even though *you* suggested that I do just that! What did you do, private-mike me after everyone else had left the ship? You knew what kind of condition I was in by then—were you hoping maybe I would follow through on your crazy idea?"

"Captain, everyone was talking to you. I was too busy watching your vital signs."

"Answer my question, Luttrell. Why did you want me to take my helmet off?"

"Captain, why would I suggest anything like that to you?" He regarded her quizzically. "But even if you did take your helmet off, it takes close to two hours to activate the kites—you know that. The only reason I want to examine you is to make absolutely sure everything is all right."

"Uh, Captain, maybe you should take him up on that

exam," Grayson suggested hesitantly. "Just to make sure, you know? You were talkin' kind of crazy out there. . . ."

"What's wrong with you?" Kate turned on him. "You afraid I've got mites? Here!" She rubbed her arm on him, and laughed when he actually pulled away. "Luttrell's really got *you* going! What's he been telling you about me?"

"Goddammit," Grayson sputtered, blushing furiously, "you oughta go, just to let him check you out. We're worried about you, y'know?"

"You jumped back quick enough, just now." Kate ran her hands through her short hair, making the wet curls stand on end. "What do you think I *am*, anyway, Grayson? What the hell do you think is wrong with me?"

She stared about her, saw them staring back, wondering, maybe even afraid, waiting for what she would do next. What must she sound like, raving at her crew like this? Very slowly she took a deep breath, then another, and made a deliberate effort to pull herself together. "George, I'm sorry. That was completely out of line. Here you guys saved my life, and I'm giving you a hard time." She smiled. "I guess I'm still a little rattled. Suffocating isn't a very nice experience."

Grayson shrugged. "You did all right," he mumbled, but she noticed he wouldn't meet her gaze.

"Luttrell, you and I will talk later," Kate said. "I'm going to bed. Somebody wake me in about two hours?"

They were drinking beer in the mess—Teresa, Grayson, Pete, and Al. Nobody seemed to want to start a conversation.

"Hey, Mac, you mad at me?" Grayson finally asked, blowing a smoke ring.

"People are going to be mad at you when you act stupid," she snapped.

"Stupid? Now wait a minute!" He sat up. "Careful, maybe, but stupid? I don't think so. Christ, we don't know what happened out there! It pays to be careful when you don't know what you're dealing with!"

"You don't really think she took her helmet off, do you?" Pete asked.

"Of course she didn't!" Teresa said. "She knows better than to take that kind of risk. Besides," she added more quietly, "Luttrell said the mites were probably dormant when the kites were. So even if she did take her—"

"He also said he could be wrong!" Grayson interrupted her. "The plain fact is, and I keep going back to it, that we don't know. We don't know enough about any of this!"

"Don't you think it's pretty unlikely that she'd take her helmet off and then put it back on? She was wearing it when we got there, and all the closures were fastened," Al said tiredly. "What's your beef anyway, Grayson? Why are you so hot to think the captain would do something that stupid?"

Grayson inhaled deeply on a cigarette. "Look at how she acted out there."

"For God's sake, George, she was hallucinating!" Teresa said. "You expect somebody to act sane when they don't have any air? Did you ever get caught with a low tank?"

"What about the way she acted back aboard ship?" he persisted. "She had plenty of air by then."

"You were asking to be jumped on."

"No, no, not that. I mean before, asking Pete if somebody could've rigged her suit on purpose. Now that," he straightened, "ain't normal. You don't come off an accident like that lookin' for somebody to blame, unless you're talkin' maintenance, which she wasn't. She thinks somebody is *after* her! That's paranoid, man, that's a bad sign."

"Maybe it would be, if this was the first accident," Teresa admitted. "But what about the winch?"

"What's that got to do with anything?"

"Don't you think it's strange that so much is going wrong with certified equipment in such a short time?" Teresa asked. "Even Pete thinks it's strange, and he ought to know!"

"Don't tell me you're going to bring up that sabotage shit again—"

"What do you mean 'shit'? Pete looked at the winch and found the same problems I did! Are you calling me a liar?"

"Ah, c'mon, Mac, cool off and stop takin' this so personal. I'm not talking about you."

"Look, Mac, we'll all go along with what happened to the winch, Pete said reasonably. "But you can't jump to conclusions about the suit. It could happen to anybody. The air-supply design is pretty shitty—it invites that kind of trouble! It's happened before, too, but Guil-Pro is just too cheap to come up with something better."

"Shit!" Teresa rose abruptly and got another beer. "I'm sorry, I just don't believe it was coincidence. You're asking me to accept too much."

"Do you know something we don't?" Grayson asked.

"What do you mean?"

"You're so goddamn set on this sabotage idea, I figure you know something the rest of us don't. So what's going on? Who's after her?"

Teresa was silent.

"Another thing about the captain," Grayson leaned back in his seat and regarded her thoughtfully, "she's really gone too far with this thing she's got about Luttrell. And I think you've been talking to her too much about this shit."

"You mean we're both crazy, is that it?"

"Oh, hell, leave y'self out of it, will you? She's got problems with Guil-Pro, she had a bad trip out here last time—she's just reacting normally. That's something to think about." Grayson stopped to take a long draught of beer. "And when you listen to her every word like you've obviously been doing, it means you're taking her seriously. I don't know if that's such a good idea."

Teresa stared at him. "I don't think I like what you're saying."

"She was looking right at Luttrell when she let everyone know she thought someone was tryin' to kill her. You just don't *do* that!"

"She didn't accuse anyone. . . ."

"We all got the picture!"

"Will you guys knock it off?" Al asked. "You're giving me a headache."

Luttrell chose that moment to walk into the mess. He paused and looked around. "Am I interrupting something?"

"Be my guest." Grayson gestured. "Want a beer?"

"No, thanks, coffee'll be fine." He poured himself a cup.

Teresa moved around the table and picked up a magazine. The men started a conversation around her, and she was left to fume in silence. What the hell was Grayson talking about, anyway, saying she was paying too much attention to what Kate said? She had half a mind to tell him who she really was, just to see the expression on his self-satisfied little chauvinist face!

"Well," Luttrell was saying, "she was in the room next to Rory's crypt when you found her, wasn't she? Perhaps she was hallucinating that he was coming out after her to take her helmet off—I don't know."

Teresa was about to disagree when a movement at the door caught her eye, and she looked up to see Kate standing there.

"All right, who's been fucking with the computer?" Kate demanded in a shaky voice.

"SINS turn off the hot water again?" Grayson turned, smiling, but the look on her face froze all of them.

"Read this." She thrust a printout at them.

—OH, FRABJOUS DAY,
CALLOOH, CALLAY!
CAPTAIN HARLIN
WILL DIE TODAY!—

"SINS did this? That's hard to believe—"

"Granted. I'm assuming somebody wrote a program. But that doesn't explain why, or who. And it's not the first one I've gotten."

"What were the others like?"

"Random. Some obscene, others just silly."

"Did you save any of them?" Luttrell asked quietly.

"This is the first one to leave a hardcopy record."

Teresa took the listing and studied it uneasily.

"There's got to be a simple explanation for this," Grayson was saying. "Maybe something left over from the last time the system was shaken down?" He looked helplessly at Teresa, who was shaking her head slowly.

"They wouldn't have my name," Kate insisted. "This is more than just chance, Grayson. This is malicious!"

"Malicious is a strong word," Luttrell said.

"What would you call it, mister?"

He had no answer.

Al spoke up. "If it was deliberate, then we have to look at why someone would do it. Then who..."

"I think I have an answer for both those questions." Kate's eyes blazed in her pale face. She looked disheveled, as though she had been awakened from a sound sleep. "Luttrell, I want to talk to you. Now. Outside."

Teresa interrupted hastily. "Kate, don't you think—"

"Stow it, MacKessen. Luttrell, are you coming? I just gave you an order."

"Certainly, Captain." Luttrell rose to his feet.

"Kate, wait a minute. Let me—"

"I said stow it!" Kate turned on her heel and strode from the room. Luttrell followed.

"Talk about pissed off!" Grayson said wonderingly. "For a minute there I thought she was going to punch him!"

"Couldn't happen to a nicer person."

"What's that, Mac?"

"Nothing." But Teresa watched the door anxiously.

"This *is* pretty strange," admitted Al, who'd taken the listing from Teresa to study it.

"Oh, I don't know." Grayson lit another cigarette. "At this stage of the game I wouldn't be surprised to find out she'd written it herself."

Luttrell faced Kate in the corridor outside. "You just made a fool of yourself in there."

"Not me." She shook her head. "Not this time, not ever again. You've gone too far, Luttrell. What're you trying to pull?"

"Me?" He raised his eyebrows.

"Don't give me that innocent-little-boy shit! I know what your game is, and I want you to knock it off!"

"Captain, I don't know—"

"That doesn't cut it anymore. Teresa and I had a pretty interesting talk a few days ago. She told me how *worried* you've been about pressure on the job getting to me. You've been so *worried*, you wanted to take that job away from me! Isn't that right, Luttrell?"

"Captain, I may have expressed concern at your—"

"I don't think you're listening to me. I know all about

the nasty little tricks you've been playing behind my back. I know *all* of it, y'hear me?" She paused, trying to keep her voice level. "I know Teresa's real name is Josephine Travers—does that tell you something?" She saw his face change. "Yeah, Luttrell, *that's* how much I know. So you lay off her, and stay out of my way or I'll throw your ass in the brig!"

His expression darkened. "Well, I see where you're coming from now. Maybe it's time to deal with basics and get this mission out of the way before we talk about anything—"

"Forget it, Luttrell. The only thing we're going to talk about from now on is a mutiny charge." She laughed at him. "So your ass is supposed to be on the line just like mine, is it? Well, you just blew it, my friend, and I can't wait until Kagen finds out!"

"I was hoping it wouldn't have to come to this, Captain." Luttrell pulled a small pressure hypo from a case in his pocket. "But, as you can see, I've been prepared for you all the same. Kagen won't hear about this one at all."

Kate backed away from him, her eyes on the small disk in his hand. He continued to move in on her, and she was suddenly afraid.

"Back off, Luttrell!"

He thrust his hand out, and the pressure hypo caught her on the forearm as she tried to dodge him. She stared at her arm, then at Luttrell. "You bastard!" she screamed, and flew at him.

"Written it herself?" Teresa slammed her beer can on the table. "What the fuck are you talking about?"

"You calm down and listen to me for a minute." Grayson's voice had a hard edge to it. "We know there's something going on with her and Luttrell, and I don't mean they're fucking, either. We also know the captain can be a little neurotic when it comes to Guil-Pro. Christ, maybe Luttrell's a shrink they got for her, I don't know! But she's taking something out on him, whatever it is, and it's getting a lot worse lately. Maybe she took a sleeping pill, or a drink, and now she's gone a little overboard—"

"Quiet!" Al thrust his hand up, interrupting them.

They could hear the sound of voices raised in the corridor

outside. There was a low murmuring, then sudden sounds of a scuffle.

"You bastard!" Kate, loudly, followed by the sound of a blow.

Teresa leaped to her feet and headed for the door, with the others right behind her.

Luttrell was bending over Kate, who lay still on the deck. He looked up at them and shrugged.

"What did you *do*?" Teresa demanded, moving on him.

"Easy, Mac." Grayson laid a hand on her shoulder. "Let him explain."

"Explain? Goddammit—!"

"MacKessen!" Grayson tightened his grip. "We weren't out here. Now shut up and let the man talk."

"I'm afraid there isn't much to say," Luttrell apologized. "She was furious with me. When I tried to calm her down, she went off completely and swung at me." He turned slightly, and they could see the welt on his face. "She kept on coming, so I had to hit her."

"Well," Grayson muttered, "I guess it was going to happen sooner or later."

Teresa started to say something, then changed her mind. Looking from Grayson to Pete, even Al, seeing the concern and pity on their faces, she knew there was nothing she could say to change their minds.

"If you gentlemen will help me, we can get her to her quarters, and I'll give her something to make sure she rests." Luttrell straightened.

"Shouldn't you wait until she's conscious before you give her any dope?" Teresa asked.

Luttrell looked at her. "Don't you think I know my job?"

"No."

"MacKessen, that's enough!" Grayson said. "You owe him an apology."

"Fuck that." She turned away from him.

"Hold it!" Grayson grabbed her arm and spun her around to face him. "You forget, I'm in charge now. I told you to apologize to him."

Teresa stared down at the shorter man and felt her right hand clench into a fist. "So that's how it is? I see how Luttrell talked *you* into playing his little game. Don't you see what a sucker you are?" she asked. "I thought you weren't interested in running a mission—why are you going along with this kind of shit?" Her voice quavered, barely controlled.

"Now wait a minute, you little idiot!" Grayson could barely speak. "Where the hell did you get these goddamned ideas? You're talking about mutiny!"

"I guess I am."

"What the hell do you think I *am*? You think I'm not as upset about the captain as you are?"

"You don't want to know what I think about you." There was a catch in her voice she couldn't quite hold back.

"What the hell kind of crazy talk is this?" Grayson was plainly as puzzled as he was angry.

"Hey, now," Pete stepped between them, "cool down, both of you."

"I want to know what the hell she's talking about!"

"Shut up, George!" Al grasped his shoulder. "You're not helping the situation."

"Ah, shit—" She gave it up suddenly. Grayson looked so hurt and so puzzled . . . maybe she was wrong. "Leave me alone, okay? All of you, just—leave me alone." She walked a little distance away, felt the adrenaline leave her as quickly as it had come. Tears started at her eyes; she felt tired, and stupid, standing there with her back to them.

Al started to go to her, but Pete caught his arm and shook his head. "Leave her be for now," he whispered. "We need to watch out for the captain." Al nodded.

Luttrell had watched the whole scene with interest, his fingers on Kate's pulse. "I wonder what's gotten into her?" he remarked, testing the water.

"God knows. But she's almighty pissed at you, not to mention me." Grayson looked at him sharply. "What've you been telling her?"

Luttrell started to protest, but was interrupted when Kate groaned softly.

"Why don't we get her off the floor?" Al suggested. He was concerned, both for Teresa and for the captain. Something wasn't right. . . .

"Let me give you a hand." As Pete bent to help, he

looked over his shoulder and saw Teresa watching them. He raised a questioning eyebrow, and she moved forward to follow them.

They were gentle as they carried their captain to her quarters. Luttrell bent over her as they laid her on her bed. "I'll have to examine her."

Pete and Al exchanged glances.

"We'll stay," Pete said.

"Then so will I," Grayson added after a beat.

Frowning, Luttrell gazed at them, and at Teresa standing slightly behind them, then shrugged and turned to his examination, which was very brief. "I don't think she'll need a sedative..." he murmured.

"Will she be all right?" Pete asked.

"She'll be fine. I didn't hit her hard enough to do any damage." Luttrell seemed irritated. "The best thing for her now is rest. And we should probably watch her for a few days."

"Watch her for what?" Teresa asked softly, but Luttrell acted as though he hadn't heard her.

"But she'll be all right for the job, right?" Grayson persisted, as they left the small cabin together.

"George, will you leave it alone?" Al asked.

"He's within his rights to ask," Luttrell said. "And the fact is that with sufficient rest, she'll be able to function without any problems."

"Well, I hope so. We're supposed to leave tomorrow!"

Luttrell nodded, glancing at Kate's door. "Yes, I know."

Kate tossed in restless sleep. Her tiny quarters were dimly lit, and she saw herself from above, lying half-awake in bed. Kagen was standing before her, his face a study in triumph. No, no, not Kagen...Kagen couldn't stand. She should've said Rory. But he wasn't here either. Oh, for chrissakes, what was wrong with her? She couldn't even keep the characters straight in this crazy play...or maybe she was the crazy one, like they were all saying behind her back.... She felt terrible, feverish....

Groaning softly, Kate turned her face to the wall, felt the dregs of consciousness slip away again.

CHAPTER
18

Teresa sat alone on the bridge facing the main console, playing a game of Pied Piper at the ninth level of difficulty. Not only was the game a good distraction for her, but it was complex enough to identify problems with SINS's inferencing circuits, if there were any. She was hoping to find a system problem that would explain the strange messages Kate had been receiving. So far she'd had no luck.

She refused to consider the possibility that her captain had cracked. She was positive of Kate's stability. No, Luttrell was up to something, and chance had combined with circumstance to make things go his way. But Kate was all right. She had to be.

There's only one way to find out what really happened, she told herself. *Go and talk to her! And do it now, before you chicken out!*

She climbed up out of her seat to the walkway and stood for a moment staring at nothing out the front viewport. It was quiet up here. Was everyone else still in the messroom worrying about the captain? Al's concern had surprised her, even hurt her. Now, Grayson she could understand. He had always pushed harder at Kate than any of the others (except Luttrell), and she knew he'd paid more attention to Luttrell than anyone else. Pete she wasn't sure about—he'd always been so neutral until today, when that look over his shoulder had plainly told her she'd better follow them to Kate's quarters. But Al . . . how could he even *begin* to think Kate was on shaky ground? He knew better, she was sure of it.

Apologize to Luttrell, indeed, she thought. *Fuck 'em all!*

The corridor outside Kate's quarters was empty and silent. She reached for the buzzer.

No answer.

Maybe she's still asleep. No telling what kind of dope the bastard gave her! Teresa tried to open the door; it was locked. Frustrated, she glared down the corridor, trying to remember where the electrical maintenance panel was for this section of Deck 1. If she could force the lock . . . Suddenly the door began to open, and she turned in surprise.

Pain split the side of her face before she could see what was happening. She spun into the opposite wall, hit it hard, and slid senseless to the deck.

Soft footfalls sounded down the corridor, moving away from her.

In the mess, Luttrell finished a cup of coffee and glanced at his watch. "If you gentlemen will excuse me . . ." He rose.

"You going to check on the captain?" Al asked.

"Why, yes." Luttrell smiled reflexively, and tensed as Pete stood up.

"Keep us posted, will you?" the engineer asked, getting himself another beer.

Luttrell relaxed, and his smile became more natural. "Of course."

"Goddammit, stop *hitting* me!" Kate shook her head against another ringing slap and tried to grab at the punishing hands. Consciousness was coming slowly, and it had been many moments before she had reacted to the maddening blows at all. She opened her eyes, ready to blast the son of a bitch who wouldn't leave her alone. . . .

"So, you're awake . . . Katie."

A man stood before her, with short, dark, curly hair, bright, bright blue eyes, and a smile made crooked by the little scar that drew his mouth up on one side.

"Rory!" She stumbled to her feet, almost losing her balance.

The drug Luttrell had given her made her sluggish. Impulsively she took a wild swing at Rory, but missed him completely. He let her fall to the floor, then picked her up by her collar. Her arms moved weakly in protest as he dumped her unceremoniously back onto the bench where she had been sitting.

"Damn you!" she mumbled, rubbing her face with numb hands. "What's wrong with me?"

"You've been drugged. It'll wear off." He filled a cup with water and held it to her lips.

She drank thirstily and began to wake up.

"Get into your spacesuit."

"What?" She looked around, saw finally that they were in the main airlock vestibule.

"I said get dressed."

"Fuck you."

He grasped her wrist and squeezed. "Get dressed or I'll do it for you."

She lasted less than fifteen seconds under the pressure of his artificial strength. "All right!" she gasped, her knees buckling. He released her, and she caught her balance.

"Much better," he said, drawing a stunner as she began to suit up. She didn't answer him.

"Good of you to be so agreeable." He tossed her a helmet. "By the way, don't bother trying to call for help. I've broken your transmitter, so you can only receive."

She stared at him. "Where's your suit?"

"Why, my dear, I don't need one for such a short trip, and, as we both know, the air is perfectly breathable at our destination." He fastened a throat mike around his neck. "But I must be able to communicate with you."

Silently she locked her helmet in place.

"Don't you want to know why we're going?" he asked, smiling that familiar smile.

Her expression didn't change.

"That's right, Katie, we're going to collect our sample."

Luttrell was approaching the last curve in the hallway leading to the crew's quarters when he heard footsteps behind him.

"Hope you don't mind the company." It was Al.

"Not at all." Luttrell forced a smile.

As they rounded the curve, Al spotted Teresa lying flat on the deck. He ran to her, quickly assessed that she was still alive, and winced at the ugly bruise on her face, the blood trickling from her nose.

Teresa groaned softly as the man rolled her over onto her back.

"Good God, what happened to you?" He looked up. "Luttrell, get your ass down here! She's hurt!"

"Oh, God—" Teresa's eyes flickered open. "My face..."

"Easy, kid."

Luttrell opened his first-aid kit and bent over the young woman. Peeling the back off a medipatch, he pressed it against her carotid and watched her reactions as the drug seeped into her bloodstream, easing some of the pain. The relief helped to bring her around pretty quickly, and he began to examine her.

"What happened?" Al asked again.

"I—I don't know." She tried to sit up, and they helped her. "Ouch, goddammit!" She winced as Luttrell cleaned the blood from her nose.

"Here, use this. It'll help the swelling." He pressed a cold pack to her face and tilted her head to one side.

"Can you remember anything?" Al urged.

Teresa opened her puffy eyes again. "A little. I was standing at Kate's door—"

"Why?" Luttrell interrupted.

"None of your business." She glared at him. "Anyway, I rang the buzzer, but she didn't answer. I was going to try the door, but it opened from inside and somebody hit me."

"Somebody?" Luttrell kept his voice level.

"Yeah, somebody. I never saw who."

"You know who it had to be," he said reasonably.

"I don't know anything! I told you, I didn't see him."

"Him?"

"That's right, *him*!"

"Now, Mac, you know it had to be the captain. No one else was down here."

"He's right, Teresa," Al verified. "We were all in the mess together."

"It had to be a man, the blow was so hard—"

"She's hit me in the face," Luttrell said dryly, "and I assure you she hits quite hard enough."

"But *why* would she hit me? That doesn't make any sense."

"You know as well as the rest of us that she's been under a lot of strain recently. You've seen how she's behaved—" Luttrell started.

"Bullshit!"

"Mac, that's enough," Al warned gently.

"Who's side are you on, anyway?" She jerked away from Al's touch.

"Mac," Luttrell interrupted, "if the captain's in trouble, we can't have any sides."

"You've got a good reason for everything, don't you?" Teresa tried to stand up. "We've got to find her."

"Now you just take it easy. She can't have gone far on the ship, and I'm more worried about you right now." Luttrell caught her about the waist as she stumbled. "Let's get you to the infirmary. It looks like your nose is broken, and I want to make sure you didn't sustain a concussion. You took a pretty hard knock."

Teresa pushed his arm away. "I'm fine."

Grayson's voice blared at them suddenly from the intercom: "Al? Al, where are you?"

The man rose quickly. "Down by the captain's quarters. Mac had a little accident, and—"

"Never mind that! Is Luttrell with you?"

"Yeah, but—"

"And Pete is here with me. Goddammit, somebody just left the ship from the main airlock!"

"It must be Kate," Teresa whispered.

"There's only one person still unaccountable," Grayson's voice continued. "Meet me at the main airlock. We've got to go after her!"

"Remember," Luttrell said, "she might be dangerous. All the cases on the *Black Opal* mission were reported to be violent."

"Fine," Grayson agreed. "We'll take stunners." They could hear him break the connection.

"You don't think she's got the disease the *Opal*'s crew had, do you?" Al asked.

"If he does, he's full of shit," Teresa muttered. "I'm

telling you, she *didn't* take her helmet off out there—she wouldn't do anything so stupid!"

Luttrell shrugged.

"Look," Al said, "we're wasting time. Luttrell, let's get Teresa to the infirmary. Maybe Pete—"

"You're not getting me anywhere!" Teresa avoided his supporting arm. "You need me out there. She won't listen to any of you after the way you've treated her—especially you!" She jabbed a finger at Luttrell. "If you want her back here alive, you'd better let me come along."

"Let's not start that again!" Al said, before Luttrell could offer a counterargument. "Are you sure you feel all right?"

"I'll be fine if you just leave me alone!"

"Luttrell?" He turned to the doctor.

He shrugged. "I'm a little worried about concussion, but—" He looked covertly at his watch. "Much as I hate to admit it, she's probably got a point about the captain's trust."

"Then let's move!"

Luttrell headed to the infirmary, and Al raced off in the direction of the main airlock. Teresa waited until they were out of sight, then tried the door to Kate's quarters again. This time it opened easily, and she slipped inside.

Minutes later, Teresa entered the airlock vestibule. Except for Pete, who was watching the main monitors on the bridge, everyone was there. Luttrell had a portable environment pack strapped to his chest. A collapsible stretcher leaned against the bulkhead next to him.

"You look like you've been in a brawl with those shiners!" Grayson told her, shocked at her appearance. "Are you sure you'll be all right in a suit?"

"I'll be okay." She dabbed at her tender nose, then pulled her suit from its locker and began to dress. "Besides, that patch Luttrell glued onto me has numbed the whole area. I can't even feel it."

"Here, take these." Grayson passed out low-power stunners. "If the captain is really crazy, we might have to get her from a distance."

"I think you guys are looking for trouble," Teresa said as she took hers.

"Well, I'd like to know what the hell other explanation

you can come up with for what's going on!" Grayson yanked his suit on with a series of jerks. "If she left the ship without telling anyone, then *something* is not right, don't you think, MacKessen? Doesn't that give you a little hint that we have a problem here?"

"Yeah, we have a problem, all right, and you're part of it! You should quit trying to second guess the situation, because you don't know any better than the rest of us what's going on!" Teresa clamped on her helmet.

"We're wasting time," Al said quietly. "We need to find the captain and stop her before she hurts herself."

"Somebody needs to stop me before *I* hurt somebody!" Grayson said from between clenched teeth.

Pete's voice came over the intercom suddenly: "I've searched all quadrants, Grayson, and I can't pick up her beacon. Maybe she disabled it."

"I'm sure she's headed for Roanoke," Luttrell said. "Remember, the disease, if that's what she indeed has, caused the victims to want to be near the kites."

Teresa made a fist with her gloved hand, but said nothing. Only Al saw her gesture.

"We might as well start there, anyway," Grayson agreed, and clamped on his helmet.

Kate trudged slowly toward Roanoke, staring at her feet as she walked. Rory was on her right, setting the pace, stunner held casually in one hand. She couldn't look at him; it hurt her brain to see him walking so incongruously on this planet's surface without a spacesuit.

"Don't be so depressed, my dear. You should be used to Kagen outthinking you by now."

No use saying anything . . . he couldn't hear her anyway. She didn't even turn her head.

"Pity. But perhaps I should be kinder."

Kate walked.

"Because," he continued, "I don't suppose you could really have been expected to know what Kagen had in mind for you. Even your friend Dr. Luttrell didn't know until we had landed here."

She swallowed the tightness in her throat and kept walking.

"It was very convenient, having free run of the ship while the rest of you were in deep-sleep. Seven months was more than enough time to take care of that foolish beacon you tried to leave, as well as change a few of SINS's linkage programs. Which reminds me—I do apologize for the bad poetry in my last message."

Of course he'd been responsible for all that, and not Luttrell. How stupid she'd been! Stupid enough to trust both Luttrell and SINS (what a mistake *that* had been) about the "brain-dead" LSH unit they had brought with them. Stupid enough to die now if she didn't start paying attention.

"You were very cooperative once the good doctor and I were able to work together. Though I . . . was a little surprised when you started to drink so heavily."

Oddly, she felt briefly cheered by that remark. The realization that she had been steered along a very narrow course during the entire time of this mission had depressed her terribly, and it made her feel better to know she had done one small unpredictable thing.

"Of course, that did make it easier for Dr. Luttrell to plant doubts with your crew about your ability to handle stress. Some of them are convinced by now that you suffer from a real and serious problem. In fact, if I'm not mistaken, they should be out searching for you soon. No, no, my dear," he caught her arm as she continued toward the looming alien structure, "we're not going into Roanoke. That's where everyone will expect us to be." He smiled. "We're going back to the *Black Opal*."

"How the hell are we supposed to track her without a beacon, that's what I want to know!" Grayson complained. They had just crowded into the jalopy and were starting off. "Roanoke is such a goddamned maze!"

"There are four of us. Why don't we split up?" Teresa suggested.

"I don't know if that's wise," Luttrell began.

"We'll save more time if we split up," Teresa insisted. "She's already got a head start on us!"

"All right, all right, you go with Al to the *Black Opal* rooms, and Luttrell and I will start in the room with the stairwell." Grayson swerved to avoid a hillock.

"Maybe you'd better watch where you're going," Al suggested, "and we can worry about what to do after we get there in one piece."

Rory sealed the *Black Opal*'s inner airlock and sniffed delicately. "The air is still good and quite fresh. A little chilly, perhaps."

Kate was staring about her numbly. The deck was scattered with kites. Not nearly as many as were in Roanoke, but certainly more than she remembered leaving behind over a year ago. My God, had the things multiplied?

"You weren't aware that they reproduced, were you?" Rory asked. "Simple fission—something Luttrell hasn't bothered to look at yet. There's quite an impressive little colony aboard the *Opal* now. Take your suit off, dear. We haven't much time, though I've no doubt Luttrell will keep the others away from here for as long as he can."

Kate shook her head. Not her last line of defense. If she stood exposed to the kites...

"You begin to anger me, Katie."

Rory grabbed her suit at the throat, just below the fitting where her helmet was sealed. The material bunched in his hand as he clenched his fist, and with a twisting motion he ripped her suit from throat to navel.

"You might as well take it off now, my dear."

"You bastard!" Angrily she jerked her helmet off. "I didn't know you were such an ass, Rory. You're still a lot more exposed than I am. They'll go after you first!"

"Oh, no, Katie, I'm afraid you've got that wrong, too." He smiled crookedly. "Kites are not attracted to a cyborg construction. They'll have no interest in me."

"What?" She reached out to support herself on the wall. "But Luttrell's full-function construct—"

"—was designed to simulate an entire closed cycle of

the human body, internally and externally. An LSH unit merely *looks* human. Beneath the skin the similarity ends. And the kites are very particular about their hosts."

"But, Rory, aboard the *Opal* . . ." Her voice trailed off.

Rory was nodding. "Now you know the real reason why nothing happened until Mishima took his suit off."

"But Kagen promised me an LSH-unit host for this trip, so there wouldn't be a problem," she whispered. "He *promised*!"

"Your faith is very touching, my dear." He gestured with the stunner. "Take your suit off now."

Kate did so, barely aware of what she was doing.

"And remember," Grayson gave his final instructions, "be careful when you come on her, especially if you surprise her, okay? *Don't* say it, Mac!" He turned on her quickly. "I know you disagree with me, but the fact is the captain has done something unexpected and not very sane, and we don't know why! I can't have you pulling any stupid heroics just because you think she wouldn't hurt you because you two have something going. . . ." He stopped, looked at her expression through her faceplate—anger mixed with puzzlement. He spoke a little slower. "You think she won't hurt you, but *I* don't want to be stuck picking up the pieces and trying to explain things back home. Are you clear on that, computer scientist?"

"Clearer than you think," she muttered, and turned away from them to follow the passage to the *Black Opal* rooms. "Al, are you coming?"

"See if you can keep her out of trouble, will you, Al?" Grayson called after them.

"Look, Teresa, you're going to have to cool off a little," Al began.

"Don't you start on me." She flipped to private mike. "I'm really worried about what's going on between Grayson and Luttrell."

"You think they're in something together?"

"I don't think Grayson's doing anything on purpose, no. But he's gullible enough to believe whatever shit Luttrell is handing him. I mean, what was he trying to say back there about me and Kate? Where would he have gotten the idea if Luttrell hadn't put stuff in his head? And he really believes something is wrong with her!"

"You don't think so?"

"No, I don't." She stared at him. "Look, we talked about this a hundred times—something strange is going on, but the problem is not in Kate's head. Believe me."

"Teresa, I really want to believe you. I don't like the way things are falling out, either. But if you know something I don't, I wish to hell you'd tell me."

"Al, I—" She stopped. "I can't. I'd be breaking a confidence."

"Did it ever occur to you I might be able to help?"

"Of course it has! But—well, the biggest help you could give me right now would be trust. And support, in case Luttrell talks Grayson into doing something really stupid."

Al was silent for several minutes as they walked on.

"Was that too much?" Teresa finally asked.

"No, that's not it at all. I was just thinking."

"And?"

"I'm with you." He smiled. "But only if I get to know what's going on as soon as you can talk about it."

She returned his smile. "You'll be first in line, I promise."

"I've got a question for you, though," he said after another pause.

"What's that?" She tensed for a moment. If he pursued Grayson's clumsy insinuations, it might really damage her faith in him.

"Why do you think she left the ship? That's—well, it's the one thing nobody can come up with a reason for. And it makes her look really bad."

Teresa was almost relieved, and shrugged in her suit. "I don't know. And that scares me."

"Well, let's keep an ear out and see if we can stay one step ahead of the others," Al said quietly. "If we can find her first, we might be able to help."

Kate forced herself to walk calmly around among the kites scattered on the deck. Her soft-soled shoes made no noise as she moved, and she was careful to disturb the creatures as little as possible. No point in letting Rory see how squeamish she was about them—at least she could handle her last hours with dignity.

"I'm sorry we have such a wait for things to happen," he told her. "I realize the anticipation must be very unpleasant—"

"How do you know that?" she asked. "Where the hell do you get off talking like you've ever experienced anything a human being could?"

He regarded her somberly.

"Yeah, you put on a good show, all right," she continued. "You had me fooled."

"You do me an injustice. This is planned to cause you the least amount of pain you could experience under the circumstances. It will be very quick, I promise. Dr. Luttrell will put you into protective deep-sleep as quickly as possible, so that you'll barely be aware of the discomfort."

"Kagen has plans for everything, hasn't he? How thoughtful of him."

"Katie, *I* made these arrangements. You don't think Kagen cares about what will happen to you as long as he gets his sample, do you?"

She stared at him. "You did that? You—you can act independently of him?"

"He doesn't know the half of what he created when he brought me into existence."

Those blue eyes were so open, so honest, so like the Rory she remembered.... "If you're that free of him, then why do you follow his orders at all? Why don't you—" she nearly swallowed the words in her anxiety, "why don't you help me?"

He cocked his head at her. "What would you have me do?"

"*Stop* all this stupidity!" She took a step toward him. "We can go home, file our report like good claim-stakers, pick up our pay and our bonuses—and go back to business as usual! What could be simpler?"

"Business as usual," he repeated. "Do you mean that, Katie? Just like it was before?"

"What do you mean?" she asked slowly. "What do you know about before?"

He smiled, and she could feel the tug of his old charm. "It was very touching the way you kept checking on me when I was frozen on Deck Two. I did the same for you, during the seven months it took us to get out here. I watched you quite often while you slept."

She shivered. "Why did you do that?"

"Because I still care about you."

"But you—you can't! You're not Rory, you're not my friend—"

"I might as well be. I know everything he knew, I remember everything he remembered—I feel everything he felt."

"How?"

"Rory filed reports aboard the *Opal* by doing periodic memory dumps into SINS. Of course they were more than simple memory dumps, for such complex creatures as we are. They included sensations and a whole range of feelings. It was Kagen's substitute for not being there himself." Rory smiled slightly. "All of this was transmitted back to the Consortium and given to me. Surely you knew such transmissions were being made."

"Yes, but I had no idea. . . ." Her voice was so faint as almost not to be heard.

"So you see," he smiled, "I am Rory."

She had to look away from him; his face was unbearably familiar when he smiled at her like that.

"Then help me," she whispered. "Don't let Kagen do this to me. Don't let him do it to us."

"Now you give me too much credit, Katie. Yes, I am Rory, as much as the others you knew were Rory, but," his expression shifted subtly, "I am also Kagen."

"And what does Kagen want?"

"I have two directions on this mission. I must collect a sample—and you must be the host."

She could not speak.

"After that, the decisions are his. I will do what I can to help you, Katie, as I have done so far. When you awake from deep-sleep to leave the *Pegasus*, you will still be groggy—"

"What do you mean, when I wake up? I thought you said I'd be frozen."

"Only for the trip home." He looked at her, his eyes almost innocent—Rory's eyes again. "Kagen expects you to walk off the *Pegasus* with the rest of the crew, in a spacesuit, but awake and aware."

"You can't mean that! It's too dangerous! Suppose the kites come to life?" She had to stop. She could not imagine herself trapped in a suit with live kites swarming over her, covering every part of her.

"No, we will be quick, I can promise you. SINS has calculated the timing—it will still take approximately two hours for the kites to become animate once you wake up." He looked at her in seeming sympathy. "They won't be alive, Katie. You won't really know they're there."

"How can you say that?" she whispered. "Of course I'll know!"

He gazed at her calmly, and it was Kagen who looked out from his eyes again.

"You won't change his plans?" she asked softly, staring at him, feeling her throat close, knowing before he spoke what he was going to do.

"Some things cannot be changed," he said. "I'm sorry."

"You're a bastard," she whispered.

"Perhaps you should remember that."

She scuffed about in the litter of kites on the deck. Although she had been here for a little while now, she still had to muster every gram of her control to walk among the creatures without showing her horror. The Loon whispered constantly in her ear, until she began to find it a distraction—a welcome distraction now. Why shouldn't she give in to the madness, after all? What else was left her?

Rory was watching her, and he *was* Rory now, head cocked slightly to one side in a posture she remembered well. How dare he? How dare this piece of electronic junk look at her as a lover had once looked at her? How dare he—*it*, goddammit—how dare *it* taunt her with the possibility of going against its own creator, to watch her beg one last foolish time for help where none would ever be?

Fear and revulsion twisted in her gut, and for a minute she nearly gave in to the soft hooting of the Loon, nearly allowed the vision of what had happened to Mishima to overwhelm her as she stood among the creatures that would soon overwhelm her in reality. Indeed, what else was left her?

Dignity, she told herself. *Dignity! And . . .* she felt a surge of adrenaline so strong it made her shudder, *maybe a way out!*

Rory was still watching her.

"It's cold in here," she said, wrapping her arms about her, making a show of her frosty breath.

"I expect so. The heating system's been off for over a year."

"Can't we do something about it? I might as well be comfortable while I wait." She looked at her watch. "How much time do I have?"

"Slightly more than an hour, I would think. Of course, you know that the length of time needed for the kites to waken after their exposure to living heat is not precise. I may be a few minutes off." He smiled.

"Be a champ. Give me your best guess."

"You have sixty-seven minutes—give or take five. Or," he watched her curiously, "perhaps give or take fifteen. Is that good enough?"

"It'll have to do." She began to set her watch. "There." She showed him the watch face, with the oversized numbers winking off a countdown. "Now I know what I'm dealing with—give or take something."

"I'm pleased you've decided to be reasonable about your situation."

"As long as you don't make me freeze to death!" She rubbed her arms briskly. If he thought she was giving in, perhaps she had a chance. "Can't you tell how cold it is in here? I thought LSH units had skin sensors or something."

"Oh, I could give you an accurate reading of the ambient temperature in here. But what would be the point? You already know you're cold."

"That *is* my point, sweetheart. Can we do something

about it? Like jump-start the *Opal*'s heating plant, or something?"

He cocked an eyebrow at her. "Very clever, my dear. A little something for the *Pegasus*'s sensors to pick up, so they'll know where you really are?" He shook his head. "I'm afraid you'll have to deal with the chill."

"Fuck you," she whispered.

"We do have enough time, Katie," he said with a smile. When she wouldn't rise to the bait, he merely raised his eyebrows and gestured to her to follow him.

"Where are we going?"

"Away from the main airlock. There's a chance Luttrell will underestimate the time and arrive early. I'd rather we not be near a likely entry port."

"Suppose I'd rather stay here?"

"Have you already forgotten my strength?" He thrust his hand out and flexed it so she could see the artificial tendons move under the skin covering of his arm. It was something Kagen himself could never do, she realized.

He began to walk, and she followed him wearily.

"What are you going to do when everyone else gets here?" she asked after a pause. The countdown on her watch had just slipped below sixty minutes.

"I will reboard the *Pegasus* during the excitement. No one will notice, believe me. And then I'll clean up after the rest of the crew is in deep-sleep for the trip home."

"Clean up?"

He smiled slowly, warmly, as Rory would have smiled—but Rory would never have spoken as he spoke. "A number of people know too much about what's going on, just like Dickenson and Westman knew too much. I appreciate how badly you must have needed to tell someone your story, but surely you realize that we cannot allow others to know the truth of the situation."

"You did kill them!"

"Not I, personally, no."

"I don't think I believe you." She turned her back on him. "Who else has been 'cleaned up'?"

His smile was nasty. "Mr. Lars became a bother shortly after we left on this mission."

Kate clenched her fists, but she wouldn't turn around. "Go on," she whispered.

"Need I mention more names? You know who you talked to after the *Opal* mission. So do we."

She spun back to face him. *"Who else?"*

"James Travers's little sister will be very easy to take care of on the trip back home. I don't believe any of the others will be a problem—though we may have to watch out for Mr. Juli in the future."

Kate fought against tears, against the feeling of defeat that threatened to overwhelm her. He was doing this to her on purpose. He was doing exactly what Kagen would have done, and she knew she had been truly betrayed. He was Kagen; he was not Rory.

"You're telling me this because you know I can't do anything about it. You're *enjoying* this!" she said furiously. "God damn you, Rory, God damn you. And Kagen! I'll get him for this. I don't know how, yet, but I'll get him." She looked him square in the face—it was Kagen's face, and she relished that. "You can give him that message from me!" She shoved past him and bolted down a side corridor.

Rory stood and watched her go. He knew she would head for the spare suit locker, and he began to move slowly in that direction. He could handle her. If need be, he could rip every suit in that locker.

The countdown had slipped to fifty minutes.

CHAPTER
19

"What do you *mean*, you want to search the basement room?" Teresa asked.

"It's the one area none of us is really familiar with," Grayson said. "Luttrell thinks she may have run there because of its association with the creators of this place."

"Yeah, well, Luttrell thinks with his asshole. How the hell was she supposed to get down there on the winch without someone to help her? Does it even look like it's been touched?"

"Teresa, take it easy on him." Al laid a gloved hand on her shoulder.

"You know the thing can be radio controlled," Grayson was saying.

"Fine. Has it been used at all recently?"

"Well—"

"You're doing real well, Grayson. The captain is bugfuck crazy, and you want me to think she'd take all the time to run away from us down in the hole, and better yet that she'd send the winch cable back up so it wouldn't look like she used it?"

"Teresa!" Al shook her shoulder, but she knocked his hand away.

"We're going down there," Grayson said stubbornly. "I can man the winch while he rides it."

"Listen to me!" Al finally spun her around to face him. "This is exactly what I was trying to stop. Now you've made him feel like an idiot, so he's going to go down there anyway, just to be stubborn."

"So, let him look like a fool! I know she didn't go down there."

"Grayson?" Pete's voice, coming from the *Pegasus*, interrupted them. "Grayson, I've got a reading on an emergency beacon. I think it's the *Black Opal*'s!"

"The *Black Opal*? But that doesn't make any sense!"

"That's where she is!" Teresa grabbed Al's arm. "She never came here at all—she went to the *Opal*!"

"But why?" Al shook his head. "Grayson is right, it doesn't make any sense. Besides, why would she run away from us, and then let us know where she is?"

"Precisely my question," Luttrell's voice joined in the conversation. "You heard yourself, Teresa, how much she objected to going aboard the *Opal* when I first brought it up. I think we should continue our search here."

"Why didn't she just contact us by radio if she's aboard the *Opal*?" Grayson asked.

Teresa switched to private mike. "Al, are you with me?"

"I told you I would be," he said.

"You can do whatever you think is best," she said, switching her suit radio back to broadcast, "but Al and I are going to the *Black Opal*. If she *is* there and we miss her, think how terrible we'll all feel."

"Wait a minute, you can't do that!" Grayson protested. "That's an order, MacKessen! Stay put!"

"Shove it up your ass, Grayson! I don't care whether you come with us or not, but we're going to the *Opal*!"

"Signal's still coming in steady," Pete reported. "I'd vote for your idea, Teresa. There's no way that signal could've been turned on unless somebody aboard the *Opal* did it."

"All right, all right, wait for us!" Grayson said. "Luttrell, get out of that damn harness or I'm leaving you behind."

"In a moment, Captain, in a moment."

Teresa looked at Al. "Did you hear that? Calling him 'Captain' already."

Al merely shrugged as they climbed into the jalopy to wait for the others.

"Pete, can you give us a bearing on the *Opal*?" Teresa asked. "I'm not exactly sure which direction to head from here."

"Give me a minute to work it out."

"Still getting that signal?"

"Loud and clear."

In minutes Grayson and Luttrell appeared through the airlock.

"You can move now," Grayson said. "I'll drive."

"I've already got the bearing to the *Opal*, Captain," Teresa said sweetly. "Wouldn't it be easier if I just stayed put?"

Grayson muttered something the rest of them could not understand, and climbed into the backseat.

Minutes later, following Pete's careful directions, they arrived at the derelict ship. Teresa noticed immediately that the bridge area was brightly lit.

"Look!" She pointed. "See the lights—someone's aboard her!"

"Let's not waste any time," Al said. "I've got a bad feeling about this."

"I don't understand what the concern is," Luttrell was saying. "Surely the ship's batteries..."

Al boosted Teresa up to the airlock, which she cranked open manually. The rest of them followed once she had let down the ramp from inside.

"Jesus, lookit the kites, will you?" Grayson remarked, kicking aside several in the airlock vestibule. "The buggers must reproduce!"

"What about this?" Teresa bent down and grasped a suit in her hand, nearly shoving it in Grayson's face. The insignia on the back plainly marked it as belonging to the *Pegasus*—and the front was ripped from throat to navel.

The last thing Kate did before she left the bridge of the *Black Opal* was to open the shipwide intercom and damage the circuits sufficiently so it couldn't be closed. She had already taken a headset and throat mike from one of the bridge stations so she could listen in on suited conversations.

She glanced at her watch. Eighteen minutes according to her countdown before the kites would come alive and engulf...someone, anyone unfortunate enough to be unsuited. They were everywhere.

Somehow she had to get to a suit, to some kind of protection. The emergency suit locker wasn't far from the bridge—but Rory knew the ship as well as she did, and she knew he would expect her to go there. Even if she discounted his incredible strength, he still had a stunner, and she didn't have time to come up with a diversion now, assuming she could fool him at all. She remembered all too clearly the earlier mission, when Greg had taken the last stunner and had gone off to attempt to block the bulkheads against their maddened crewmates. She'd never found it or his body. There were no other weapons aboard the *Opal*....

The wrench! Kate shuddered with the memory. She had killed Alicia Chavez, the *Opal*'s physician, with a heavy wrench from the bridge's toolkit. The wrench would still be near the woman's body. It was an incident Rory knew nothing about, so he wouldn't know the weapon was there. Not much against a stunner or his superior strength, but it was better than nothing! Kate crept from the bridge, her only fear that of running into Rory before she could find what she wanted.

"Let's split up," Luttrell suggested. "She knows this ship better than any of us, so in two groups we can cover more ground."

"Why not search singly?" Teresa asked. "That way we would be four groups."

"*I* don't wish to run around this ship unaccompanied," Luttrell said pointedly. "Do you?"

"How was I supposed to argue with that?" Teresa asked Al moments later as they went down a corridor away from the airlock vestibule.

"Hey, he's got a point. I don't care how crazy he thinks the captain is, she couldn't have ripped a spacesuit like that." Al shook his head. "We've got company!"

"I'm glad I didn't have to be the first one to say that. What worries me is—well, who, or *what*, could it be?"

Al paused in the corridor, head tilted to one side in his helmet.

"What's the matter?"

He held up his hand. "Listen!"

"I don't hear anything—"

"I'm getting just a trace of interference—it's the ship's intercom. Someone's opened the shipwide intercom!"

Teresa turned down the volume on her suit radio. "You're right, I can hear the others, just barely."

"I'll bet the captain did that. She had to be on the bridge when she activated the emergency beacon, and I'll bet she opened the intercom so she could hear what was going on. Keep your suit-radio volume down—we may be able to track her."

"Don't you think she'll try to be extra quiet? She knows the sound will carry."

"She may assume we'll be too busy concentrating on our suit radios."

"Well, it's worth a try. But the others can do the same."

"Ah, they're in too big a hurry—they probably won't even notice. Besides, we need all the help we can get. I don't even know where to start looking for her!"

"The emergency suit locker," Teresa said immediately. "Where would *you* go if your suit was ripped down the front and there were kites all over the place? We don't know how long she's been here—we have no idea when the two-hour countdown started!"

"We don't even know if two hours is a good number or not. Do you know where the locker is?"

Teresa shrugged.

Proud of himself for managing to become "separated" from Grayson, Luttrell wandered down a corridor, trying to decide where he would be going if he were Kate Harlin.

"Would you like to be of some assistance in this effort?"

Luttrell jumped. Even though he knew there was an LSH unit aboard the *Opal*, he hadn't expected to be approached from behind by the thing. "Well, where is she?" he countered. "Don't tell me you've lost her. I thought you had the situation under control."

The biomechanical man regarded him coldly. "Are you interested in pretending to be in charge, or in doing something useful?"

Luttrell cleared his throat, recalling belatedly that his stunner wouldn't work on the cyborg. "What did you have in mind?"

"Do you know where the emergency suit locker is?"

Luttrell nodded. "But why—?"

"Go there if you want to intercept Kate Harlin. She hasn't much time left, and she'll be looking for protection."

"What will you be doing?"

"You know I can't be seen by the others if the plan is to be carried out properly. I'll be nearby if you need me—but I don't expect you to need me."

Luttrell turned and headed for the emergency suit locker. He looked back over his shoulder once, and the LSH unit was still standing there, unsuited, watching him. He shuddered and walked on.

Kate walked slowly up to Alicia's body. Everything was just as she had left it, except for the proliferation of kites in the area. There had been none when she had . . . when Alicia had died over a year ago. The body itself was a shriveled husk, in no way resembling the woman who had once been her friend. Kate bent to retrieve the wrench, noting that it was stained with blood. She then bowed her head briefly and said good-bye.

Minutes later, Kate cautiously approached the emergency suit locker. She knew Rory would expect her to come here. She only hoped she had thrown him off by detouring to the bridge. A glance at her watch showed less than five minutes—she was well inside Rory's period of uncertainty.

Slowly, so slowly that she was almost unsteady on her feet, Kate rounded the last curve in the corridor. Rory's artificial hearing was so acute that she couldn't afford to make the slightest sound. . . .

Someone had gotten there before her. A spacesuited figure stood near the wide entrance to the locker area, back turned to her. Not Rory, but . . . who?

The figure must have been listening intently to the conversations on his (her?) suit radio. She crept as close as she dared, the wrench hefted in both hands.

"*Hey, you!*" she called.

The figure before her turned, startled, and she could see his features through the faceplate. It was Luttrell.

Kate leaped at him. She swung the wrench wildly as he raised his stunner, and the heavy tool caught him on the side of the head. He staggered and fell, though she could see his helmet was undamaged. He raised his stunner shakily.

And the dam burst inside her. She hit him again and again with the wrench, willing him to drop the stunner but he wouldn't drop it his arm wouldn't go down he kept trying to shoot her if he'd only drop it she could stop...

She heard his helmet crack, heard it split, saw pieces flying away with the force of her last blow, and the sound was enough to make her realize that if she didn't stop she would kill him. Panting, her shoulders heaving, she pulled away from him, drew back on one knee, and saw Rory standing a few paces away, stunner cradled in his hand, gazing at her. His head was cocked on that familiar angle, and he smiled, the scar on his lip pulling it slightly higher on one side—

"Kate! *Duck!*"

The voice was Teresa's. Kate obeyed, diving to one side, and heard the beam of a laser crack overhead. Rory went down, the expression on his face unchanged in that last instant.

For the briefest of moments there was no sound, no movement, then Kate rolled to her feet and bolted for the locker room.

"Help me!" she called, and pulled desperately at the first suit locker she came to. Teresa and Al understood what she was trying to do and came to her aid. With their help she suited up in record time...and screams came from the corridor.

It was Luttrell.

Kate didn't need the timer on her wrist to tell her what had happened. They crowded around, speechless, watching as wave upon wave of black diamond-shapes rose up from the deck to flow on and around Luttrell's twisting form, disappearing in through his shattered helmet.

"Do something, for God's sake! Help the man!" Grayson whispered, barely able to speak.

"Teresa?" Kate held her hand out for the young woman's stunner. She fired once, and Luttrell's struggles ceased.

"Is that all you can do?" Al asked matter-of-factly.

"I'm afraid so. Unless you want me to kill him now."

No one spoke. Calmly, Kate went into the suit locker and chose a spare helmet. She bent next to Luttrell and began to remove the damaged one.

"Here, let me help." Al crouched next to her, and together they worked on the unconscious man. The sea of kites shifted, burying Luttrell's face completely. Al looked away.

"Can you hold him up by the shoulders?" Kate asked levelly.

"Mm? Oh, yeah, sure."

While Al supported the limp figure, Kate brushed away as many of the kites as she could to make room for the new helmet. Only when it was secured in place and she was assured of a clear airflow inside Luttrell's suit did she rise to her feet.

"So," she let out a long breath, "what took you guys so long?"

Everyone except Grayson tried to talk at once. The pilot was standing a little to one side, shifting his gaze between Luttrell's suited form and the prone LSH unit with a gaping hole in its vitals. Kate stood still amid all the noise, and she began to grin until her face hurt as it occurred to her that everything was really all right now.

"Stop, stop!" she finally said, laughing. "One at a time!"

"Good, I claim the first question," Grayson said. "What the hell is this thing?" He pointed to Rory's still form.

Kate's smile disappeared. "It's a thinking frankenstein."

"But that's—not possible!"

"There he is, without a spacesuit, too. What kind of proof do you need?" Teresa burst out.

Kate looked surprised at the outburst.

He shook his head. "I don't get it."

"Yeah, and you never will, either! I swear to God, Grayson—"

"That's enough," Kate said quietly. "We'll talk about it later."

Grayson cleared his throat to break the uncomfortable silence. "What're we going to do with Luttrell?"

"Take him back to the ship."

"What for? He's as good as dead, isn't he? Why don't we just kill him?"

"Yeah," Pete's voice came through their earphones from the *Pegasus*. "Croak the bastard. He's caused enough trouble already."

"He won't be any more trouble than the frankenstein would've been," Al said reasonably. "We came out here to collect a sample; it's in our contracts. We've got a good one— I vote we take him home."

"Who said anything about voting?" Kate asked quietly. "He goes home with us. Somebody help me get him on the stretcher."

"Shit, Captain, he ain't worth the trouble!" Grayson finally exclaimed.

"I don't want to hear that from you, Grayson. Two hours ago you'd have followed him to hell through high water!" Teresa said.

"You can all just stow it!" Kate snapped at them. "I'm not interested in anyone else's opinion. We take him home— got it?"

"But—" Grayson started.

"I will not kill someone in cold blood, and I will not order someone else to do it. Enough people have died for this filthy cause already—I want no more death!" She stared at each of them, and one by one they looked away. "Anyone want to say anything else?"

"Uh, don't you think we should get back to the ship?" Grayson asked after a beat.

"Good point," Pete's subdued voice came through their earphones. "You guys have been out there a long time. The captain's the only one with a decent amount of air left."

Al and Grayson unfastened the medical pack from Luttrell's suit and strapped him to the stretcher. Kate watched them for a few moments, then walked over to where Rory lay. His face was frozen in that familiar half-smile, his eyes were wide open, and she could almost believe he would climb to his feet in a minute and laugh at all of them.

"Teresa?" Without turning around, she held out her gloved hand. The younger woman seemed to understand; she handed Kate the laser. Kate drew a deep breath and very calmly crisscrossed the body with precise laser fire, until the chest area was a smoking mass of useless electronics. The head she left untouched.

"Kagen, one ... Harlin, one," she murmured to herself. "Even game, you bastard."

"Ohh ..." Teresa stumbled suddenly and nearly fell.

Kate caught her by the arm. "You okay?"

"It's my sinuses—shit, my nose is bleeding! How'm I supposed to wipe my nose in a goddamn suit?"

"Why is your nose bleeding?"

"I came to your room to talk to you, but when the door opened somebody punched my lights out. I guess it was that thing." She pointed to the frankenstein.

Kate peered through her faceplate. "Good lord, your face is puffed up like a balloon!"

"Captain, we're ready now," Al said. "Maybe for Teresa's sake we should make it quick."

"Absolutely. Al, can you manage this thing by yourself if I help George carry Luttrell?" Kate indicated Rory's still form.

"I can help—" Teresa started.

"You're in no condition. Al?"

"Sure, no problem."

They traded places at the end of the stretcher, and began to move slowly away from the nightmare.

CHAPTER

20

The crew of the *Pegasus* sat around the mess table and tried to relax. Kate had produced a bottle of Chivas from her quarters (her last unopened "gift" from Rory), and it now sat in the middle of the table, surrounded by five glasses. They drank in silence.

Kate sat quietly, the calmest of the group, chin propped

on her hand, eyes closed. Talking required more energy than she had right now, though she could feel the rest of the crew watching her. She knew she would have to break the silence soon.

The meter-wide monitor off to one side showed a closeup image of Luttrell, frozen in the frankenstein's cubicle on Deck 2 where Rory had been kept. The doctor had still been unconscious when they had removed his life-support pack and plugged him into the special controls in the freezer compartment that allowed him to be frozen in his suit. He would stay there until they arrived home.

Kate opened her eyes, saw the rest of them tense expectantly, and smiled a little. "I guess you're ready to talk."

"Yeah," Grayson agreed. "But before we get into a long story, I got a question."

"Go ahead."

"Did you know about that thinking frankenstein?"

Kate looked at him for a long moment. "You're a damn untrusting son of a bitch, you know that?"

He returned her look. "We've been through a lot of shit. I want to know where I stand."

Teresa slammed on the table the cold pack she'd had against the side of her face. "You know, Grayson, it's a long walk home, and I'm about ready to invite you to take it. Haven't you ever heard of trust?"

"Look, honey," he thrust his finger at her, "I don't know what's going on here yet, so I don't trust nobody!"

"If you'd wait a minute like a decent person, you might find out—"

"That's enough." Kate's voice was very quiet, but they stopped immediately. "You'll get your answers, Grayson. I'll even answer your question first, though I don't think it deserves one. No, I didn't know about the thinking frankenstein. Kagen had promised me a brain-dead LSH unit for a host on this mission, and like a fool I believed him. I only found out Rory was alive and active a few hours before the rest of you did."

"Rory? Wait a minute." Grayson frowned. "Wasn't he the engineer on the *Black Opal* mission?"

"A fuckin' genius, he is," Teresa muttered. Grayson shot

her a look, but neither of them was willing to start the argument again.

"That's right," Kate agreed.

"You mean this guy we had in the freezer on Deck 2 and the *Opal*'s engineer were the same thing? But I thought you said he was killed here!"

"They were the same type of LSH unit, not the same unit, although they shared knowledge and memories. But the Rory I knew had been in the space service for years. Pretty good dry run for the model, don't you think? He passed with flying colors." She swallowed—some memories still hurt.

"How many of these guys are there?"

"I don't know, but the ones I've seen have all been dead ringers for Kagen."

"Kagen? Oh, Jesus . . ."

"It proves what I've been saying all along—you can't trust Kagen, and you can't trust Guil-Pro. The kites can't even use a frankenstein as host. Rory told me that himself after we were on the *Opal*."

"Why were you there?" Al asked.

"*I* was supposed to be the host." Her hand shook slightly as she drank. "It was a nifty idea—I'm sorry I didn't figure out what Kagen was up to from the start. God knows Luttrell caused enough trouble on this mission, but things happened he either didn't know how to do or couldn't have gotten away with doing.

"Rory didn't need a hibernation unit, of course. He was up and around the whole trip out here. You can do a lot in seven months." She smiled. "He programmed SINS with the random messages I kept getting. He screwed with the winch, messed with the air supply in my suit—even my presence aboard the *Opal* was going to look like an accident. He meant to be gone by the time the rest of you got there, and no one would've known about him except Luttrell."

"You mean Luttrell was on—on that thing's side?" Grayson asked.

Kate nodded. "Luttrell would've seen to it that he got back aboard the *Pegasus* and into the chamber while you were busy with me—he *could* live in that freeze chamber, you see—and you'd have been real busy, chasing my ass all over the *Opal*." She shuddered. "Poor Captain, gone crazy from the strain, running around stark naked and covered with kites. Your sample for Guil-Pro, wrapped up all nice in a spacesuit with a bow on top."

"This is—this is crazy!" Grayson sat back. "Why? What the hell's been going on?"

Kate told her story one more time, to the most attentive audience she'd had yet. She explained everything, from what had really happened to the *Hercules* right up to the fight Luttrell had forced on her in the corridor outside the mess room. They were silent when she finished.

"So," she finally said, "now you know where I stand. I tried to keep you guys out of most of it, but things got out of hand at the end. I'm sorry."

"You can't blame y'self for it," Grayson said, somewhat embarrassed. "It happened, and we *are* involved. Let's leave it at that."

Teresa curled her lip. "What's the matter, George, you going soft?"

"No," he said, for once not rising to her bait, "I'm trying to apologize. That okay with you?"

She flushed. "Fine. But it sure took you long enough."

"Can you kids knock it off for a while?" Kate's tone was light, but they took the hint.

"Well." Grayson cleared his throat and tried to start afresh. "Seems to me we still have some decisions to make. Like about Luttrell, for instance. I mean, what do we do with him when we get him back home? He ain't exactly what Kagen's expecting."

"Kagen might not be expecting anything," Al pointed out. "By the time we get home we'll have been gone almost a year and a half. A lot of things can change in that time."

"Yeah, usually for the worse," Pete muttered, and they all chuckled.

Kate looked around the table and saw everyone nodding in agreement, and she relaxed a little. "I can tell you what Kagen is expecting," she said. "Rory laid it all out for me while we were on the *Opal*. He's expecting all six of us to walk out together. He's expecting me to be awake and aware, in a suit full of kites."

"I don't think we should do that with Luttrell, though," Pete said. "It's a hell of a risk, especially when you consider that we're not even sure how long it takes for the things to wake up. Suppose freezing them so close to a body changes them somehow, speeds up their animation process? The thawing procedure itself takes two hours or more!"

Kate nodded. "That's exactly why we can't follow Kagen's scenario. It's just too dangerous. We'll have to keep Luttrell frozen."

"Now wait a minute. I think thawing him out is a *great* idea!" Grayson broke in. "Look, we're real worried about the reception we're going to get, right? You think Guil-Pro is going to get anywhere near us with live kites around? Hell no, they'll be running in the other direction, and that'll be our chance!"

"George," Kate said tiredly, "we're dealing with a real problem of contagion—we can't risk letting those things loose, even on a station as far away as the *Orphic Angel*." She spoke more softly. "Even to guarantee our own safety."

"Well, I still think it's a good idea," he grumbled, "but I guess I see your point."

"That settles it, then. He stays frozen." She looked around. "Any more questions?"

"Can we expect any help from the Authority?" Al asked. "You said Lars had your proof."

"No." Kate's face closed up suddenly. "I—I don't think the information ever got to them. They won't have a case without it—they won't even know what's going on at all, so . . . no."

Teresa looked up quickly. "What do you mean, never got to them? How can you be so sure?"

"Rory told me Lars was dead," Kate said flatly. "Just like everyone else who knew too much."

"But they didn't know about him! How could they—?"

"Teresa!" Kate's voice was harsh. "Dickenson and Westman died, didn't they? You were with me when I got the news. How did Kagen know about them?" She paused, her jaw working. "An hour ago *I* was a *host*, with no way out. Why would Rory have lied to me? It gained him nothing."

"Pleasure."

Kate stared at the table, knowing that Rory was only a machine, yet more than a machine . . . but the thought gave her no hope.

Teresa's voice shook when she spoke again. "I'm sorry, Kate."

"So am I." She shaded her eyes with her hand, avoiding Teresa's gaze, beginning to wonder why she was knocking herself out when there was no longer any reason to.

"What about Watson?" Pete asked.

"I don't even know if he's alive or not. Rory didn't say he'd been hurt, but . . . Besides, the *Orphic Angel* is too far away for him to easily deal with Earthside Port Authority, and he gave the information to Lars anyway."

"So we really have to do this on our own," Pete said.

"You didn't expect it to be any other way, did you?" Teresa asked. "We haven't gotten many breaks all along. Why should this be any different?"

"I guess we need to figure out what this means to us now," Grayson said.

"I've got some ideas. You may not like 'em, but they're pretty realistic, I think." Teresa glanced at Kate, who was still staring at the table, and continued. "We'll probably get an escort from the terminus all the way back in. There'll be armed guards at the airlock of wherever we debark, and you know they'll search the ship as soon as we're off it to make sure we haven't fucked up—"

"Which we have, and royally." Grayson looked at Luttrell's image in the monitor again. "Plus destroying a very expensive LSH unit—faugh, have we got a mess!"

"Yeah, we sure do." Teresa smiled tightly. "And that's my whole point. Kagen will be able to figure out real quick just how much all of us know about everything, and when he does, he's not going to mess around. If *I'm* going to be eliminated for the good of the Consortium, it better be because I've done something, not just because I was in the wrong place at the wrong time."

"I like your style, Mac." Grayson grinned. "What d'you got for us?"

"So far we haven't really done anything to Kagen except inconvenience him. That LSH unit is expensive, sure, but it's not even the only one he's got. I mean, we're even bringing back the damn specimen he wants! Maybe it doesn't matter to the rest of you, but I really want to stick it to the bastard. I want to rub his face in this so bad I can taste it!" She pressed her palms flat on the table and leaned forward. "The way it stands right now," she said more quietly, "Kagen will just send somebody else out here to do what we didn't, unless—"

"Unless there's nothing here for him to get!" Al finished. "You want to get rid of the kites? Get rid of everything?"

"Hey, I like that idea," Grayson agreed. "Blow the whole works—go out with a bang!"

Pete looked over and frowned as though he disagreed, but said nothing.

"Well, that's not exactly what I had in mind," Teresa said. "It's the first thing I thought of, but now I don't think it's such a good idea."

"*Now* what's the problem?" Grayson wanted to know. "It's a good idea—and what choice do we have?"

"Will you stop thinking like an asshole, George? I really do like you, but sometimes you drive me crazy, you know?" Teresa shook her head. "Listen to me—*think* about this. We can't destroy an artifact like Roanoke! Pete, you understand about the Lost Colony and everything—this may be the only legacy of an entire race! Or, as the captain pointed out to me, these people may still be around. When they come after us to find out what happened, do *you* want to explain why we blew up their property?"

"Ah, c'mon, d'you really think—?"

Kate looked up. "Teresa's right. It doesn't matter what we think. We can't afford to destroy what may be the only heritage of this race—nor can we afford to destroy something that doesn't belong to us, just because it's dangerous and we don't know how to handle it. It's the easy way out of our problem, but it's the way we always seem to choose, and I don't think it'll really solve anything. What did you have in mind, Teresa?"

"I played twenty questions with SINS the other night. What I was looking for was a way to destroy the kites without hurting Roanoke itself. Doesn't look like we can do that. But in the process of answering my questions, SINS asked a few of his own—have any of you ever used SINS in inferencing mode?"

Everyone shrugged.

"SINS can actually carry on an interactive conversation while it's trying to figure out how to answer what you've asked it. Kind of like making you get to the point, or making you ask what you really mean, as opposed to what you think you mean. Am I clear?" She looked around, saw nods.

"Okay. So after about fifteen or so exchanges, I'm down to asking not how we can destroy kites, but how we can hurt Kagen and Guil-Pro the most. That's what we want to do, isn't it?"

"Well, yeah, I guess, if you put it that way," Grayson agreed.

"So get this! SINS tells me the *only* way we can hurt Kagen and Guil-Pro is to make them lose money. Our asses are already in the fire, right? Nobody's going to jail over this, except maybe us—nobody else is going to suffer. But if we work it right, Kagen will have wasted all this money on three ships and won't have a thing to show for it! He can get into a lot of trouble with higher Consortium management for being so inefficient."

"Am I thick?" Pete asked. "You still haven't answered the real question. *How* do we make them lose money?"

"Yeah. Wouldn't blowing up the whole works do that?" Grayson added.

Teresa grinned. "The answer is so easy I almost didn't believe it. Kagen has broken the law all down the line with this place. He lied about the *Hercules*'s discovery, he lied about what *happened* to the *Hercules*, he lied to the crew of the *Black Opal* about the true nature of their mission—and all along he's been trying to get somebody to bring back a sample of the kites from here. That's against the law! Sure, we're working for the government now, supposedly, which makes bringing back a specimen okay, but none of the earlier missions were. SINS has all those records, so we can prove it!"

"So, big deal, what'll that get him, a slap on the wrist? A fine? He won't care about that," Grayson said.

"No, but he *will* care that the find no longer belongs to Guil-Pro."

There was silence in the room.

"What do you mean?" Kate finally asked. "Why won't it belong to Guil-Pro?"

"Because they've broken the law. You can't profit from a crime."

"Are you sure? That sounds so—so simple!"

"I can show it to you straight from SINS's legal library."

"Then who does it belong to?"

"It defaults to the men who staked the claim originally—and their heirs."

"Well, that's just great!" Grayson said in disgust. "What the hell good does that do us? Those guys are dead, we haven't the faintest idea who or where their relatives are—"

Teresa looked at Kate, who raised her eyebrows slightly. "The captain didn't tell you the whole story about the *Hercules*." She hesitated. "Jamie Travers was my brother. His claim defaults to me."

"Oh, my God." Grayson said it very softly.

There was a silence, and Al laid his arm across her shoulders. She smiled up at him briefly.

"What does this buy us, Teresa?" Kate asked.

"Kagen can't make any use of what we discovered here. It doesn't belong to Guil-Pro anymore—he can't touch it."

"Uh, how do we substantiate this?" Al asked.

"I can file an amended claim right now. It should get there before we do. After it's processed, it'll land on Kagen's desk. He won't know what to do when he gets it! He won't even know where it came from."

"Why won't he just ignore it?" asked Pete.

"I don't think he can afford to," Kate interjected. "He'll go to Legal about it, and they'll have to tell him." She smiled a little. "If we're on the right track, he's going to be *very* unhappy."

"Well, that's what we're looking for, right?" Pete asked.

"Damn straight we are!" Grayson poured another round from the almost empty bottle. "Let's give 'em hell."

They drank on it, touching glasses solemnly.

Some time later, Kate sat in her quarters with her feet

propped on her bunk. It was dark except for the green glow of her clock.

She wondered how Lars had died.

She sat in her quarters and didn't cry because she couldn't cry until it was all over, so she thought about how good it would feel to strangle Kagen with her bare hands.

It was 4:00 A.M.

Kate sat at her station on the bridge and waited for Pete to report the final takeoff sequence from engineering. The *Pegasus* thrummed beneath her as power grids generated the energy they would need to lift away from the planet.

"Surface thrusters are go, Captain," Pete's voice came to her. "All quadrants are green for light-plus."

"Thank you, engineering. Environmental?"

"Luttrell's condition is stable. All cryo systems are green," Teresa reported.

"Thank you. Navigation?"

"Return course locked in for return via Outer Terminus Sector Five," Grayson reported. "That'll put us in the neighborhood of the *Orphic Angel*, as you requested."

"Thank you, navigation. Engineering, we are go for takeoff. Engage surface thrusters."

The *Pegasus*'s muted rumbling rose to a thunderous pitch, and the ship lifted slowly from the planet's surface.

"All surface thrusters nominal!" Pete reported.

"Landing struts retracted," Kate said. "Bay doors sealed."

"Altitude six kilometers," came Grayson's voice moments later. "Velocity six hundred meters per second."

"Artificial gravity engaged—now!" Kate threw the switch.

"We've just cleared the planet's atmosphere, Captain," Grayson said. "That should do us."

"ETA at the safety limit?" she asked.

"Three hours and thirty-five minutes."

"Thank you. How's life support look, Teresa?"

"Everything is green."

Kate pushed back in her seat slightly. They could relax for a while.

Several hours later they had reached the safety limit and

engaged the light-plus engines. The crew met in the central life-support chamber.

"SINS will wake us about an hour outside the outer terminus," Kate told them as she applied her medical sensor patch. "You know we won't really be sneaking in. All the rim beacons we pass will report our configuration, so anyone who's interested will know we're on our way." She pushed her hands through her hair. "We'll wake up before we drop into normal space. That way we can watch out for what might be on the other side."

"What'll we tell them?" Teresa asked nervously.

"I'm working on that." Kate smiled.

The crew settled into their individual hibernation units with only their own thoughts to keep them company. Kate double-checked the link between the freeze chamber that held Luttrell and the emergency wakeup alarm, and pressed the switch that would close the life-support link.

"Good night," she called softly, and laid back.

CHAPTER
21

Geoffrey Kagen pressed a button on his intercom. "What is it, Martin?"

"We have a report from the Taurus Sector rim beacon, sir. A light-plus pattern matching the *Pegasus* configuration passed it at O-one-thirty hours Earth Greenwich Time."

"Excellent. They are within ten hours of their filed schedule. Keep me informed of their progress, and have logistics begin preparations for their arrival." He paused. "Has everyone been briefed?"

"Oh, yes, sir. Everyone knows exactly what to do."

Kagen doubted that, but he took Baker's assurances in good faith. "Very good, Martin. That will be all." He broke

the connection and looked down once again at the paper on
his desk:

"I, Josephine Travers, as the sole living heir of James
Travers, late of the L.P.S. *Hercules*, registered to the Guilford
Production Consortium, do . . ."

Legal had already told him that, if circumstances were
indeed as she claimed them to be, and if she had the evidence
she referred to, her claim was valid. But these were annoying
details that could be dealt with later—what disturbed him
was not knowing where the claim had originated. Other de-
partments of the Consortium were investigating, but had no
results as of yet. Where had this Josephine Travers been?
Where was she now?

And how timely the claim had arrived, just before the
Pegasus itself was to return from its year-and-a-half mission.
He was beginning to wonder if the two occurrences were not
more closely related than he had first thought. Particularly
since the *Pegasus* had filed a flight plan that would have it
arrive at station *Orphic Angel* instead of coming into Equator
Station as had been originally planned.

Most of all, it annoyed him not to know exactly what
was going to happen when the *Pegasus* docked and her airlocks opened. Despite all his careful orchestration, all the
blinds and double blinds and contingencies, he had no way
of being sure that things had turned out as he had planned.
It might come down to the very end, right down to who would
be the first member of the crew to step through the airlock
into the station.

"Geoffrey, is this trouble for the Consortium?" Thomas
Guilford turned away from a window.

Kagen shook his head. "This is nothing, Mr. Guilford,
I can promise you. Nothing!"

He ran his hand over the document one more time, then
turned to the intercom. "Martin? It's time to make arrangements for our travel to the *Orphic Angel*. We must be there
before the *Pegasus*."

As usual, deep-sleep had not been restful. Kate lay in
her open hibernation unit and massaged the bridge of her
nose, trying to shake the headache she had gone under with

seven months ago. No such luck. Wearily she crawled from the unit and grabbed her clothes from the nearby hook. Maybe a hot shower would get rid of the headache.

Less than an hour later, Kate gulped two aspirin and scalded her tongue on her first cup of coffee. The rest of the crew wandered into the mess one by one and either sat or paced as their nerves dictated.

"Everybody all right?" she asked.

Teresa dribbled cream into her coffee. "The way I feel right now, I think Luttrell's better off than the rest of us."

"So he's still alive."

"Oh yeah. And his body has maintained better muscle tone than people usually do in a long freeze. If it's because of the kites, maybe those little bastards are worth something after all."

"Can't we talk about something else?" Pete complained.

"Sure," Kate obliged. "How're your eyes, Teresa? Looks like the swelling is gone."

"Still tender."

"Yeah, you've got two good-lookin' shiners there." Grayson smiled as he lit his first cigarette. "They'll be great for the news coverage. 'Captain beats crew in a fit of rage.'"

"He thinks he's a real wit." Teresa sighed.

"What's the agenda?" Al asked.

"Depends on what's waiting for us when we drop out of hyperspace," Kate told him. "We'll be about one normal-space hour away from the *Orphic Angel* at that point. By the way, SINS recorded an I.D. request from the Taurus Sector beacon. They reported us when we passed." She glanced at her watch. "We've got about half an hour before dropping into normal space."

"That evasive course you requested is locked in," Grayson said.

"Good." Kate swirled the coffee around in her cup.

"Don't we have to worry about being spotted right now?" Al asked.

"No." Kate smiled. "Except for our heading when that beacon reported us, they have no way of telling exactly where we are. They know we'll end up at the *Angel*, but that's not enough data for them to go by. And, since George programmed a kink into our course, they can't track us on a probability curve. Besides, we'll hit normal space outside the terminus staging area—they'll have no way to register our drop. It'll be a little tricky without the staging beacons, but it's worth it to be able to surprise them."

"This waiting is getting on my nerves," Al said.

"Nothing we can do about that." Kate glanced at her watch again; barely five minutes had passed. "Well, we can't put business off any longer." She leaned forward and put her elbows on the table. "I want Kagen to think up to the last minute that this mission went exactly the way he wanted it to."

"You mean you're supposed to be crazy by now."

"Not necessarily. Just not in command." She rubbed her forehead. "I'm not sure how much Rory was on his own, but I think we should be as indefinite about my actual condition as we can get away with. Teresa, you take the communications console. You'll field all the first contacts."

"Great. I'm so nervous I'll lose my voice."

"You'll do fine. Grayson, as exec you'll have to be in command. Don't tell them anything you don't absolutely have to, especially not if the Port Authority comes on. We don't want to give them the wrong impression, either, just in case," she swallowed, "they might be there to help us."

"Okay. What do we say about Luttrell?"

"Don't say anything."

"Suppose they want to talk to him?"

"Don't worry, they won't ask for him, not right at first. They have to follow the book, too, you know. They can't afford to act like anything is different about this mission until we tell them it is. That means they talk to the captain first. But if they do ask for him, tell them he's with me. Say I'm not feeling well, but don't be specific unless they push. The idea is to make them think I'm buried in kites somewhere without coming out and saying it. Let them jump to the wrong conclusion."

"Okay." Grayson sighed. "I hope this works."

"It has to," Kate assured him. "Kagen can try to prepare himself all he wants for problems—especially if he's as worried about Teresa's counterclaim as we hope he will be—but he's basically going to assume that everything went his way. Believe me, he's an incredibly confident son of a bitch who thinks no one would dare interfere with him. That's where we're going to trip him up."

"And you're sure he's going to be on the *Angel* when we get there?" Pete asked.

"That's what Rory told me."

Teresa spoke after a long silence. "I wish I had your confidence." She checked her watch nervously. "How much time left?"

"Less than fifteen minutes to normal space. Let's get to our stations and start checking things out."

Kate slid into her seat on the bridge and powered up her console. Pete's voice came to her as she slipped her headset on.

"Engineering is green, bridge. All light-plus units in full functioning order. Sublight thrusters ready to engage."

"Good." She flipped various toggles and watched as her consoles began to register the ship's condition. "Teresa, scan ahead. Do you get anything from normal space?"

"Just the usual interference." She tried to sharpen the focus. "Garbage. Nobody there."

"Then we still have the edge."

"Two minutes, forty-five seconds to disengage light-plus," Grayson reported.

"Okay so far," Kate murmured. "Got your story figured out yet, George?"

"Pretty much." He grinned at her. "Thought about it while I was in the shower."

"I'm getting some chatter out there now, Captain," Teresa said. "Not specifically about us, but they know something's on the way."

"Okay. George?"

"Thirty-two seconds and counting."

"Thank you. Teresa, stay on those scanners."

Kate's eyes strayed to the bridge viewport as Grayson continued his countdown. The port was more than big enough to see the stars through when they were in normal space, though now all she could see was the violet-hued interference pattern of their hull passing through normal space at light-plus speeds. Even as she watched, the wavering field shifted and her vision blurred. Blinding white streaks resolved into an unchanging starfield. They had achieved normal space.

"Normal space achieved," Grayson verified. "Right on target, too, if I may say so."

"Good job, George. Teresa?"

"No clear signals yet, and nobody out there waiting."

Kate checked her console. "Engineering, give me one-half speed on the sublight thrusters. We're . . . just about a hundred thousand klicks from the staging area. You should be getting something pretty soon, Teresa."

"I can't wait."

But wait they did, silently and with increasing nervousness, as they approached the staging area.

"This is Control Center for Outer Terminus Station *Orphic Angel*. Please identify yourself."

Everyone jumped when the voice blared from the speaker, and Teresa backed the volume down hastily. Kate took a deep breath to calm herself—the voice belonged to Billy Watson.

"As if they didn't know who we were," Teresa muttered, and flipped the talk switch on her console. "This is commercial Light-Plus Ship *Pegasus*, registration number GPC-1242, class J, requesting clearance to cross the outer terminus."

"Welcome home, *Pegasus*. The Taurus Sector beacon reported your configuration a while back. We've been expecting you."

The crew exchanged glances.

"Clearance granted, *Pegasus*," the voice continued. "Can we have your captain?"

Grayson thumbed his talk switch. "This is the exec, Control Central. Our captain isn't, uh, feeling too well right now." He glanced at Kate, who nodded, though she wished she could tell Billy she was all right and they needed help.

"Sorry to hear that, *Pegasus*." Billy's voice was perfectly neutral. "Was your mission successful?"

"Yes, it was."

"Very good, *Pegasus*. Do you wish clearance to dock?"

Again Grayson glanced at Kate. She shook her head slightly. "Not at the moment, Control Central. We're carrying some, ah, unique substances, and I think we need to deal with a Guil-Pro official before we can link up."

"Very well, *Pegasus*. I believe some officials are on their way, but I have no arrival information as yet. We'll keep you informed, and we'll be here if you need us. Control Central out."

"Thank you, Control Central," Teresa responded. "*Pegasus* out." She cut communications. "That wasn't so bad."

"Yeah," Kate pushed back in her seat, "but that was Billy Watson. Take my word for it, that was just the start of it!"

Kate had just ducked onto the bridge with a steaming mug of coffee when a voice crackled over the loudspeaker.

"*Pegasus*, this is Control Central. We have a Mr. Martin Baker here from the Executive Board."

"Go ahead, Control Central. Our exec is standing by," Teresa said, and looked at Kate, who made a face.

"This is Martin Baker, *Pegasus*. What's your name, exec?"

Grayson rolled his eyes. "George Grayson, sir."

"Thank you, Mr. Grayson. What is your mission status?"

"I was told to report directly to Mr. Kagen only."

Kate drank her coffee and listened.

"I am his confidential personal assistant. You report to me for now."

Grayson stretched back in his seat, arms folded behind his head, a wicked grin on his face. "I don't know, Mr. Baker, are you sure it's—?"

"It's all right, Grayson!" Baker sounded as though he were speaking from between clenched teeth.

"Touchy bastard," Teresa remarked softly. Kate merely smiled.

"Well, if you're sure. I'm happy to report the mission was a success."

"Excellent, excellent. Mr. Kagen will be very pleased to hear that." A pause. "By the way, I've received reports that your captain isn't feeling well. Can you give me any details?"

"Not really, Mr. Baker. We think it's just a hibernation reaction, but—that's all I know."

Kate grinned at him and winked.

Baker's tone was clipped when he next spoke. "I can appreciate your discretion, Mr. Grayson, but Mr. Kagen will most assuredly not. He expects a full report."

"Fine. I'll be glad to talk to him," Grayson said placidly.

They could hear Baker's exclamation of disgust as he broke the connection.

"This is Control Central, *Pegasus*. We have a break in the transmission signal. Did Mr. Baker cut you off?"

"Roger," Teresa replied. "Didn't even say good-bye."

"Do you want me to repatch?"

"Negative. There's nothing else to say."

"Roger, *Pegasus*. Control Central out."

Teresa thumbed the switch and started to laugh. "Boy, did he sound pissed! I bet he runs crying straight to Kagen."

"That was exactly the way to handle him, George." Kate finished her coffee. "You did all right."

"I'm getting really tired of waiting around," Teresa complained. "When are we going to hear from Kagen?"

Kate shrugged. "He may be doing this on purpose, trying to make us nervous."

"Well, it's working," Al remarked.

"*Pegasus*, this is Control Central. Mr. Baker asked me to inform you that preparations for receiving you are almost complete."

Grayson cleared his throat. "What kind of preparations, Control Central? This is news to us."

"Baker was supposed to explain everything to you."

"He never got back to us." Grayson nodded at Kate's mouthed instructions. "Can you fill us in on what they're doing?"

"They're sealing off your docking area. It looks like a quarantine bay. You guys must have some pretty hot stuff."

Kate pursed her lips. This was the most informal Billy had been in all their conversations with the *Orphic Angel*. She leaned over and whispered in Grayson's ear.

"Yeah, you could call it that," Grayson agreed. "Say, Control Central, are you on a tight beam?"

"You're all right, *Pegasus*. Yeah, I am."

"Good. I've got somebody here wants to talk to you." Kate traded places with Grayson. "Hi, Billy."

"Kate! But I thought—what the hell's going on?"

"Sorry, Billy, we don't have time now. Just pretend you've never had this conversation after it's over, will you?"

"No problem."

"Can you tell me more about what they're doing there?"

"Only what they've told me, Kate—I haven't seen any of it myself. They're sealing off a whole area around one of the docks, and they're only going to admit a few people when you guys come in."

"That shouldn't be any problem," Kate said with a laugh. "There's only a few people on the whole station!"

"Boy, they *are* keeping you guys in the dark! This place is crawling with media reps waiting for Kate Harlin's return!"

Kate sat back abruptly. "No kidding."

"Hey, Guil-Pro is really pissed about it, but they couldn't stop it. They know how important media relations are. They've promised a press conference and all sorts of stuff after the fact, but I don't know if that's going to flow with this bunch— they want to be on the spot when you guys debark. They know there's a story in this mission."

"Who's going to win that one, I wonder?"

"Well, it's a Guil-Pro station, after all."

"Yeah, I was afraid you'd say that." Kate sighed. "How much time do we have?"

"No more than two hours, they've told me."

Kate was silent for a moment. "Billy, do you think you could get through the security?"

"Hell, Kate, I don't know. Why?"

"We're going to have trouble, and we're going to need somebody on our side. If you could get some of those media people in there, Guil-Pro'll have to behave themselves."

"We could give it a shot, but—" She could almost hear his shrug. "I'd hate for you to rely on it."

"You may be all we have, Billy."

"I'll try, Kate. That's all I can say—I'll try."

"That's better than nothing, Billy. I'll let you go now. Don't want anything too irregular to show up on your logs."

"Hell, if I couldn't falsify that kind of shit, I wouldn't be in this job! Good luck, *Pegasus*. Station out."

"Well," Kate said, "looks like it won't be long now." She glanced over to Teresa's station. The younger woman was flipping switches with an air of desperation. "Is everything all right?"

Teresa turned to look at her. "No. Luttrell is starting to thaw."

"What?"

"SINS has taken over. I can't stop it, I can't break in— I couldn't even cut off his oxygen right now if I wanted to! He'll be thawed by the time we're ready to debark."

"Okay, *Pegasus*, you're grappled in," Control Central reported. The voice was strange—someone other than Billy was on duty. "Seal your umbilicus and you'll be ready to debark."

"Roger, Control Central." Teresa looked at Grayson.

"We may need some extra time," he spoke up. "We'll be offloading a sick crewmember."

"Roger. A med team is waiting."

Kate grimaced.

"Acknowledged," Grayson said. *"Pegasus* out."

Teresa stretched and pulled herself up from her seat. "God, I'm nervous!"

"Well," Kate smiled briefly, "you're not the only one."

The four of them walked slowly to the spare suit locker, where Pete was to meet them. They would all have to be suited before they handled Luttrell again.

CHAPTER

22

"Are you sure there's no way to reverse the process?" Pete asked. "Maybe we can wait until he thaws, and then freeze him again?"

Teresa shook her head. "I've already looked into that. SINS has it locked up tight."

"We just have to be careful," Kate said.

"Yeah, but he'll be a little—well, crazy, won't he? I would be, knowing I was walking around in a suit full of those things."

"It'll be okay. It'll have to be."

Minutes later, the entire crew stood grouped around the freeze chamber in the cubicle on Deck 2. Pete monitored the final stages of the dehibernation process.

"Do you think he'll know us?" Teresa asked.

Kate shrugged. "How much longer?" she asked Pete.

"Ten minutes. He'll be groggy."

They peered anxiously down through the plastex cover of the infirmary's freeze chamber. Mercifully, Luttrell's face was free of kites, and they could see none through the faceplate of his suit helmet.

"Come on," Kate said, her voice steady, "everybody loosen up a little. We're stuck with this; it's not our choice. If what Rory told me was true, chances are he won't even be aware of what's wrong with him." She eyed the monitor screen on which SINS displayed Luttrell's vital signs as his body temperature returned to normal.

Finally, with the sound of quiet hydraulics, the lid of the freeze chamber began to slide open. Everyone took a step back, then looked at one another and smiled sheepishly. But no one stepped forward again, until Kate did.

"He won't know where he is at first," she said. "Let him come back slowly."

Luttrell groaned—they could all hear it in their suit radios. His eyes flickered, then opened wide. For a moment he seemed not to recognize the helmeted faces clustered above him, then he smiled.

"Wh-what's wrong?" he asked weakly, raising his gloved hands over him. "Why am I suited?"

"We had a problem with your unit," Kate said levelly. "You'll be all right. Just give yourself a chance to wake up."

"Why am I suited?" he insisted. "Why are you? What's wrong with me?" He struggled to sit up, and they let him.

"Kenneth, you need to stay calm," Kate told him. "We can't help you if you get all excited. It's time to leave the ship now, and you have to be able to walk. We'll help you, but we don't want to have to carry you out. Can you do that for us?"

"What's wrong with me? What's *wrong* with me?" He seemed to become suddenly aware of the strangeness of the situation. An edge of desperation crept into his voice. "There's something in my suit!"

"Can you guys handle him?" Kate asked.

"Yeah, if he don't get too squirmy," Grayson said.

He and Pete lifted Luttrell by his arms, disconnected his suit from the chamber's life-support system, and fastened his standard suit-pack in place. Then they helped him to stand.

"Can you walk, Kenneth?" Kate asked him. "We're going to help you, but you must try to walk."

"Maybe we should just knock him out," Teresa muttered.

"No! No, don't knock me out!" Luttrell pleaded. "I can't go to sleep again! I had nightmares—terrible nightmares! Please, don't make me go to sleep again!"

"Okay, Kenneth, we won't make you go to sleep again. Just walk with us, won't you?" They began to make slow progress down the corridor to the airlock vestibule.

"What's in my suit? You . . . you never told me."

"It doesn't matter, Kenneth," Kate soothed him. "Just walk with us."

His eyes were wide and staring. "Yes, it matters. What's in my suit? What happened to me? I—I remember someone hit me, we fought ... and ... and ..." He looked at each of them as he suddenly remembered. "Oh, my God, they came on me! It was like vermin, like big black bugs ... oh my God ..." he screamed, and began to thrash. "Why did you let them get me? Why didn't you kill me?"

Kate took him by the shoulders. "Pull yourself together, Luttrell. We're trying to help you, do you hear me?"

"Oh, but you can't ... I know how it works, you can't do anything for me ..." He grasped one of her gloved hands in his own. "Please help me, *please* ..."

"Listen to me, Kenneth—"

"*Please*, Captain, I never did anything to you, I never meant to—"

Her face changed at his words. "You never what?"

He babbled at her, eyes so wide she could see the whites all around his pupils, even through the faceplate of his suit. Foam flecked one corner of his mouth.

"You never *did* anything to me?" She grabbed him by the arms and shook him, punctuating her words. "Is *that* what you said?"

"Oh, please God, nooo ..."

She went on, oblivious to the fact that he was beyond understanding her. "You listen to me, you yellow-assed coward—*listen* to me! You're going to walk off this ship—do you hear me, *walk* off this ship like a man, like a member of this crew! You're going to look Kagen right in the eye and tell him you've got what he wants—do you understand me?"

Luttrell only mumbled now. "Please, I would never have ... I didn't mean ..."

Kate stopped, made herself let go and step back away from him. She could see the others watching her as she blinked sweat from her eyes.

"We could stun him," Al suggested quietly.

"No! No, we're going forward with their plan." She jabbed the controls on Luttrell's suit to polarize his faceplate. "SINS figured out this scenario for them, and we have plenty of time before those things wake up. If they were wrong, it's on them. Now, let's get out of here." Kate took a deep breath and let it out, and suddenly she was very calm. The entire situation came into unnaturally sharp focus, and she knew she was doing the right thing.

"I'll go first. George, Pete, you take him by the arms and follow right behind me. Al, can you and Teresa get the frankenstein? Use the stretcher, and keep him in the bag. I don't want the whole world to see what we've got just yet."

"No problem," Al agreed. "Will you be all right with him?"

"We can manage," Grayson assured him. "Just hurry up and get that thing, will you?"

Kate would never forget that endless walk through the corridors of the *Pegasus* on their way to the main airlock vestibule. Always waiting for that faint rustling sound in her earphones that would mean the kites were coming alive, over-whelming Luttrell in his suit—even though she knew they should have more than enough time to get him out before that happened. She tried not to think about how the closed environment of the suit might affect the animation sequence of the kites. SINS had said they had enough time.

So she waited, as he muttered softly in her radio and walked obediently between George and Pete, who held his arms tightly. There was no pleading in his voice now, no hint of sanity . . . he could only gibber quietly and shake as though he were freezing. Things were moving in his suit, they were alive—but she knew it wasn't true, she knew it was only the helpless mutterings of the deeply insane.

Teresa operated the controls and they passed through the airlock chamber into the umbilicus.

"Polarize your faceplates," Kate told the others. "I don't want them to know who's who."

She went first, ducking through the small opening into the station itself, and stepped out alone at the top of the ramp to the receiving area.

There were few people waiting to meet them. Kagen in his automatic chair, his face scowling with puzzlement and anger; Baker, standing immediately behind him, looking vaguely shocked by their appearance—but no sign of Billy.

"What is this? Why are you suited?" Kagen demanded. "Remove those helmets at once—I order you!"

Kate unlatched her helmet and lifted it slowly. The look

on Kagen's face as he recognized her almost made the whole of her terrible effort worthwhile. She smiled.

Kagen gestured, and Martin Baker pushed his chair forward. "Welcome home, Captain Harlin. Congratulations on a successful mission."

"Thank you, Mr. Kagen. But I'm not sure the mission is truly over yet." Kate looked about her, began to really take in her surroundings.

They were almost alone in the receiving area. Besides her crew of five there were a few scattered Guil-Pro security men, Kagen, and Baker behind him. A medical rescue team hovered in the background. The blue-gray uniforms of the Port Authority's Station Security Force were nowhere in sight, and she became even more nervous about the odds she and her small crew were facing. How easy for Kagen to have them placed under protective quarantine, with no one outside this room the wiser. They were really on their own.

"Not over? Well, we can discuss that later, in more congenial surroundings," Kagen was saying. He seemed to be completely recovered from his initial shock at seeing her.

"I'd like that, Mr. Kagen, because you and I have a lot to talk about."

"Perhaps we'd best deal with your injured crewmember first. Who is it?" he asked, peering behind her to the stretcher carried by Al and Teresa.

"Dr. Luttrell can probably discuss it better than any of us," she said. "But I don't know if he's up to that right now."

"What do you mean?" Kagen asked.

Suddenly there was noise and movement at the back of the receiving area. A voice blared over the intercom.

"This is the Port Authority Security Force! We have a warrant to inspect cargo aboard the L.P.S. *Pegasus*!"

Kagen's face darkened. Baker turned to look over his shoulder, then bent and whispered something in his boss's ear.

Kagen gestured angrily with his good hand. "You three," he ordered his security men, "get back there and talk to them! Delay them!" He turned his attention back to Kate and her crew. "I hope you had nothing to do with this, Harlin."

"You flatter me," she said, peering anxiously to the back

of the receiving area. The Port Authority had entered, but they were being successfully blocked by Guil-Pro security. She could hear the puzzled and worried voices of her crew in her headset. If Kagen's men delayed the Port Authority for too long...

"No!" Luttrell screamed and lunged, and everyone turned, startled.

"Captain, watch out!" Grayson yelled.

In a single frenzied motion, Luttrell had worked one arm free with unexpected strength. Al and Teresa dropped the stretcher and tried to help, but Luttrell was too quick for any of them.

"Hang on to him!" Kate said, trying to help, but the crazed man pushed her aside, knocking her into Grayson, and they stumbled frantically for balance. Luttrell jerked his other arm free of Pete's grasp and ran forward while unfastening his helmet. He wrenched it off, tossed it to the ground, and stood there, his entire head completely buried under a mass of swarming, fluttering kites.

Everyone stopped, arrested for a moment in shocked silence by the terrible sight. The Guil-Pro security force stood, weapons drawn, unsure of what to do. They could kill the spacesuited figure, but what would happen to the hundreds of alien creatures engulfing him? Would they then invade the entire area, attaching themselves to anyone not protected by a spacesuit? Trying to kill all those things would be like trying to stop a flood of cockroaches—if they could even kill them at all. The security men began to edge nervously backward.

"You!" Luttrell's voice sounded muffled, coming as it did from under a layer of crawling shapes. He brushed them aside, seeming almost careless of their presence on him. "You did this to me, you bastard!" He gestured at Kagen. "Look at me! Look what you've done to me!"

Kagen was rigid in his chair, staring at Luttrell. Baker was so frightened he forgot to move, forgot to get his superior out of harm's way.

Kagen knew in that instant that he was looking at kites, and at a man who could expose him to a horrible disease, to insanity...who might already have exposed him. In that instant nothing mattered to Geoffrey Kagen but that he was in danger and could do nothing to get away from it.

"You!" Luttrell shrieked and flung his arms wide, and several of the diamond-shapes fell away from him, fluttering down to the floor. Baker howled and fled. Panic erupted as everyone scrambled to get as far away as they could, leaving Kagen sitting alone. Screaming, Luttrell dived at him.

Knocked backward out of his chair, Kagen sprawled with Luttrell on top of him. More kites squeezed from the opening of Luttrell's suit, slithering to the deck as the two men rolled about, pinning kites beneath them. Suddenly the creatures began to swarm over Kagen, as though realizing that a second host was now available.

Kate got her own immediate reaction of panic under control when she realized what was happening, and snapped her helmet back on. Gesturing at her crew, she ordered, "Pete, get back in the ship and get a couple of sample cases. Everybody else, grab up those strays. If they get away they'll reproduce and this place'll be crawling with 'em!" Her orders broke the spell everyone seemed to have been under, and they moved to obey her quickly. Then she went after Luttrell.

One of Kagen's security men had left the rear of the receiving bay and was already running forward to help her. The Port Authority took advantage of the confusion and moved into the area, followed quickly by reporters, though they all stopped a safe distance away when they saw what was going on.

"Are you crazy?" Kate hollered at the security man through her helmet while trying to motion him away. "Get out of here, let us handle this!" But he ignored her. Together they subdued Luttrell, who gave up as soon as they pinned him to the floor. He seemed to have lost his force of will—it was as though he had accomplished his one goal and now had nothing more to do. He lay still on the deck and let Kate secure his helmet.

She looked up over her shoulder. "Grayson, hold on to him! Come on, move it!"

Kagen, however, was not in nearly as calm a state. Out of his chair and helpless on the ground, he thrashed and wailed, screaming, "Martin! Martin, help me!" But the little man had fled in terror to the farthest reaches of the bay. The lone security man worked frantically at a seemingly Sisyphean task—as fast as he could brush the kites from Kagen's face, they swarmed back to secure themselves against his warm flesh.

Turning her attention to the struggling men, Kate marveled that this one man could maintain the loyalty he'd been hired for and was willing to handle the live kites with such calm.

"Kate, here you go." Pete tossed her a sample case, which she caught deftly. "I'll take the other one over to Al and Mac and help them round up the loose ones." She nodded at him, and saw for a moment her other two crewmembers frantically scrabbling after several single kites that still fluttered about the deck like bizarre butterflies. The whole scene was so chaotic that she had to stop for a moment and squeeze her eyes shut. But the sounds of Kagen's frantic screeching snapped her out of it.

Placing the sample case between them, Kate and the one security man worked rapidly, in silence, pulling the kites off Kagen and tossing them into the plastex case, where they fluttered aimlessly about. Unsuited, the security man was incredibly efficient, searching Kagen's clothes, his pockets, anywhere a stray kite might be hiding, while Kate, somewhat clumsier in her suit and gloves, removed the most obvious ones. Kagen had stopped screaming by now; he lay there panting, pasty-faced, his good hand clutched in the fabric of the security man's suit, his withered one waving feebly about, like a hermit crab's claw.

"Listen," Kate turned to her assistant and shouted through her helmet, "we've got 'em all now. Go tell those medics they have to spray everyone with a disinfectant! Any kind will—!"

"I'll take care of it," he said, and moved away.

Kate turned back to look at Kagen and saw that he lay gasping on the deck, his one good hand now clasped to his chest, his face white and pinched. Just as suddenly, he was unconscious.

Pete, who had come over to tell her they'd captured the last kite, mumbled a soft, "Oh, shit," while Luttrell's high, loonlike giggles rang in the crew's ears. Everyone's attention was focused on the prone figure, but no one moved. He had touched the alien creatures; he may as well have kissed a plague bearer. The medics were busy donning their contagion suits while the one security man assisted them.

Kate, realizing that Kagen was having a heart attack, stared and wondered, for just a moment, what it would feel like to watch him die of fright.

"Goddammit!" she swore, and began to strip away her suit.

"Kate, don't!" Teresa almost screamed at her, but Al muttered something and she became quiet.

"Captain—!" Perhaps Grayson? Pete? She couldn't tell.

She ignored them and bent to begin resuscitation. The security man returned, and began to pump on Kagen's chest while she breathed for him. In the background she was vaguely aware that the medical team had begun spraying the area, the reporters, the Port Authority officers, the rest of the *Pegasus* crew, and even Martin Baker with a foamy, sweet-smelling stuff.

"You'd better get disinfected!" she gasped in the pauses between her rhythmic breaths. "Make sure they cover you—!"

The man looked at her and smiled. "Oh, don't worry about me. I'll be all right . . . Katie. . . ."

Her heart slammed so hard that she nearly lost track of what she was doing. Suddenly she and Kagen were doused with spray by the rescue team, and the security man (who didn't look like Rory but *should* have) slipped away in the confusion. A moment later Kate herself was pulled away from Kagen as protectively suited medics took her place. Another pair was leading the helpless Luttrell back into the ship, no doubt to secure him in the infirmary.

"Where's my crew?" Kate pushed away the helping hands. "Teresa? Al? Make sure the Port Authority gets that bag!"

"Don't worry—!" She thought she heard Grayson's voice in the background.

"Kate! Kate, are you all right?" someone called from the back of the room.

"I am now!" She laughed and turned to hug Billy Watson.

"Nothing like waiting till the last minute! Did you plan it that way?"

"Hell, yes! Had to make sure we were gonna get the bad guys redhanded! What's this shit all over us?" He pulled away from her, grinning, and wiped his shirtfront with his hands.

"I don't know." She wiped some from her sleeve. "Doesn't matter, though, as long as it does the job. *God*, it's good to see you!"

Someone grasped her shoulder. "I hope it's just as good to see me."

Kate spun around, her eyes going wide. "Lars!" She choked on the word, trying to laugh and cry and talk all at once. She finally threw herself at him and hugged him fiercely.

"Hey, hey!" He laughed. "Easy, there, you'll crush me. Are you all right? Lord, woman," he held her at arm's length, "you look like you've seen a ghost."

"I—I have." She swallowed, all the tears she'd been saving up running freely down her face, mixing with the dripping disinfectant. "Lars, they told me you were dead."

"Not the last time I checked." He looked closely at her. "You're serious. Kate, what the—"

"Later, I think." She smiled weakly. "We'll talk about all of it later." She hugged him again, and pulled Billy into their circle. The rest of her crew had stripped off their suits and endured the disinfectant spray again, for safety's sake. They wandered over one by one.

The docking area was a mess. White foam was everywhere, making the deck dangerously slippery. Everyone in the room was soaked with it. Reporters milled about, recorders whirring, trying to get interviews, looking incongruous in their wet clothes and dripping hair. Members of the Port Authority police were circulating, making sure no one left the area. But Kate looked in vain for the man who had helped her with Kagen.

"Who're you looking for, Kate?" Billy asked her.

Before she could answer, someone called her.

"What is it?" Kate turned to see a medic.

"Mr. Kagen wants to see you."

"You don't need to talk to him!" Teresa insisted.

"He said it was an order, ma'am." The medic looked uncomfortable as the rest of her crew gathered close around her.

Kate smiled wryly. "He doesn't give up, does he? All right, I'll see him. He's not the only one with something to say."

Kagen's voice was hoarse, and he looked incredibly fragile attached to the portable heart machine, still dripping with disinfectant. "I understand . . . I owe you my life."

She folded her arms. "I've done worse."

Teresa, Billy, and Lars stood with her, and the others were right behind them.

"I hope you realize . . . how . . . inextricably . . . we are tied . . . together . . . by your act of mercy."

She regarded him silently.

"We . . . are not finished, Katharine," he whispered. "I made the mistake . . . of underestimating you . . . and some of those close to you . . . once. I shall not make . . . that mistake . . . again."

Before she could answer, the doctors bent over him again, closing her out.

"What was that all about?" Lars asked.

"I don't know," she said, but thought of the man who didn't look like Rory or sound like Rory, but who had called her Katie. "And I don't care right now. Can we go somewhere else? Is it all right for us to leave yet? I've got to get this crap off me." She ran her hands through her hair, and they came away wet and foamy.

A man Kate didn't recognize approached.

"Kate, it's Meitner!" Lars exclaimed, grinning, and grasped the man's hand. "You guys were right on time! Everyone, this is Port Authority Chief Patrick Meitner. He's responsible for pulling your asses out of the fire today."

"I had a lot of help," Meitner smiled, "especially from Mr. Watson, here, and the station's Port Authority officer, Ms. J. D. Cort, who refused to be intimidated by Guil-Pro roughnecks." He indicated a young woman standing beside him.

"So what's going on?" Kate asked.

"Everything is proceeding smoothly. That burned-out

LSH unit I just looked at is a powerful piece of evidence in your favor, Captain Harlin. Our specialists have already started working on it."

A shadow passed over Kate's face.

"With that," he continued, "and the data from the *Black Opal* mission, as well as the new data from this mission, some heads will roll at Guil-Pro. Our preliminary investigation has already found things in the computer system that were locked away from everyone but Luttrell and the LSH unit. And, of course, we'll learn a lot more once everything is brought back to our main facilities at Equator Station."

"Do you know about my claim?" Teresa asked.

Meitner smiled. "It'll take a while to research, I'm sure you realize, and we'll have to find the families of the other crewmembers from the *Hercules*, but it looks like it'll hold up."

"And Luttrell?" Kate asked. "What happens to him?"

Meitner shrugged. "I don't know, that's out of my jurisdiction, but I can assure you he'll have excellent medical care."

"What about the rest of us?" Grayson asked. "What kind of protection do we have?"

"There are well-grounded laws to protect whistle-blowers, of course—"

"Kagen is outside the law!" Al interrupted. "Look what he and Guil-Pro have already been getting away with for the last ten years! The law will give us nothing."

"You're right, of course. But publicity will. The discovery of a complex alien life and the existence of thinking frankensteins will hold the public's interest for a long time to come."

"I don't know. Once the excitement wears off . . ." Grayson sounded very doubtful.

"Look, Guil-Pro is in a lot of trouble. If anything happens to any of you, we look at them first and they know it. It'll be in their best business interests to keep their hands clean." Meitner took a deep breath. "You can't hurt them any more than you already have. They can't stop what has already begun. You'll be all right."

Kate thought of the man who hadn't looked like Rory

but who should have, and she shivered. Meitner didn't know Kagen like she knew him. He didn't know.

"What should we do in the meantime?" Pete was asking.

Meitner steepled his fingers. "Guilford may drop your contracts, they may not—the issue hasn't come up yet. I would advise you to relax here for a few days, then go back to Earth, collect your pay, and go on whatever vacations you can afford. Get away for a while, let us do our job."

The group nodded in general agreement.

"A vacation sure sounds good to me," Kate said, running her hand through her hair and grimacing as it came away sticky. "But what I want more than anything else right now is a shower!"

Later that night, Kate lay in the dark with her head on Lars's chest, listening to his heart.

"What's the matter, Kate? You seem distracted," he said quietly.

"I'm still getting used to the idea that it might really be over." She sighed. "I guess it'll take a while."

"You've got all the time you need. I'll even help, if you want."

She raised her head to look at him. "Why did you do all this for me?"

"I still care a lot about you, Kate. Are you so surprised?"

Kate winced at his choice of words, remembering when Rory had said the same thing, and she was glad Lars couldn't see her face. "No." She laid her head back down. "When do you go back out?"

"Not for another month and a half."

"Good. Take vacation with me?"

"Your place or mine?" he mumbled against her hair, and they laughed softly.

EPILOGUE

Kate had been alone for three months in the middle of several thousand square kilometers of trees and mountains and lakes in the far north-central part of the United Americas, in the old Canadian Northwest Territories. She owned property there, had a small underground house—such dwellings were allowed as long as they didn't interfere with the wilderness.

She and Lars had shared their first month, until he'd had to return to Equator Station for his next assignment. She had been sorry to see him go, yet hungry for the time alone that she hadn't been able to have in many years. Time alone to write, to read and relax, time to use her telescope in the clear and unblemished darkness—time to try to forget.

At first she had forgone all contact with the outside world; she had a radio, but left it disconnected. There was not even a computer terminal in her house. She didn't miss it much after the first few weeks, especially when she thought of how easy a data connection, even by satellite, would make it for someone to find her if they really wanted to. She was especially interested in not being found, though as time went on she grew gradually more curious about what was going on in the world outside.

Kate powered up her receiver and prepared to eavesdrop on the world. It had become a once-weekly ritual for her, consulting the charts and aiming the dish in the direction of a likely satellite. She wasn't much for tradition, but she believed a regimen was necessary in life, so she listened to the satellites every Thursday evening, an hour after sundown.

When a call signal came through one Thursday evening, she was startled.

"This is 99734-23-KH," she acknowledged cautiously. "Please identify yourself."

"Kate, is that you?" The voice was surprisingly clear, and Kate laughed in relieved recognition.

"Teresa!"

"That's right. God, but you're a tough person to get hold of!"

"Had it occurred to you maybe that's the way I wanted it?"

There was a laugh from the other end. "I knew *that* before I started trying! But I figured if I stuck it out I'd eventually find you. So how are you?"

"Now that I'm over my surprise, fine. You?"

"Oh, not too bad. Although—well, yeah, I'm all right."

"What's that supposed to mean? Either you are or you aren't. What's up?" Kate had a sudden vision of Teresa set upon by Guil-Pro thugs.

"Don't sound so worried!" Another laugh, but sheepish this time. "I'm embarrassed to admit it, but I broke my leg skiing two weeks ago—in four places!"

"My God, you did it up right! Let me guess—you gang-tackled the mountain?"

"No, only a tree."

"Sounds painful."

"It was at the time. I think I made the ski patrol blush with what I was saying until they knocked me out."

"Will you be all right?"

"Oh, sure. It'll keep me out of trouble for a while, that's all."

"I guess."

"Must be awfully quiet there," Teresa piped up, as if uncomfortable with the long silence that had ensued. "What do you do for a good time?"

"Stay out of trouble."

"Oh."

There was another long silence, broken only by a faint hiss in the background. It was raining again, Kate noticed idly.

"Well," she shook off her mood, "you couldn't have

called just to chat. This must be costing you a bundle, not to mention all the searching you must've done."

"No, it's really not." A brief pause. "It'll be easier if I start this at the beginning. I'm on Equator Station right now."

"I didn't know you had quarters there."

"I don't; I'm staying with Al. He's got a—"

Kate chuckled.

"We were skiing together when I ran into the tree," Teresa explained. "It's a little hard for me to get around with the exoskeleton they've got my leg strapped into, so he said he'd help me out while he's still here. His next assignment isn't for another month, so he got a temporary job here at the station to tide him over, and one of his benefits is free communications. Which is why," she finished triumphantly, "this call is being paid for by Ma Bell Satellite instead of me!"

"His benefit, not yours. You must not be too worried about getting caught."

"Nah, he's standing watch right now."

"My rates better not go up because of this kind of thing!" Kate laughed briefly. "So Al's got work again. I'm glad to hear it."

"Uh—yeah. He's with Guil-Pro again, you know. They renewed him."

"Oh?"

"Kate, it's not like that!" Teresa came back hastily. "Guil-Pro is bending over backwards to make up to us. They've offered everybody jobs again, with extra sweeteners, even."

"Everybody?"

"Even you, Kate."

"What's the matter, their public image hurting?" She was surprised at the bitterness in her voice. "Something must've happened." She sighed. "You'd better tell me."

Teresa's excitement fairly poured from the speaker. "Well, to begin with, the Port Authority arrested Kagen while he was still in the hospital. That would have been—oh, almost three months ago, now."

"They've hauled his ass in?" Kate rose abruptly and went to pour herself a scotch. "Now *that's* news. What charges?"

"Creating and owning an LSH unit that wasn't brain-dead, and encouraging the study of intelligent cybernetics."

Kate stared at the speaker. "That's all?"

"Well, for now, yeah."

"Shit." Kate stared at her drink, then brought it to her lips and downed it in one gulp.

"You don't sound very happy."

"Oh, I am. But—those charges miss the whole point of his operation, the whole *depth* of his—!" She thought of Rory, a thing she had not done in some time. "What about all the people who died? The *Opal*'s crew, your brother? What were Guil-Pro's plans for the kites—aren't they worried about that?" She laid her head on her arms. "What about me?" she whispered.

"Kate?" Teresa's voice was tentative. "It's better than nothing, isn't it?"

"Like getting a murderer for tax evasion!"

"But at least you've got him! Hell, it worked with Al Capone, and he died in jail! Besides, it's not like that's all they're going to do. Meitner said just a few weeks ago that the investigation is going ahead full speed, and they plan to hit Kagen with the real heavy charges as soon as the evidence is assembled."

"Those magic words—'as soon as.' But I guess you're right. It looks like everything is moving along." She couldn't quite keep the sarcastic edge from her voice. "Kagen's been busted, Guil-Pro's running with their tail between their legs for now, you've all got your jobs back...."

"Does that bother you?"

Kate couldn't answer, and Teresa plunged into the silence.

"Kate, what more do you want? *You* did everything you could. You held us together, you got us back home in one piece—you even saved Kagen's life, which was above and beyond the call of duty as far as anyone is concerned. What more—"

"How's Luttrell?"

There was no answer.

"Teresa? Have you heard anything?"

"Well, yeah. I wasn't going to bring it up, but..." Teresa

sighed. "They gave him something to try to counteract the toxin, but it didn't work. He had a reaction from it and died about two days later."

Kate felt a tension leave her. "I'm glad it happened fairly quickly."

"Yeah, you can stop worrying about him. Besides, I have more news." Teresa sounded the slightest bit smug.

"Well, let's hear it."

"They've reopened my brother's case. Meitner says it's pretty much just a formality. His survivor's benefits should be reinstated—and it looks like my claim on Roanoke is valid."

"No kidding? That's great news! What's the next step?"

"I don't know yet, it's all too new. I can sell the rights, or sell the rights to work the place, or rent them out, or hire someone to do it and keep my interest in it—a ton of things."

"Looks like you've hit fat city."

"If I work it right." Teresa paused. "Kate, I was wondering—when are you coming back to work?"

"What? How did we get on this subject?"

"I want to know."

"Well, I . . . I hadn't thought about it yet."

"You've had a bunch of job offers. You're hot property!"

"Oh yeah? I don't exactly expect my previous employer to give me glowing references."

"Oh, screw Guil-Pro. The publicity from this thing is what's *made* you look attractive! Especially—well, there's one offer in particular that really interests me. I assume you've got some money stashed away?"

"Enough." Kate grew interested. "Got a good tax shelter for me?"

"Better than that if it works out right. There's a small company just starting in the business. Actually they're about five years old now, but you've been gone most of that time, so you probably wouldn't know them."

"Try me."

"Phoenix Enterprises. It's run by women. They've gotten in touch with me several times, and I told 'em I was interested." Teresa hesitated. "Last time they asked me specifically about you."

"Did they?"

"Sure did. Kate, you'd love it! They're in the mining and exploration business, only on a smaller scale, of course, which means less overhead. They've been able to undercut some of the bigger corporations on their project bids. And they do good work."

"It's tough to build a deep space reputation in just five years," Kate said doubtfully.

"Well, they don't have one yet. They've only done short hauls until now. But they want to get into deep space—and that's where you come in!"

"Ahh..." Kate let her breath out slowly. "What about equipment, ships worthy for interstellar travel—?"

"They're working on that right now."

"Got any jobs lined up?"

"I own a major percentage of Roanoke. I figure that can be our first job—if you're with me."

"Well, this gets interesting." Kate stared out the window. "You sound as though you've really researched them."

"I'm not going to throw Roanoke to just anybody."

Kate laughed. "I like your style, Teresa. Got a name for me to get in touch with?"

"Oh, this is great! You don't *know* how I was hoping you would ask that!" Teresa gave her the information.

"Mmm." Kate gazed thoughtfully at the name. "Gabrielle Jacobs."

"She's is a very interesting person."

"I'll bet she is. And I'll get to this—soon." She could almost see Teresa's grin through the speaker.

"Great!"

There was a brief pause.

"You know," Kate said, "the longer you stay on, the easier it'll be for them to catch you."

"Yeah, you're right." Teresa hesitated. "Maybe I'll see you around on the station? Soon?"

"More than likely."

"Good. You take care, Kate."

"You do the same, Teresa. And...thanks."

"Anytime."

The connection faded. Kate stared once more at the name

Teresa had given her, then rose and walked over to her big sliding plastex doors.

The rain had stopped and the stars were out. Kate stepped out onto her deck and smelled the crisp air. In the distance across the lake she could hear the laughing cry of the loon, and she thought what a truly beautiful sound it was.

27 million Americans can't read a bedtime story to a child.

It's because 27 million adults in this country simply can't read.

Functional illiteracy has reached one out of five Americans. It robs them of even the simplest of human pleasures, like reading a fairy tale to a child.

You can change all this by joining the fight against illiteracy.

Call the Coalition for Literacy at toll-free **1-800-228-8813** and volunteer.

Volunteer Against Illiteracy. The only degree you need is a degree of caring.

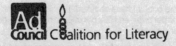

Ad Council Coalition for Literacy